VOLTARA: BATTLE FOR THE GALAXY

METANOIA MOIRAI A CHANGE IN DESTINY

ALICE MEEKS

authorHOUSE®

AuthorHouse™
1663 Liberty Drive
Bloomington, IN 47403
www.authorhouse.com
Phone: 1-800-839-8640

This is a work of fiction. All of the characters, names, incidents, organizations, and dialogue in this novel are either the products of the author's imagination or are used fictitiously.

Published by AuthorHouse   12/12/2014

ISBN: 978-1-4969-5237-0 (sc)
ISBN: 978-1-4969-5236-3 (e)

Library of Congress Control Number: 2014920341

Contents

THE BEGINNING OF OUR UNIVERSE AND THE ASTERS

Humans thought they were alone in their universe. In the beginning, there was the old galaxy, before the planets were created, before the stars and moons it was the time of Gods, Titans, and Ancients. They decided to create multiple galaxies in the universe. The gods were the creators; they made the various creatures we see before us now. They spread them across vast galaxies, but their favorite was ours. It was where they spent most of there time. When they created the planets in the human solar system it was left to one, the goddess of all the elements her name was Relana. She was the most beautiful goddess, with raven hair and eyes as blue as the seas. She created all the planets, including your Earth. There was one planet she created for the Titans, which were their guardians, it is known as Voltara. All was well in the in the galaxy until, a God fell in love with a Titan. On the planet of Voltara, the surface was made of mostly rock and there were multiple volcanoes. The creatures that dwelled here started out as Dregons. A Dregon is a creature with an impenetrable stone like skin, like the planets surface and had a humanoid form, and long wings for flight. As they evolved they began to take on a more humanoid appearance, but their skin would be a deathly pale due to the lack of sunlight. Their planet was mostly dark and dreary during the limit of a 6-hour daytime, there is one in particular that ruled them all, and his name was Delarous. All other titans feared and respected him, when the goddess Relana visited she noticed something about him. She decided she did not want to be alone in this galaxy any longer. Their love would anger all other gods, Titans and even ancients. As their love grew word spread of her defiance, she was summoned to the ninth galaxy where all the other gods had decided to make their home. They made the decision that they could no longer be together. Delarous in his anger would wipe out most of the gods, leaving the ancients to flee into the depths of the universe. After the destruction of the Gods Relana began to question what she had done. She also discovered she was with child. In fear she sought out the ancients to ask for help. They decided to take the remaining Titans and seal them away, where no one could find them or free them. Relana returned to Voltara itself where she would raise their child, Vonken Aster. When the child was six, she began to notice his appetite for destruction and his lust for power. She tried to teach him the ways of the gods, but as he grew older and learned what his father had endured at the hands of them. He swore that he would be the ultimate power in the universe. When he turned twenty-one, he had set a plan in motion with the creatures he created, one of which was known as a Moneconda. They have a beastly appearance, dark gray and dinosaur type with quills along there back, which they use for paralyzing and rendering their victims unconscious or even killing them if they desire. They can shape shift into whatever or whomever they desire. He gave them a home in a place known only as the Monster Zone, a dark series of caverns with deep caves and dark forest surrounding it. So as his plot unfolded, the Ancients spoke to Relana and demanded she either destroy him or lock him away in another galaxy. She decided to imprison him in a tomb of which only one of his own blood could release him. While all this was being planned, Vonken would go to his beloved, a queen from the new galaxy named Kariana. She too wished to rule, what she considered the lesser beings of this universe. Relana cast her curse to transport Vonken into his tomb, where he would remain for centuries. As she sealed the tomb he cursed them all. He swore he would return and that his blood would rule the universe. Now as centuries past, we find ourselves in my time the year is 2239. The entire universe is still yet to be discovered by the humans, they have only just begun to discover this galaxy. The one planet, which will be the focus of the universe's fate, is Voltara. We would begin the story that starts with an Aster known as, Volkren, he was like his father an arrogant powerful creature, with the ability to be both man and transform into a fierce Dregon, a secret that Kariana kept even from Vonken. His eyes brown his hair was black his skin deathly pale. He would travel the galaxies in search of his father's tomb, while he had begun his mission of terror throughout the universe back in our galaxy his son Volkren Aster Jr. created his own legacy. He did not start out as evil as his predecessors. He would soon have darkness in his heart. He had two sons, Voltar and Volrin. When they grew up one would rule Voltara, the other would be lost in the monster zone for many years. Voltar was a cruel dictator and his lust for power had become legend in this galaxy. Voltar would first marry Alena, where he would have a daughter named Valtra and a son named Alden. Their marriage would not last, due to his uncontrollable lust for power and women. He would then keep a mistress Amelia, a beautiful humanoid female of their sister world Voltia. She would give him two sons Rick being one of them. Voltar would then find his true love, a princess born on Voltara, Terina. She would soon pass when Voltar Jr., their son, tuned three. Now we go to the future, where a new fate would embark on the Aster clan. As thirteen years have passed, there is now mostly peace in our galaxy thanks in part to the creation of the Galactic Alliance. The Alliance is made up of all the planets in our galaxy except for one, Voltara.

Chapter 1
JOURNEY OF THE SON

It started with me; I was the one who was determined to defy my legacy, my birthright to prove not all Asters were created evil. This is my story to tell you and many of those to come soon after me. My journey will take me to a world of beings that have a will as strong as my own, I would join and fight with them, and I would end up changing my fate and the fate of those who succeed me. I am the one to change the Aster destiny and define future generations as good. I will rise above the darkness of my blood and show this galaxy that Asters should not be feared but followed. My name is Jon and I am an Aster.

My life was typical of a prince. I never wanted or needed anything, except my father's attention. I did not know then why he was never there. He was always out with my other siblings. I thought it was because my mother died when I was three. I thought he could not stand the sight of me; the constant reminder of his late wife. With my emerald green eyes and jet-black hair. The day I turned sixteen was the day my life would forever change. It was a good day; I walked into the city as I typically did every week. It was the only place on Voltara that I was allowed. My planet was nothing but dark and dreary in most places, although the city was of technology and very modern. The planet's surface was made of molten rock with charred mountains, volcanoes, and murky seas. While on a stroll through the city, which was the only place, I was allowed. While I strolled I saw an odd vessel in the distance. As I continued to walk the street, my curiosity grew. That's when I saw them, Humans. They looked similar to us except not as pale. I made my way to the docking station. My heart pounded when she stepped out, I felt nervous because of her beauty, Her raven hair was smooth around her ivory skin and her eyes a deep sapphire. She smiled at me when she looked up. I worked up the nerve to go over and speak to her. "Excuse me but, who are you?" I asked. "My name is Carla, I am on a mission from Earth, a member of the Galactic Alliance." It was then that she told me of her mission here and opened my eyes to the truth about my family and the terror and destruction they caused. "Are you not familiar with Voltar Aster and his destruction?" She explained. "You are lying!" I firmly informed. I felt a hot boil in my blood but it ran cold as she showed me proof, of all of it. She had photos of my father and siblings killing and raising chaos. As Carla stayed on Voltara I would sneak out to meet with her and she told me all about her home on Earth. It all sounded so amazing to me, I sometimes dream about leaving here.

As that year went on, I fell hard for her. My father had returned from one of his trips to see I was different as he strutted in his silk suit with a stern cowl brown hair and hazel eyes. "Junior I'm home!" He called from his throne room. It was the only part of our castle that showed off his arrogance and expensive taste. As I came in he could tell I was acting more like a human. "Welcome home father." I replied. "What has put a smile on your face?" I told him not realizing the consequences. "I met the most amazing girl, she is from Earth the Galactic Alliance." I answered in content. He was disgusted and had a look of disappointment. Carla had started to grow on me. "You are never to see her again." He commanded. I was bold and rebellious. "I love her, we will be together," Jon informed. "You cannot stop me!" He became quiet and walked away. I should have known then that my life with Carla would never be. I managed to slip out of the castle and back to the docking station. That's when I met her brother Tommy who was my age. "I am joining the Alliance." He told me. I decided at that moment that I would join too. I made the mistake of trusting my brother Rick with the news of my decision. As I stood in the main hall of the castle Rick entered. "I have decided to join the alliance." I announced. He stood in displeasure with his light green eyes and long blonde locks. This would not go so well. He was enraged by the thought.

"You would join with our enemies?" He interrogated. "They are not our enemies if you would just hear what they have to say!" I argued, my brother silenced and gave a cold look that this wasn't over yet. After our argument I snuck off to see Carla and told her what had happened. She said, "It is time to go!" Carla insisted. I agreed without hesitation. Tommy had it all planned out. He got the ship ready for us to escape to Earth. That night I met Carla at the docking bay, ironically where we met for the first time and our last.

When I arrived, my brother Rick stood before me with his thugs, his fan club wannabe's with their straight blonde long locks and brown eyes, The Nelcon twins, two brothers that would die for mine. They had Carla in hand. "Let her go Rick!" I yelled. He became even angrier to see this display of my defiance. I would see a side of him that I'd never want to see again.

We are similar to humans except for one thing, our Dregon, a creature we can shape shift into as a defense. It is a different color of our essence for each of us but in all a similar creature form. They represent your inner soul. I only ever saw my father's dregon, which was black as night. My brother's was a fire red. His wings expanded outward with his claws extended. His eyes went from green to a soulless black. I knew what would happen next. I tried to stop him. I charged at him but he threw me back. I hit the wall so hard I was seeing double as I tried to focus my vision was blurred. When I finally saw clearly in the chaos I tried to stand but I winced in pain. I saw my brother use his claws to stab Carla in the chest. Her blood seeped out staining he very uniform. He turned his hand and pulled out her heart. "Carla!" I cried. The light faded from her eyes as she fell to the ground. I stood there frozen in horror. My own brother had brutally murdered my first love. Tommy saw what happened and ran towards me. He was pulling me up yelling but the noise was drowned out. "We need to get out of here!" He shouted. He led me on the ship and as he hurried to start the controls. I sat staring out the window as we lifted off and slowly flew farther away from my home. I did not notice my father yelling for me "Junior!" He roared. All I could see was her murder playing back in my mind over and over again. As we traveled to Earth, we sat in silence. I could not sleep and

I continued to gaze out into space until I saw endless colors of blue and green that mesmerized me.

When I saw Earth for the first time, I was amazed by it all as I took it in. A wave of clam fell over me a sort of independence too. I only wished that Carla were here, as I exited the ship, I saw a vivid blue sky and a sun that felt so radiant as its rays heated my cold pale face so opposite to my home world. The sun was a symbol of comfort and my journey into the light. This is where my new life will begin.

Tommy and I went to the Galactic Alliance building. When I walked inside, it was a typical structure with stations and desks all around. I saw a mural on a high wall of all the planets in our system all accept my own. My father would never side with the Alliance. He was too busy craving power and control. I then noticed how many of the different species looked at me as I walked through the building. Some had a look of fear and others a look of hope. My name although was a reminder of death and destruction. I decided from that day forward I would not be judged by my name so I changed it from Voltar Aster Jr. to Jon Aster.

The general of Earth would be the first to welcome me. "Welcome I am General Jameson of the galactic alliance, we are so glad to have the first Voltarian here." "Hopefully not the last." He added. "Thank you for this opportunity, to prove not all Voltarians are evil." I replied. While I was becoming familiar with my new home, my old one was full of chaos. My father and brother went on a killing spree leaving a trail of blood in the streets. I was oblivious to all of this, at least for the moment.

I would begin my training and study with the Alliance. When we entered the academy it was like another world. There were so many different creatures. The only one missing was Carla. Tommy and I shared a room, which was smaller than I was used to but still feels like where I belong. I will honor Carla by becoming one of the most influential beings in this Alliance, in this galaxy. The academy is intense. As they trained us hard I was starting to make friends. No one really knew who I was or where I came from. For now I am going to keep it that way, as I am becoming my own man now. "So new recruits, are you ready for the most intense training of your young lives?" Capt. Milcroft exclaimed as he stood 6'5 he was a Neptune refter, a creature of blue skin and fur covering his massive body. Meanwhile my father and my siblings were searching the planets for me. They had no idea I was on Earth. Even if they did they could not come here, it's protected.

So Tommy and I were sure when we graduate we'd be assigned to the best Alliance base in the galaxy, which is stationed above Voltia sister planet to Voltara. So now it's finally here, graduation day. This was the day we had worked and suffered for. Tommy was the first one to arrive at the assignment board. We spent two years training for this day. I am now eighteen. I was ready to fight for what I believe in, and what Carla died for. I knew once I left Earth I would have to deal with my father and brother except this time we are on opposite sides. As I arrived Tommy was so excited. I could tell we got in because he had a look of pride. "We were accepted to Qualteran!" Tommy exclaimed, I knew we could do it. So as I began to pack up I held a photo of Carla and I on Voltara. I knew she was always with me. We arrived at our shuttle to take us to our new home. I feel like I've come full circle. I grew from a naive boy of royal blood to a noble, enlightened young man humble to be around these beings.

What a journey it has been for me, for Tommy as well we both only wish Carla could have been with us. When we arrived on the base it was massive as it hovered above Voltia. I could see my former home from its windows. It has been two years since I've seen it. What must it be like now? What has my father done to it? What has become of its people? I will soon find out. We were now headed to our briefing room. We entered a room that was more like an auditorium. We were seated and waited a few moments then the doors opened. Two very different looking humans stood there. One was dark skinned with brown eyes and heavy built and the other was fair skin with Hazel eyes and a little slimmer.

The first was our commander Biscus Brown, His brown short hair with streaks of gray. He looked like he'd seen battle. The second was our pilot commander Dylan McKay. He had light brown hair. He looked somewhat sad like he lost someone he loved. I would discover soon just who she was and her connection to me. "Ok lets get started, we have reports of Rick

Aster at his Gentlemen's Club." Biscus informed. We are to go there and take him down. I could feel my heart pounding. The thought of seeing my brother again after all this time, I don't know if I will be able to control this dark vengeance I feel inside.

After our briefing "So grab your gear and head to the docking bay," Dylan stated. As we went down the corridor I saw her. She was beautiful. Her blonde hair shining and her eyes like emeralds. Her name was Jessica, and she was from Voltia. She was one of the first women to join this team. She was brave and tough. She would become my reason for living. She will be one of the reasons why I will not be my father's son. "Am I late?" She asked. "We are headed to the docking bay." Tommy replied. As we left the base, Dylan briefed us on our mission. "Ok we are gonna go in and scope out the club once we see him we take him down." Dylan instructed. I was busy trying not to show my fear. Tommy knew what this day would mean. He also looked forward to it. I knew he wanted his sister's killer dead. I just wanted to hate my own brother but deep down I was conflicted. When we landed we split up. Jessica was my partner. We made our way into the club. Of course I have never been in it, but I have heard all about it. Rick would tell me about the beautiful women he kept in his employee. It reeked of liquor and sex to me. The women were indeed beautiful as he described but they were also hired assassins and criminals. The table off the corner of the main bar was where my brother sat with his sinister grin and women on each side.

Also seated there were the Nelcon twins. I could feel my blood run cold. I wanted to become my dregon, use my abilities and slaughter them for what they did to Carla. "Ok hold it galactic alliance!" Ralph shouted. All the people ran for the exits but we took them down. "Nice, did you have to cause panic?" Mitch replied. As they were cuffed with the Mandistan Bracelet, which suppressed any abilities like ours, just then they walked Rick by me. He just smirked not saying anything. Jessica asked. "Is something wrong?" "First mission jitters". I responded. Although she could tell it was more. Back on the base I was in sickbay for my physical when he walked up.

This skinny nerdy guy, wearing standard issue alliance uniform and he introduced himself "I am Dr. Paul Schwartz". Who knew he'd become my best friend later. He scanned me and he was fascinated to find out I was Voltarian and he was not afraid. He only wanted to study me and learn "Why would a being with your power, want to join the Alliance?" He asked. Making me realize that after all that happened I could never return home. "The alliance and earth are my family now". As he kept chatting I could hear my brother in my thoughts summoning me.

"I will kill everyone in this base if you don't come to me now." Rick vowed. So I excused myself abruptly and left. I went to our Cell Block. I knew what I wanted to tell him. I had rehearsed it for two years. However when I got to the cell I just stood there, "It is time for you to come home". Rick ordered. I lost my temper and blasted him back with my telekinetic powers. He got up and smiled looking unfazed by it. "Our father will be seeing you soon." Rick replied confidently. As I left the Cell Block, I came upon Jessica. She was waiting at my door. "Why are you here?" I asked, "I know everything." Jessica confessed. She then proceeded to tell me about her telepathic abilities, which all Voltians possess. All I could think of was how beautiful she was. How her eyes seemed to glow when she was engaged in conversation. Then I thought, could I risk my heart again? What if my family killed her? I politely excuse myself and went to the Mess Hall.

All of the other team members were gathered here eating, laughing, and drinking. I came up to them. They informed me of their victory celebration. I sat to join them. They are a very different bunch from all types of beings. Ralph is our comedian and also the commander's son. He always saw the lighter side and was quick to come up with something that would make us all laugh and a good friend to have in the thick of battle. "I didn't know if I should arrest him, for murder or prostitution his hair confused me". Ralph said. He was not the only one on the team to know battle. Mitch Trent, he was twenty-five and the oldest of us. His skin is a light gray color, his eyes brown. He's from Jupiter. He also used to run with my father's gang until he realized that path was the wrong one. "Tell me about it, here is to bagging an aster". Mitch said as he raised his glass. Cole clings his with him. Cole Babor we met briefly at the academy. He has brown hair and green eyes. He is humanoid from Mars. I did not realize it then but he too was running away from his own past. He had come from a line of criminals. His sisters Cora and Cara, twins, caused more death to the male population than any before them, we will meet them soon enough.

Our next mission was the Babor Twins, beautiful but deadly women. "They are the most unstable women we'll meet." Dylan replied as we sat. "There are a trail of dead handsome young men all over Mars." Biscus added. Cole was sure he could get through to them. I hope he was right, although in my heart I knew they could not be changed, as I knew that of my father and brother. This is where Jesse comes in. He is the youngest of us at sixteen but don't let that fool you he is extremely smart. He can track anyone anywhere. "I found the twins sir." He informed as he entered small tech device in hand.

There will also be another to join us he too was young. Shane Laurence. With his light green eyes and straight short sandy blonde hair. He is from Voltia. I felt like we should know each other but I could not place where. "Also we have a new member." Dylan replied as Shane entered in his uniform and strong presence. "This is Shane Laurence." He adds. We all got acquainted on our way to the docking bay. Later we landed on Mars to find the Babor Twins, we walked to a local tavern where they were last seen. "Please let me go in first." Cole begged." "Alright you got five minutes." Dylan agreed. As he entered he saw them at the table looking over a map. It would seem they were looking for someone. Turned out that was Cole. He was never raised by them but by a kind older gentleman, which is why his heart is pure.

He came up to them. "Cole?" Cora replied. "It is him." Cara realized. It was actually strange to see them smile, that was until the rest of us came in. They realized that their brother was in league with the enemy and they were really pissed. "You work for the good guys?" Cora screamed in a rage. A battle broke out guns blasting everywhere. I didn't even realize I was hit, until I felt a sense of confusion; it was blood loss. I fell hitting the ground and the last thing I saw was Jessica. "Jon stay with me!" As she kneeled to him on the floor, the rest of the team managed to capture the sisters. It was while I was in Sickbay the rest of my team would learn my true identity. I thought for sure they would hate me.

I'm glad I was wrong. They told me I was brave even thought at the time I did not feel like it. Jessica stayed at my side the whole time. "I was unconscious for two days?" I replied as I sat up in the hospital bed. "Yes healing up your lucky you got that immortal mojo going for you". Paul responds. This was enough time for my father to learn of this. When I was cleared to go to my own bed that night as I slept, Rick had escaped prison and appeared at my bedside.

I woke up when I felt his presence. He had an actual look of fear and concern in his eyes. "What are you doing in my bedroom?" I said. "I am glad you're ok, I heard you were shot." Rick replied. For a moment it was the brother I knew. Not a monster that I last remembered, until he insisted that it was time to go home. "Its time to end this nonsense with the humans." Rick stated. I then remembered who he is. "You can leave now." I responded. He was angered. I did not know what he would do.

He just walked out. I got up to follow. I went to the living room to see he was gone. In his place was my father. He stood in judgment. "This ends now." He announced. "You are coming home with me." He ordered. "No I am not." I replied firmly. "I am not the naïve boy who left two years ago." "I've seen the horrors you have done." "I'm not like you and I will never be." I asserted. In a rage, he blasted his power at my wall putting a hole in it.

It was at that moment my team arrived. He could see that I had allies now. I was no longer under his control. "I will always love you junior, this is not over. Then he vanished. Jessica hugged me tight. "It will all be okay." She said. I wanted to believe her but I also know my father, he will never give up. He would not allow me to become one of them.

As I healed, there were other things going on that would impact us all. As I rested, Rick made his own discovery. He would visit Shane, which it turns out to be his half-brother. Shane seated in his quarters when Rick appears. "So I thought I felt your presence." Rick replied. "You can leave." Shane ordered. They share the same mother, a beautiful Voltian who comforted my father before and after, my mother died. Rick admired his defiant tone. I would also learn during my time on this base of my sister's love of a human and the son that they shared.

My sister Valtra was my father's finest warrior. She has beautiful auburn hair and light green shimmering eyes. Although she was a woman, he raised her like he did with my brother and me. She was cold and brutal. It was always believed she took no prisoners but she did. She fell in love with a human Galactic Alliance member. She had a child with him. I would meet my nephew with my sister's eyes. He also has his father's stubborn mind. His name is Steven and his father is our Pilot commander Dylan McKay. I only wish I could've known sooner for my sister had a rare disease which will take her life.

As I continue on this path, I will always question myself. I still love my family and I also love my new one. How can I exist in both of these worlds? Especially when one family wants to hurt the other, I can only follow what is in my heart, which is good. I will try to save them but in the end I must defend this galaxy. It is what I pledged to do and what Carla wanted.

Chapter 2
DARKNESS VS RIGHT

My story began in darkness. Now it will end in the right. I found my true home among the humans. I would find a family here. We will join together to rise up against all those who would see the alliance destruction. With that said let me take you through a typical day. The scene is set this time in the Control room, which is not much for décor just chairs at each console station, large vid screen in front of that. This is where our day starts. As Biscus stands at the Helm with a look of frustration yet determination "Alright we have our biggest threat yet." "There is word that Voltar has found the beast known as body parts. "What is that like Frankenstein?" Ralph asked. As he made the team all laugh. Biscus replies "In a way yes." Jesse is quick to add, "I've seen his photo he is massive." Just then Dylan enters the room "its time to move out there has been a sighting." We all headed out into the corridor, and headed toward our docking bay where our fighter jets are kept. I noticed that Shane was somewhat distracted. I walked up to him. "Hey is everything alright?" Shane looked to me with a sense of appreciation for my concern. "I'm fine". He stated. Then we loaded up into our individual fighters to find out what my father was up to. As he was already devising the alliances demise. At his castle, which stood, tall and dark with it's walls made of our planets strongest rock from its mountains and caverns. We go inside to find an older gentleman standing in a laboratory. His mind as twisted as it is genius. His name is Kravitz. He is a scrawny, short little man with brown hair and streaks of silver. He has worked as my father's chief scientist for all of my life. "I have him my lord". He replies with a devilish look in his eyes. He then pushes a button on a sidewall to reveal a glass floor beneath there feet. As my father looked below he saw bodyparts a creature of seven feet tall lying flat on a slab. He consisted of various parts of creatures from different galaxies and worlds. Carefully and intricately sown together with a type of unbreakable thread. You could see he was alive as his openly revealed chest rose and fell. "I am impressed." Voltar stated in his self-serving tone. "We will crush the alliance now." Kravitz adds. "Let me know when he is awake." Voltar replies as he walks out of lab. Now outside of the castle near the forest our team landed. I was nervous myself. I had not been back here since Carla died. "Be careful, were on his world now." Dylan reminds us. We made our way toward the castle on foot, as we walked Amanda another member of our team with beautiful auburn hair and green eyes who is from Voltia. She also has psychic abilities. We also have another new member to our team. His name is Charlie. He is younger than us at sixteen. He is smart and an excellent marksman. He had a familiar arrogance about him with his dark brown hair and green eyes. As we made our way to my father's castle He emerged from the top of it in his cruiser ship and dangling from it was bodyparts himself. "He has revived him!" Dylan shouts. "We need to move." He adds, as we hustled back to our fighters. We followed them. They arrived to Jupiter and released the beast. It landed on its feet and began its reign of terror on the innocent creatures of this world. We tried our hardest to stop it. As we fired on it our weapons had no affect. "We didn't even scratch him" Cole replies. Then biscus called to us on our com-link. "We need to regroup." Biscus ordered. "I know how to stop it." He added. We made our way back to the base where we all disembarked and headed to the control room. "How do we stop it"? Ralph asks." I've done it before." Biscus responds. As biscus stood at the helm of the control room we all gathered to hear the tale. He told us that many years ago. He and my father had to join forces to stop bodyparts. I found it hard to believe my father could help any human. "We had a weapon, a device that is no longer made." "A tissue disrupter." "I need some of you to go find the last man in the galaxy, that may actually have one." Biscus instructed. So he chose Shane, Cole, Mitch and Charlie to go. They loaded up there gear and into their fighters to head to a remote part of Venus. As they landed Cole pulled out a hand held tracker. "Not getting any life signs yet." He replies. "Great, so he's dead?" Shane responds. Mitch says with confidence. "Relax he is alive my god wouldn't let us down." As they make their way threw a dark, murky swampland. "Yeah well my god, has a bad feeling about this." Cole says. "Cut the chatter." Charlie insists. Just then Cole's tracker goes off. "I got something due west." "It's a life form." He adds as they follow the signal. Meanwhile back on our base we had a situation of our own. Bodyparts arrived within feet of our base. Jesse seated at his console. "Whoa, he's going to ram us!" he calls as Bodyparts slams into our base sending everyone flying Back, meanwhile on Venus, as they get closer to signal. "I hope this tardo is that life form." Cole replies they arrive at a small modest hut type home. "Nice quiet mud hole." Mitch accounts. "Should we knock?" Shane questions. "It would be the polite thing to do." Cole responds. Charlie proceeds to knock. It swings open. Mitch draws his weapon from side holster. "Let me go in first." He contends. Charlie stops him. "He is not our enemy". Charlie reminds him. "I'll watch your back". Mitch adds. Shane responds in jest. "Sure there's a few beluin bugs behind us that could pose a problem." As they enter. "Everybody's a comedian. Mitch answers. As they are all inside it is wall-to-wall filled with all types of trinkets, gadgets and bobbles "this guy is a real packrat." Cole reasons. "Lets just hope he has this weapon." Charlie replies. Just then a young girl steps out of the clutter in front of them. Shane and Mitch react on instinct and draw there weapons expeditiously. "Hold it"! Mitch barks. "It's ok I don't think she's armed Cole claims. "Put them away". Charlie commands. As they do. "I apologize my name is lieutenant Charlie Carile of the galactic alliance. We are looking for Tardo". He states. "You are too young to know of him". She answers. "Our commander Biscus brown sent us". He adds. Just then an older humanoid creature of about sixty comes out of shadows. "Why didn't you lead with that?" He argues. "Come in. How is he"? He inquires. "He is fine." Charlie states. "Where are my manners"? "Tara, go get them some refreshments." He demands. "We don't have time". Charlie insists. "Well a cut to the chase man huh"? Tardo reacts. "I apologize but bodyparts is back". Tardo clutches his chest in fright and disbelief. "Are you alright"? Cole inquires. Tardo regains his composure. "I'm fine". "You did say bodyparts"? He questions. "Yes he has been revived". Charlie clarifies. "What do you need form me"? He asks. A weapon used to stop him". "A tissue disrupter." he instructs. Tardo begins to search his piles of items. "It won't do you much good without a sorcerer". He contends. "We have one". Charlie answers. "So Voltar is still in charge"? He inquires. "No he's not in charge, his son Rick handles his affairs now". Charlie informs. "I should go check in with the base". Cole communicates. He goes outside. As Tardo manages to find the weapon, "Here it is". He yells. As he blows off all the dust it has accumulated. Everyone coughs. Charlie takes it from him. "Thank you" he acknowledges. "We will return it". He vows. "Keep it". He maintains. "Tell your friends about us"! He calls. As they head out. "Yeah ok". Mitch says Cole rushes to them out of breath from his long trek back to the fighters. "What is it"? Mitch responds. "Bodyparts attacked the base". Cole bellows. "Lets go". They shout. Tara comes out behind Shane. "May I go too"? She inquires. "Take her she is an excellent pilot". He brags. "Ok come on". Shane approves. Meanwhile back on the base. There are pieces of dabree all over the place as Ralph rushes to biscus who is pinned under his computer console. "Pop are you ok?" He Inquires. "I think my leg is broken". He recognizes, as you can see the exposed bone emergent from his skin. Ralph lifts console off of him. Amanda checks what few computers are still functional. "He's gone for now". She gauges. "I'll try to track him". Jesse asserts, as he checks computer. The others arrive back. "Everyone ok"? Charlie said as he sees the chaos. "Who is she?" Amanda requests. "Tara. She's a good pilot". Shane defends. "You're hired." Biscus states. "We can use all the able bodies we can get". He replies. "We'd better find Rick to help". Cole reminds. No one noticed the look of distress on Charlie's face. Why I wondered. On Voltara my brother was invested in his own personal interests. Rick had discovered where his long lost love was now living. He was about to confront her and find out about a secret that will change his destiny as well. Rick landed his private vessel on earth near a small town. He came by this information by one of his loyal men Matt Nelcon one of a set of deadly assassin twins. As he made his way to on particular modest home he seemed a bit uneasy. He actually cared about this woman. He never really cared about anyone woman before but Charlene she was diverse. She was also gutsy. She was one who would not be kept. I dare say he may have loved her for a moment in time. He knocked on the door. Charlene opens it. Her eyes expanded. Her heart raced. She tried to slam the door. Rick positioned his foot in the entryway.

She stood with a look of panic, as he forced his way inside. "How did you find me"? She commanded. "I have my sources". He countered. "My question is, why did you leave me"? "Did I not treat you well"? He enhanced. "As well as all of your other women." she snapped. Rick then smiled his overconfident way. "So it was jealousy then". He implied. Charlene moves her body to cover a photo of a young boy on her side table. "You again assume with that aster ego, larger than any man". She alleged. Rick noticed she is agitated. "Are you expecting someone"? He probed. Charlene became angered and defensive. "None of your business." She stated. Rick notices the photo on table. He moves swiftly toward it, Charlene in a fright Screams at him. "Just leave"! He then grasps she is trying to redirect him away from the table. "What is it"? He demands. He then seizes photo from the table. He glances at it. "Who is this"? He inquiries. "No one. My nephew." She answers. "You have only one sister". She has a daughter if I recall. He states. "I've met them." He concludes. "I'll ask again, who is he"? He becomes aggravated, as he moves in her face, She frantically tries to get him to leave. He final comprehended what he suspected. "This is my son." as he set photo back on table. "Does he know of me"? He inquires. "Yes, he knows all about you". She clarifies. "What did you tell him"? He pressures. "Did you tell him only the bad things"? He feared. "No I didn't have to he sees it everyday". Rick has a look of confusion. She shows him a recent photo it is of Charlie in full galactic alliance gear. He takes it from her hand and throws it furiously to the floor. "He serves the alliance"! He roars. Charlene gestures yes. "I will fix that". He states. Then he leaves; As Rick was in a fight to get to our base. We were busy contending with Bodyparts. With the help of my father we are able to divided Bodyparts into fragments. We then sealed him inside the monster zone. Which is a void at the end of our galaxy where we place our most dangerous of villains. There are other beasts, which dwell inside. There is only one way in and one way out which is forcefully shielded. Now back on the base it is business as usual. Charlie is at a station in the control room looking over monitors. After he is done he heads to his quarters to rest up. As he walks in he takes off his jacket and hangs it on a bracket on wall. When Rick appears before him. Charlie not startled by his presence. "So you know". He conveys. Rick attempts to come closer to him. When Charlie causes his hands to radiate a glow. "That is close enough." He states. Rick halts. "So, this is how it will be"? Rick probes. Charlie lets out a chuckle. "Did you think I would embrace you?" Charlie responded. "Call you father". He says conclusively. "It does not need to be this way". Rick indicates. "Are you going to change your ways"? He questions. "Serve prison time?" He catechized. "Don't be absurd." He responds. "I will however be your father." "That will not change." He recaps. "You need to leave we are done." He decides. "We are family we will never be done". He inserts. As he gives him a smile then in an instant he vanished, later I was seated in the mess hall. Charlie enters. He proceeded to grab a bottle of rum from the kitchen area. Then he sat down. I rose from my seat and came to him. "What's going on?" I inquired, As Charlie poured a drink into a glass. "I guess you'll find out, soon enough". He informed. "What is it?" I asked as I sat beside him. He takes a moment then replies hesitantly "Rick aster is my father." as he sips his drink. I was speechless. Another aster, and he is on the side of good. I can finally feel like my decisions were the right ones. "Are you going to be ok?" I asked knowing the answer to that question. "Oh yeah, I'll be just fine". He suggests. Well while my newfound nephew was drowning his knowledge of his lineage. At the prison on Earth, Cole was desperately trying to save his sisters. He entered the visiting room. After the guard closed the door a few moments later Cora and Cara were brought in. "Hello brother." Cara replies. "Why are you here?" Cora demands. "I came to see my sisters." Cole responds. "You did, so you can leave alliance officer." Cara barks. "I will always try to save you." Cole reiterates. "You're wasting your time. "Cora indicates. As they head back to door guard opens it they go. Cole stood there struggling with his heart. He was not alone in his struggles. Shane had to return to his home to deal with the death of his mother. He would also find Rick there. In a rage he punched Rick in the face. "You killed her"! He shouted. "I want you out of here." He demands. Rick in his self-importance. Exclaimed, "She was my mother too"! Shane walks away. Now we skip a few years ahead. The battle with my family still rages on. At least I am not alone in this fight. I have my nephew Charlie, Who is determined not to have anything to do with my brother. Then there is Shane who is my brother's brother. There is still another secret to be discovered, One which will shake up our team and his world forever. It started on a routine mission, Shane now nineteen, I am twenty-two. We were just picking up some minor criminals when things go horribly wrong. As we entered an abandoned building or so we thought. We would split up. Shane went around back as Charlie approached from the front, as one of our suspects attempted to escape. Shane fired his weapon and hit him. Only problem was the suspect got off a shot as well. Shane was hit in the chest. We rushed him to sickbay. He was barely breathing. Paul did what he could to stabilize him. Still we were loosing him. Danny our chief medical officer would discover why. He told Biscus and Dylan, who then called me into sickbay asking for my help. I was confused as to why. "He has DNA that is almost exactly like yours Jon." Paul described. "It is exactly a match to Rick's." He stated. Which could mean only one thing. That Rick and Shane were not half-brothers but brothers. Which makes him my brother too. When Shane finally woke up after a day. We told him the truth. He reacted like anyone finding out your father is Voltar Aster would. With rejection and anger. We could see the pain in his eyes. "I will never be an Aster." He shouted, as Shane was healing. My father was being his usual arrogant self. He came to see Shane in his quarters. "Get out!" Shane shouted. "I don't want to see you ever!" He asserted, Voltar in defiance "You have no choice." He implied. "I am your father." He affirmed. "You will never be my father." He instructed. Then suddenly he felt a rush of fever over his body. As he clutched his head and collapsed. When he came to he was in sickbay lying on a bed. "What happened?" He asked in confusion and uncertainty. "You collapsed." Paul informed. "It was your Voltarian power surging throughout you." "Fortunately Voltar was here, only a Voltarian father can calm the first transition." Danny replied. Shane catches a glimpse of Voltar at the sickbay entrance. "You should of let it kill me." Shane contended, as he turned over on his side toward the wall, as we dealt with the tension in sickbay. Rick was also being an Aster father. He came up to Charlie in the docking bay as he put up his gear after a mission. "What is it you want?" He demands. "To make sure you're ok." He declares innocently. "You are my only son you know." He reminds him. "Does not mean I have to like it." Charlie replies, as he walks past him into the corridor. Rick proceeds to follow him. "You are so like me." Rick brags. Charlie stops turns to him. "Lets get something straight, I am nothing like you." Charlie rebels. Rick smiles smugly. "I am also stubborn." "I will wear you down." "I am lovable." He states. Charlie exhales in weariness. "Just go." He demands. Rick vanishes and Charlie walks down corridor. That night Shane was fighting his inner darkness. A battle I know all too well. He tried to understand his mother's betrayal of truth, the discovery of who he really is. It is about to take its toll. He left the base and flew his fighter to Voltara. Perhaps out of curiosity. He walked the city streets. He was full of darkness and wrath. I knew we had to save his soul. So he would not be lost. We went to Voltara to locate him. We were not the only ones looking for him. One of Voltar's enemies would find him first. He would beat him within an inch of his life. We would discover later it was part of our father's design. He was about to show us his true agenda. Jessica woke me as I slept. She saw a vision of this. She had them often foretastes of the future. She said my father was coming for all of us. I should have taken them more seriously. I guess even now, I was still in some denial of what he was capable of, I am a married man now I should understand my father will, never let his blood go. There was only one man who could help us now. A man my family has not met yet, my grandfather Volkren Aster Jr. Known to most as Moondeath. A name he used when the darkness ruled his heart. His turn was mostly due to a beautiful but domineering witch. He would out live her as we all do. We are immortal. We had to travel to a remote part of Voltara. A place none have gone and made it back. I took Shane and Charlie with me, as we were on our quest. My father was using Kravitz to find and resurrect bodyparts, as we flew in a shuttle down to the planet. "Can we trust him?" Shane questioned. "Yes we can." I echoed. We landed in the middle of swampland, as we exited. "It's a swamp." Shane replied in revulsion. "He likes mysterious and dreary places." It's an aster thing." I replied. Charlie used a hand held device to scan for life forms. "I'm picking up someone ahead." He stated. "Lets do this". Shane says.

As we made our way toward the structure "I hope he's on our side." Shane replies. We came upon a small hut in the middle of this abyss. "This is it." Charlie answers. "He lives in that?" Charlie adds, as Jon knocks on the door. "Grandfather?" Jon calls out. No response. "Maybe he's dead?" Shane questions. Just then an older not very challenging man comes up behind them. "Not yet ". He answers. He smiles. I gave him a big hug. "Where is your pretty wife?" He asks. "She is back on the base." I answered. "I really like her." He adds. "We need to talk." I said moving the subject.

Moondeath opens the door. "Then come in." He pronounces. When we walked in it was a huge elegant home fit for a man of his stature. "Now I met Charlie, who are you?" He asks Shane. "I'm Shane I would be your other grandson." He answers. "Another one?" He questioned as he looked at me. "Welcome to the family." He said to make him feel at ease. "So what did my son do now?" He says already believing it was not good. "He is trying to resurrect bodyparts, again." "To destroy the galaxy." Shane disclosed. "That is my son, always using big weapons." Moondeath said. "Will you help us?" Jon pleaded. "I will." He said without hesitation. "He will not listen to me." He reminded us, As Charlie and Shane looked in discontent. "I will try." He says with reassurance. "Besides it's too quiet around here." He adds. "I like him." Shane says, as we made our way back to base. The team was discovering another weakness to bodyparts. "We need to aim for the heart. Biscus instructs as he stands in front of a monitor with a display of Bodyparts's structure. "Should we wait for the others?" Amanda inquires. "There is no time to waste." Dylan counters, the rest of them head to docking bay. They take off to encounter bodyparts who was awake and back together reeking destruction. "Alright aim for the heart." Mitch calls over the com-link. They blast weapons from the ship. It directly hits his heart. It then explodes inside his chest, as bodyparts falls down onto the planet below. "Lets make sure he's toast." Cole replies Meanwhile Voltar is watching this all unfold on his vessel. He then turns to Kravitz in rage and disbelief. "Explain yourself man." He demands. "They discovered his weakness my lord." He responds hesitantly. "I thought he had none." Rick queries. "We will find another way." He vows. "For now we retreat." He adds grudgingly. As they fly off. Back on the base everyone greeted and hugged Moondeath. "Well I'll be." Biscus says in delight. "Your still alive." He adds. "Yes immortality is a good thing." He responded. Jessica comes up and hugs him. "Now that is a sight for sore eyes." "I only wish we knew what he was up to." I said eagerly. "Allow me to help with that." Moondeath replies. As he concentrates his eyes begin to glow. He creates an image in the air in front of them of the inside of Voltar's castle. "I can get cable too." He adds in jest. "You are the man." Ralph contends, as we continued to monitor them. Voltar would reveal his next plans for us. He discovered an android created centuries ago but disabled and hidden he was named Zonebot, as he was support to keep the monster zone criminals and creatures in line. He is planning to go after it. We knew we had to get there first. We will. There are still more battles to be fought with my father, our father. At least I am not in this alone any longer. I feel a sense of confidence in the future that we will triumph over my father and his cohorts, to stop them from ruling the galaxy.

Chapter 3

FATHERS AND SONS

As our team deals with all the twists and turns of our lives, my brother Shane is taking it the hardest. He cannot accept my father as his. I fear he is headed to darkness, which my father would love. I must save his soul. I will save him. In the Control Room, Biscus stands at the head of the room. Tara says, "I should talk to him." Biscus replies, "He feels betrayed. His life as he knew it was a lie." Charlie says, "Let me talk to him. I can relate to his state right now." Charlie then goes off.

In Shane's quarters, Charlie enters. Charlie calls out, "Shane?" He looks over to see Shane seated on couch still in stained and worn t-shirt and sweatpants. Shane replies surly, "She lied to me. How could she? She was my mother. She could've told me before she died." Charlie sits beside him, "She wanted you to be free of the burden of being an Aster." Shane then snaps back in anger, "Free?! I'm not free! I don't know who I am! How can I forgive her?!" Charlie replies, "The same way I forgave my mother." Shane adds, "At least she told you the truth."

Charlie sighed, "No, I actually figured it out when I came into my powers. I knew my father could not be who she claimed." "I appreciate it but I'd like to be alone now." Shane responds. As Charlie respects his wishes and leaves, Voltar appeared at the doorway. "May I enter?" he asked in his arrogant tone. Shane looked to him and responded, "I really can't deal with you right now!" Voltar comes closer and says, "Look I'm just as angry as you. She never told me." Shane says, "I don't want to be your son." Just then Rick appears, "Can I come in?" he asks, Shane says, "Great why not one more Aster?!"

As Voltar is trying to convince Shane he would be a good father, we were dealing with our first of many psychotic females that would be coming after us Aster men. It's a long story. You see a woman scorned cursed our father. Now we all will pay the price, even my brother Rick. Biscus gathered us in the Control Room. He put up a photo on the screen, a beautiful female with blonde hair and blue eyes.

Biscus says, "This is Lolara. She is a sorceress from Saturn and she's escaped from prison." Rick then happens to be passing by when he sees the photo. He enters, "She's free?" he asks. Everyone turns to look at him in confusion. Charlie responds, "You know her?" Rick then says, "Yes she loved me once but I had to break up with her. She was unstable!" Cole says, "She was unstable?" Biscus replies, "Let's get out there and find her!" As they do, Lolara appears in the corridor as Rick turns to her. She gives him a look of pure rage yet lust.

Rick replies, "So Lolara, how has prison treated you?" Lolara in anger, "How dare you!" She then uses her power to blast him into the wall with a loud thud! Danny then sees her and calls over communicator, "We have trouble here!" Biscus comes to see the fight. He calls to the team over communicator, "Get back here she's after Rick with a vengeance!" As they arrive back on the base, Lolara has Rick hovering in the air with her telekinesis. Rick replies in a tone of fear, "Well do something!" Amanda fires stun weapon. Lolara falls to the ground.

As Rick is dropped to the floor, the team restrains her. Charlie helps rick to his feet, "Are you okay?" he asks. Shane replies, "Well you sure have a way with the ladies!" Rick says with disgust, "She was no lady." Charlie adds, "I think we got that." Rick says with a smirk, "Well I think I should stay here until she is back at the prison." Charlie responds, "What? Why?" Rick adds, "I was just assaulted in your base!" Ralph says, "Seriously you could've killed her if you wanted to!" Biscus replies, "He is right, at least until we get her off the base."

Rick comes to Shane, "So can I stay with you brother?" he asked slyly. Shane replies, "My quarters are…. Sort of small so…." Rick interrupts, "Good! I don't take up much room!" He proceeds to head to Shane's quarters. "Great." Shane mutters. "He's your father!" he says to Charlie. "Well you wanted your big brother back before so…" Charlie adds. Charlie goes, Cole pats Shane on the back. "Have fun!" Amanda says, "Play nice!" Shane yells, "Come on! Why me?" As he opens the door, he finds women seated by Rick on the couch.

Shane responds in shock, "What the hell is this?" rick replies, "Just a few friends, you don't mind do you? You can have one." He added, Shane replies, "No thanks. I have a girlfriend." He then sees photo of his mother on the table. He takes it and throws it in the trash angrily. Rick asks, "What are you doing?" Shane says sternly, "Nothing." Rick responds, "Ladies time to go." They leave. Rick asks, "Why did you do that?" Shane responds, "Why? I can't look at her right now! I need to go." He goes out. Shane then goes to the docking bay and in his ship. In the Control Room, alarm sounds.

Biscus replies, "Who just left?" Jesse checks computer, "Shane did sir." He replies. Biscus hits communicator on console, "Shane what are you doing?!" he demands, Shane responds, "Just blowing off steam!" Biscus says, "Get back here ASAP!" Rick enters as well as the others. "He's mad." Rick says, Charlie responds, "What did you do?" Suddenly ship alarms go off. Biscus calls over console, "Shane what's going on?" Shane does not respond. Jesse tracks ship, "He's going down sir!" Charlie says, "Let's go!" They head out to the planet. Shane is unconscious.

The cockpit door is opened and a shadow pulls him out. Shane then comes to and looks up as he tries to focus, "Hum who are you?" he questioned. Moondeath removes hood, "So that Aster temper getting the best of you?" Shane mutters out, "Sorry I was angry." He sits up and clutches head. Moondeath says, "Easy, you hit your head pretty good! So feel better?" Shane says, "No just stupid." Team arrives and Charlie comes over to him, "Are you okay?" Tara runs over and hugs him. Shane, "Yeah sorry about this." He breathes. Charlie says, "Thanks. Um Moondeath right?" he asks as he looks over at him. Moondeath responds, "So, you're

Rick's son? You're a handsome boy." Charlie says, "Yeah thanks." Let's get back!"

As we headed back to the base, we would also find out about another woman. Her name was Tracilla. She is a goddess. She can seduce men with ease and she will. For now she is out for revenge on my father. She'll try to use us to do it. "Her name is Tracilla." Jesse states as we are all in the Briefing Room with her photo on the screen. "She is beautiful with raven hair and fair skin with green eyes. Biscus says, "We have reason to believe that she is back and will be coming after us."

Ralph asks, "Why us?" Biscus replies, "She hates all Asters thanks to Voltar." Jon says, "I remember her. She is very beautiful but also dangerous." Jessica says, "We'll capture her." Biscus adds, "Won't be easy. She's a goddess." Shane asks, "Why doesn't she just kill Voltar? Why target us?" Jon replies, "What better way to hurt him then to hurt his family?" Charlie asks, "So how do we stop her?" Voltar and rick appear. Voltar interrupts, "It will take all of you to stop her." Just then the base shakes as the team struggles to stay on their feet. Jon replies, "She's here!" Just then she appears inside the base.

She is dressed in a short skintight red dress. Tracilla then replies, "Well Voltar it's been too long." She then causes the walls to blow outward with her power. Voltar asks, "What do you want?" Tracilla looks around at all the team, "I see many handsome young Asters here." She walks up to Jon, Shane, and then Charlie. "Very handsome." She adds. Voltar responds, "Now we'll end this!" Tracilla turns to him, "Yes we will." Voltar exclaimed, "All of you now!" Just then Rick, Charlie, Shane, and Jon glow and blast at Tracilla.

Just then she explodes in a flash of light. Cole asks, "Is she dead?" Voltar replies, "For now." Biscus says, "Ok then back to work!" The team disperses. Voltar comes to Jon, "You saved the day." Jon says. "Yes I did junior." Jon replies coldly, "Don't call me that. I still want to trust you." Voltar says, "I know I will earn it one day." Jon goes out. Shane comes to Voltar; "I don't really know what to think about you right now." He says. "I'll try my best." Voltar replies as he smiles then goes off. Charlie speaks with Rick, "So can I ever trust you?" he asks. "When it comes to you yes. You know we are not so different." Rick answered.

Charlie replies, "You should go now." Rick vanishes. Now on Voltara, Rick says, "The old man is ready for us!" Voltar replies, "I hope our sons can forgive us." Rick responds, "They will." He reassures. Now back on the base, Shane and Tara are in Shane's quarters. Shane says, "I've been awful to you." Tara replies, "You were angry. I understand." Shane responds, "It's no excuse. I am trying." Tara kisses him, "We will handle this together." Now it's another day and Mitch is in for a surprise.

In the Control Room, Jesse at the computer, Mitch comes in. "Hey Mitch!" "What's up kid?" he asks. "I got a message for you from a Brent Trent." Mitch looks surprised, "My brother? Why is he calling?" Jesse says, "He said it's urgent." Mitch goes to quarters; "I'll take it in my quarters." Ralph comes over to Jesse, "Wonder what's up?" Now in Mitch's quarters, he pulls up vid phone. Brent is on the other end. He is fifteen years old dressed in torn clothes with brown hair and green eyes. Mitch says with concern, "Brent are you okay?" Brent replies with worry, "Ok look don't be mad okay?" Mitch replies curiously, "What did you do?" Brent, "See you always assume the worst!" he said frustrated. Mitch says, "Ok what happened?" Brent replies, "I need to see you."

Mitch replies, "Ok come here now." He clicks off. Brent arrives at Docking Bay. Amanda comes up to him, "Who are you?" Brent replies slyly, "Whoever you want me to be." "Watch it kid she's spoken for!" Cole says. "Sorry I'm Brent Trent." Ralph replies, "You're Mitch's brother!" Brent says, "Yes I am." Mitch comes in, "So you're here." He says. Brent says, "Nice friends you got."

Mitch after everyone goes out. "Okay what's wrong?" he asks. Brent says nervously, "Did I say anything was wrong?" Mitch replies, "You haven't contacted me in three years. So what did you do?" Brent explains, "Nothing big I just need a place to lie low for a while." Mitch says, "If you're going to stay here I need to know more kid." Brent sighs, "Fine but I need to promise to be calm." Mitch replies, "I can't." Brent says, "Fine. Well…. I sort of stole a shipment that I should've now the owner is after me. They already tried to kill me once!" Mitch stops him, "Okay slow down! Who's the owner?" Brent answers, "Cora Babor!" "Cora Babor! How can you be so stupid? I told you never to get involved with them!" Mitch yells.

Brent pleads, "I'll go straight I swear just help me please." He makes a sad face that would melt your heart. Mitch replies, "Fine. You can stay." Brent hugs him, "Thank you! I promise I'll be good. You won't even know I'm here!" Mitch comes over to team in Control Room, "My brother will be staying for a little while." He says. Biscus asks, "Is everything okay?" Mitch answers, "He's got himself into some trouble with the Babor twins." Jesse says, "Was he crazy?" Mitch says, "All we can do is give back the goods before they notice."

Jon replies, "Of course we'll help." As we were planning to help Brent had his own dangerous agenda. He is in Mitch's quarters on vid phone, "Yeah so tell Cora if she wants her stuff she's got to make me a better offer." Cara is on the other line, "Kid you've got some nerve." Brent replies, "Better believe it!" He then disconnects the vid phone. Mitch enters, "Okay the team will return the property no problem." Brent responds, "Are you nuts? That's my deal of a lifetime!" Mitch responds, "Are you nuts? You don't mess with the Babor Sisters you'll end up dead!" Brent argues, "I need those supplies Mitch!" Mitch replies, "What is so important? Tell me everything!"

Brent explains, "There's a staff in that shipment. It's very powerful or else they wouldn't have tried to kill me." Mitch replies, "I'll call my team." He calls over vid link. The team returns to the base. Now in Control Room, Mitch says, "That shipment is valuable to Voltar." Shane asks, "How do you know this?" Brent replies cocky, "I'm just that good." Mitch gives him a scolding look. Jon asks, "So what now?" Charlie replies, "We hold that shipment and check it out."

Cole asks, "What if they come looking for it?" Charlie replies, "We start making arrests." Biscus replies, "Okay Jesse analyze the staff." Jesse says; "I'm on it!" he goes. Mitch grabs Brent by arm, "You come with me!" he said angrily. Mitch asks, "Who did you call?" Brent replies, "What?"

Mitch adds, "I know you made a call. Who was it?" he questioned again. Brent sighs, "Fine. I called Cora Babor to make a deal." Mitch replies, "You don't care that they'll use it against us?" Brent replies, "Okay I'm sorry I'm a jerk." Mitch responds, "You'd better be telling me everything!"

Brent replies, "I am! I just wanted to make some money." Mitch responds, "Not at the expense of others." Brent sarcastically, "You go good for a few years and think your Mr. clean." Mitch grabs him up and yells, "Hey that life was the wrong one. I got a second chance to do it right!" Brent gulps, "You were the best." Mitch replies, "I still am just on the right side." He lets him go. Brent responds, "Gone soft is more like it." Mitch says, "You really think being bad is right? Come with me tough guy." They go to Docking Bay. Brent asks, "Where are we going?" They load up in ship. Mitch, "You'll see." They fly to Voltara itself and then they exit.

Brent asks, "What is this?" Mitch takes him to village where people are lying on the ground mostly dead and others beaten. Mitch says, "This is what the Babors do!" Brent replies, "I want go." Mitch replies, "just remember this." They go back to ship. Now as they fly back Brent says, "I'm sorry. I'll go straight." Mitch says, "You'd better or I'll take you back there." Brent asks, "So what will I do here?" Jesse asks, "Well what are you good at?" Brent replies, "I'm a good shot and I can fix things." Biscus says, "Okay you can work on fighters." Brent asks, "I'm hired?" Biscus replies, "Yes so go!" Jesse says, "I'll show you." They go.

Now later that night, Brent is on a vid phone in the Rec Room. "How much?" he asks, Cora replies, "We'll meet to discuss it." Now in the morning, Brent is in the Docking Bay suiting up when Mitch comes up to him. "What are you doing?" Brent turns, "I just wanted to see how it feels to be a pilot." He says. Mitch replies, "Okay well Jessica's ship needs an adjustment so get on it!" He smiles. Brent goes over to ship. Mitch leaves so Brent goes over and gets into ship and flies out meanwhile,

Jesse is at computer in Control Room when alarm goes off. "Captain we have an unauthorized departure!" he says. Biscus asks, "Who is it?" Jesse replies, "It's Mitch's ship." Just then Mitch enters Control Room, Biscus asks, "If you are here then who is in your ship?" Mitch replies, "What?"

Biscus says, "Open a channel." Jesse does. Mitch realizes and says I know who it is. Brent get back here now!" Brent responds, "I can't got a big deal going." Biscus replies, "I can shoot you down."

Brent responds, "You won't." He closes channel. Mitch replies, "I can't believe him! He's acting like me when I was his age." Charlie replies, "Well let's go get him." Mitch says, "I need a ship." Jesse replies, "Take Jessica's she's off today." Charlie and Mitch head to Docking Bay. Cole and Ralph enter Control Room. Cole asks, "What's going on?" Jesse replied, "Mitch's brother stole his ship to make a deal with the Babors." Ralph says, "Is he crazy? Let's go they'll need back up." They head out as they do Brent lands on Mars. He exits ship and looks around, "Where are they?" he asks as Cora comes out.

Cora asks, "Where is my property?" Brent turns around, "I'm not stupid it's somewhere safe. So let's deal." Cora comes closer and says, "You're confident." Brent asks, "So how much is it worth?" Cora replies, "What are you asking?" Just then the team flies over head, "A set up huh?" Cora replies. She fires her weapon at Brent as she runs. Brent looks up to see Jessica's ship he says, "No she'll crash!" Charlie over com-link, "Okay let's pick him up." Mitch says, "I'll handle it." He goes in to land but landing gear does not respond.

Mitch replies, "My gear won't open!" Cole yells, "Look out!" Mitch crashes on the planet. Everyone else lands and heads towards the ship. Charlie says, "We got to get it open!" Brent runs to them, "Is Jessica okay?" he asks. Ralph says, "Jessica?" Brent says, "Yeah it's her ship." Ralph explains, "Mitch borrowed it when you took his." Brent's eyes widened in fear, as they lift open the hatch to find Mitch unconscious and bleeding from head to chest. Charlie replies, "Mitch can you hear me?" Ralph says, "We need to get him to Danny."

As they lead him on Charlie's ship Cole comes over to Brent, "You ride with me." Brent asks, "It's bad isn't it?" Cole replies, "He's been through worse." Now back at the base the team is outside Sick Bay. Brent is pacing, "Why is it taking so long?" he asked impatiently worried. Jesse replied, "Take it easy kid Danny is the best." Biscus comes to Brent, "You are in big trouble!" Brent with tears in his eyes, "I am so sorry!" Biscus scolds, "You could've done much worse to you and this team! You either work with us or not at all!" Brent hugs Biscus and sighs, "I'm sorry."

Danny comes out of Sick Bay into hall. Brent comes to him and asks, "Is he okay?" Danny answers, "He's asking for you." Brent goes in. Charlie comes to Danny, "Is he okay?" A look of sadness in Danny's eyes said something else. "No his chest is collapsed his rib punctured his heart. He is dying." Danny says. Jessica exclaims, "Oh my god!" she hugs Jon. Amanda begs, "Is there something we can do?" Danny says, "No I'm sorry but the damage is too extreme." Shane replies, "I can't accept that!" Jon adds, "Maybe we can help?" Charlie asks, "Use our powers?"

Jessica replies, "Maybe if you all do you can repair the damage." Danny says, "Try it. We have nothing to lose." They enter Sick Bay to find Brent holding Mitch's hand; he is hooked up to machines. Brent says, "Please don't die I know I screwed up… I let you down." He sighs. As tears roll down his face he continues, "But I need you. You're my brother." Mitch opens his eyes. He says weakly, "I'm out of the game kid. I know because I can't feel anything. I love you. This team will be your new family now." He closes his eyes and dies as the machines go off. Brent yells, "No!" Charlie comes over to him, "Hurry let's do it!" They all join hands.

Their eyes glow as they put their hands on Mitch. Brent asks, "What are they doing?" then it stops. Mitch opens his eyes. Danny comes over and scans him with a small device, "The damage is completely healed." Shane smiles, "Welcome back!" he says. Mitch replies, "I'm alive?" Cole says, "We should leave these two alone." They go out Brent comes over to Mitch, "How did they?" he asks, Mitch says, "I'll explain later." They hug, Brent says, "I will go straight I swear this time!!"

Mitch responds, "I know you will. I love you." Brent says, "I love you too." Biscus comes in, "Okay mister you have ships to repair!" Mitch replies, "Take it easy on him sir." Brent says, "No I'm a member of this team I need to act like it and except my punishment." He goes out. Mitch replies, "He's a good kid." Biscus says, "I know. Now get some rest." Biscus goes to Loading Bay and comes over to Brent, "Okay here's your list." Gives him paper. Brent replies, "Yes sir." Biscus responds, "And when you're done pick up your uniform!" Brent looks at him, "My uniform?" he says confused. Biscus says, "Yes you wanted to be a part of this team right?"

Brent responds, "Yes sir! Thank you." Biscus goes. Jesse walks in Control Room when Biscus walks in. "You're a push over captain." Jesse jokes. Biscus replies, "Zip it!" Now as we were celebrating our newest member my father was up to no good. In the castle in the main throne room, Voltar says, "We need a plan." Rick replies, "I'm thinking. I know we can release all the criminals in the prison and cause chaos." Voltar asks, "How are we going to pull that off?" Rick replies, "Kravitz explain to my father." Kravitz comes up, "Well I have a device that could handle that!"

Voltar replies, "So it can't be traced back to us?" Kravitz says, "Exactly my lord they will be tracking your movements." Voltar responds, "I like it. Gentlemen get suited!" Now in the Mess Hall, Ralph is sitting at table with Jesse. "Boy is it dead around here!" Jesse says, Ralph replies, "Yeah we're just too good." Meanwhile down in the Rec Room Amanda is in work out gear with Cole on the mat. "Okay let's practice!" She says. Jessica replies, "Yes some of us are getting rusty!" Amanda responds, "Now let's not embarrass the boys!" Cole asks, "What do you mean by that?"

Just then alarms sound as Voltar's henchmen have gone to each planet to use Kravitz's device to unlock all of the cells in the prisons. Jesse at computer, "Sir we've got multiple breakouts on all prisons!" Biscus replies, "How is that possible?" Shane replies, "Its Voltar! It has to be!" Charlie asks, "But how?" Jon replies, "You are talking about my father." Mitch adds, "We can't handle this many prisoners!" Biscus replies, "Which is just what Voltar wanted." Brent asks, "So what do we do?"

Charlie replies, "We try to recapture as many as we can." Jesse adds, "I'll work on how they got out!" As he checks the computer, Shane thinks, "What about that scientist of his?" Jon says, "Of course! Kravitz, he's brilliant. He can do something like this!" Charlie says, "I say we question him!" Biscus says, "Yes after we round up these prisoners!" the team heads out as we attempted to round up all the criminals my father set free there was someone in the wings planning.

Here name was Sarella. She was the first girl my brother ever kissed when they were thirteen. He fell hard for her but my other brother Rick knew she was a demon from hell itself or as we call it the Underworld. We will battle many of their kind as they escape the dark depths. This one wants the power that Asters possess and she'll do anything to get it. I must join with Rick to save his life. I just hope we can stop her and send her back to hell.

Chapter 4
WOMEN EVERYWHERE

You will learn that with Asters, There is never a shortage of beautiful women of all species. Unfortunately most of them that come to us are evil and psychotic bitches. We can thank our father for this problem. He pissed of a powerful ancient once so she placed a powerful curse on him and all his offspring to have these special types of females fall for us. It will not end well. In the control room, Jesse is at his console. As we returned from a mission, Jesse gestured Shane to him. "I received a message for you, From a Sarella"? Shane is astonished. "I haven't seen her in years". He indicated. "I was thirteen". "Old girlfriend?" Jesse queries. "First love." He responses. Amanda hears conversation and comes to them. "Tell us more". She probes. "Leave the guy alone it's personal". Ralph asserts. "So was she hot"? Ralph solicits. Shane answers with a smile. "Yes she was". He conveys. Amanda insists he go on. "I met her at my school, we were close". "She was my first kiss". He recalls. "What happened"? Jesse probes. "For some reason I still don't know, Rick just showed up." "He dragged me off and told me I can never see her again". Shane conveys. "He threatened to kill her". He resumes. "I never saw her after that day". He finalizes. "Why did Rick do that"? Amanda questions. "I don't know he never said". Shane accounts. "So maybe she is here to answer that". Jon supposes. "I guess I'll find out". Shane answers. He then proceeds to his quarters to call Sarella privately on his vidlink. She responds she is picturesque with golden hair and sapphire eyes. "Shane is that you?" as she stares at his solid jawline and jade eyes with light brunette hair. "Yes it is". He answers. "Can we meet"? He inquires. "Of course". She stresses. Then he ends call as Brent walks in. "What's going on"? He asked. "I'm going to Voltia if anyone asks". Shane states, as he goes out. Brent then proceeds to the control room to apprise the others. "Shane is on his way to see Sarella". Brent states. "Keep an eye on him". Charlie conveys to Jesse. "I think we should talk to Rick". I proposed. As we headed to Rick's club. Shane made his way to Voltia. He made his way to one of there favorite spots in the open grass near his old school. "Are you here"? He calls. Sarella comes out from behind a tree in a stunning short dress and level shoes. Shane turns to see her. She spellbinds him. They make way to each other meeting in the middle of the open field. "You are so beautiful". Shane accounts. "You are as handsome as I remember". Sarella complements. They then kiss passionately. We arrived at Rick's club to find him engaged in other pursuits. We knocked on his Room door. He came to it opened it. "What do you want"? He demands. "Relax your not under arrest...yet". Charlie dispatches. "We need to talk about Sarella" I identified. Rick's face goes absolute and his eyes enlarge in alarm. "Is she here"? He reacts in unease. "I will destroy her". He apprises. "What is it about her"? I commanded. "Who is she"? "What has she done"? Charlie asks in simplicities. "She is pure evil" He educated. "She is a demon of the underworld". "She targets formidable males". "She makes them evil". He adds. "We need to go now". Charlie demands. "Is she with him now"? Rick inquires. I shook in agreement. We loaded up to get to Voltia expeditiously, as Sarella was working on Seducing Shane into her trap. They are lying on the grass gazing into each other's eyes. "I missed you". Sarella articulates. "I always wished we'd meet again" Shane responds. Sarella caresses his cheek. "Now nothing will keep us apart". Sarella pronounces securely. Just then we arrived overhead. Sarella rises. "What is that?" She examines, as Shane rises as well. "It's fine it's my team" Shane assures. "Not again". Sarella whispers. Shane looks to her he can tell she is frantic. "Are you alright"? Shane questions. "I will not loose you again"! She screeches. Shane observes in confusion. "They are my family and friends" Shane assures. We landed and rushed to him. "Shane"! Listen to me, you must get away from her". I implored, as rick came behind me. "What did you say about her"! Shane commanded "The truth Shane" Charlie echoed. "She is evil". He added. "So please come over here I insisted. "No"! Sarella shrieks as she grabs Shane by arm and hurled him toward nearby tree knocking him out with the intensity. "He is mine". She acknowledges. "I'll handle her". Rick notifies. "Get him out of here" Rick demands. We made our way to Shane. "Now I will kill you as I should have so long ago". Rick accounts. "You can try". She says in arrogance as the battle commences with powerful blasts as Rick becomes his rubicund dregon and she turns into her revolting true form. "He can handle it lets get Shane to sickbay." Charlie instructions, as we loaded up into a shuttle, Rick advanced to slash Sarella apart. Now back on the base in sickbay Danny tended to Shane. "He'll be fine". Danny communicates. "Where is Rick"? Cole asked curiously. Rick then materializes in sickbay. "Is he alright"? Rick probes. Charlie comes to him. "He'll be ok", "Just a concussion". He adds. "Where is Sarella"? I inquired. "She is dead and back where she belongs". He indicated. Shane begins to awaken. "What Happened"? He asks feebly. I walked up to him. "It's a long story". I replied. "I think Rick should explain". Rick comes to his bedside. As the rest of us give them privacy. "What did you do to her"? What was she"? He asked in discomfort and puzzlement. "She was a demon of the underworld". He educated. "I guess I owe you one". Shane responds. Rick touches his arm slightly. "You are my brother, you owe me nothing". He reminds. Well as Shane rested. We had our own drama with female advances. It was a new day. We were all gathered in the control room. "We have a unidentified vessel landing on Voltara". Jesse expresses. "Our first catch of the day". Ralph boasts. Cole reacts with a sigh. "Really"? As the two of them head out and down the corridor toward the docking bay. Shane comes to docking bay as well. "Are you cleared to return to duty"? Charlie questions. "Yes I'm good" Shane replies. At that moment the power goes out, Biscus in the control room. "What is going on Jesse"? He demands. Jesse struggles to check the equipment. "Power failure all stations sir". He responds. The rest of the team makes way back to control room. "What happened"? Cole asked, "Something took out all our systems". Jesse responds. "We're defenseless". He added. Just then a huge explosion is experienced and heard thought the base. "What was that"? Cole shouted. "What ever it was it's not friendly". Mitch responded. Then instantaneously the power is restored. "Get me intelligence people". Biscus orders, as Jesse scans the data. We split up to investigate the source. Jesse guides them over the com-links. "It originated from sector five". Jesse instructed. Charlie with Ralph are closest so they investigate. "Set weapons for stun". Charlie insists. "At least until we know who or what we're dealing with". He adds. When they make way into Sector Five they come upon a small shuttle that crashed threw their outer wall. They secure the wall with a second barrier door so they can breathe. "I've never seen a craft like this before". Ralph reported. The hatch then springs open catching them off guard. They point weapons toward hatch. "I guess we will see who's inside". Charlie replies. About eight very mysterious, youthful, beautiful women emerge. They are clothed in battle armor and gear." I love my job" Ralph delights. "Why did you attack our base"? Charlie demands abruptly. The first young woman comes to him she is there leader. "We are in need of assistance". She pleads. The rest of the team arrives. "Always blast your way in to achieve that"? Amanda demands. "I respectfully apologize". "We needed to assure you where an ally". "Where are you from"? Ralph probes. "We are Valdred from Valdar four". She revealed. "It is outside of your known galaxy". She enlightened. "How did you end up here"? Mitch investigates. "We were attacked we had to flee here". She said. "Who were they"? Charlie questioned. "We do not know". She responded. "Lets get them to sickbay" Amanda insists observing fresh wounds on them, now in sickbay. Danny examines them thoroughly with scanners. "I am Dr. Danny Mihal". He states. "So many men here'. She says in interested and shameless manner. "This is a small base". Jessica informed. "So you are equals in this galaxy"? She probed. "Yes of course". Jessica solidifies. "On my world we ruled". "Men worked for us". She boasted, meanwhile in the control room. "They claimed they were attacked". Charlie says with distrust. "So are they friend or foe"? Biscus asks, "I'll check over their vessel". Jesse undertakes, as he goes out. "I'll help him". Brent offers. Biscus nods in agreement and Brent go out. Now in Sector Five. They both study the craft intensely. "It sure looks like it's been in battle". Jesse concurs. "I'll go over the data logs" Jesse states. Now back in sickbay Danny relays his findings to the others. "Well they appear normal by my scans". Danny apprises. "We should question them," Cole advises. Charlie goes up to woman. "So what were you carrying in your vessel that they were after"? Charlie questions. "They were after us". She professed. "To own us." She added. "We can protect you in our galaxy, if you want us to"? Charlie assured. "We thank you but we must get to our home world." She declined. "What if they find you again"?

Amanda expresses. "We are warriors, we will fight till our last breath." She responds. "Well I guess that's all we can do." Cole declares. "We could scout ahead make sure there path is clear." Charlie recommends. "Yeah it will take only a few hours in our fighters." Brent chimes in. "We can make sure their vessel is repaired by then." He adds. "Be careful, don't go starting a war". Biscus cautions. "Only if they shoot first." Mitch responds. As team heads out Jessica interrogates our guests. "So tell us about your world." Jessica asks. "We are a peaceful people." She says in innocence. "The ones who attacked us were cowards and savages". She confirmed. As our guests stayed behind we flew into their galaxy and made our way to there home world, which they gave us directions to. "We are almost to there planet." Ralph informed. "I'm not picking up any other craft in the vicinity." Cole determines. "Well maybe they've moved on." Mitch answers. "Did you not see those women?" Ralph reminded. "We should head back then." Charlie ordered. Just then a similar vessel came upon them. It omitted a tractor beam at there fighters and ensnared them pulling them toward their world. As the team tries to get free and radio for assistance with no success, they landed hard onto the planet. They are roughed and thrown about in there fighters. "Is everyone ok?" Charlie asks with a minor laceration above his right eye bleeding. "Yeah I'll live." Mitch adds as he opens the hatch to his cockpit. "All bones are in place." Ralph responds as he checks. All exit their fighters. "Just a hard landing". Shane states. "Where'd the ship go?" Cole asks. "Lets pair up and find out" Jon recommends. "Ooh a first date who do I choose?" Ralph says sarcastically. "Very funny" Charlie responds. "Mitch with me" Charlie says. As Jon and Shane agree to pair up. "Great I'm stuck with him" Cole reacts. "Trust me you are not my first choice either." Ralph returns. As we head off in different directions to evaluate our situation. On the base Brent and Jesse return to the control room. "Well it's all fixed." Brent informed. "Any word from the team?" Jesse inquired. "Not yet." Dylan replied. "You ladies are free to go". Biscus states. "Thank you commander." She replies with a smile. They head to their vessel and get aboard. "Is it done"? She commanded. "Yes my queen." Second girl replies. "Then let us make haste." She instructs, now after there departure. "Shouldn't they be back by now"? Brent questions. Jesse attempts t contact there fighters. "I have nothing but static." He says. Just then an incoming message flashes on Jesse's monitor screen. "Sir it's a message from

Valdar four." He replies. "They are keeping our men." He reads. "No they are not," Jessica answers. "Lets suit up people." Biscus declares. Meanwhile back on Valdar four. Cole and Ralph walk along a desolate path surrounded by an uninhabited small town. "Is it me or is it way to quiet around here?" Ralph examined. "Your right where are all the people?" Cole questioned. Just then underneath there feet the ground collapsed down into a waiting enclosure below. Where they would realize the others were as well. "I get the feeling this was all planned." Cole replies. As they get to there feet. The woman soon entered a few minutes later. "Now you are ours." She conveyed. "I demand you release us from here now." Charlie ordered. "Why are you doing this?" Cole asked. "You are here to protect and serve us." She justified. "I think they took our offer too literally." Ralph whispers. "Their only women, we can take them." Mitch says in certainty. Meanwhile above us the rest of our team was arriving. Only to be welcomed by our same fate. "I have all of their life readings sir." Jesse conveyed thankfully. "Good it means they're alive." Biscus rejoiced. Just then the tractor beam is activated from the planet and locks onto their fighters. "Whoa they're pulling us down!" Brent shouts. They land hard on the surface. "Everyone ok?" Biscus asks all acknowledge him. "We need to take out that beam to get off this planet". Amanda apprised. As they get out of their fighters Jessica and Amanda use their Supernatural telekinesis to find and blast the beam. As they accomplished that below in the underground lair we resided in. "I hope they get here fast." Charlie expresses. "Guys is it really so bad?" Ralph deliberates. "They will probably use us for slave labor Romeo." Mitch enlightens. "Whoa hell no we got to get out of here." Ralph grabs at bars. The rest of the team above made their way to us. "We need a distraction." Biscus contemplates. "Leave that to me sir" Jesse says assertively. He then pulls out gear in his equipment bag. "Do we even want to know?" Brent asks. "It's just a small explosion I'm whipping up." He states. "Of course it is." Brent accounts. Then Jesse throws it into entranceway. It explodes and knocks out the women. The others hear the explosion. "Sounds like the team is here." Jon responds. "Lets get off this rock, I prefer my own galaxy." Ralph asserts. Now back on the base. "Ok lets catch our breath people." Biscus instructs. All disperse and head to various locations on the base. Charlie heads to his quarters. Enters sits on couch and begins to relax when Rick appears seated beside him. "Well it was almost a good day." Charlie moaned. "I just wanted to check on you." Rick replies innocently. "I'm tired what is it?" Charlie complained. "Can't a father just say hello?" Rick maintains. "You are up to no good, always." Charlie prompts. "My son you know me too well." Rick acknowledges. "I'll let you rest up." Rick adds as he touches Charlie's shoulder and vanishes. Now it's a new day a day filled with more feminine dilemmas. It would start when a fellow member of the galactic alliance someone who was a mentor to Shane would crash his fighter in a battle into the monster zone. Where no one can return. Shane will not accept that as finality for his fallen comrade. This is the day that we would encounter two sisters who will be a never-ending problem for generations of asters to come. Let me explain. They are called Moneconda. In their original form they are quite gruesome and grotesque, but they can also change into a humanoid form, which is quite seductive and alluring. Once they fall for a male. They do so until they die. They cannot and will not love another until they are dead. They can also be regenerated, but the next recreation will not remember their former existence and can fall for another male they see. Scary isn't it? Now in the control room, the call comes in. "Mayday, Mayday this is this is Captain Alec Darren. I am going down in the monster zone repeat going down in the zone god help me." Transmission goes dead. "He was a good man." Biscus says with distress and despondency. "He could still be alive." Dylan indicates. "We cannot risk going into that place for one man." I'm sorry. He responds. Shane is also present he rises to his feet. "I'll go in." He states with sincerity and faith. "Are you sure?" Biscus probes. "He would do it for me." "He was like a brother to me." Shane conveys. "You understand this would be a solo mission no one can go with you inside." Dylan reminds. "I owe him." Shane adds. "Jesse will try to configure where his fighter would have crashed." Biscus says, As Shane steps over to Jesse to review the data. Charlie comes to Dylan. "He cannot go in there." Charlie contends. "Maybe I should go." Jon volunteers. "Don't talk about me like I'm not here." Shane interrupts. "I didn't mean to offend you." Jon replies. "I just think I'd be faster." Jon indicated. "I can do this." Shane insists. "He is my friend." I'm going to be the one to bring him home." He concludes. "Don't treat me like a kid, I know you didn't appreciate it when our father did that to you." Shane added, as he walked out of control room. "If I told our father maybe he'd stop him" Jon proposes." "If you said anything you would not be going in either". Charlie settles. As they finalize their plans. In the zone itself we find a fighter crashed and severely damaged In the midst of a dark and dreary void with a black as night forest in front of it. Alec is lying in front of his ship gravely injured bloodstained and battered his left leg exposing a deep wound that is slightly protruding bone. He makes an attempt to use his com-link earpiece but it is damaged as he pulls it out and drops it to the ground. "Damn it." He utters. He then hears a horrific snarl coming form the forest. He grabs his side arm in his hands as he scans the immediate area. "I am armed." He shouts in alertness. The noise then stopped. Meanwhile back on the base Jesse is at a clear glass table instructing with digital map the coordinates to where Alec should be. "He should be right here before the entrance to the dark woods". Jesse contends. "Be careful, there is only one small tear in that void." Dylan recaps "It is heavily guarded." He adds. "Jon and Charlie will give you cover fire to get inside." Dylan continues. "I'd rather have Cole and Mitch, if it's ok?" Shane requests. "That will be fine." Biscus states. Danny then entered with a large case of medical supplies. "Incase of injuries." Danny described. Shane takes the case then heads out to the docking bay. Jon and Charlie standing near by as he just walks past without a word. Mitch and Cole follow suit. "You are cleared for departure." Jesse instructs. Now as they fly threw space toward the monster zone. "Coming up on the target, be ready." Mitch communicates. "Ok we will keep them busy." Cole adds. As Mitch and Cole fly to the Zone's guarded segment. They capture the attention of the guards in ships. Shane slips inside and into the zone. He then lands on the surface and exits his fighter. He grabs the medical case in hand and makes way to crash site in the distance. "Where are you?" He questions as he scans the surrounding area with hand held tracker. He picks up a life form ahead. He rushes toward it, to see Alec being attacked by two Garlocks. They are similar to ogre type creatures only more blood thirsty and slobbering. Shane discharges his power from his hands at them. As the brutes escaped back into the forest. "Thank you." Alec sighs. Then as Shane kneels to him he grasps it is him. "Shane?" He voices in disbelief. "It's good to see you too." Shane replies. "I'll be a son of a bitch." He grins. Shane opens up the medical case. I'm here to take you home." He declares. "Just go kid, I'm too far gone to save." He contends, as Shane is bandaging Alec's wound. "I didn't come all this way to leave you." Shane instructs.

"Now lets get you back to my ship." He adds as he helps Alec to his feet. Just then more Garlocks would arrive, with them a moneconda a dark scaly shade of green. They are surrounded. Shane assumes it is Monzee, one of whom we'd dealt with and arrested. "Monzee? He questions "It can't be you your in prison." He added as the Garlocks grab them. Meanwhile back in our control room. "He has been gone too long". Dylan insists. "We need to go after him." Charlie demands. "That's going to be a problem." Biscus explains. "They doubled the guards since he went in." He added. "We can't just sit here." Jon commands. Meanwhile back inside the monster zone, Shane and Alec are brought into a cavern with a large throne in front of them. She is seated upon it. "I still don't get how you escaped?" Shane demands. "I am Montra, Monzee Is my sister." She explains. "There are two of you?" Shane reacts. "Silence!" She roars. "Or I will kill you." she added. "What's stopping you?" Shane probes. "I think you're worth more alive than dead." She pauses "My sister tells me everything that happens out there." She enlightens. "Look the alliance will pay you what ever you want." Alec interjects. Montra rises to her feet, she comes down to them. "Not as much as Voltar Aster will." as she looks to Shane with desire in her eyes. Shane's eyes broaden in shock and dread. "You think I don't know about the newest Aster?" She indicates. "Is that true?" Alec asks, "I found out not too long ago." Shane replied. "Voltar is my father." He identified. "Your father I'm sorry." He replies in compassion. "Not as sorry as I am." Shane replies. Montra lets out a snicker, she then called us. Dylan puts her on the large monitor for all to see. "Is that Monzee?" Dylan asked, "I am Montra!" "Ruler of the zone." She added. "I have captured these alliance intruders." She detailed. "I wish to speak to Voltar Aster, to discuss negotiations."

"Why Voltar?" Biscus asked. "I'm sure he will pay very well for his son, don't you?" She responded. All have a look of panic and uneasy about them in the control room as she cuts off broadcast. "What do we do?" Jesse anticipates. "We call Voltar." Biscus says hesitantly. "Wait, I know the zone better I have been inside." Jon offers. "No, that bitch does not need two of his sons to bargain with." Dylan interrupts. "He's right." Charlie hesitantly agrees. "The rest of you suit up." Dylan advises. "Yes you cover us from above." Biscus says then looks to Jon and Charlie "You two will go in with me." He shocks. "Thank you sir." Jon responds. Dylan stops and expresses his concern. "Are you sure?" Dylan asked. "We need them." He stated, "Besides with Voltar going in we will be covered." He poised. They head to their fighters; meanwhile back in the zone Alec and Shane are taking a pounding form the Garlock goons. As they have been strapped down onto a block like table. Then one of them proceeded to gnaw on Alec's wounded leg, as he cried in torment. Shane fights to get free to try and stop them without success. "Let him go." He shouts. "I'm the Aster!" He added. Montra comes up to him. "Yes I know, but it is much more fun to torcher the weakest link first." She relishes. As now two of the beast are feeding on his leg. The team makes way in their fighters to the zone's entrance. As Voltar's cruiser also emerges. Voltar materializes aboard their main shuttlecraft. "I will go in alone." Voltar declares. "I'm going too." Jon disregards. "No you are not." Voltar demands. "This zone is her domain." He reminds them. "How can we trust you?" Charlie grills. "Your commander will go with me." He assured. "Be careful." Jon whispers to Biscus. "I will." Biscus stated. As Voltar Takes Biscus's arm they vanish and rematerialized inside the zone. They make their way to the cavern to Montra's lair. "So where is our hostess?" Voltar queries. Then Montra makes her presence known as she comes form the shadows. "Well Voltar Aster, we meet at last." She conveys. "Another moneconda the poor galaxy." He adds. "Watch your tongue or the boy dies." She affirms. "Where are our men?" Biscus stresses. "They are being torched as we speak." Montra clarifies. She then signals two Garlocks to hit a control imbedded in the wall, to reveal her torcher chamber. Biscus rushes to Alec's side and fires at the beasts. "You're going to be ok Alec." He assures him, as he unties him first. "I can't feel my leg sir." He mutters, as Voltar uses his powers to break the bonds on Shane. "You?" Shane says in irritation and disbelief. "Yes your annoying father." Voltar replies mockingly. "Ok Voltar pay the lady." Biscus states as he has Alec and Shane off the slabs and beside Voltar "What is it you want filth?" Voltar responds. "Half of your empire." She says with seriousness. "Your insane as well as determined." Voltar replies. At that moment Jesse locks on to Biscus and the others and beams them out and onto shuttlecraft above. "No!" She screeches, as Voltar smiled and vanished as well. Now back on the base. In the sickbay, Danny is tending to Alec. "We had to amputate his leg." Danny regretfully informs Biscus.

"Thanks doc." Biscus replied. Shane is standing by Alec's bedside with scratches and bruising on his face. "I'm sorry, what will you do now?" Shane inquires. "I will be fine, you saved my life man." Alec acknowledged. "You saved mine once, I owe you." He recapped. Shane then proceeded to head out of sickbay into corridor where Biscus stood. "You have a visitor in the briefing room." Biscus apprises. "Lets get it over with." He groaned, as Shane goes into the briefing room. "What is it you want?" Shane asked. "I just wanted to tell you how brave you were." Voltar stated. "You risked your life for a friend." He adds. "Of course if I had known sooner, I would've stopped you." He prompted. "What do you mean stopped me?" Shane expelled angrily. Voltar smiled as to be impressed with his defiance. "We will talk more later." Voltar interrupts. Then he vanishes. Jon comes by and notices Shane he enters. "Is everything ok?" Jon asked. "Yes just another father-son moment." He replied in sarcasm. Shane heads out, now later that night. Shane had powerful vicious recounts of his captivity in the zone; he could feel the pain, smell the blood. He woke up in a pool of perspiration and panting profoundly. As he tried to get back to sleep in the zone Montra was planning her agenda. She was in love with my brother. She will soon learn as they all do. You cannot keep an Aster for long. As I know my father will not sit still for it either. We will also have to prepare yet again for one of my father's attempts at a hostel take-over of the galaxy. I won't let that happen.

Chapter 5

LAW OF THE ASTER

As we continue on our journey in this galaxy. We start off with typical day like any other; only this day will not end so well for someone. I should explain by beginning with my nephews, the next generation, Steven my sister's son with Dylan, and Charlie Rick's son. Today relationships will be tested. Father's will attempt to lay down the law their way. Good luck with that scenario. In the briefing room where we are all gathered for our missions. Biscus displays a photo of our next capture. He is a crilcrak a creature with shear bruit strength. He escaped from an alliance prison on Saturn. "He has not been out long twenty-four hours." Biscus informed, "He did not escape without help." Dylan deduced. "We'll find him." Charlie directed. The team then heads out. Dylan goes to his quarters to see Steven sitting on couch reading his tablet. "How are you doing?" Dylan inquires. Steven stops looks up. "Fine, just finishing my homework." He said. "Good I'm going on a mission so you stay put got it." Dylan expresses. "Ok dad." Steven responds. Dylan heads back out. Then Voltar appears. "Hello Steven, I thought I'd visit." Voltar says. "Does my dad know about that?" Steven advises. Voltar is amused. "You are your father's son." He indicated. "So what can I do for you?" Steven asked. "I make it a point to visit all of my kin." Voltar informs as he sits beside Steven on couch. "I need to ask something." Steven requests. "Of course." Voltar replies. "I'd like to go to Voltara, I would ask my dad but he would say no." Steven tells. "I don't know your father hates me enough as it stands." Voltar shows. "He never needs to know." Steven implied. "How can I say no to you." He rationalizes, "I already told my dad I was going to take the Alliance entry exam, so tomorrow morning?" He appeals. Voltar nodded in agreement. Now the next day Steven is at the docking bay about to load up on shuttle. "Ok dad I'm off." Steven indicated. Dylan standing before him "Good luck." He delights. "I am so proud of you." He added, as he hugged him tightly. "Ok dad cutting off circulation." He mutters. Dylan lets go. Steven gets onto shuttle it leaves. Biscus comes in. "They grow up too fast." Biscus recalls. "Don't remind me." Dylan refutes. Now on Earth as Steven exits shuttle near the Alliance building. He anxiously looks around. "Where is he?" He pondered. Just then Voltar materialized in front of him. Steven is surprised. "Sorry I'm late, are you ready?" Voltar inquired. "Yes." Steven stated as he took his hand and they disappeared. Meanwhile back on base, in the control room Jesse is at his monitors scanning for Drycil. "He'll be out for Aster blood." Dylan reminds. "Should we call Voltar?" Give him a heads up?" Jesse asks. "Lets find him first." Dylan expresses. Jon then enters "What's up?" He asked. "Just trying to find our escapee." Dylan answers. "He has no powers, my father can handle him." Jon affirmed. "Yeah, it's not like he can use one of us to barging with." Charlie reminds, meanwhile on Voltara in Voltar's castle. He opens the doors to a beautiful bedroom. As he and Steven enter. "This was your mother's room." He educated. Steven sees her photo on the bedside table. "I miss her." Steven describes. Voltar glances at photo too. "So do I." He answers. "Look around for awhile I'll be back." Voltar voices. As he leaves him alone, he goes to his throne room where he finds rick waiting. "Father, Dylan called to say Drycil has escaped." Rick abreast. "I should have killed that bruit long ago." He identified. Just then a crash is heard coming from Valtra's room. They rush to find the window demolished and Steven gone. "Steven!" Voltar cried. Back on the base the com-link flashes. Jesse checks it. "Sir Voltar is calling us." He says in disbelief. "On screen." Dylan responds. You can see the despair and terror in Voltar's eyes. "Drycil has kidnapped Steven." Voltar reveals. The team is in confusion, fright and commotion. "What!" Dylan shouts. "He begged me to visit, to see Valtra's room." Voltar disclosed. "He was at your castle?" Dylan utters in unawareness. "I warned you, to stay away form my son." Dylan says. "If anything happens to him." Dylan vows. Meanwhile on Voltia at an isolated abandoned location. In one of the smaller structures, we find Steven seated in a chair hands tied behind his back. With abrasions and nicks on face and hands from window. Drycil stands off to side a large Minotaur type beast. "So your Valtra's boy?" He understands. "I loved your mother once." He claims. "She was a feared and formidable warrior." He added. "My dad will find you." Steven says in self-assurance. Drycil places his face in front of him. "I think not little one." He refutes. "I'm betting, Voltar we'll offer more for your safe return." He added. He elevates his chin. "I'll destroy Voltar." He declares. Steven jerks away. Meanwhile the team is using Steven's Tracker to locate them. They land on Voltia near where they are. "Spread out and be careful." Charlie says. Voltar also appeared before them Dylan runs up to him and decks him. "This is on you." Dylan shouted. "When he is safe you never talk to my son again." Dylan instructs. Shane steps between them "He's upset you shouldn't be here." Shane requests. "I am sorry, I would never want him hurt." Voltar maintained. The team makes way to building. "I got two life readings." Cole notifies. "I'll lead the way." Dylan orders. Charlie steps in front of him. "You are too close to this." Charlie reminds him. "He is my son." Dylan responds. Jon comes over. "We need focus to get him out of this." Jon reiterates. "I'm the captain here." Dylan says. "Let us do this, we'll get him out." Charlie assures. Dylan assesses the truth of what they are saying. "Fine." He concedes. As the team divides up and take their positions to surround the building. "Drycil will not kill him, he loved Valtra once." Voltar attempts to comfort him. Dylan looks at him with an icy glare. The team then makes way in to where they are. Jon uses his power to elevate Drycil off the ground as Mitch and Shane go to Steven and free him. "Are you ok?" Shane asks. "Yeah where is my dad?" Steven notices he is not there. "So Voltar's sons that went good." Drycil snarls. As he pulls out a gun hidden in his pants. He tries to shoot at Shane but Mitch shoves him out of way and is hit. "No!" Steven yells, as Mitch falls to the ground, Jon then Blasts Drycil with powerful blast to render him unconscious. Dylan rushes in to Steven. "Get him out of here." Jon says, as Dylan hugs Steven tight. Cole and Ralph drag Drycil out. Brent kneels to Mitch. "Mitch?" He cries. "Open your eyes!" He demands. No response from Mitch as he lies silent and motionless. "Don't do this to me." Brent cries with tears in his eyes. Shane tries to pull Brent up but he pulls away. "He's going to be ok, you guys can fix him." Brent insists. Dylan leads Steven outside. Shane looks to others. "Give us a minute." Shane asks. The others go out. "He died a hero Brent." Shane recaps. "He is not dead!" Brent shouts. "Where is Paul?" He looks around. "You, you can heal him." Brent recognizes. "I can't I'm sorry." Shane responds, as Brent wipes tears from his face. "I need my big brother." He stated. "You have a team of big brothers, thanks to Mitch now." Shane shows. "How do I go on with out him?" Brent questions. "You make him proud, you become an alliance officer just like him." Shane voices. "You keep him here." Shane gestures to his heart. Brent looks back down to Mitch's lifeless body. "I'll be ok, I'm not alone." Brent grasps. Now back on the base as the sad truth of this horrific day is sinking in. In Dylan's office Steven is standing in there as well. "I am so angry right now." Dylan vents. "I want to yell at you, but now is not the time." He added. "I'm so sorry dad." Steven begs as tears roll down his cheek. "I just wanted to know her." He voiced. "You never talk about her." Steven resumes. "I know and I'm sorry," Dylan replies. "You need to talk to me first from now on, ok?" Dylan says. "I will." Steven states as they hug, meanwhile outside office in control room. "He will be missed." Biscus expresses. "He would not want us to be sad." He added. "He would want us to move forward." He left behind this vid disc." Biscus tells as he plays it for all. You see Mitch seated in his quarters on couch. "Well if your watching this, then I am gone." "I hope it was in battle, which is how I want to go." "I know it will be saving a life." He stated. "I will miss every last one of you brats." He added the team let out a little laugh. "I will miss Biscus morning meeting, "Most of all I will miss my family." "Brent I hope you know you have a family here as I did." "They will keep you safe and straight." "This is Mitch Trent signing off." Now next day in Control Room, Biscus asks, "Are you sure you're ready?" Brent replies solemnly. "Yes sir I'm okay." "Then lets go." Charlie replies. They land on Venus to see a Galactic Alliance building and four women entering it.

Brent asks, "Are they looking for weapons?" Charlie says, "Let's ask them." They go in the side door. Ralph says, "Well I'll be damned ladies." Jenna replies, "So Galactic Alliance?" Charlie says, "You better believe it." Just then they open fire. Jon yells, "Spread out!" They go for corner. Ralph shouts, "So tough girls huh?" Brent replies, "I like tough girls." Shane asks as they battle, "Where did they learn to shoot so well?" Cole says, "Military school?" Charlie yells, "Give it up we have more officers coming!" Jenna yells, "You'll never take us alive!"

Ralph says, "Okay she's trouble huh?" Charlie says, "I am a Galactic Alliance officer, surrender your weapons now!" "Come and get us if you can!" Jenna replied as the other three girls make it to their ship. Jon yells, "They're getting away!" Charlie rises, "Like hell they are!" He runs over to stop Jenna. Shane calls out to him, "Charlie!" Charlie gets to her, "Ready to come quietly?" he says as he puts weapon to her head. Jenna drops the gun, "Fine you win officer." Lisette is in ship, "What do we do?" Cheryl in pilot seat, "We've got to leave, we'll get her later!" They fly off., "Looks like your pack left you." Charlie replies. Jenna smirks. Now back at base in Locking Bay, Jenna exclaims, "This isn't over!" Charlie snaps, "Yes it is, Speak proper English or did you not finish kindergarten?" he goes. Jon replies to him, "Just a little harsh there?" Charlie retorts, "Don't say it." Jenna in cell, "Is he always like that?" Jessica replies, "Yes he is, it's an Aster trait." Jenna in shock, "He's one of Voltar's kin?" Jenna asks. "Yes, Why?" Jessica answers. "Never seen one before." Meanwhile on Mercury,

Lisette as they are in ship, "We need to go back." Mary, a little younger with dark hair brown eyes and Asian features says, "How?" "The Galactic Alliance has her." Cheryl replies, she has light brown hair brown eyes and is African American, "Yeah we can't just walk in there!" Mary says Meanwhile back on the base; Charlie is seated at his desk in Control Room when Jesse comes over, "Ah Charlie?" Charlie looks up, "What is it?" He responds, "The prisoner has requested to see you." Jesse answered.

Charlie in confusion, "What?" he says, "The pirate we captured earlier?" Jesse reminded. Charlie looks back to charts and paper work, "I'm busy." He says. Jesse asks, "Does that mean no?" Charlie looks back up, "Yes it does!" Jesse walks back to station. Jessica comes over to Charlie. He looks up, "Jessica? What's up?" Charlie says, "You tell me." Jessica asks, "What are you talking about?" Charlie replies. "I'm a telepath Charlie, I felt that spark between you and Jenna." Charlie inquires, "Who?" "Jenna the pirate we captured on Venus." She explains. "Your reading that wrong Jessica." He responds. Jessica smiley, "I have a feeling about you two." she replies. "Jessica, I love you, you are my family but you are way off!" Charlie responds. "She's not as bad as you think, she has a good reason behind that attempt." Jessica says, "Please don't try to play matchmaker." He replies. "Really? Right now the only woman in your life is Monzee!" she explains. Charlie replies, "Thanks for that frightening thought." "Don't you at least find her attractive? "That much I got." Jessica states, "She's a criminal." Charlie reminds. "So is your father!" she added. Charlie replies, "Yes, but I don't find him attractive either."

"She stole the weapons out of desperation." "Go talk to her". She insists. Charlie drops his pen. "Fine I will, if it will get you off my back." Charlie says as he rises. He heads out of control room down the corridor toward the cellblock. He enters and goes down the hall to the cell Jenna is in. "I need you to release me" She pleads. "Are you out of your mind?" Charlie suggests. "You stole millions of dollars in Alliance weaponry, I'm support to just let that go?" He added. "I only took them to save my sister." She informed. "Why didn't you just ask for our help?" He replies sincerely. "I couldn't, if I involved alliance she'd be dead." She clarified. "Look you seem like a nice guy, just let me go," She begs. "If you do you'll never have to see me again." She added. "No I have a better idea." Charlie suggests, meanwhile above the base itself. A ship is flying at them. "Sir I have an incoming vessel." Jesse notifies. "Open a channel". Dylan instructs him. "Identify yourself or you will be shot down". Dylan demands. Charlie enters with Jenna behind him. "Stop Dylan let them land." Charlie commands. "They need our help." He ends. "What?" Dylan asks in confusion. "Just trust me." Charlie assures. "Sir?" Jesse confirms. "Let them land." Dylan says. "Send security to escort them here." He added. "What is going on?" Dylan questions. "I'll explain everything." Charlie promises. Now as everyone is gathered, we see our newest ladies Mary, Cheryl, and Lisette, Some tough yet beautiful strong girls, who have been through a tough life. Charlie proceeded to explain the situation to us. How her sister was kidnapped into a slavery ring, which is operating on Mars. As Ralph, and Brent are busy drooling over the girls and as Jesse was also distracted. "I will need Steven if that is ok?" Charlie requests "Why me?" Steven is interested. "Her sister is your age you can help to talk to her." Charlie states. Dylan reluctantly agrees. "Be careful." He reiterates. As they prepared for their mission; On Mars a creature named Tred with scaly skin and an enormous potbelly protruding from his filthy shirt. He propels his way to a cell full of young humanoid looking girls. "Now my lovelies you will bring me lots of money." He chuckles, as he sniffs one of their locks of hair, drool drips from his lips. The girls' huddle together frightened, the team lands on the outskirts of the place were Tred's building stood. The team makes there way right outside of his doors. "All right Brent and Shane cover me, I'm going in." Charlie orders. "Jesse you and Lisette go back to the shuttle have it ready." Charlie directs. They head back. "Let me do all the talking." Jenna insists. "We'll get your sister." Brent confirms. Then Charlie and the rest go inside, as Tred is seated at his computer console. He glances up to see them. "Well Jenna did you come with my supplies?" He barks. He notices Charlie dressed in street style clothes. "Who is he?" He distrusts. "He is the one who will get your weapons." She reveals. "He has connections in the alliance." She adds. "Well then lets talk terms," He continues. As they distract him Brent and Shane with Steven make way inside to the cell with the prisoners. Just as they move to touch the bars alarms blare. Tred grabs his weapon at his side. "What is going on here?" Tred commanded. "You're trying to double cross me?" Tred Verifies. "Hit the floor." Charlie shouts as he quickly used his powers to shove Jenna to the ground as Tred fires at Charlie hitting him in the chest. He falls to his knees, the rest of the team busts in. Ralph points weapon at Tred, as he was attempting an escape. "Hold it tall dark and scaly." "You will never take me alive!" He yells as he tries to turn back, but Brent is there to take him down with one shot to the head. He falls dead. As the others free the girls. Lisa runs to Jenna who is leaning over Charlie as he struggles to keep alert and breathe. "Jenna!" Lisa cries. "He's hurt!" Jenna cries. "Hang on." She pleads. "Working on it." Charlie replies. Now on the base, Paul and Anilla his nurse work on him. Jon comes to sickbay. "What happened?" He exclaims. "Weapons fire sir." Ralph confirms. "Is he ok?" Jon asks. "We don't know he took a shot to the chest." Brent informs. "He'll be ok." Steven states confidently. Jenna stands by the entrance to sickbay. "This is my fault." Jenna indicts. "No it's not," Jessica states. "He wanted to help that is who he is." She added. Rick appears in the corridor "Where is he?" Rick asks anxiously. Jon comes to him "Relax he is in surgery." Jon informs. "Why does he do this?" Rick questions. Shane comes over. "He is strong, he'll be fine." Shane insists. "He is all I have." Rick worries. Paul comes out. "I cannot stabilize him!" He says in concern, Just then Charlie codes on table. Paul rushes back inside. Rick has a pale look of panic. "My son cannot die." Rick begs. As they continue to work on Charlie If he survives, will Rick allow his only child to be an Alliance officer? Paul comes back out. "He is out of surgery, but critical I think Rick should go in first." Paul chooses. All agree. Rick goes in walks up to the bed to see Charlie lying there weak and still blood soaked onto the bandages covering his chest. Tubes coming form his nose and IV's in his arm his eyes closed. Rick takes his hand in his. "I'm here son." He stated. "I know I'm not who you expected or maybe even wanted, but I need you. "You are the only good thing about me." He confesses. "So don't you leave me." He demands. Jon, Shane, and Steven enter. "It's ok to cry." Steven reminds him. As Rick's eyes are watered. "I know kid." Rick replies. "We are all here." Shane added. As we talked to him, Charlie was at the gates to the underworld at least his spirit was. He walked up to gates. "Hello?" Charlie calls. "Where am I?" He questions as he looks around, just then an older humanoid looking gentleman comes up to him. "Hello their Charlie horse". He says. Charlie recognizes him. "Grandpa Jake"? He says. "Wait your dead." He adds. "As a hammer." He verifies. "So are you." He informs. "What, I can't be dead?" He challenges. "I haven't lived, I haven't fallen in love." "I need to go back, "How will they end up with out me?" He asked. "That I can show you." Suddenly he whisks Charlie away to a cold dark cemetery. "Why am I here?" He asked. Jake points to the headstone with Steven McKay's name on it. "No, How?" Charlie demands "He was angry, he lost that part of him that kept him positive." "He went after criminals with a vengeance, he was shot down and killed." Jake replied. "I have to go back." Charlie demands. Meanwhile back in sickbay. "I don't understand it he is just not here fighting." Paul explains. "We need to think about what to do next." He added. Just then Charlie opens his eyes. Anilla rushes to Paul, "He's awake!" She shouts. Paul and others come to him. "Charlie?" Charlie looks to Paul. "What happened?" He asked. "We thought we lost you" Paul replies. "Yeah don't scare us like that again" Jon smiles. Jenna walks up to his side. "You sure know how to impress a girl, for a cop" Jenna winks. Charlie lets out a laugh. "Your not so bad yourself, for a criminal." He jokes. "I'm going legit," She informs him. "Wow was it something I said?" Charlie responds. "You saved my life." She says as she kissed his lips. "I'll go find Rick." Shane says as he goes out into the hall. Rick looks nervously "What is it?" "He's awake." Shane replied with a smile. Rick feels a great relief. Now back inside sickbay. "Once your back on your feet, "I'll show you some real action." Jenna indicates. "I like the sound of that." Charlie replies as Rick walks in. "Can I have a minute alone?" Charlie asks. Everyone goes out. Rick touches his forehead. "Your really ok?" He inquiries. "Yes I'm an Aster that way." Charlie makes light of it. "As soon as you are on your feet, you need to come stay with me." Rick demands. "I'm going to be busy and back to work but I could take time of to…" Rick interrupts "No, I mean quit the Alliance and live with me." He exposes. "This job is too dangerous." He added. "I don't want to argue with you." Charlie asserts. "There will be no further discussion." Rick decides. "I will not allow you to risk your life." He apprises him. "I'm not a child, do not start that Aster I'm in charge of your life crap with me." Charlie declares. "I'm only trying to protect you." Rick justifies. "I know you are, but this is my choice my life." Charlie tells him. "We all die even Asters will eventually." He adds. "Not if I can stop it." Rick defies. Paul comes in after hearing the agitation. "He needs to rest." Paul states. "This conversation is far from over." Rick ends. "I'm not doing this now." Charlie added. "You need to go!" Paul demanded. Rick goes out. Charlie tries to calm down. "You need to de-stress." Paul insists. "Tell that to my father." Charlie responds. Meanwhile in the control room the team is gathered. "Well our two favorite monsters have escaped the zone." Biscus informs us. "No don't say it." Shane pleads. "Monzee and Montra. Dylan ends. "Lets go find them." Jon replies. As they headed out Jesse is at his console when Lisette comes over to him. "So you take care of all the technical stuff huh?" She says. "Yeah it's just a boring job." He stated. "I think the smart guys are the real heroes." She indicates. "Especially when they're as cute as you." She ends. She then leans in and they kiss. Biscus comes over to them. "Excuse me!" He shouts, as they jump apart. "He was just…" Biscus interrupts "Showing you his tonsils?" "Back to work!" He goes into his office. "Yes sir!" Jesse yells. Just then an incoming transmission comes over. "The sisters are on Jupiter." Jesse calls over the vidlink, now on Jupiter in a small hut that sits in the middle of the woods. Monzee and Montra are inside. "So now what?" Montra inquired. "We get our plan set, on how to get into that base and claim our men." Monzee declares. The team lands on the planet near the woods. "Shane are you sure about this?" Jon asks, "It is you she's after." He added. "I know that, I have an idea." Shane enlightens. "I'm not gonna like this am I?" Jon questions. "I'll go to the door they won't hurt me." Shane reminds him. "I hate this idea, but you are right it would get them to show themselves." Jon admits. They make way to hut, Shane knocks on the door. Montra says, "Who is that?" Monzee replies, "A villager. Tell them to go away." Shane replies, "It's important!" Montra goes up to the door, "I'll deal with it!" She opens it and replies, "Well a social call?" Shane puts gun to her head, "What do you think?" Montra tries to escape but Shane shoots her. Jon rushes over, "Are you okay?" Cole checks Montra, "She's bad!" he exclaims. "We have to help her." Shane insists. "Are you crazy?" Jon asks

"Look all she's really guilty of is falling for me." Shane says. "He's right!" Jessica replies. So we took Monzee and Montra back to the base. Unfortunately that was their plan all along, to try and kidnap Shane and Charlie. Luckily we stopped them this time. There will be more villains to come. It's only just the beginning of the Aster legacy. It will definitely be a bumpy ride but as long as we stick together as a family we will be just fine.

Chapter 6
NEW ADDITIONS

Every aster will have an advisory, that one that hates them so much. Mine is Octo, he is what we call an Ocktakiran he was born from the seas of Jupiter. He is part amphibian and humanoid. He actually hates us all. I just seem to be his target of the week. We also will welcome some new additions to our team, don't worry there not secretly Asters. We will also have a very pleasant surprise as well. We begin in the briefing room. "Alright listen up." Biscus broadcasts. "We have two new members to the team, so lets make them feel welcome." He added. He introduced us to Xavier Nerys and Marco Santana two humans from Earth. Xavier has Brown hair and Brown eyes, with a trim build, while Marco has jet-black hair and hazel eyes and a stout build. "We heard this was the base to be on." Marco claimed. "Well we try." Jon replies. Paul then enters. "Ok gentlemen follow me for your physicals." "Now be nice Paul they are rookies." Ralph jokes. As they head out. "We have new trouble on Earth." Dylan reveals. "A group of terrorist are attacking the Galactic Alliance buildings and other properties." "Biscus concurs. "Any ideas who they are?" Cole asks. Dylan brings up a photo on the screen of an older human Hispanic gentleman of a stealth build with brown hair and eyes. "They call him "The Bull." Dylan adds. Just then Xavier comes back in to see photo and recognizes him. "That's Miguel." He states. "You know this guy?" Shane asks. "Yes, we grew up together in the same town in Philadelphia." He explained. "Well your friend is a known terrorist." Biscus tells. Xavier is stunned. "I can't believe that." Xavier replies. Dylan has a thought. "Do you think you could go to Earth and meet with him?" Dylan asked. "You mean spy on him?" Xavier questioned. "If he really is then, yes he would not consider me a threat he does not even know I joined up." He adds. "Then lets go." Charlie responds. Just then Jessica clutches her forehead feeling lightheaded. "I feel strange." She replies. Jon hurries to her side. "Are you alright?" he asked. "I think so." She responds. "Have Paul check you out." Biscus insisted. "I'm fine it's passed." She assures him. "I would feel better if you did." Jon appealed. She nods in agreement. Meanwhile on Earth in a large bunker underneath an abandoned city near the Alliances main building, Miguel "the bull" addresses his comrades. "We have them running scared my friends." He boasts, as the crowd cheers. "Now our goal is to free our planet from these aliens that have seized control and put it back where it belongs in human hands." He claims, as the crowd roars. "No longer will humans be cast aside." "The Earth will be ours again!" he shouts. Just then a young girl in her twenties enters. "Bull there are some alliance ships landing with supplies at the building." She communicates. "Well more good news." He responds, now at the alliance building. "Ok Xavier and Marco will infiltrate their group, to find out where they will strike next." The two of them head off. Meanwhile as Jesse scanned the Alliances files he learned that Miguel use to be one of us. "So he was on our side?" Charlie examined as he looked through the records on the tablet he held. "Look at his list of metals." Jesse added. "So why did he go rouge?" Brent inquired. "Not enough in the paycheck?" Ralph jokes, as the team dug deeper into Miguel's past. Xavier and Marco made their way to the abandoned city. The young girl would discover them; She takes them to Miguel in the bunker bellow. "This guy says he knows you." She claims. As the two of them come in. "I'll be dammed Xavier!" He exclaims, as he hugs him. "Who is your friend?" He asked. "This is my pal Marco." Xavier replied. Miguel shakes Marco's hand. "So how did you find me?" He probed, as the girl exits. "I saw your face on the news scanners." He admitted, "We believe in humanity my old friend," It's time to take our planet back from the aliens." He stated. "Not too long ago we were the aliens." Xavier reminded. "Earth has been overrun with them there is no room for us now." Miguel added. "It is time to fight back." He replied. "There are too many of them in power now." Xavier tells. "So how can I help?" he added. Miguel smiles. "I was hoping you'd say that." He replied. "Come to my briefing in a few hours, we'll go over my plan tonight." He explained. Meanwhile back at the alliance. "Charlie is studying tablet. "I hope their ok." Jon indicated. "They've only been gone a few hours." Brent replied. "I think maybe we should go in after them." Cole suggests, just then Xavier and Marco enter. "No need to go in guns blazing yet." Xavier replies. Charlie rises from seat. "So what happened?" Jon asked. "Well Miguel is a total lunatic." Marco stated. "Yes he is planning on attacking the alliance building itself, he's gone off the deep end." Xavier informed. "He is crazy that is a suicide mission." Shane confirms. "He doesn't care if he dies, it's like I never knew him. "Xavier explained, "He was why I joined up." He added. "So what's our plan?" Amanda inquired. "Xavier and Marco go back, let them come here and attack us. We'll be ready to arrest them." Charlie responds. "You think it's safe for them to go back?" Jon asked. ""If we don't Miguel will be suspicious and call it off." Marco states. "Go we'll be ready." Charlie insures. As they get back to town girl comes up on them. "Where have you two been?" She interrogates. "Were ready to leave." She added. "We scouted ahead to find a way in." Xavier replied. "Now that is thinking ahead my friend." Miguel replies as he and his comrades emerge from the bunker. "Ok let's move out!" She yells. As they all make way back to the alliance building, Marco suggests they go on through the side entrance hidden in some trees. They make way to door when the girl spies Xavier's alliance issue weapon in his jacket. "It's a set up." She yelled, as she grabs Xavier's weapon from him. "Your alliance scum." She adds. Miguel comes to him, sees the weapon in her hand. "This hurts me deeply." He stated as he takes the gun and places it to Xavier's temple. "I once called you a friend." He expressed. The team hears the conversation over com-link and spring into action. "He's been made!" Charlie exclaimed. They come out of the back door. "It's over!" Jon stated. Young girl fires at them "Die alliance scum!" She shouts. As they go for cover battle ensues. Xavier managed to flip Miguel over to the ground and get the gun, as he was distracted by the chaos. "You're done." He says. "You're a fool." He replies as he reaches in his side pants pocket discretely to pull out a dagger. "I'll kill you!" He yells as he goes to throw it at him but Marco Fires at him hitting him in the head killing him instantly. "I don't think so." Marco responds. Then the young girl sees Miguel and screeches a deathly holler. She then jumps on Marco's back attacking him. Xavier helps him and pulls her off flinging her to the ground, as he points his gun at her. "Your under arrest." He informed, now as the team subdued the other members of his gang. "Nice moves there." Brent observed. "Well I try not to always use my weapon." Xavier acumens. "Lets get back." Jon replies. Now back on base as the others head for the mess hall. Jon heads to sickbay to check on Jessica. He finds Danny at his station. "How is she?" Jon asked. "Paul is gathering up the test results now." Anilla tells. As Jessica is seated on a bed Paul comes out of lab area. "I have your results." He replied. Jon comes to Jessica as Charlie and Shane came to inquire as well. The others are waiting outside. "What is it?" Jon asks anxiously. "Is it bad?" He feared. Jessica smiles. "No everything is fine." She states. "Then why were you dizzy?" Shane replied. "I'm pregnant." She informed. "Your pregnant?" Jon says then he proceeded to faint. "That's great!" Shane shouts. "Yes congratulations." Charlie added. "Should we help him up?" Shane says. Then Shane and Charlie help him to his feet as he comes around. "You ok?" Shane asked. "Yeah I'm fine we're just having a baby." He then realized what he said and fainted again. They lay him on bed next to her. The team all enters and give their blessings to Jessica. "Ok all people not having a baby back to work." He stated. As they shuffle out of sickbay, Jessica comes over to Jon as he comes around again. "Hey there you." She smiles. "I'm sorry I guess I'm so overwhelmed. Jon replied. Just then Voltar and Rick Appear, Outside of sickbay. "I sensed some good news." Voltar interrogates. "Yeah I'm gonna be a cousin!" Steven exclaims. "Jessica is having a baby." Shane confirms. Voltar goes inside. "What are you doing here father?" Jon replied. "Nice way to say hello junior, really?" Voltar answered. "I just heard the news, congratulations Jessica." He added. "Thank you." She replied. "You and I will talk later junior." He says as he leaves. "So we are going to be parents?" Jon grasps. Jessica kisses him. "Yes daddy, are you happy?" She probed. "Of course I am, I'm just worried about my father you know how he gets." Jon reminds her. "I will deal with that." She guarantees. Jon smiles. "I love you." He added. They kiss. Meanwhile on Voltara the team is called to a fight that broke out in the city creatures are attacking the citizens. "Who is the ring leader?" Xavier shouts. "Who knows their all crazy." Ralph replied as they attempted to restore order. Cole spies Montra and Monzee in the distance. "I think I have an idea." Cole replies, as he directs their attention toward them. "No way." Brent replies. "Who are they?" Marco asked. "They are trouble." Amanda clarifies. "Where are Charlie and Shane?" Cole replied. "Why?" Xavier inquired. "No reason, other than the fact their obsessed with them." Ralph interrupts. "Your kidding right?" Marco replied. "I cannot even make that up man." Ralph responds. "Why don't we just capture them?" Xavier asked. "We have more times then we can count." Cole replied. Meanwhile back on the base; Moondeath heard about our newest addition to come and came over, he knocks on door to quarters, Jon opens it. "May I come in?" He asked. "Of course." Jon replied. "I understand your going to be parents." He affirmed. Jessica is glowing and smiled. "Yes." She replied. "I am so glad for you two." He said. Meanwhile back to the action on Voltara. Charlie and Shane are using their powers to take down the creatures, when they noticed a few Garlocks. They went after them to find Monzee and Montra. "Are you kidding me?" "They escaped again." Charlie says in irritation. Monzee sees Charlie and Shane "Their here." She squeals. Mary noticed the situation "We'd better cover their backs." She informed. "Oh I got this." Jenna replies in annoyance, as she fires her weapon at them separating them. "Nice shooting." Shane replied. "It's nothing really." Jenna responds. "Lets load them up for transport back to prison." Charlie requests. As they are caged and loaded onto shuttle, "We'll be out fast." Montra stated. "Not if we can help it." Brent replied. Now back on base Amanda goes to Jessica's quarters. "I came to check on you." Amanda replies. "Thanks I've been so bored." She stresses. "What not enjoying desk work?" Amanda jokes. "No I am going insane." She vented. "Jon thinks I need to stay off my feet." Jessica added. "All men think like that." Amanda replied. Meanwhile in the Mess hall, Jon and Shane sit together. "So dad." He chuckled. "I've got to get used to that." He adds. "So do I." Jon replies. "Where is Charlie?" Jon questioned. "He is resting, we just caught Monzee and Montra on Voltara this morning." Shane informed him. "You two ok?" Jon worries. "Yeah they are locked up." Shane replied. "Sorry I hope I'm not coming off too overbearing." Jon responded. "What you?" He says sarcastically. "You are just being a dad." He smiled. "I know Jessica is not too happy about desk duty." Jon added, "Of course not she is a fighter like us." Shane concluded. "Speaking of dad's have you seen ours recently?" Jon asked. "No not since yesterday, why?" Shane probed. "I know he is up to something." Jon replied. "When is he not?" Shane responds. "I guess I'm just a little tense." Jon stated. "You're the only guy I know, who has been a father before you were one, you take care of all of us." Shane replied. "Thanks for that." Jon says. Now in the briefing room; Biscus brings up a mug shot of Octo. He is half octopus half human. "This is Octo he escaped from the monster zone a few hours ago. Biscus informed. "He has been reported on Jupiter." He added. "So why do we need to find him?" Cole asked. "Well he took out the Jupiter base so it falls to us now." Dylan explained. "So what's this guys problem?" "I mean other than his face." Ralph replied. "He has a grudge against the Asters." Biscus responds. "Since all of the good ones are here, He'll most likely come here first. "Dylan replies. "We need to be ready." He added. "I think I should confront him." Jon advised. The team looks at him in confusion. "I don't know about that." Biscus replied. "I've dealt with him before." Jon recalls. "I'll go too, to back you up." Shane insists. "No I can handle him." Jon replies. "No way you're going in alone." Shane responds. "Fine." Jon concedes. "Just be careful, he is volatile and a genius that is never a good combo." Dylan replies. "I know all too well." Jon remembers, as Shane and I headed to the docking bay. "So tell me about this guy?" Shane asked. "It was just as I joined the team." Jon recalls. "He was a scary guy, he hated all life forms especially humans or anyone similar." Jon continues. "He wanted us all to be like him an superior species of his designing." Jon concludes. "Sounds like a real psycho." Shane determines. "He nearly destroyed earth and the alliance." Jon added. "So how do we capture him?" Shane asked. "We bait him in with the one thing he can't refuse, power." Jon informs. "How did he get out?" Shane deliberated. "I would ask Monzee and Montra about that." Jon replied. They load up into their fighters and head out to Jupiter; we arrive at an isolated location that I believed to be his kind of place, an abandoned cave near by. As we landed near the cave we got out and made our way to it. "You think he's in there?" Shane asked. "It's dark, it's moist it probably leads out to the ocean, so yeah I think so." Jon replied. As the walk inside a gate drops behind them "He knows we're here." Jon states. Just then Octo comes out of the shadows. He has the body of a humanoid although his limbs are that of tentacles and his head is that of an octopus. "Well look what I caught two alliance pigs." He boasted. "So how did you escape Octo?" Jon asked. "Well Jon Aster, or is it back to junior now? Octo checked. "I will relish killing you," He added.

"In your dreams squid head." Shane replied. "I don't know you boy but you have a familiar arrogance to you, you will die just as painfully for that remark," Octo replied. Meanwhile back on the base in control room. "We're going in." Charlie declared. "Take him down and be careful." Biscus replied. Jessica walks in. "Jon is in danger." She informed. "Don't worry we'll handle it." Dylan responds. "Octo is out for Aster blood." "I'm going with you." She declares. "I'm not so sure about this." Charlie replied. Jessica gives him a firm look of determination. "Ok go but damm it be careful." Biscus cautions. They head out. Meanwhile back in the cave, Octo has placed them into two separate modular pods. "I'm so glad you will be the first to test my device, I devised it with Asters in mind." He brags. He presses a control on a console he is standing in front of. "I'll make all of you like me, so you can live in the seas and on land." He snickers. "As long as I look nothing like you." Jon required. "You're going to love this." Octo claims. "I think we're in trouble." Shane replied. "I will enjoy watching, as you shed your humanoid skin for some gills and tentacles." Octo celebrated. "You will never get away with this." Jon vows. "Yeah our team will stop you." Shane replies. "I think the one who insulted me should go first." Octo responds. "No!" Jon shouts. "I'm the one who sent you to the zone." Jon reminded. "Yes but this one annoys me." Octo replied, as Octo comes to his pod to turn it on. "I really don't want to be like him." Shane panics. At that moment the team burst in. Brent shoots octo's hand before he can touch the pod. Jessica rushes to Jon. "Are you alright?" She asked. "I'm ok get Octo." Jon stresses. "There will be a next time alliance." He replied. He then pulled a panel on the wall beside him quickly it released the trap door bellow him and he went down it, it lead out to the ocean. "He got away." Cole replies. "We'll get him." Charlie insists. As they get the pods open to free them. Now back on the base. Jesse is frantically checking the planets for any trace of Octo. "Any sign of him?" Biscus asks. "Not yet sir." Jesse responds. "Well get out there and find that fish." Biscus shouts. The team heads out. "Sir he is actually a cephalopod." Paul educated. Biscus looked to him in irritation. "Never mind sir." Paul withdrew. Meanwhile back on Jupiter in the cave Octo surfaces in another cavern. Where Monzee and Montra are waiting for him as they have yet again escaped. "Hello ladies." Octo replied. They help him out of water. "I almost had them." Octo snarls. "We need to work together." Monzee advised. "So what do you ladies desire?" Octo inquires. "All we want are our men." Montra demands. "Of course but Jon Aster and the others are all mine." He specifies. As they smile. Meanwhile back on the base. Jesse is seated at his console. "Still no sign of Octo sir." He stated. "He couldn't have just vanished." Biscus replied. "Is he still underwater?" Lisette believes. "No he still needs some air, he is half humanoid." Jon informs. "Lets hope he drowned." Dylan says. "Now that's a nice thought." Shane replied. "This guy sounds too tough for that." Charlie responds. "I agree." Jessica said as she comes in. "You should be resting." Jon maintains. "I can't you're the one he wants to kill, or turn into a fish." She stated. "I can handle this." Jon assures. "I've got his back." Shane replies. "Guys I'm getting an incoming communication." Jesse interjects. He puts it on the audio-link. "Attention Galactic Alliance, This is Montra." "We will be conquering your galaxy." She continues. "So be warned most of you will die." She ends. "You think she is working with Octo?" Shane asked. "We'd better find out fast." Dylan replied. Just then an alarm flashes on console. "Sir it's a distress call from earth." Jesse freaks. "On screen." Biscus demands. Jesse puts it on the vidlink. It shows the streets of a city near the Galactic alliance main headquarters. People see a smoky substance in the air then they begin to turn into cephalopods, similar to Octo himself. "Oh my god." Biscus gasped. "He released that formula as gas." Dylan exclaimed. "He has to be working with them, he doesn't have the contacts." Jon recognized. Just then Montra and Monzee can be seen in the distance. "Your right." Shane agrees as he points to them on screen. "We are in trouble." Charlie declares. They rush out of the control room and get to the docking bay, and then they departed for Earth. Montra sees their ships from the ground. "It worked there here." Montra thrills. "Remember our men are not to be harmed." Monzee looks to Octo and recaps. "I know the rest of that team will be plenty." Octo replied. The team lands and exits fighters. "Ok move out." Charlie orders. They make way to the city. "Alright Monzee come out!" He shouts. They emerged from the shadows. "I love it when you take charge." She thrills. "Should I blast a hole threw her?" Jenna replied. "That would be an improvement." Ralph responds. "You won't be talking when your fish!" She shouts. As Octo comes out of shadows with his weapon and fired it at them emitting a gas. Which begins to turn the team into cephalopods. Meanwhile back on the base. "Get me eyes on that planet Jesse." Biscus commands. "No one is answering my calls." Jesse replied. Just then the vidlink comes on. They see the team lying on the ground with fish type bodies and heads. "Oh no." Lisette cries. "We've got to do something." Steven pleads. "What can we do?" Biscus asked. "We need to get there." Dylan replied. As they head out back on the planet. In a cave, Montra has Shane chained against wall. "I hope you like our getaway." She jokes. "It suits you anyway, dark and disgusting." Shane replies. Montra moves closer. "Face it you've lost it's over." She boasts. "I will make you pay for that." Shane promises. "I look forward to that." She whispers as she licks his face with her tongue. Over in another part of that cave Octo has Jon in his pod. "I saved you for last." Octo delights. Meanwhile the rest of the team lands on earth. They make way to cave as Paul and Anilla tend to the team. "Be careful." Dylan replies. "We need to get them to water." Paul states. The team moves them to the near by water. "How do we change them back?" Lisette worries "We need to get the antidote, Octo has to have one." "Why can't they talk?" Lisa asked. "Their vocal cords are changed." Paul replied. "Lets go ask him." Dylan insists. Meanwhile back in the cave Monzee has Charlie chained against the wall as well. She strokes his cheek. "Don't be angry, I saved you." Monzee implores. "What is he gonna do to Jon?" Charlie asked. He's going to make him just like him." She replies. "Now forget him lets talk about us." She suggests. Just then the team bursts in. "We've got to get him out of that pod." Dylan replied. "Leave that to me." Jessica states. She uses her power to blast Octo against the far wall, as Dylan gets the pod open. "I'm ok." Jon replied. "Charlie and Shane are in here with them somewhere." Jon added. Jesse goes after them. He sees Montra lusting over Shane. He blaster her with his weapon, she falls to the ground. "Hey you ok?" Jesse asked as he frees him. "Yeah I'm good." Shane answers. Meanwhile Brent finds Charlie with Monzee. He knocks her out. He unchains Charlie. "We've got to find the antidote." Charlie replied. They make way back to where Octo was. Octo rises to his feet. "Is this what your looking for?" Octo replies as he dangles a bottle in front of him. "Give it up Octo." Jon said. "I never lose!" He shouted. Jon blasts him against the wall as Jessica used her powers to secure the bottle out of his hand and to hers. Now outside they use it on the team and citizens. "What happened?" Ralph asked. "Why are we wet?" Cole replied. "We'll tell you on the way home." Dylan replied. "I will never be able to eat seafood again." Ralph added. Meanwhile as the team went home and celebrated a victory back on Voltara My father was plotting. "What is your plan now father?" Rick inquired, "Patience my son, I'm working on it." Voltara replied. Cora enters. "I'm tired of sitting here." She states. "I agree it's time for action." Rick responded. "I think it is time I went back to the old ways." Voltara replied. "It's good to have you back boss." Cara says. "Lets destroy something." He stated. Now back on the base Biscus is getting an incoming audio-link. "Looks like the Asters are back." Biscus stated. Jon comes over to him. "What is going on?" Jon asked. "He just attacked a village on Voltia." Biscus answered. "Why I thought he was trying to be better?" Shane says in unease. "We had to know they wouldn't stay quiet for long." Charlie replied. So they loaded up and flew to Voltia where it was a war zone, total destruction of everything even resembling a village. "What set him off?" Xavier questioned. "What a mess." Amanda replied. "I'm going to ask him." Jon replied. Jon, Charlie and Shane fly to Voltara and arrive at Voltar's castle. Rick is there to greet them. "Well hello brothers, Son." He smiles. "We are here as Alliance." Jon stated firmly. "Where is he?" Shane asked. "Relax he's wanting to talk to you too." Rick replied. They head down hallway to the throne room. "What the hell are you doing?" Jon demands. "What I have always done junior, take care of business." He replied. "By killing innocent people?" Shane interrogated. "They owed me a debt, and no one is innocent Shane." Voltar replied. "It is time to get back to what asters do best." He bragged. "Which is?" Charlie asked. "Ruling this galaxy of course." He replied. "So it begins." Jon responded. "The old Voltar is back boys, and he takes no prisoners." Voltar smiles ominously. "Is this for real?" Charlie asked. "This is son." Rick replied. "Then we need to bring you in." Jon stated. Voltar laughs. "Take me in?" "You will have to capture us first." Voltar and Rick then transform into their Dregon beasts. Voltar's is Black as coal. As Rick's is a fiery red, Then They fly straight up and threw the ceiling. "What do we do now?" Shane asked. "We find them and take them down. "Jon replies. Now back on base in control room. "I guess it was too good to be true." Ralph states. "I knew it would come to this." Jon replied. So now my Brother and nephew will witness what I have already seen, the darkness that is Aster. I myself wanted to believe they could change, but his lust for power is too great. It is something I still struggle with when I must use my abilities. I'm not sure if we can stop them or even save them. Now the next day in the control room Jon is standing at console going over the last sightings of Rick and Voltar. "So do we look like those creature, when we change?" Shane asked. "Our Dregons are a part of us." Jon replied. "Ours reflect what we are in our hearts, so not exactly like theirs." Jon added. "Mine is of a blue reflective light." He assured him. "Good I didn't want to think I could be like him." Shane replied. "You're not like him, we maybe Asters by blood but we are a unique kind." Jon ended. So as we continued our constant battles back and forth with our father and Rick, we would see more of their darkness emerging. Shane would question the darkness within himself. As we slept on the base that night, our father made an attempt to lure Shane to his side. Lucky for us he has no intention of joining him. Which on the down side only increased my father's rage. Unfortunately we have another issue. We are about to discover yet another Aster, Moondeath had another son. Voltar's younger brother thought killed long ago in the Monster zone. His name is Volrin. He will prove to be more sinister and cold than my father ever was. For he has a wraith inside of him, that even he cannot escape. It started like any other day. Biscus had us in the briefing room. "Can we talk to Moondeath?" "Maybe he can help." Dylan asked. Moondeath then appeared to them. "I think I may have found a way to save Voltar's very soul, Volrin." He replied. "Who is Volrin?" Shane asked. "He is my son." Moondeath informed. "Father never mentioned him." Jon replied. "He was lost, as a young boy long ago in the zone, he followed Voltar everywhere." "He wanted to be just like him." Moondeath recalled. "I thought he was dead." He added. "So what makes you so sure he is alive?" Shane asked. "I can feel him, I never stopped but I can not find him I need your help." He requests. "We each have a bond with our children we know when they are hurt or dead." He stated. "Then lets go find him." Charlie vowed. "There is just one problem, it's the zone only two creatures now it best." Dylan says. "Then I'll ask her." Charlie replied. "Lets remember who were dealing with." Jon prompted. "She will only talk to me you know that." Charlie replied. "Ok just be careful." Jon pleads. As we prepared for a trip into the monster zone, Volrin was preparing as well, for revenge on all of us. He has had too many years to sit in that cold dark void and remember who left him there to rot. This will not go well for any of us.

Chapter 7

NEW POWER RULING

Say what you will about my father, but he always puts family first. So if there is a chance his young brother could still be alive? If so, how has being imprisoned in the zone changed a once naive boy now a man? How cold does that make your heart? Well we are about to find out. In the zone deep in the bowels of it's darkest caverns we see chained to a wall a young man scrawny and malnourished his clothing ripped and torn. "Someone hear me." He pleads. Now as we land inside the zone, where by the way Monzee and Montra have returned to escaping our prisons. We made our way to a cave at the entrance stood a goblin like creature with a bit of an attitude. "What?" He complained. "No visitors allowed." He added. "Who would ever want to visit here?" Ralph replied. "We need to see Monzee and Montra." Charlie demands. "No visitors." He repeats. "Don't you know who we are?" Shane asked. "Should I?" He snaps back. "I am Shane Aster." Shane replied. "Alliance!" He screeches. "Let us in." Charlie repeats. "Ok if you insist." He moves, as they go past him into cave to come out in an open cavern with Garlocks and many other creatures all around. "Should've got my rabies and tetanus shots." Ralph replied. As they made there way to the center. There is a large slab of rock, which is used as a table and seated at it are Monzee and Montra. "We need to talk." Charlie stated. "You are coming to us?" Monzee replied. "Look we are here for information." Shane added. "You can have what ever you want." Montra smiles. "We know you have Volrin Aster here somewhere, we want him released to us." Charlie orders. "Who"? Monzee replied. "If we had an Aster here we'd be married to him." Montra suggests. "Ok first off never, second your not lying are you?" Shane replied. "I would never lie to you." Montra swears. "Then you won't mind if we check your lower caves." Charlie requested. "If you wish." Monzee replied. "Are you sure it's safe?" Shane whispered to Charlie. "It's possible they don't know they have him, he was a young boy." Charlie responded. "Lead the way." Jon insisted. They follow Monzee and Montra to a wall, which they release a lever and open to reveal a pathway with stairs made of rock spiraling down. Amanda uses her psychic power to try and read the minds of the creatures they came upon in the many small caves along the way. "I'm getting something." She replied. She follows the voice she can hear in her head to a cave, at the end of the path it is Volrin brown hair, brown eyes. "It's him." She informed. Jon entered first. "Volrin." Jon replied. "Do I know you?" Volrin asked. Shane and Charlie come in as well. "No actually, but we are related." Jon stated. "I am Voltar's son. And so is Shane." as he pointed to him. "We are here to take you home to Voltara." Jon added. As Charlie and Shane unchain him from wall. "He has children how long has it been?" Volrin replied. "You have been missing for twenty years." Shane answered. Just then Moondeath made his way inside. "Father?" Volrin asked. Moondeath comes to him and sighs in relief and touches his cheek. "My son." He responds. "Lets get him back to base." Charlie replied. As they all head back up to main cavern. "So we did help, what do we get?" Monzee desires. "We won't arrest you this time for kidnapping." Shane replied. Now back on the base. "So all of you work for the alliance?" Volrin asks. "Yes." Jon replied. Danny was scanning him with hand held scanner. "Well other than the usual dehydration and malnutrition he is ok." Danny assured. "Thanks Danny." Jon replied. Just then Voltar and Rick appeared before them. "My brother is alive?" Voltar says in amazement. "I searched everywhere for you." He continued. "I am sorry, it was all my fault." He ended. "It's in the past brother." Volrin replied. "You will come back with me, to my castle." Voltar vowed. "I am just glad to be free." Volrin declared. "He needs to rest." Danny encouraged. "Fine rest awhile then we'll talk." Voltar replied. They all go outside. Volrin gives a look of loathing and a snicker. "Revenge will finally be mine brother." He replied. "All of your family will suffer as well." He added as his hands began to glow. Meanwhile Jon is in his quarters with Jessica. "I can't believe how nice he is, considering all he has been through." Jon replied. "He is just glad to be free." Jessica responds, now in the docking bay, where Voltar has a ship ready to transport his brother to Voltara. Volrin has managed to slip out of sickbay unnoticed. He then made way to the docking bay and surprised Voltar as he rested. "You will die excruciatingly at last," he muttered. Just as Volrin was going to blast him with a deadly dose of his power, Rick walks in. "Volrin your awake?" Rick replied. He stops his hands from glowing. "Rick your with him." Volrin stated. "I thought you needed to rest." Rick says confused. "I'm feeling stronger now." Volrin replied. Then without warning he uses his power and puts rick to sleep with one touch of his hand to his temple. "I never liked you." He replies as rick falls to the floor. Then as he turns back to Voltar, who is on his feet and angered. Volrin then uses his power to blast Voltar to the far wall of his vessel. "You will know the pain I've endured brother!" He bellows. He then lifts him in the air with his telekinetic abilities and throws him into another wall. "The years of torcher by those beasts." He ranted. "While you enjoyed your wealth, your power, your whores." He comes close to him as he has him pinned against the wall. "Power that should be mine, it will be mine." He boasts. Voltar manages to break his hold of him "So you've become a true Aster in your captivity, my brother." Voltar replied. "I survived on my hatred for you, Brother." Volrin responds. "That is how my power grew stronger." Volrin added. "Allow me to show you." Volrin insisted. As he took all his power and harnessed it then blasts him right threw the vessel wall into the docking bay. The alarm sounded. "Soon your good sons will come, who do you think they'll believe?" Volrin embellishes. Voltar grabs him up by his hand, which has now become a Dregon claw. When the team enters. "Let him go!" Jon exclaimed. Voltar released him. Jon comes to Volrin. "Are you alright?" Jon asked. "Are you trying to kill him?" Dylan replied. "It's alright he was angry, I can forgive him." Volrin replied. "He attacked me!" Voltar maintains. "Why would he do that?" Shane asked. "Yeah he's still weak." Jon added. Volrin then clutches his head to sell his performance. Dylan helps him back to sickbay. "You need to leave." Biscus demanded. Just then Charlie noticed Rick lying in the vessel unconscious. "Dad?" Charlie replied as he heads to him. "Danny!" He calls. Danny comes kneels to him checks him over. He's in some sort of comatose state." Danny replied. "What did you do?" Jon demands. "I would never hurt my son." Voltar replied. "It was Volrin." He added. "Who do we believe?" Charlie asked. "Only Rick can answer that question." Danny stated. "Lock him up until we get answers." Dylan orders. Security comes and escorts Voltar to cell block. Now back in sickbay. "How are they?" Dylan asked. "Rick is still unconscious." Danny replied. Charlie comes up to Rick lying in bed. "Volrin is ok." Danny added. Shane comes to Volrin's bedside. "Your sure your ok?" Shane asked. "I'll be fine thank you, how is Rick?" He probed. "We don't know yet." Shane replied as he glances to him. "You have to be ok." Charlie says to rick. "I know we fight every time, but your still my father, I don't want to loose you." He added," "This makes no sense." Jon scrutinizes. "Was it during the fight?" Jon questioned. Jessica enters. "Jon I need to speak to you." She insisted. They step out into the corridor. "I read both of their minds, Volrin is mad with revenge." She indicated. "He is the one who put Rick in that state." She added. "I don't understand, why?' Jon replied. "Volrin has let his hatred for Voltar over come him." "We need to gather everyone away from Volrin now." Jon orders. The team is regrouped in control room. "So your telling me Volrin is insane?" Shane replied. "Yes." Jon answers. "Well I never thought I'd say these words, but release Voltar from cell block." Biscus ordered. "What do we do with Volrin?" Dylan replied. Just then an explosion is felt and heard. "What the hell?" Biscus exclaimed. They run toward it to sickbay they arrive to see a hole punched into the wall and equipment being sucked out into space. "Danny!" Jon yells as he makes his way to control panel and seals the breech to the hull. He then helped Danny to his feet. "Volrin blasted his way out." Danny replied. Voltar comes in. "Allow me to deal with him." Voltar informed. "I'm the one he wants." He added. "We will help." Shane replies. "What about Rick?" Charlie asked. "Well make him fix it once we capture him." Jon promises. Now on Voltara in the main throne room of Voltar's castle. Volrin proceeds to sit on Voltar's throne. "This feels right." He indicated. Voltar appears in front of him. "So, making yourself at home brother?" Voltar replied. "Of course." Volrin boasts. "Don't get comfortable." Voltar replied. "Give it your best shot." Volrin replied. As Volrin rises to his feet, they blast power at each other, then became their Dregons Volrin's is a dark purple. As they each throw each other around the room hard. "Had enough?" Volrin questions. "You're getting soft in your old age, brother." He added. "It's time for a new power to rule this galaxy." He declares as he flies up to the ceiling as Voltar lies on the floor stunned and returns to humanoid form. The team then bursts in. "I will be much worse than he could ever be children." Volrin vowed. As he lets out a sinister laugh and glows then flies straight up and threw the ceiling sending the roof falling in all scatter to avoid Fragments. "Were in trouble." Jon replied. Then Volrin flies back and hovers over them "I've made short work of my brother." He stated as Voltar gets to his feet. "Why are you doing this, he's your brother?' Shane demands. "Poor naïve Shane, your father let all of us down." He replied. "Instead of protecting us he sits back and watches from his throne." He added. Moondeath appears. "Volrin stop this." He commanded. "You never wanted to be like Voltar, this is not you." He replied. "You don't know me!" He shouted. "He left me to die, you both did, but I lived, I saved myself." He stated. "You've gone mad is what you've done." Voltar replied. "You went on with your life brother, you made me what I am now, your worst enemy." He announced. "Please Volrin, is there nothing left of my son?" Moondeath pleads. "Your son is dead old man." He replied. "I like this Aster I think I'll keep him." He laughs. "You don't want to be like him, your letting the power win." Shane insisted. "Sorry kid." He replied. He lands and goes back to throne and sits. "Now I wish to be alone." Volrin demands. He uses his power to make them all vanish and reappear back inside of the base. "How did you get here?" Biscus asked. "He has more power than we realized." Jon replied. "Volrin did this?" Dylan replied. "What do we do about Rick?" Charlie asked. "I will try to wake him." Voltar replies. They go to sickbay. "He won't be able to." Jessica states. "How do you know?" Jon replied. "Volrin's power is too strong." She responds. "Then we need to get Volrin." Charlie demands. Meanwhile back at the castle, Volrin is working Voltar's underlings to the bone, as Charlie is sitting by Rick's bedside. "You need to sleep." Jon replied. "I need to be here." Charlie asserted. "Trust me he can feel that you're here with him." Jon replied. In the control room, the team tries to come up with any type of plan to stop this new threat. "What we need is a more powerful being." Dylan replied. "May I speak?" Moondeath asked. "We welcome any insight." Biscus replied. "If we combine our power together I think we can weaken him." He suggested. "Will it kill him?" Shane asked. "No, he is immortal like any Aster he will live a long life." Moondeath replied. "Then we'd better move." Jon replied. The team heads back to Voltara,

They make their way to the throne room but it is empty. "Where is he?" Jon replied. As they search. "Did he leave?" Shane asked. "No he is here." Amanda replied. Just then the double doors swing open that lead to the garden. "Well back for round two?" Volrin replied. "We want to help you." Shane answered. Then they all join hands and blast him with a commanding bolt of supernatural energy. It knocks him to the ground. Then he passes out. "Lets get him locked up." Jon replied. Now back on the base in sickbay due to Volrin's debilitated state the spell he placed on Rick was broken as Rick wakes up, he looks to Charlie seated beside him. "Did you miss me?" He replied sarcastically. Charlie hugged him. "Volrin's weakened state released the spell he put on you. "Jon replied. "I never thought, I'd be glad to see you two back in charge of the criminal element in this galaxy." Jon replied. "Why junior that was the nicest thing you could ever say to me." Voltar replied. "What happens to Volrin?" Shane asked. "It will take time but I will help him." Moondeath vowed. "Good luck." Jon replied, as Moondeath takes a power-binding bracelet wearing Volrin and they disappear. "Well I hate to break this up but I have evil to spread." Voltar replied. He walks away. "Wow and he's back." Shane responds. Meanwhile off to the side Charlie and Rick are speaking. "I'm glad your ok." Charlie said. "So now you see how I feel when I see you hurt." Rick smiles. Before Charlie can respond. "We'll talk more later." He added as he goes, so as we recover from the drama that is my uncle Volrin. We will now discover that one of our team has ties to one of Voltar's henchman. Scene on Earth Matt and Gunner enter a brothel. There are wall-to-wall women scantily dressed very beautiful of all kinds of species and sizes. A young blonde humanoid approaches them. "What can I get for you gentlemen?" She asked. "We're looking for Diana." Matt replied. "She left a long time ago honey." She says. Gunner becomes angered and grabs her up in his arms. "What do you mean left!" He yelled. "Where the hell is she?" He demands. "Relax brother we'll find her." Matt says calmingly. "Now lets put the lady down?" He replied. Gunner lowers her back down. "I do apologize for my brother, no manners, we really need to find her if you can help?" He asked. "I can tell you where she is now." She replies. "Where!" Gunner says angrily. "Well after she found out she was pregnant she went where all the girls go." She informed. "I knew it!" Gunner irrupted. "They go there to give their babies away." She added. "She gave away my child!" Gunner says in fury. "Your child?" She replied. "Where us she now?" Matt probed. "She gave the baby to a good family I'm sure." She assured. "What was their name?" He demanded. "I'm sorry you'll have to ask her." She replied. "Believe me I will." Gunner indicated. As they leave, they follow her directions to a small modest home just a few blocks away. Matt knocks on the door. "Forget formalities brother." Gunner said as he blasted in the front door. "She gave away my child." He added. "Diana!" He shouted, as he searches the rooms. "Where are you?" He demanded. He finally makes way to a back bedroom where he saw her laying in a bed frail and sickly with an I.V. in her arm and tubes in her nose for oxygen. "I always knew you'd come eventually." She mumbled. Gunner is stunned by her ghastly, weak appearance. "What happened to you?" Gunner asked. "This is my punishment for the life I lead, I have Trailax syndrome." She replied. "I will be dead soon." She added. "How could you not tell me?" Gunner ordered. "Did I not treat you like a queen when we were together?" He reminded. "Yes until you joined up with the Aster clan." She replied. "Where is the child now?" Matt asked. "I don't know, I lost track of him few years ago." She replied. "The last name of the family was Trent." She added. Gunner has a moment of familiarity. "Where have I heard that name before?" He ponders. "Mitch Trent." Matt remembered. "He use to be one of us before he went soft." He added. "I think he had a kid brother." Matt replied. "My son." Gunner stated. "It is time to go." Gunner informed. He heads toward door, as matt followed. "What are you going to do?" Matt questioned. Gunner stops and looks to him. "He is my son, I'm going to get him." He replied. "How he is alliance, they will protect him." Matt reminds. "Not to mention he hates us." He added. "I am his father, he is still young." Gunner recapped. They load up on their vessel and leave Earth. Meanwhile back on the base in the control room. "All is quiet sir." Jesse informed. "I know it's too quiet." Biscus fears. Just then the doors to the docking bay are blown open setting off all kinds of alarms. Jesse brings up vidlink. "It's the Nelcons." Jesse replied. They make their way to the control room. "Where is Brent?" Gunner demanded. "Why would we tell you?" Jesse asked. "Don't be stupid kid." Matt replied. "I'm not here to hurt him." Gunner replied. "Why would we believe you?" Biscus asked. "He is my son." Gunner identified. "You're lying, what game are you playing?" Jesse replied. "We can prove it." Matt says. "I'll go get the team."

Lisette replied. She goes out. Then a few moments later the team walks in. "What is going on here?" Dylan asked. "What the hell do you want Nelcons?" Dylan added. Gunner walks up to Brent. "I need to speak to you." Gunner replies. "What for?" Brent questioned. "Someone want to tell us what is going on?" Shane asked. "I'll explain everything." Matt informed. "Fine." Brent said they go to the briefing room. "So what do you want?" "I don't know you, is this about Mitch?" Brent inquired. "No this is about you." Gunner replied. "What about me?' Brent asked. "I only just found out." "She never told me until now." Gunner explains. "What are you talking about?" Brent says in confusion. "It was fifteen years ago, I fell for a young girl I thought she did too." Gunner replies. "I am not interested in your conquests dude." Brent responds. "Her name was Diana." He continued. "She is your really mother, and I am your father. Brent has a look of revulsion and disbelief on his face. Meanwhile back in the control room Matt explained everything to us, which I must say, was unnecessarily detailed. "That poor kid." Dylan replied. Brent rushes in to get away from gunner. "He has to be lying, it's not true." Brent rejects. "I know my parents." He added in denial. "I wish we could say he was lying but he has proof." Biscus stated regrettably. "He has your original birth certificate." He shows him. "I don't care what that says." He looks to Gunner as he walks in. "You will never be my father." Brent walks passed him and out into corridor. Gunner follows him. "All I want is a chance to know you." Gunner pleas. Brent stops. "I don't need you." Brent responds. "Look, I know I've chosen the wrong side here but I'm new at this." He admits. "I can't trust you." Brent stated. "You're my son, you can trust I will protect you with my life." Gunner insures as he walks away and comes up to Matt with a sad expression. "It will take time brother, I know you won't give up." Matt replies. "Now get off my base while I let you." Biscus demands. "You will be getting the bill for the doors." He added. They go. Now as Brent struggles with his newly discovered lineage. We will find that something worse is coming. My father has been gathering his evil army; he even managed to recruit Monzee and Montra. It almost seems like the Darkness will over take us. Today will be the darkest day of my life. A day it will take me years to recover from. The day I almost gave into the darkness myself. My heart will never be the same. Scene Jessica heads to the Docking bay. "Where are you going?" Jon asked. "I'm going to help

the people on Voltia, I won't be gone long." She replied. She kisses him on
the lips and goes. As she is flying to Voltia a battle is breaking out between
Voltar's armies and us. As they fired upon each other a blast hit Jessica's
fighter. She crashed down onto the planet below. As the team headed to
the wreckage it exploded into flames. "No!" Amanda screams, as Jon is at
the docking bay in a state of dissolution and disbelief. He collapses to his
knees. "I lost her, just like before, all the women I love die." He appraised.
"I'm going to be like my father alone." He added. "No you won't, don't let
your father win." Dylan insists. "What is left for me?" Jon asked. "Jessica
was my light, my life." He cried. "You are not alone, your family, your team
is here with you." Dylan replied. "All I can feel now is darkness." Jon
affirmed. As biscus comes in Dylan comes to him. "We are losing him."
Dylan fears. "He is shutting down." He added. "Stay with him." Biscus
insisted. Just then Moondeath entered. "Jon." He said. "It's me I am here."
He added. "I'm here to help you." He replies as he kneels down to him.
"Can you make the pain stop?" Jon looks to him eyes filled with tears.
"This is my fault, if I would've stayed on Voltara they'd be alive." Jon said.
"You would be evil if you did, that is not the boy I know." Moondeath
recaps. "I am Voltar Aster Jr. there is only evil in that name." He replied.
"We all have lost someone we loved, it does not make us evil. Moondeath
said. "Yes it does, my heart is deadly to anyone I let in." Jon deems. "No,
your heart is full of love and compassion, it is strong and good." Moondeath
confirms. "I don't want to fight anymore, I just want to give in it's easier."
Jon remarks. "I killed my wife and child." Jon replied. "Don't become your
father." Moondeath pleads. "I am his son." Jon responds. "I just want to
be alone please." Jon insists. Moondeath touches his shoulder and then
rises he comes back over to Dylan. "We must pull him out of this darkness."
Moondeath asserted. "Or it will destroy him." He added. As my family
and friends fought to save my very soul, my father was busy planning his
takeover of the galaxy. He would use all the villains we'd ever fought; he
even managed to convince Volrin to join him, all this as I struggled, with
burying my wife and child. It will take all that I have to survive this, but
Shane and Charlie are counting on me, my strength to keep them strong.
While inside I am falling apart, I cannot let my father win. I won't let that
happen. As our battles with them got more destructive and intense, my
father kept trying to lure me back to that darkness. He appeared in my

Quarters that night. "Junior?" He called. "I came to check on you I am sorry about Jessica." He replied. "I know what it's like, to loose a love." He added. "Do not think that you and I can bond over this." Jon confidently stated. "I just want you to know I'm here." Voltar claims. "I'll survive, I always do." Jon replied. Now as a few months have gone by it has gotten easier to get up in the morning, remembering why I left home in the first place is a good reminder. I did meet a woman her name is Leana she was out for some revenge at first, her mother was a witch the one who actually cursed Moondeath all those years ago. I helped to convince her to let that go. She will never replace Jessica in my heart; unfortunately I would discover she was not all she appeared to be. She would end up being one of our families greatest enemies she is a goddess. She is so beautiful yet so deadly. I only hope I can escape her myself, now in the corridor. "I'm having dinner with her tonight." Jon replied. "So you and her are getting serious?" Shane asked. "I'm happy for you." Charlie stated. "She makes me feel alive again." Jon responds. "You deserve it bro." Shane replied. Now in the mess hall a special table is decorated for a romantic dinner for two. Leana is seated in first chair her raven hair set perfectly above her neck with pins, Her brown eyes deep and alluring. Jon enters and is immediately spellbound by her beauty. "You look incredible tonight." Jon replied. "I wanted to make everything perfect for us." She informed. He sits at the table in the chair across form hers. As they enjoy their meal, Jon cannot help but to stare at her. "I'm sorry, am I making you uncomfortable?" Jon asked as she noticed. "There is just something about you." He added. Leana smiled. "Thank you." She replied. Now after dinner is over they head to the entrance of the mess hall. "I should go." She replied. Jon takes her hand. "No you should stay." He insisted, as he pulls her in close and kisses her passionately. "I don't want to be alone." Jon replied. "Are you sure?" She asked. "I will always love Jessica but she is gone." Jon answers. He leads her back to his quarters where they kiss even more passionately it is like a supernatural seductive force that rushes through him. They make their way to the bedroom, where they would have the most powerful foremost sensual experience like none he'd ever had before. As they lie in bed together after, Jon touches her neck to gently move her hair back "That was, Incredible." Jon said. "Yes it was, so much better than any of the Asters before you," She replied. Jon sits up and looks to her in bewilderment and surprise. She then rises up out of the bed and glows she transforms herself into her true form her skin is that of glimmer and her hair still raven in color but her eyes are a brilliant shade of brown that is almost crystal like. "Remember me?" She asked. "I must admit you are the best Aster I've ever had." She informed. As she smiled, Jon realizes who she is, Tracilla he had heard of her from his father a very seductive goddess who went after only the most powerful of beings. "You can't be her?" Jon replied, "My father said he destroyed you." He added. "I am a goddess, I can only be killed when I choose to ascend." She replied. Jon goes to get out of the bed but she swiftly climbs in and pins him down. "You can't think of leaving not after tonight." She smiled. "Let go." Jon demands as his eyes glow. She lets him go, as he proceeds to grab clothes and get dressed. "No need to cover up lover." She replied. Jon looks back to her in anger. "You do realize I can suspend time?" She replied. "One of my many talents." She added. "I mean we were having such a good time, I didn't want anyone to ruin it." She stated. Jon takes in a deep breath and sighs. "Just shut up." He demands. "I'm having too much fun with you." She replied. "Why did you choose me?" Jon inquires. Tracilla rises out of bed with her dress of glittery black diamonds short and form fitting. "I've always wanted to meet the Aster that went good." She replied. "So there never was a Leana?" Jon determined. She comes closer to him. "No." she replied. She touches his cheek. "You're trembling, was I everything you wanted and needed?" She asked. Jon moves away from her. "No." He replied, she comes back in his face and she caresses his cheek. "Stop." Jon demands. She pulls him in and kisses him intensely you can feel the power between them. "I can change back to her if you'd prefer?" She whispers. She tries to kiss him again but Jon pulls away. "No, this was a mistake. Jon replied. "What have I done?"

Chapter 8
TRACILLA THE POISON

I've always struggled with the darkness inside of me. My heart is strong and moral but with the loss of Jessica and our child I have begun to let the darkness consume me. It was why she so easily seduced me, a dark goddess one of the few remaining in this galaxy. She will never have my heart that only belongs to Jessica. As for my body and soul I was hers. She is toxic, her powers of persuasion are unmatched, she maybe the one person who brings out my Aster. Scene in the bedroom "Why didn't Amanda sense you?" Jon questioned. "That weak telepath?" "I am a pure goddess, I control what people see." She replied. She tries to touch Jon's shoulder. "It is magical between us Jon, I know you felt it." She recapped. Jon pulls away from here. "No it's not." Jon stands firm. "Don't deny your true nature." She replies. As she turns his body toward hers "There are no feelings." Jon answered. She pulls him in closer "You wanted me as much as I did you." She identified. "I wanted a woman I thought you were." Jon replied. "You know there was a connection between us." She replied. "No." Jon decisively said; as he attempts to walk away form her. "You are the Aster I should have been after all along." She declared. "Your power is strongest, it is pure." She replied. "You are of two parents of Voltara the first world." She recognized. "So your after my power then?" Jon asked. "No we should be together to rule these lesser beings." She implied as she sits on the edge of the bed. "We can stop Voltar's reign of terror." She added. "This can't be happing." Jon refuses. "When do I wake up?" he asked. "Am I really so bad?" She replied. "We belong together tonight proves that." She added.

"Admit it, you never felt such fire such desire before." She replied. She rises and comes in his face touching his cheek. "I am your equal, no others will satisfy you as I can." She affirmed. She kisses him he kisses her back intensely but then he pulls back. "No this is wrong." He replied. "I am yours Jon." She declared, as she tries to kiss him again. "Stop, your evil I'm not." Jon indicated. "I am just misguided but you can save me." She replies innocently. She kisses him again and once again leads him back to the bed where they have empowering sex again, now after. "What spell have you cast over me?" Jon insisted. "What you have done to me." She replied. "I will see you again soon." She added as she gently kissed his lips and then vanished. "What is wrong with me?" Jon demands. As he lies back in bed, just at that moment Voltar appeared before him. "Exactly my question junior." Voltar replied. "How did you get in here?" Jon demanded. "Never mind that, How could you?" Voltar asked. "She is very beautiful and seductive apparently you did." Jon reminded. "Yes but I am a womanizer son, you are not." He answered. Jon sits up in bed. "Don't you think I feel sick?" He replied. As he grabs clothes and gets dressed. "I can help you with her." Voltar indicated. "No, I can handle this." Jon replied. "You, son you're helpless in this situation." Voltar observed. "I am not talking to you about this." Jon replied. "Then you'd better talk to your friends." Voltar insisted. "No, they will think I've lost my mind." Jon replied. "I've got news for you son, you have and I say that because I love you. "He added. He then vanished. Then Paul knocks and entered. "Jon?" He calls out, as Jon emerged from his bedroom. "Hey, where is Leana?" Paul asked. "I made a big mistake, now I'm going to pay for it." Jon replied. "I don't understand?" Paul inquired. Now next scene is in the control room the team is gathered. I told them all about Tracilla, from what I knew and what happened between us. "Whoa as in the dark goddess?" Charlie asked. "It's obvious she tricked him." Biscus replied. "She said I'm the Aster she should be with." Jon indicated. "She is so twisted." Amanda fumes. "I feel like such a fool." Jon replied. "Hey she is beautiful." Shane stated. "We will figure something out." Dylan replied. "I don't think I can resist her again." Jon admits. "Then maybe you should go to Voltar or Moondeath, someone who is familiar with her." Charlie replied. Just then Moondeath appears. "So you were caught in her web too." He replied. "How do they do that?" Cole asked. "They have a connection." Amanda replied. Jon goes into the briefing room with Moondeath. "I've never felt like this before, I think I maybe obsessed." Jon admitted. "You need to get control of your inner power." Moondeath replied. "I don't think I can with her." Jon replied. "Then the only other solution is to destroy her." Moondeath replied. "How do you destroy a goddess?" Jon questioned. "Your power is the strongest of us Jon, only you can do it." Moondeath replied. Meanwhile over at Rick's club, Tracilla appears in a sexy dark red dress with black lace trough out it. Sitting on the couch in the back is Voltar. "Well hello future father in law." She replied. "You sick bitch." He said as he rises. "Careful you're not as young as you used to be." She replied. "I'm sure I can take you." She adds with a smile. "Leave my son out of this." Voltar appeals. "He is good not your type." He added. "OH but he is. He is perfect." She replied. "I'm keeping him." Her eyes glow red. Voltar lunges for her she vanishes and reappears behind him. "I'm too fast for you." She replied. "Jon is mine." She asserts. "I will make you a deal." Voltar insists. "Not interested, Jon is leader material but you knew that, it's why you're so desperate to get him under your thumb." She replied She winks at him then vanished. Rick comes over. "Was that Tracilla?" Rick asked. "Yes and she has got her claws into junior." Voltar replied. "If she can get him to use his true power, he will rule us all." Voltar added. "I must get him away from her." Voltar realized. "I'm glad I never slept with her." Rick replied. Meanwhile back on base, Moondeath steps out leaving Jon alone in his living room. Tracilla appears. "Hello lover." She affirmed. "You need to leave." Jon demands. "I stopped time just for us." She replied, as she walks up to him and slipped off her dress. "So what do we do know?" She smiled. "I told you we couldn't do this." Jon replied. She kissed him he pulled free of her grasp. "No, this is over." Jon replied. "You really don't want to make a goddess angry." She fumed. "Things could get ugly." She added. "I won't." Jon declared. She pulls back and her eyes glow red she transformed into a gruesomely devilish ghoul, almost titan like, red in color with sharp teeth and claws. "I warned you," She growled. Jon's eyes widen in disbelief and fright. "I always get what I want." She hissed. She then changed back to her humanoid form. "Now, where were we?" She replied. "I can't do this your like a poison, I will find a way to stop you." Jon vowed. "You are mine." She replied. Then she vanished, now next day in rec room. "You must learn to use your power Jon, you can manipulate time too." Moondeath informed him. "Both your mother and father were of a long line of pure Voltarians, it is the purest magic in this galaxy." He added. Jon closes his eyes and concentrates, his whole body begins to glow a brilliant luminous light. He then froze moondeath and everyone in the base. He opens his eyes and noticed moondeath not moving. "I did it?" Jon questioned. He touches moondeath and he moves Jon jumped back. "How are you moving?" Jon asked. "When you touch someone they will be brought back into your time." Moondeath replied. "Now you can deal with her." He added. Now that night as Jon slept she came to him. Jon wakes up "I'm ready for you." Jon replied. His eyes glow. "Then we'll just have to play in my cavern." She stated as she grabs his hand and they vanish, reappearing in a cavern. Meanwhile the team hears the alarms go off and rush into Jon's room. "She took him." Shame exclaimed. "To her cavern in the monster zone." Moondeath replied. "We are going to need all of us to enter it." Moondeath informed. "We can't just walk into the zone." Shane replied. "We have to." Charlie responds. Now inside the zone, the team and Voltar, Rick and Volirn are present. "All this over a woman?" "How pathetic." Volrin replied. "Shut up Volrin." Rick ordered. They make their way to her cavern meanwhile Jon is still asleep as Tracilla touches his cheek "You will learn to love me." She states. "I wouldn't bet on that." Voltar replied as they entered. Voltar blasts her with a jolt of his power slamming her into the wall and on the floor." "Lets get Jon out of here." Shane replied. "Jon?" Shane says. Jon wakes up he looks around "Where are we?" Jon asked as he sits up. "We're in her cavern." Shane replied. "Where is Tracilla?" Jon asked. "She is down for now." Charlie replied. "This time, I'm going to train you junior." Voltar asserted. Now in Voltar's castle. "You must release all of your power junior, do not fear it embrace it." Voltar replied. "Your power is pure and not evil son, you are a true Aster like your great grandmother was." Voltar informed. Jon concentrates his body glows radiant and he blasts his power outward and threw the castle wall. Then he stops. "Whoa sorry about the wall." Jon replied. "Now your ready for her." Voltar replied. "Your sure I can resist her?" Jon asked. "It's all up to you." Voltar replied. I would find that I could not resist her, at least this time. In fact I slipped closer to her grasp and further from my family. She was taking over my very soul. There was only one thing left to do, my father made a terrible deal to free me from her. At the castle a desperate Shane and Charlie try to figure out what they can do. "I can make a deal with the overlord." Voltar proposed. "I'll get Jon back." Voltar insisted. "Who is that?" Shane asked. "The ruler of the underworld." Voltar replied. "Only the overlord can enhance my powers so I can destroy Tracilla once and for all." Voltar explained. "Are you sure that's a good idea?" Shane questioned. "I'm doing it for junior." Voltar replied. He then vanished; meanwhile Jon is with Tracilla in her cavern. They are lying in her bed, her head on his bare chest. "We can't keep doing this." Jon insisted. "Why not we're great at it." She replied with a smile. "I'll never be dark and you can't be good." Jon stated. "I will try for you." She replied, she sits up looks at him. "Your serious?" Jon asked. "I am in love with you Jon." "I'll do what I have to, to keep you." She replied, as she kissed him. Meanwhile in the dark caverns of the underworld, beneath the very core of the planet of Voltara, Voltar arrives at gates made of bones and flesh of those long dead. "I'm here my lord." Voltar called. The gates then opened inward as he stepped threw. The overlord came form the black shadows A large beast whose skin was red as fire, eyes as black as death and whose face was so grotesque, it would make any mortal cringe, the embodiment of darkness and pure evil. "Well, my most favorite creature of darkness Voltar Aster." Overlord snarled. "I need to be more powerful." Voltar pleaded. "So, finally ready to destroy this galaxy?" Overlord replied. "I will, once I save my son from Tracilla." Voltar vowed. "Then we have a deal." Overlord replied. Then the Overlord takes the power from inside her very flesh, it is a ball of red fire and throws it at Voltar as his body absorbs it, and his eyes glow the darkest of red. Now back at Tracilla's lair. "I don't want to loose you." She says, as Jon is asleep beside her. "I'll make it so you cannot leave." She replied. She gets up, and glows she creates a field around the castle. "Now you are mine forever." She smiled. Just then Voltar explodes threw the wall of the cavern. "So trying to seal him away." Voltar exclaimed. Tracilla transforms to ghoul, As Voltar becomes his Dregon, which is even larger than before and more powerful. Jon wakes up and sees them. "Father?" Jon questioned, as Voltar and Tracilla exchanged powerful blows. "He is mine!" She shouts. "Not as long as I breathe." Voltar replied, as he gathered his new power and concentrated a blast at her she turns to a mist of golden dust. Jon jumps to his feet. "You killed her?" Jon replied. "Yes I did junior, I made a deal for you." He replied. "A deal for me?" Jon stated in confusion. "With who?" Jon questioned. "With the overlord of course." He replied. Jon surprised by what his father has done. "You gave up your soul?" Jon asked. "I'd do anything for you son." Voltar declared. "I don't know what to say." Jon replied. Now back on the base. "Are you ok?" Shane asked. "Yeah I will be." Jon replied. Jon comes to Voltar "I guess I owe you." Jon replied. "I am your father, you owe me nothing junior." He answered. "What about the overlord?" Jon asked. "I'll deal with that." Voltar replied. Jon hugs him. Then Voltar goes back to castle, just then the overlord appeared in front of him. "Now about our deal." She replied. "I will conquer this galaxy as I promised." Voltar confirms. As I again believed something good about my father, he again let me down. He attacked multiple planets with his newly gained power. Now I must confront him, scene on the base. "Your sure you want to go alone?" Shane asked. "It's my fault, he did it for me." Jon replied. "He did it for more power too." Shane reminded. Now at Voltar's castle Jon enters, and makes his way to the throne room. "Father?" He calls out. Just then the overlord appeared before him. "Well the son of Voltar." Overlord replied. "Where is my father?" Jon demanded. "He is out celebrating my victory." Overlord indicated. "He is growing old his power is weak." Overlord replied. "You on the other hand, have pure power." Overlord salivated, as she moves closer to Jon. "Whoa back up." Jon replied as he moved back. "I don't need him, but I can use you." Overlord decided. "I don't think so." Jon replied. The overlord lets out a snicker. "I have all the control here, I will own this galaxy." Pauses "And you." Overlord replied. She then grabs his left arm, and uses firepower to burn a unique symbol into his inner wrist. Jon pulls arm free. "What the hell?" As he sees looks at it. "You are marked, I own your soul." Overlord replied. We'll talk again soon." As overlord smiled then vanished. Voltar then enters. "Junior what are you doing here?" Voltar asked. "What have you done"? Jon demanded. Voltar has a look of confusion. "What are you talking about junior?" He inquired. Jon showed him his wrist. "You sold my soul too." Jon replied. "No I would never son." Voltar insisted. "The overlord was here, she did this to me." Jon informed. "I'll handle this." Voltar maintained. "How the overlord wants me, wants my power." Jon comprehended. "I swear to you, I did not know her true intentions." Voltar replied. "You brought me down with you." Jon indicated. "I will go to her." Voltar directed. Now back on the base, Jon is in sickbay where Paul is scanning Jon's wrist, as Shane is present too. "How do we stop her?"

Shane asked. "I don't know if we can." Jon replied. "He'll fix it, you'll be fine." Shane insurers. Meanwhile in the caverns of the underworld, Voltar walks in. "Where are you?" He shouts. "You are not taking my son!" He exclaimed. Overlord comes out of cavern. "I don't need you any longer, I will rule the galaxy now." Overlord replied. "Your son belongs to me as well." She added. "I will never allow this." Voltar replied. "He is part of my plan, to rule the entire universe." She added. "Over my dead body." Voltar replied. The overlord blasts him with her power and absorbs it. "Now your weak." She affirmed. "I will find a way to end you." Voltar vowed. "You can try." She laughed. Now back on base in the control room. "So, we got rid of one psycho for another?" Dylan replied. "The overlord will come here next." Charlie informed. "Why do you say that?" Biscus asked. "I'm here." Jon replied. "She wants me to rule by her side." He added. "Did she not see herself in the mirror cause she is ugh a lee." Ralph replied. Just then Jon feels a psychic connection to Voltar. "My father he's hurt." Jon replied. Now at the castle, they come inside to see rick standing outside his bedroom. "He's in here." Rick stated. They go inside as the bedroom is dark and dreary Voltar lying in the bed portraits of Voltar line the walls. They come upon a faded and pale Voltar. Jon sits at his bedside. "Father?" Jon replied. "Junior, are you alright?" He asked. "What is happening to him?" Shane questioned. "The overlord she did this she is killing him." Rick answered. "He is immortal, he can't die." Shane insists. "She is the overlord, she controls the life and death of all beings even Asters." Rick replied. "I will go to her." Jon stated as he rises. "Are you insane?" Rick replied. "It's the only way." Jon stated. "We can't let you do that bro." Shane replied. "If I don't he will die, then who will she target next?" Jon questioned. As rick and Shane look at each other in query. "I'm going." Jon replied, as he vanished. "What do we do?' Shane asked. "We gather, my side and yours for battle." Rick replied. Meanwhile as Jon appears in the caverns of the underworld. "Where are you?" He commanded Overlord comes out but she is different her skin is a dark sultry red her hair black as night her eyes a hazel glow she is beautiful. "So my assistant." She says. "I've come to make a deal, for my father's life." Jon replied. "No deals I own you." She stated. "I am the original darkness in this galaxy." She replied. "Then why do you need me?" Jon asked. "You are powerful, a power I can feel within you, almost as pure as the gods themselves." She replied. "You are born for the darkness Jon," She added. "No!" Jon roared as the ground beneath them shook with the force of his inner power. "I make my own destiny." He vowed. Then he used his power to open up the ground beneath her very feet. "I know how to stop you." Jon informed. As it swallowed her up and he sealed it back. Suddenly the mark on Jon's wrist glowed then vanished. Now back at the castle Jon enters the room. "What happened?" Shane asked. "I destroyed her for now anyway." Jon replied. He walks up to Voltar in bed, only now he is stronger and has some color back in his face. "Junior are you alright?" Voltar asked as he sat up. "I am now, I stopped her." Jon replied. "I am sorry for this, my son." Voltar apologized. Jon kissed his father's forehead. "I know." Jon replied. "No matter what, you are still my father and I love you." Jon added. "I love you to junior." He smiled. Jon heads out to Shane and Rick. "So you ok?' Shane asked. "I'm getting there." Jon answered. As the team enjoyed this one short victory, Monzee and Montra were up to no good as usual. For the lust of a Moneconda is intense and lengthy. There about to go after Shane and Charlie in full force will there be wedding bells in their future? Not if I can help it. Now in the Monster zone. "With Tracilla gone and the Overlord out of commission, it is time to rule." Monzee stated. "We need to capture our Asters too." Montra reminded. "We will sister." Monzee smiles. As the team is out on they're usual missions, battling the criminals. Shane and Charlie are paired up on Voltara, where they are in the process of arresting a band of pirate dealers. "Alright lets go." Shane replied as they load them up onto an alliance transporter. Just then Monzee and Montra appeared. "Great not you two." Charlie replied. "We are here to claim what is ours." Monzee stated. "I will never be yours." Charlie responded. They then swiftly grab hold of their arms and vanish. Now in the control room Jesse looses their trackers. "I lost Shane and Charlie's signal!" Jesse yelled. "Those damm sisters." Dylan replied. "Lets go kill um this time huh?" Ralph endorsed. As we prepared to go after them, in the zone Shane pulls free from Montra. "Don't you ever give up?" Shane asked. Montra caressed his cheek gently. "I never give up on love." She replied, as Charlie also pulled free from Monzee. "The team will be here any minute." Charlie affirms. "They won't make in time." Monzee replied, as she hits a switch on wall, it moved away to reveal a large computer. She then goes to it, and punches in a code, a shield is emitted that surrounds the outer caverns of the zone. "In time for what?" Shane asked. They both smile sinisterly. "For us to be married." Montra replied, and then she hits another button, to reveal another room with a chapel style to it. Charlie and Shane replied in unison. "Oh my god." "They will never make it." Monzee spewed confidently. "Ok any way we can discuss this?" Shane appeals. "We are in trouble." Charlie replied. Hopefully we will make it in time, I can't imagine those two as my in-laws. As the team heads to the zone it was not easy to even land. "They are planning on marrying them." Amanda read from their minds. "Not on my watch." Jon replied. He then used his power to freeze time, so that Jesse could disable that shield. He does and we get to the caverns unfreeze them. "So did she look really hot in her wedding dress?" Ralph asked. "Not even funny." Charlie glared. Now as we went back to the base, after we locked up the sisters yet again in my father's castle. "You need to get control of your son." Volrin demanded. "Don't be jealous." Rick replied. "Relax I will handle junior." He replied. "You'd better, or we won't be running the galaxy." Volrin added. "What are you going to do father?" Rick inquired. "I mean his powers are stronger." Rick says reluctantly. "He is still naïve, he has yet to master all his power." Voltar recapped. Now back on the base in Jon's quarters. "I still can't get over your powers, I'm so jealous." Shane replied. "I won't be making it a habit to use them." Jon maintained. "It would make it easier to capture criminals." Shane suggested. "No." Jon stated. Shane goes out and Paul enters. "What is going on?" Jon asked. "We need to talk." Paul replied. "Should I sit for this?" Jon asked. "Your power is growing." Paul stated. "When I did your last scan, your body was glowing on the inside." He added. "Am I going to explode?" Jon asked nervously. "No, look have you ever heard the tale of the Valr Te Nesk?" Paul replied. "The what?" Jon said. "Its been written, about a ruler of Voltarian blood, who would lead the galaxy into peace." Paul expressed. "I'm not a ruler." Jon indicated. "There is a way to confirm it." Paul specified. "How is that?" Jon asked. "You will have to go to the mountains of Voltara, and confront the Volesk, if you can defeat him with a touch, you're the one." Paul concluded. "Your insane that creature is huge and hungry, it would never let me near it." Jon replied. "Many men have gone to attempt to prove their valor." Paul stated. "Yeah that is called suicide." Jon replied. "You are not a normal being Jon." Paul insisted. "I suggest you ask your grandfather, "Your mother's father he lives in those mountains." Paul added. "Look, I know I'm not this Valr Te Nesk, but I am curious to see my grandfather." Jon replied. Now the next morning Jon enters the control room and everyone stops and looks at him. "You told them didn't you?" Jon replied. He looked to Paul. "I think it's incredible, you could be the one." Dylan recognized. "I am not "The One!" Jon insisted. "My man the Valr Te Nesk." Ralph replied he goes for a high-five. Jon looks at him angrily. "You gonna leave me hanging?" Ralph added. "Ok stop!" Jon yelled. "I'm going to meet my grandfather, so he can confirm to all of you, I am not the Valr Te Nesk." Jon replied, he walks out. He heads to docking bay and gets into his fighter and flies to the mountains of Voltara. He climbs out to see a cave entrance; he walks to it and goes inside. "Hello!" He called out. A voice called out of the darkness. Come in!" "I'm looking for Sel?" He asked, he sees a light up ahead. "You found him!" He replied. When Jon enters to find a beautiful royally decorated room. "Come in young man." He added. He comes out from back; he is an older man white hair and brown eyes. "My name is…Sel cuts him off. "I know who you are." Sel replied. "You're my grandson, come sit next to me." He stated as he sat in chair by a table. Jon comes and sits in chair beside it. "How did you know?" Jon asked. "I felt your presence." He replied. "The last time I saw you, you were two." Sel remembered. "Sorry I don't remember you." Jon replied. "I am glad you're finally here, to claim your galaxy." Sel stated. "Whoa, I am not The Valr Te Nesk." Jon says firmly. "I just came here to see you." Jon replied. "Your journey begins with me." Sel said. "I will set you on your path, to your destiny." He added. "I'm sorry to disappoint, but I'm not a leader" Jon replied. "You will, you have it in you to tame the beast." Sel stated. "You have the wrong guy." Jon insisted. Sel rises. "Come with me." He said. He leads Jon to another cavern with a large sealed door. "It is time." He replied. "What, wait now?" Jon replied. "Yes, it is time to embrace who you are meant to be." He added. "He is waiting for you, I can not go with you." Sel replied. "Look I'm not going to tame it, it is going eat me." Jon implied. "Yes you will." He said. He then opened the doors, and pushed Jon threw and locked it behind him. Jon bangs on the door. "Hey this is not funny!" Jon yelled. He then stopped and looked around. "Great my grandfather is insane." He replied. "Now I'm going to die." He added. Just then he hears a profound and mighty growl coming form just ahead of him in the dark abyss. "Why me?" Jon asked. "It might not be so big." Jon hopes. Just then he hears and feels heavy footsteps. "Or not." Jon replied. Suddenly some light emerges form the cavern, as he can see a large creature blocking another door. He is at least 7 feet tall, with lava rock type skin and larger horns on either side of his head, wearing black pants. I could feel my heart racing and pounding threw my chest. "I took a wrong turn sorry!" Jon yells. "You dare to challenge me boy?" It asked. "You talk?" Jon asked. "Of course, don't you?" He replied. "Well yeah." Jon responded. "Are you prepared to die?" He asked. "No not really, so how about I just go out the way I came." Jon replied. Then a thick wall comes down over those doors. "Look someone made a huge mistake." Jon insisted as he turned back toward him. "Yes you did." He replied. The beast then reached down to grab Jon, Jon then put his hand up to defend himself as soon as the beast touched it he felt the surge of power and backed away. "Forgive me." The beast begged, as he fell to his knees. "I did not realize it was you." He added. "You can get up, this is awkward." Jon replied. The beast rises and the doors behind him opened. "You may go." He replied. Jon sees a palace of pure gold in the distance with Sel standing in front. "What just happened?" Jon asked, as he walked to Sel. "Come with me and I will explain it all...Valr Te Nesk." He replied. We went inside he told me all about the ones who came before me how they helped to rule this galaxy. I was the first whose heart was as pure and good as my power. I just sat in disbelief, wondering what will happen next? How do I go on as Jon Aster? Now everyone will know I am The Valr Te Nesk. What about my Father, my brothers? This is all happening way too fast. Am I really ready to try and rule a galaxy, or even to defended it? Sel is right about one thing my destiny has just begun, I'll have to see where this path takes me. It is time to see what I can do.

Chapter 9

VALR TE NESK

Now that I know my destiny, that is the easy part. The hard part will be going back to a normal existence. The entire galaxy wants to know, which side I'm on. I know in my heart I am meant for good, which will only end in disaster for my family and team, scene on the base in the control room. "I hope he's ok." Shane replied. "We would know if he wasn't." Charlie encouraged. "I am not sensing any danger for him." Amanda disclosed. "I still can't believe, he is going to be the ruler of the galaxy." Jesse replied. "Hey he is the guy for the job." Brent responds. Meanwhile in Biscus's office he is with Dylan. "The general wants to speak to him." Biscus informed. "He says he's getting calls form every planet." He added. "If Jon is really the future of this galaxy, you can bet Voltar will try to influence him." Dylan replied. "I have faith in him." Biscus stated. "Yeah, but can anyone really take down his or her own father?" Dylan asked. Meanwhile on Voltara in the castle, all of the villains are gathered in the throne room demanding answers. "I have everything under control." Voltar claimed. "How your son is the Valr Te Nesk?" "He has no equal." Volrin exclaimed. "He is still my son." Voltar replied. "If he accepts his destiny, we will all be screwed." Cora responded. "My son hates power, he will not want to rule." Voltar trusts, Meanwhile in the caverns of Voltara in Sel's castle. "You will rule us all." Sel celebrated. "Look I'm not the ruler type, I'm just happy to be a member of the alliance." Jon replied. "Your course has been set, all the beings of this galaxy will respect and bow to you." Sel informed. "I don't want them to fear me like my father." Jon replied. "They will have no reason to, they have witnessed the kind of man you are." Sel stated. "You have a lot of faith in me, I'm not so sure I do." Jon confessed. "You will be fine." Sel insisted. "I have been tempted by darkness." Jon replied. "We all have but your heart guides you." Sel guarantees. "This is all just, way too much." Jon replied. "How do I lead a galaxy?" Jon feared. "The way you always have, by protection and servitude." Sel replied. "You are our future Jon." He added, now back on the base Jon has returned he entered the control room. "Hey your ok." Dylan replied. "Yeah, considering." Jon said. "The general wants to talk with you, seems the word is out." Dylan replied. "I'm not sure, I'm ready." Jon responded. "I don't think you have a choice." Biscus informed. "Sir the general is here." Jesse interrupted. The general walks in Human and older with white short hair. "You wanted to see me sir." Jon replied. Dylan and Biscus allow them to use the office, as they step out and close the door. "I heard of your new found destiny." He replied. "I really didn't do anything." Jon insisted. "I always knew, there was something about you since the day we met." General replied. "I never asked for any of this sir." Jon replied. "No one asks for their destiny, it just is." General responded. "I believe, you can join our galaxy together." He added. "I'm honored sir, I will try." Jon says humbly. General extends his hand Jon shakes it. The general comes out of office and leaves. "What did he say?" Dylan asked. "I'm going to give a speech, at the conference in a few days." Jon replied. "That's great." Biscus added. "What am I support to say?" Jon worries. "Say what you feel." Dylan replied. "What if my father is there?" Jon asked. "He chose his destiny, it is time for you to do the same." Biscus replied. Jon goes to his quarters, to find Voltar standing in his living room. "What are you doing here?" Jon demanded. "We need to talk junior." Voltar replied. "I already know what you're going to say, I am not helping you." Jon stated firmly. "I love you, no matter what you do son." Voltar replied. "What about your partners?" Jon asked. "What is good without evil, remember that junior." Voltar replied. "I know what I have to do father." Jon state. Now a few days later on Earth, at the Galactic Alliance building the auditorium is full of all types of beings good and evil, back behind the curtain Jon is waiting. "Good luck." Biscus replied. "I know what I'm going to say." Jon responds. General steps out to the podium as all settle down. "Now we will here form, the Valr Te Nesk." General stated Jon walks out all applauded, he steps to the podium all-quiet down. "Look I am no leader, this system has always been divided by light and darkness." He replied. "I know, you all expect me to say peace is the only way, but it is not that easy, I know." He continues. "I am one man, I cannot give you that. "All I can say is, I will try to keep the balance in this galaxy, and protect those who cannot protect themselves." He stated. "So that no one side, is in absolute control." "Good will always have evil. "I have seen both within myself and it is in all of us, you must listen to your heart." "That is how we can save this galaxy, form total chaos." He concluded, then all the crowed erupted in applause. "What kind of speech was that?" Volrin smirked. "Shut up brother." Voltar replied, now back on the base in the control room. "I think I shook every hand in that auditorium." Jon replied. "You did good." Charlie stated. "Yeah I even saw father clapping." Shane replied. "Why didn't you get that on video?" Ralph asked. "Lets get back to work people." Dylan replied, meanwhile on Voltara in the castle "That speech made me ill." Volrin replied. "Now you know how we feel, when you talk." Rick responded. "I can still work this to our advantage." Voltar insisted. "I'm all ears great leader." Volrin says in sarcasm. "I'll be back." Voltar replied as he vanished. Voltar reappeared in Jon's quarters. Jon is in his kitchen. "Hello son nice speech." Voltar replied. "What do you want father?" Jon asked. "I must always get to the point with you?" Voltar inquired. "Yes." Jon replied. "I came to see my son." Voltar justified. "I'm fine I am an Aster." Jon replied. "So, are you going to claim the throne?" Voltar asked. "Not my style father, I don't need your throne to protect this galaxy." Jon replied. "So, how do your minions feel about this?" Jon asked. "They feel how I tell them to." Voltar stated. "I wouldn't bet on that." Jon replied, meanwhile on Mars at a circus type tent, a carnival is taking place. Inside the main tent people are seated all around, for a very unique show, an older gentleman not human. He is tall in stature with a face that looks like a rat and long dark hair with beady eyes. "Ladies and gentlemen!" He shouted. "Witness the power of a child." He stated. "You will be amazed by what he can do, with a mere touch." He added. The crowd looks on with curiosity and intrigue. "You will love this show." He replied. "I have a tale to tell, a mysterious and powerful young boy, who wandered these very streets until, I saved him." He replied. "This boy can give life or snatch it away, in an instant." He continues. "All he needs to do is touch with his hands." "A boy blessed with a gift and yet also a curse." He goes on. "Are you ready to meet him?' He asked. "Yes!" The people shouted. "I give you…Keyes!" He exclaimed, he then opens a curtain behind him to reveal a cage, in which sits a young boy of barely sixteen, his eyes a dark green his hair dark blonde. "He is caged due to, the unpredictable and dangerous nature of his power." He insisted. "Now to prove his power." He replied. He goes over to a corner grabs a bag, opens it and walks over to the cage. "Inside is a dead cat." He replied. He comes to a crowd member. "Please good sir, assure us all that the cat is indeed dead." He asked, man checks it and agrees it is dead. "Now witness the miracle." He replied. He takes cat to Keyes gives it to him, Keyes concentrates and his hands glow and then the cat jumps up and out of the cage. The crowd is amazed and goes nuts. "Now watch as he takes the life back." He stated, as he grabs up the cat and brings it back to Keyes. "No!" Keyes shouted. "Do it or I will whip you boy." He whispers Keyes uses his power to blast at the cat, making it run out of cage and out of tent as the crowd laughs. "Show is over!" He exclaimed in anger. "You will pay for that." He added now at night as all were sleeping, man comes to Keyes in the cage. "Who do you think you are?" He asked. "I found you half dead, I fed you." "All I ask is for a few tricks and this is how you repay me?" He replied. "I won't kill animals anymore." Keyes said firmly. "Really?" Man replied as he pulls whip from his coat Keyes stands up, when the man swings it at him he grabbed it, pulled the man close and touched his arm using his power to kill him. "I will kill for you, one last time." Keyes replied, he then drops him and blasted the cage open. One of the workers comes in a girl and screamed, as she saw man lying on ground. "You killed him!" She screamed Keyes then runs out of the tent, into a crowd of workers. "Murderer!" One shouted. "Get him!" Another said, meanwhile back on the base. "Sir I got a call from Mars, a murder." Jesse replied. "Lets go people." Dylan ordered now on Mars the team arrived. Charlie and Ralph went in first to Asses the scene. They come upon a crowd by a large tent. "Wonder what happened." Charlie said. "Freaks gone wild?" Ralph joked. They walk into crowd, to make their way to the front. "Galactic alliance, what is going on?" Charlie demanded. "He killed Marlin." Girl replied as she pointed to Keyes. "Did you kill him?" Charlie asked Keyes said nothing. "Tough guy huh?" Ralph replied. "Lets get him back to the base." Charlie insisted. Now back on base they place

Keyes in cell in cellblock. "Run his prints." Dylan replied. Jesse checks database. "He didn't say a word the whole ride back." Charlie stated. "If he did it, that is a hell of a magic trick." Ralph replied. "There was no mark on the victim, and he had a whip in his hand." Charlie stated. "I got a hit sir." Jesse replied, as they come to screen "Keyes no last name, he was born on Voltia and abandoned at age six." "This Marlin guy found him at age twelve and made him into a side show freak." Jesse replied. "What can he do?" Dylan asked, as Jesse read further. "He can give life or take it with a touch." Jesse read. "Well, the crowd did say in the show he brought back a dead cat." Ralph replied. "He doesn't look like a killer to me." Charlie stated. "No one ever does." Dylan replied. "No, I have a feeling about him, he is not bad." Charlie responded. "I think it was self-defense." Charlie added. "Well if he would tell us that, it could help his case." Dylan replied. "Get Amanda she can read him." Biscus ordered. Charlie headed to cellblock goes up to his cell. "Mind if I ask a few questions?" Charlie asked. "Ask all you want, I have nothing to say." Keyes replied. "Did this Marlin whip you?" Charlie asked. "We found a whip in his hand." He added. "Am I under arrest?" Keyes asked. "I thought I was asking the questions?" Charlie replied. "Look, I want to help you, if you'll let me.' Charlie added. "He whipped me everyday, make you feel better?" Keyes replied. "Now can you just send me to prison, so I can at least have a place to sleep?" Keyes insisted. Charlie goes out and heads back into control room. "He has anger, I sensed that." Amanda replied. "What else are you getting?" Dylan asked. "He hates himself, and his power." "He can't always control it." She added. "Explains his attitude." Charlie replied just then Paul entered. "What is it?" Dylan asked. "I ran the usual work up on this kid, he is not form Voltia.' He replied. "Then where is he from?' Dylan asked. "He is Voltarian." Paul replied. "There is something else, his DNA matches Charlie's." "He is your brother." Paul added. "He is what?" Charlie replied. "Can't be, Rick said I was his only child." Charlie added. "He is only a few years younger than you." Dylan replied. "Whoa, I have a brother?" Charlie absorbs. "I can't believe it, another aster?" Biscus replied. "We have to tell Rick." He added. "Let me talk to him." Charlie insisted. Charlie calls to Rick telepathically, as he headed into docking bay. Rick appears a few seconds later. "What is it?" "Are you alright?" He panics. "Yes I'm fine." Charlie replied. "I need to ask you something." Charlie added. "What?" Rick asked. "How do I ask this, when you were about twenty, did you have a serious girlfriend?" Charlie probed. "That is a little personal son." Rick replied. "Its important." Charlie answered. "If you must know, there was a girl after your mother left, why?' He asked. "I have a surprise for you, you have another son and I have a brother." Charlie replied. "Excuse me?" Rick says in shock. "His name is Keyes." Charlie added. "That is not possible, she would have told me." He claimed. "Right, because my mom told you." Charlie reminded. "I want to see him." Rick demanded. "Wait, he doesn't know any of this yet." Charlie informed. "We need to do this slow." Charlie replied. "Why?' Rick asked. "He was abandoned and abused for many years, he is not ready for a family let alone ours." Charlie replied. "Who did that I'll kill them?" Rick insisted. "I'm afraid he already did that." Charlie replied. "Just let me handle this." Charlie asked. "Fine, I trust you." Rick conceded Rick then vanished as Charlie returned to control room. "What did he say?" Dylan asked. "I told him to let me handle it first." Charlie replied, just then Jon and Shane entered. "What's going on?' Jon asked. "I have a brother and Rick has another son." Charlie replied. "Does he know?" Shane asked. "Yes I just told him." Charlie replied. "His name is Keyes." He added. "Gees your family is like rabbits, they keep multiplying." Ralph replied. Charlie sets up a meeting with Keyes, he is brought into the briefing room, Charlie enters. "I am done talking to you." Keyes insists. "Good then you can listen.' Charlie stated. "Ever heard of the Asters?" Charlie inquired. "Of course, who hasn't?' Keyes replied. "They run the criminals in this galaxy." He added. "Well I am an Aster." Charlie informed. "You're an alliance officer?" Keyes replied in confusion. "I never said I was that kind of Aster." Charlie replied. "So why you telling me?" Keyes asked. "It would seem, you are an Aster too." Charlie replied. "No way." Keyes denied, meanwhile back in the control room "Another one?" Brent asked. "So I hear." Cole replied. "Does Rick know?" Mary asked. "Yes, Charlie told him." Lisa replied. "How is Charlie handling it?" Cheryl asked. "He seems happy actually." Jesse replied. "I'm afraid Rick, will see this as an opportunity.' Jon said. "Yeah, a son he may be able to manipulate." Shane replied back in the briefing room. "My father is Rick Aster?" Keyes replied. "Trust me, I was not happy when I found out either." Charlie stated. "No offense but, I don't want to be an Aster." Keyes replied. "I would like, to get to know you?" Charlie asked. "I never had a brother." Charlie added. "There is nothing to know about me, other than I can kill people." Keyes replied. "You should stay with us, we can help you control it." Charlie insured. "I am not ready for a family. "I don't want one." Keyes insisted, he stands up and heads for door. "I need one." Charlie replied. "I thought, I'd always be on my own with being Rick son, but here you are." Charlie added, "I think, we were meant to find each other. Charlie implied. Keyes turned back to him. "Look, you seem ok, but I am trouble I'm jinxed." He replied. "At least now, I know where I got it from." He added. "I am not kid brother material." "I had the kid beaten out of me long ago." He replied. "You don't know what it is like, to be called a freak." Keyes added. "You don't belong in a cage." Charlie replied. "I can't control it." "If I get angry?" "I could kill someone." Keyes stated. "We can help you, if you'll let us.' Charlie pleads. "You really are pushy." Keyes replied with a smile. "Ok, I'll try it but don't expect a miracle. Keyes added. "Come on, you should meet the others." Charlie replied. They go out and head to the control room, where Voltar and Rick are also. "What are you doing here?" Charlie demanded. "I am here to meet my son." Rick insisted. "He is not ready for this." Charlie replied. Voltar comes to Keyes. "I understand you have quite the gift." He stated. "I call it a curse." Keyes answered. "He is not strong enough to handle this, father." Jon replied. "Fine, we will go for now." Rick replied as they vanished. "Is he always like that?" Keyes asked. "What, you mean an overbearing pompous ass?" Charlie replied to change the mood. Shane walked up to Keyes, extended his hand. "I guess I'm your uncle Shane." He stated. "I am your uncle too." Jon added. "I'm Dylan my son is your cousin." He informed. "That would be me." Steven replied. "It is weird, how you all ended up here together." Keyes observed. "So did you." Charlie added. "Can I go lye down?" Keyes asked. "Yes of course, my room is down the corridor 316." Charlie replied. "It is going to take time, before he trusts us." Jon replied. Keyes made way to quarters goes inside, goes to second bedroom and lies on the bed closing his eyes, when Rick appeared before him Keyes jumps to his feet. "Sorry, I didn't mean to startle you." Rick insisted. "I just wanted to speak to you in private, if it's ok?" He asked. "The great Rick Aster, I don't think I could stop you." Keyes replied. "It's just, you here is so incredible, I thought I could have no more children and yet you're here." He rejoiced. "Glad I could help?" Keyes replied. "Look, I know you have been threw hell, so I will let you rest, but if you need to you can stay with me." Rick suggested. "I'll get back to you on that." Keyes replied Rick then vanished as Charlie entered and came to his door. "You have a job here, if you want it?' Charlie asked. "I am a jinx, I can't accept it." Keyes replied. "Please Ralph is a jinx." Charlie responded. "I am not ready." Keyes informed. "We will go slow and train you." Charlie replied. "I am liking the big brother job." Charlie added Keyes lets out a laugh. "See I am getting to you." Charlie replied. "You are something else, oh by the way our father was here." Keyes replied. "What!" "Did he bother you?" Charlie asked. "No, I can see how you two are father and son though." Keyes stated. "You guys have issues." He added, now back on Voltara. "Neither one of you can control your children." Volrin observes. "Well, when you have some of your own then we'll talk, till then shut up." Rick replied. "Quiet both of you." "I'm thinking." Voltar stated. "Don't hurt yourself brother." Volrin remarks. "It is time we get our children back." Voltar replied back on the base, Charlie brings Keyes to mess hall. "This is the worst food in the galaxy." Charlie replied. "Not to mention, the ugliest wall paper." Ralph added. "I'm Ralph by the way." He replied. "Yes your the comedian right?" Keyes replied. "I do try." Ralph replied as Charlie and Keyes sit at table. "So what do you think of our base?" Steven asked. "It's nice." Keyes replied. "We will give you the full tour." Jenna replied as she comes to them. "I'm Jenna, Charlie's better half." She replied. "And the owner of his leash." Ralph added Jenna kicks his leg under the table. "Damm girl." He replied as we enjoyed our lunch, my father was up to no good sending his pals out to cause havoc. Cora is shooting into crowds of people on the city streets of Mars. "This is more like it." She stated. "I feel alive and evil again." Cara added, as she was shooting with her. The team arrived on Mars to the chaos. "Ok your father is going all out." Cole replied, as they see the injured people lying in the streets. "I'll say." Brent agreed. Danny and Paul tended to the people. "We need to put an end to this" Jon stated, as people came up to him. "You're the Valr Te Nesk, come to save us." Man cried. "Yes you must free us of Voltar's tyranny!" Woman shouted. "I think its past time, to lock him up." Shane agreed. "Your right it is time, to take him down." Jon replied. "Now Voltar's reign will end." Man sighed. "Our true savior has come." Woman stated. "I think your father is in trouble." Ralph replied. Meanwhile back at Voltar's castle. "This is not good dear brother, you'd better do something or your empire will crumble." Volrin commanded. "Will you shut up, so I can think!" Voltar ordered. "While you take time to think, he will become king." Volrin replied. "He is the Valr Te Nesk." Rick stated. "I know, my son he does not want to be a king." Voltar replied. "You may as well just give him this galaxy." Volrin declared. Meanwhile outside the castle in the city streets of Voltara, the team is assessing their situation. "What are you gonna do?" Dylan asked. "I'm not sure yet, but I am gonna stay here to help for awhile." Jon replied. "I'll stay to help too." Shane insisted. "Ok the rest of you back to base." Dylan ordered as they load up and go. "So does it feel right?" Shane asked. "What do you mean?" Jon replied. "Your destiny." Shane stated. "I am just here to help." Jon replied. "Your not like him, you would be a good king." Shane believes. Meanwhile back at the castle. "So now what?" Volrin asked. "I will talk to him." Voltar replied. "Yeah that will work." Volrin replied sarcastically as Voltar vanished, he then appears to Jon standing by a building watching. "Enjoying the view junior?" Voltar asked. "What is it you want father?" Jon replied. "You don't want to be a king, it is not you." Voltar stated. "I'm going to help them to defeat you and lead themselves." Jon vowed. "I know what my path is now father, I'm not running from it this time." Jon replied. Now back at the castle Voltar returned. "I will figure out how to stop him." Voltar insists. "Well were all screwed now." Volrin replied. "I am still his father, he doesn't have it in him to destroy me." Voltar replied. Meanwhile back on the base. "So, we are really gonna move our base down to Voltara?" Ralph asked. "Yes, we are a family and team we stick together." Dylan answered. "Besides, we would have a great strategic angle on the planet." Biscus replied. So it was set. We build a strong and fortified base like none before it on Voltara itself, near its vast forest. "I am glad the alliance agreed to do this." Jon replied. "So, has father been around?" Shane asked. "Yes, he is not backing down and neither am I." Jon replied. "So he is planning something?" Charlie asked. "He is Voltar Aster, when is he not?" Jon reminded Keyes comes out and looks at the skeletal structure of the base. "Well few more weeks, we may have a roof." Keyes stated. "This base will take awhile to build." Charlie confessed. "I think I can speed things along." Jon replied. He concentrates and his body glows as he uses his power to put the entire base together in minutes. "Man, anything you can't do?" Ralph asked. "I don't know." Jon replied as the team grabs their gear out of shuttle. Trina a very beautiful young lady comes to Jon, she has raven hair and blue eyes. "Your friends are loyal." She noticed. "Yes, I am lucky." Jon replied. Trina makes a bold move to kiss him. "I'm sorry, I hope I was not too forward." She asked. "No, its ok." Jon smiled. It is now time to face my father, he has always tried to manipulate me and control my power, I must defeat him to be free. Charlie, Keyes and Shane come out of the base doors. "So what is this about a fight?" Keyes asked. "It is my battle alone." Jon replied. "Your not alone anymore we got your back." Shane stated. "Its about time, we all took a stand to be free." Charlie added. "Fine, but I will handle my father." Jon stated. "Got it, its your fight." Shane replied. "Perhaps, you should eat before your battle?" Trina suggested. "Sounds good to me." Keyes agreed as they did, at the castle. "Its about time you realized we had to kick butt." Volrin replied. "The battle is with me and junior." Voltar dictated. "No one is to interfere." He added. "Father, he will defeat you." Rick stated. "No one can defeat me son." Voltar replied. "Not for long." He added. "We will take out his team and the resistance." Volrin replied. "They want a fight, we will give them one." Rick responded as they donned their battle gear the team was in a small house at a dinner table. "So, when is this battle?" Ralph asked. "It will be soon, I feel it." Jon replied. "You will win." Trina stated. "How many will die?" Amanda asked, just then an explosion occurred outside of the house, a man runs in. "They are here!" He shouted as they all get up and rush outside, to see people running and screaming toward them as those loyal to Voltar are firing at them, in the chaos a large vessel landed in front of them. "Let me guess, welcoming committee? Keyes replied as the hatch opens and Cora, Cara, Matt, Gunner Volrin and Rick emerge. Voltar appears in front of them. "It is time to finish this." Jon replied as a battle erupts, Jon using his power and Voltar uses his at they manage to keep each of their power in a collected ball of energy, they then let it go and come face to face in the center of the fighting around them. "You sure about this junior?" Voltar asked. "Yes I am." Jon says firmly. Jon concentrates and blasts his power at his father sending him flying back. Voltar rises and blast his power back at Jon as Jon is thrown back but rises as well. "So, is this how it is going to be?" Voltar asked. "Its that anger toward me, that makes your power stronger." He added. "Still trying to manipulate me?" Jon replied. "We don't need to fight, it is pointless." Voltar insists. "We can compromise."

He added. "No deals, Voltara will not be ruled by you any longer." Jon replied. "I am the only king they have known." "You defeat me, others far worse will come." Voltar stated. "I can protect my people now.' Jon declared. The team manages to take down Voltar's henchmen. "Alright lock them up." Charlie replied. "How is Jon doing?" He added. "They are talking." Shane replied. "You ran away from responsibility once son, it got people killed." Voltar reminded him. "You bastard." Jon said in anger as he grabs him by throat and begins to choke him. "I will end you." Jon shouts his eyes glow a shade of red the team runs over. "Its your fault they are dead!" He exclaimed as Voltar falls to his knees. "Jon stop!" Shane yells. "He is not worth it." Dylan stated. "Don't be like him, let it go." Charlie replied. Jon looks to them and lets go as Voltar coughs and catches his breath. "Take him to prison." Jon replied. "Are you ok?" Trina asked. "I need to be alone for a moment." Jon answered. Now back in the base, after the dust settled in the mess hall. "So why did he stop?" Brent replied. "Its his father." Mary said. "He deserved it." Ralph added. "So where is Jon now?" Cole asked. "He is trying to calm down." Shane replied. Meanwhile on a transporter bound for Earth's prison, they each are in cells, which bind their powers. "So I missed it." Volrin said disappointed. "Shut up, he was just angry he loves you." Rick replied. "You did not see his face, his eyes in that moment he wanted me dead." Voltar grasped. "Well you did ask for it." Volrin replied. "I need to see him." Voltar insisted. "I would wait on that brother." Volrin replied. Meanwhile back on Voltara Jon is sitting on a bench in the middle of the city. Sel appeared to him. "Having trouble young one?" He asked. "I almost killed my father." Jon comprehended. "I never got that angry before." Jon replied. "All of us have the capability of light and darkness." Sel reminded. "But you did not kill him, you stopped." He added. "Only because of my team, my family Jon replied as he stood up. "I am becoming my father here." Jon added.

Chapter 10
OWNING A LEGEND

As the months went on, I learned to control my power, balance my darkness and light. My family helped a great deal. Trina and I became closer but as Sel explained to me, I am meant for the galaxy not to rule Voltara. I am a protector, not a king. As I truly embraced my destiny, I was unaware that the Overlord was fully regenerated and about to come after me yet again. I managed to keep her confined to hell for now anyway. My challenge was still yet to come; for we discovered a large mass outside of the system we know another planet, which we will investigate only to find trouble. On the base we go into control room. "Sir I just got word, Voltar and his pals escaped the prison." Jesse informed." I'm picking them up, leaving our system." He added. "He is exploring." Jon reads his thoughts. "Does he know something we don't? Charlie asked. "I suggest we find out." Dylan replied. The team goes and suits up and flies off to the end of the system. "It would be incredible, if we find another planet." Brent replied. "You think its possible?" Jenna asked. "If my father and the others are out here, then yes." Charlie replied. Meanwhile Voltar and his followers have landed on the newly discovered world. "Let us find out if it is inhabited." Voltar replied as they exit. They see that the planet is devastated and desolate; it is desert like but with a chill to the air. "It is a wasteland, I love it!" Volrin exclaimed. "I would deem it is deserted." Rick observes. "We can claim it as ours." Voltar replied. Meanwhile back with the team as they are in flight. "If there is one planet out there, there will be more." Shane replied as they come up on planet, all stare in amazement. "It is another planet." Jenna confirmed. "You can bet my father and the rest of them are down there, planning to take it." Jon replied. "I'll call the base, we will need more men." Charlie answered as he brought up com-link. "So a new world, any life readings?" Biscus asked. "We don't know yet." Charlie responded. "We are landing now, we will let you know." Charlie replied as he ended transmission. They land on the planet. "Looks like its been destroyed." Jon judged. "I have life readings ahead." Jenna says as she is scanning. "It has to be father." Jon replied. "Lets go find out." Shane stated as they head toward it. Voltar and his associates come upon a ruined city. "We will need troops to get started." Voltar commanded. "Guess again." Charlie replied as team comes up on them. "So, trying to take over defenseless worlds out side of the system?" Jon asked. "We found it first." Volrin replied. "Doesn't mean you can just claim it." Charlie informed. "There is no one to stop us." Voltar stated. Just then the ground beneath them rumbled and splits open behind them, to reveal an elevator rising up from it. The doors then opened and an odd small creature gray in color emerges followed by six others. "Who are you?" Leader demanded. "How dare you invade Seltran"? He added. "We come in peace, we just discovered your world." Jon replied. "I believe you, I can tell when someone lies." He informed. "Give me a break." Volrin replied. "You!" He shouts as he points to them. "I can smell the evil in you." He replied. "Really shorty?" Volrin asked. "Allow me to handle this." Voltar stated. "We only wish to better your planet, your society." Voltar added. "How eloquently you explain bulling and overtaking our world." Leader replied. "Let me handle it." Volrin demanded. As he goes to leader and lifts him up, the creature then gives Volrin a powerful jolt and he drops him back down as Volrin yells. "You deserved that." Rick replied. "You and your evil followers need to leave." Leader ordered. "You heard the man get out," Ralph replied. "We will be back, count on it." Voltar stated as he and the rest of them go back to their ship. "You are an amazing young man." Leader replied. "You are the kind of leader we need." He added. "We would be glad to help you rebuild." Jon replied. "Yes we will go get more supplies." Charlie added. As the rest of the team headed back to their fighters, Jon stayed behind. "My name is Berbril." He informed. "I knew Sel, I can tell you are related." He added. "You did?" Jon asked. "Yes, he was a legend." He replied. "Now, we have our new ruler here and no one will take you away." He informed. "Excuse me?" Jon replied. "All will be explained." He replies as he touched Jon's hand and gives him a powerful jolt, rendering him unconscious. "Take him below." Berbril replied. "They lift him up and take him to elevator. "I will deal with the rest." He added. The elevator then sealed and lowered back into the ground. Meanwhile at the fighters the team was getting ready to head back, when the ground beneath their feet heats up. "What the?" Charlie exclaims. "The ground is heating up, get in the fighters!" Amanda yells. They load up and lift off as the ground is almost on fire. "Where is Jon?" Shane replied. "We can't land on the planet." Charlie replied. Just then Berbril appeared on their vidlink. "Leave my planet and do not return." He commanded. "Where is Jon?" Charlie demanded. "He is ours now." He replied. "The grandson of Sel is taking his rightful place." He added. "You can't keep him." Shane replied. "We already have." Berbril stated. He then ends transmission. "We have a problem." Jenna replied. "They are in for a fight, they are not keeping Jon." Charlie replied. Meanwhile down under the planet in a series of caverns and tunnels. Jon is lying on a bed in one of the rooms. Berbril is sitting by his side in a chair. "You are here to save us." He stated. "You will not be leaving." He added. Jon lay unconscious; back on the base the team is gathered in the control room. Voltar was also present. "You just let that little beast take him?" Voltar exclaimed. "He heated up the entire planet." Shane explained. "We need some history on that planet." Dylan stated. "What about Jon?" Cole asked. "They won't hurt him, they need him." Amanda replied. "We will go back to that planet and circle around, see if there is a place to land." Rick insisted. "We need to figure out, what we are dealing with." Biscus replied. As they do that, back on the planet Jon begins to wake up. "What the hell?" Jon replied as he sits up dazed and looks around. "Where am I?" He added. Berbril rises from chair. "Relax young one, I will explain." Berbril replied. "Where is my team?" Jon demanded. "I sent them away." Berbril informed. "I am not staying here." Jon replied as he gets to his feet. "You cannot leave, you belong with us." Berbril insisted. "This galaxy needs me." Jon stated. "This is your true home." Berbril replied. "Sel promised us he would return." He added. "I am not Sel." Jon replied. "Our world is yours to rule." Berbril instructed. "Not interested, thanks." Jon replied. "My grandfather made that promise, not me." He added. "I will help to rebuild your world as I said but, you are not keeping me here." Jon commanded. "We are good people." Berbril said.

"Prove it, let me leave." Jon replied. Berbril opens door to room and heads down a cave into a larger command center as Jon followed. "What is all this?" Jon asked, as he looked at all the high tech computers. "It is our defense, your grandfather designed it." Brebril replied. "It kept us safe all these years." He added as he disarmed the heat mechanism. "Come, let me get you back to your team." He replied. They go to the elevator and take it back up to the surface. The team landed on planet when they discovered the temperature had dropped back to normal. "Jon are you ok?" Shane asked. "I will kill you!" Voltar shouted as he lunged for him. "Father no!" Jon exclaimed. Voltar stopped. "We have to help them to rebuild, to honor Sel's promise." He added. "Ok, we will help them" Shane replied. "I'll be keeping my eye on them." Voltar stated. We helped to rebuild their world. "You do realize when word spreads about your world, people will come." Jon replied. "We will welcome them." Berbril replied. Now back on base in the mess hall. "That was enough excitement for one day." Cole replied. "I wonder how many more worlds are out there." Amanda thought. "Let them come to us." Ralph replied. Just then alarms go off, the team heads to control room. "We have trouble on Mars." Jesse stated. "Let me guess, only the Valr Te Nesk can help? Jon replied. "They asked for you." Dylan replied. The team arrives on Mars, to find a man shouting from the roof of a building. "We will not stop until the Valr Te Nesk is here!" He yelled. "I'm here!" Jon replied. "Thank the gods." He said as he comes down. "You are the only one who can stop it." He begged. "Stop what?" Jon asked. "The beast." He replied. "A monster like no other." He added. "Show me where." Jon replied. The man led him to the sea nearby. "It will not let us fish or swim." Man claimed. Jon looks around, just then the beast emerged, it is huge black and scaly. The people run for cover. "I am this sea." It proclaimed. "No one may enter." It added. "I am the Valr Te Nesk. Jon informed. "You?" "You're a boy" It replied. "So they keep saying." Jon answered. The creature kneels to his eye level. "Prove it." It ordered. Jon then concentrated, and his hand glowed he aimed it at the creature lifting him out of the water, and into the air. "Whoa!" Creature exclaimed. Jon lowered it to the ground. "I am yours to command." He stated as he bowed to him. "Just stop attacking these people, and let them swim and fish." Jon replied. "I am Trelt, I am the last of the great guardians of the gods." He explained. "I will now serve you." He vowed. "Thanks, but I really don't need one." Jon replied as he goes to leave, but Trelt follows him. "I will guard you with my life." He pledged. "I'm fine really." Jon answered. "You will need me, especially if Mostle escapes the Monster Zone." He informed. "Who?" Jon asked. "Your grandfather sealed him long ago, in that zone he is dangerous." "If he is ever freed." He explained. "Well, if he is sealed then I'm fine." Jon replied. "I must insist, on doing my duty." Trelt replied as the team comes up. "Holy crap, who's your friend?" Ralph asked. "This is Trelt, last of the guardians," Jon replied. "He is huge." Shane added. "He'll be staying close, for awhile." Jon informed. They all look at him in stunned and confused. "Its not my fault." Jon insisted. Now back on the base. "So this Mostle is going to escape?" Charlie asked. "That is what Trelt believes." Jon replied. Meanwhile in the monster zone, Monzee and Montra are exploring unvisited caves. They come upon a sealed door of gold and they smash it open. "I've never been in here." Monzee stated. They walk inside; to see a golden chest in the distance their curiosity is peeked as they rush to it. "It must be treasure." Montra insisted. They force it open with their bruit strength, and are blown back by the blast of light and power that explodes out of it. A large devilish looking creature emerges form it, with large white teeth and humanoid features. Long sharp claws, it is dressed in black and red silk robes. "I Am Free!" He bellowed. "Time to reclaim my galaxy." He replied as he extended his dark black wings and flew over them and out of cave. "What was that?" Monzee asked. "Looks like trouble." Montra replied he flies up and out of the zone and is flying threw space. "I am coming for you, Valr Te Nesk." He vowed. As Jon was resting in his quarters Sel appeared to him. "He is free." Sel replied. Jon sits up in bed. "He is seeking you, he will destroy planets to find you." He warned. "Then I'd better find him." Jon stated. "You are powerful but so is he." Sel replied. "He is the balance for evil, his strength is only matched by yours." Sel explained. "His power comes form fear and despair. He added. "Thanks for the heads up." Jon replied. Jon heads to the control room, where the team is already tracking him. "I'm going after him." Jon informed. "You're going alone?" Charlie asked. "Yes, this is my fight." Jon replied. "Good luck." Shane added. Jon heads out meanwhile; on Pluto Mostle is flying above a city there and blasting fire at the people and buildings. They run and scream as he feeds off their fear. "Where are you?" He searches. Jon flies his fighter to Pluto and landed he exits and comes into city. "I'm here!"

He shouts. Mostle sees him and flies down to land before him he looks him over. "Is this a joke?" He asked. "No." Jon replied. "You are a boy." He stated. "I am here for Sel." He demanded. "Sorry but he has ascended, so it's just me." Jon explained. Mostle lets out a dark laugh. "You what kind of challenge could you be?" He implied. "Your about to find out." Jon replied. "You have spirit boy, I'll enjoy squashing it." He replied. "Lets see how your power holds up." He added as he sends a bolt blast at Jon throwing him back against a building wall. "So give up boy?" He yelled. Jon rises. "Never!" He shouted as Jon concentrated and sent his own powerful sphere of power toward him hitting him, and sending him flying into a building wall and threw it. "You have a kick boy." Mostle replies as he gets up. "I'm just getting started." Jon replied. "Enough games." Mostle insisted as he flies up into the sky. Jon transforms into his Dregon of pure blue light and flies up too. They grab at each other, fighting back and forth. They each glow so bright, that they cause an explosion of power, which blasts them apart. They landed on the ground. Jon returns to his humanoid form as he rises up, so do Mostle. "It appears we are equally matched kid." Mostle admitted. "So ready for round two?" Jon asked. Then Jon uses his power to create a sword of pure white light, as Mostle created a sword of fiery red. "Lets do it." Mostle replied. They battle each swinging their swords at each other and it's intense. Mostle manages to slice Jon's left upper arm. Jon then countered and sliced across Mostle's chest as black blood oozed out. "Nice." Mostle credited. Meanwhile back on the base, Jesse brings up the battle on the vidlink. "We should go help." Shane insisted. "I will go." Trelt replied. "We all will go." Dylan stated. The team heads to Pluto, as the battle raged on in the streets, both of them battered, bloody and bruised. "Looks like were in time for the last round." Ralph replied. "He is hurt." Amanda stated. "I can't believe were just gonna stand here and watch this." Shane replied. "Its his fight." Charlie stated.

Jon and Mostle lock swords. "Had enough?" Jon asked. "Why are you surrendering?" Mostle replied. Just then Jon gets a clear shot at his head and sliced into his very skull, a white light beams from it. "Think I found your weak spot." Jon replied. He then cut Mostle's head clean off, in one strike. "Yes my man!" Ralph exclaimed. Then his head began to speak. "Think you've won?" He replied. "You must still seal me in the chest." He added. "I will." Jon vowed. Mostle uses his power, to raise his body up from the ground with sword still in his hands and leads it toward Jon. Trelt sees this and rushes to Jon, pushing him out of the way as the sword stabs him in his back. "No! Jon yelled as Trelt falls. Jon goes to him. "I told you, I would guard you with my life." Trelt replied. "I meant it, Valr Te Nesk." He added then closed his eyes and dies Jon lowers his head. "Too bad, he was a fool." Mostle replied. Jon rises from the ground and goes to Mostle. "Time to finish it." Jon stated. They take his body and head and sealed them into two chests. Trina comes to Jon and hugs him. "I was so scared." She replied. "Not too bad for my first battle huh?" Jon said with a smile. "You kicked ass bro." Shane stated, as he pats his shoulder. "Lets get you back to sick bay." Paul insisted. "I will, first things first." Jon replied. They loaded up the chests and took them to the zone this time, burying them both separately and deep with in the very core of the zone. Jon used his power to seal the chests. Now back on the base. "He saved my life." Jon replied. "I Know." Trina replied. "You should get some food and rest." Charlie stated. They go to mess hall. Now later that night, Sel comes to Jon in his bedroom. "So your first test is completed." Sel replied. "First, You mean there are more?" Jon questioned. "Of course there are, many ancient creatures out in the galaxies that existed way before your time." Sel replied. "Could you give me an estimate?" Jon asked. Sel smiled and said. "Lets just say, you will have your hands full." He replied. "Then I'd better get some sleep." Jon answered. "I will visit again soon." Sel insures. Now the next day in the rec room: ralph and Brent are seated arm wrestling at a table. "So give up?' Brent asked. "I'm just getting started." Ralph replied. "I'm giving you false hope." He added. Brent brings Ralph's arm down. "Yeah sure you were." Brent replied. Charlie and Jenna are by the weights. "Your sure your ok?" Charlie asked. "Yes I'm just tired." Jenna replied. "I can help with that." Charlie replied. He leans in and kissed her, just then an explosion rocked the docking bay. "What the hell was that?" Charlie replied. They all rushed to the control room. "What was that?" Dylan demanded. "A ship just crashed into our docking bay, sir." Jesse replied. "We tried to contact it, but no response." Mary added. "Any life readings?" Biscus asked. "Yes one very faint." Jesse observed. "Lets go get some answers." Jon said. The team heads to the docking bay, where Mark the head of security for the base is already present. "They are putting out the flames." Mark informed. "Find the pilot." Dylan commanded. "We are trying to pry the door open now." He replied. The security team gets it open, they go in and pull out a badly injured young man of eighteen, light brown hair and bruised also unconscious. Dylan's jaw dropped as he recognized him. "Oh my god, get Paul now!" Dylan yells. "What is it?" Biscus asked. "Do you know him?" Jon replied. "Of course I do." as Dylan touches his cheek. "He is my son.' He replied. Security team gets him to sickbay on stretcher. Dylan followed; the rest of the team is in shock. "He just say son?" Shane replied. "Lets get to sickbay." Charlie stated, as the team arrives just outside the doors to sickbay, Paul and his Nurse Anilla are working on him. "Don't let him die Paul." Dylan pleads. "I won't." Paul assured. Biscus enters. "What is going on Dylan?" Biscus demands. "He is my son, he's eighteen. His name is Ryan, and yes I was younger than him when he was born." Dylan explained. "He ran away from home when he was fourteen." "I haven't seen him since, till now.' He added. Steven rushes in. "Is it true dad?" Steven asked as he comes closer, to see him. "It is Ryan, isn't is dad?" Steven exclaimed. "Yes son it is." Dylan replied. "What happened to him?" Steven asked. "We will find out soon." Dylan informed. Ryan opened his sparkling green eyes; he looked around to see Dylan and Steven. "Dad?" Ryan manages to utter, as he is still weak and takes a deep breath. "I am here son." Dylan acknowledges. He takes hold of Ryan's hand. "You'll be ok, Where were you?" "What happened?" Dylan asked. "I can explain it all.' Ryan replied, taking a deep breath. "You better have a great story." Dylan demanded. Ryan looks to Steven, as he comes closer. "Steven?" "Is that you?" Ryan asked. "You've gotten taller." He added. Steven grabbed his other hand. "I'm sorry I left, I screwed up." Ryan replied. "We can talk about it later, rest." Dylan insisted. "I can't, I'm in trouble dad." Ryan informed. "We will give you some privacy." Biscus replied as he and medical staff goes out of area. Paul informs the team outside. "He is stable." Paul informed. "Can I start by asking, where you've been for four years?' Dylan replied. "Traveling mostly." Ryan stated. "You couldn't call me, to tell me your alive?" Dylan replied. "If I did, you would've traced the call." Ryan answered. "I was angry and young." Ryan admitted. "I thought, I could make it alone." He added. "Well, you are home now.' Dylan replied. "If you're staying?" Dylan asked. "Are you?" Steven begged. "I have to, if I go outside these walls now, I'm a dead man."

Ryan informed. Both Dylan and Steven look at him with eyes widened in surprise. When you are young and naïve, life feels like an adventure, an unstoppable force. The galaxy is a vast wonder of the unknown, but when you fall in love with the wrong girl, you will end up a marked man. Which, is exactly what our young Ryan McKay is now. "What do you mean dead man?" Dylan asked. "Who is after you?" He demanded. "She thinks I left her, but I didn't." Ryan replied. He begins to get short of breath and agitated. He breathes deeply, as he is struggling for air. "I have to, talk to her…He pauses. "I have to tell her, I didn't leave her.' He whispers. "First, you need to calm down son." Dylan replied. "Who is she?" Steven asked. "I only left, to see you." He struggled to say as he swallowed. "I heard you were here, on Voltara." He added. "There is plenty of time to catch up son." Dylan insists. Dylan touches Ryan's forehead "Rest for now." He asks. "I will, but I need to call her." Ryan pleaded. "We will tell her for you." Steven replied. "She has to hear it form me, to believe it." Ryan explained. He closed his eyes a moment and takes a deep breath. Dylan signals Paul, as he comes back in. He checks his vitals. "He is weak, he must rest." Paul insists. "Ok I will get a com-link, so you can call her just please rest." Dylan asked. "Just tell Cara, where I am." Ryan said before passing out. "Did he just say Cara?" Steven said. "It can't be her." Dylan replied. Meanwhile on Mars in Cora and Cara's secret lair, Cara is tearing up her bedroom as Cora entered. "I told you he was not in love with you." Cora embellished. "No, he would not just leave, where did you go?' Cara asked. "He is a man, all men cannot be trusted." Cora replied. "No he is different, I can trust him. Cara insisted. Meanwhile back on the base, in the control room in Biscus office with the door shut. "What do I do?" Dylan struggles. "I don't know, Cara is not the most stable girl." Biscus answered. "How did he get involved with her?" Biscus asked. "She is a beautiful, slightly older woman at his age I would have." Dylan confessed. "Are you going to let him call her?" Biscus asked. "I can't stop him, he is eighteen, and if I try he'll leave and never come back." Dylan replied. "I'm gonna have to bite my tongue on this one." Dylan concedes. They come out of the office, where the team is gathered. "I know you all have questions." Dylan admitted. "It is not our place." Jon replied. "It is, your all my family." Dylan said. "I was only sixteen when Ryan was born." He explained. "His mother was not an option at the time, which is why I guess he was so rebellious." Dylan confessed. "He hated any rules." He continued. "He had no intention of joining the alliance, so when he turned fourteen he ran away." Dylan replied. "That was the last I saw him until today." Dylan concluded. "I guess I can relate, I did the same thing for awhile.' Brent replied. "He is not a bad kid, but he is in trouble now." Dylan informed. "We will help, what is it?" Charlie asked. "He has been, well dating a slightly older woman for a year and a half." Dylan replied. "He is a McKay after all." Ralph joked. "I wish it was that simple." Dylan replied. "The woman is Cara Babor." He added. The team is stunned. "As in my sister?' Cole asked. "That is not going to end well." Xavier replied. "He is in love with her?" Keyes asked. "Yes, I think so." Dylan stated. "He has no idea what he is getting into." Amanda replied. "My sisters are known for hating men, but if they do fall for one that love is deep and intense." Cole informed. "He asked to call her, to explain why he left before he passed out." Dylan replied. "What we need to find out is who attacked his ship." Charlie probed just then Mark entered. "I can answer that." Mark replied. "That ship is from Mars, it is one of Cora and Cara's ships." He replied. "Also, the weapons fired on it belonged to them." He concluded. "Thank you Mark." Dylan replied. Paul called from sickbay. "He is awake." Paul stated. "On my way." Dylan replied. He headed to sickbay and enters. "So, you're feeling better?" Dylan asked. "Ryan sitting up in the bed. "Yes I am." Ryan replied. "Did you call Cara?" Ryan asked. "Not yet." He answered, as the team entered. "This is my team." He added. Ryan recognized Cole. "You're her brother, Cole right?" Ryan asked. "Yes I am." Cole confirmed. "She talked about you often." Ryan stated. "So how did you two meet?" Everyone looks at Ralph in astonishment. "What, somebody had to ask, we were all wondering it." He replied. "Its fine, we met a year and a half ago on Venus." "I really didn't know who she was back then." Ryan explained. Just then over the com-link. "Sir I got trouble, it's the Babor sisters." Jesse informed. "She is looking for me." Ryan replied. He then attempted to get out of the bed, but due to his injuries and blood loss he sits back down. "You need to rest and heal." Dylan ordered. "We will deal with them." Dylan insisted. The team heads out to control room. "Dad!" Ryan calls. Dylan comes back. "Please tell her, I did not leave her." Ryan begs. "I know she is not your favorite person, but I love her. "Ryan added. "I will tell her." Dylan replied. Then goes out now as the team heads to the docking bay, the doors open to see an all terrain vehicle approaching fast. "Let me go talk to them." Cole insisted. He went out and met the vehicle half way, they stop Cora is driving. "Ok calm down Ryan is ok." Cole stated as Cara climbed out of the passenger side. "He is ok, where is he?" She asked. "What happened to him?" She demanded. "He is in our sickbay, his ship was shot down. "He crashed into our docking bay." Cole explained. "Who would've attacked him?" Cara asked. "I have no idea." Cora claims. "He came to see his father and brother." Cole replied. "What?" Cora questioned. "Dylan McKay is, his father Cara." Cole informed. "Great so he is one of them, should've seen that." Cora replied. "I don't care, I just want to see him." Cara exclaimed. "Follow me." Cole replied. Cora stayed behind. Now in the sickbay, Cara enters and sees Ryan in the bed sleeping. "Oh my god!" She gasped. "Ryan?" "Its me Cara." She replied Ryan opens his eyes. "I am sorry I left without a word." Ryan replied. "When Cora told me my father was on Voltara, I had to see him"? He added. "Cora told you?" Cara interrupted. "I didn't leave you." Ryan replied as he touches her cheek. "I know that now." She answered as she kisses his lips. "He needs to rest." Dylan comes in and replied. "I want to speak to you." He says to Cara. They step out into corridor. "Do you love my son?" Dylan demands. "Or, is this personal against me?" He added. "I had no idea he was your son." She responded. "Look, I do not like you or your sister, but I love my son, so I will tolerate this but if you hurt him in anyway, I will kill you." Dylan confirmed. "I love your son." Cara replied. "He was the first guy I met who, treated me like a lady, with respect, he talked to me." She explained. "He is special." She added. "Yes he is." Dylan replied. Meanwhile out at the vehicle Cora stands and looks on. "Don't get too happy sister, you will not have him for long, I will take him from you." She replied, "You don't deserve him, I do." She ended.

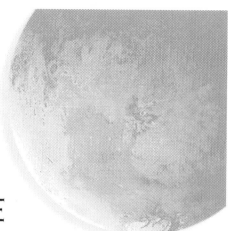

Chapter 11

HE IS THE ONE

I did not know it then, but Ryan McKay is a very special man. There is something about him; it is why two sisters would fall for him. Now in sickbay Anilia is checking Ryan vitals signs. "When can I get out of here?" Ryan asked. "When Paul says your ready." She answered. "You were bleeding internally, if you move too soon you could hemorrhage." Anilla informed. Steven enters. "So, bored with us already?" Steven replied. "Not with you here." Ryan said. "I still can't believe it, you're practically a man now." Ryan added. "I'm also, the best pilot on the team." Steven informed. "I'd expect no less." Ryan stated. "How has dad been?" Ryan asked. "He missed you, he never stopped looking, he still has your photo on his desk. "Steven replied. "I have a photo of us too." Ryan said. "I guess I've just been a stubborn McKay." He replied. "You are here now that's what counts." Steven comforted. "Yes I am." Ryan replied. "When you're better, I'll give you the tour." Steven stated. "I will try to speed that up." Ryan smiled. "Can I ask a question?" Steven probed. "Of course." Ryan replied. "Why Cara Babor, I mean she is evil." Steven reminded. "I have seen her true side, what is in her heart." Ryan replied. "She is just, wanting to please the wrong people." Ryan added. "Well if your happy, I will try to like her." Steven replied. "She is Cole's sister too. Steven added. Just then Dylan entered with Cara beside him. "Everything ok?" Ryan fears. "Yes, I will give you two a moment alone, come on Steven." Dylan ordered. Steven hugs Ryan and they head out. Cara sits on bed beside him. "I was so scared." Cara confessed. "I should've talked to you before I left." Ryan apologizes. "Its over now, you just get better." Cara replied. "Did my father threaten you?" Ryan asked. "He is just being a protective father, I wish I had one." Cara answered. "I am not an angel you know." She added. "Half the galaxy knows that." Ryan smiled Cara lets out a giggle. "I should let you rest." Cara insisted. Cora steps in the doorway of sickbay, with a look of loathing. "Cara we have business." Cora barks. "I'll be back soon." Cara replied. She kisses Ryan passionately and gets up and walks to Cora, as she looks angry. "Always a pleasure Cora." Ryan replied. They leave. Meanwhile in the rec room Amanda is punching the bag, suddenly she gets a wave of emotion that overwhelms her she sits down on bench. Cole puts down his free weights and comes to her. "What is it?" Cole asked. "I felt something, a powerful and dangerous wave of emotions." She replied as she collects her composure. "Is it Voltar?" Cole asked. "No, this was jealousy, loathing, anger and love." She stated. "Who were you picking up on?" Cole asked. "Their sister, one wants what the other has, always wants it." Amanda channels. "I don't like the sound of that." Cole begins to realize. "Cora wants Ryan." Amanda replied. "We have to warn him and Dylan." She replied as she rises. "This will not end well." Cole feared. They head out of rec room and to the control room. They go to Dylan and revealed what she was reading telepathically from Cora, while she was in the base. "Damm it, I knew the Babors would be trouble." Dylan exclaims. "Cara is not trying to hurt Ryan." Cole reminded. "Our main concern is to protect Ryan." Biscus stated. "I'll have Mark post guards in sickbay." Jon replied. "We should warn him." Steven replied. "I will call Cara." Cole informed. Meanwhile back in sickbay Ryan is asleep as Paul checks him, then he heads down to his office on the other side of the room. Cora uses her Teleportation device, which she and Cara have on their wrists to appear to Ryan's bedside. She moves in close and strokes his cheek. "She does not deserve you, I am the smart one, and you will love me." She vowed. She then uses her device to transport her and Ryan out of sickbay. As Dylan and the others enter. "Ryan we need to…." He sees he is gone. "No!" Dylan shouted. "She has taken him." Amanda senses Just then Cara returned to see him. "What is going on, where is Ryan?" She questioned. "Your sister took him." Dylan replied in a fury. "What?" Cara is confused. "She wanted him because, he was yours its why I was calling you, to warn you." Cole replied. "He should not have been moved, he is still recovering from his injuries and it is dangerous." Paul informed. "How dangerous Paul." Dylan asked. "If he begins to hemorrhage again, he will bleed out and die." Paul replied. "I will kill her." Cara swore. "We have to find him." Dylan ordered. "We better hurry." Cole added. Meanwhile, Cora had reappeared in one of her remote cabin hideaways in the Mars Mountains. "Now we are alone." She replied. Ryan begins to move and wakes up he looks around to see Cora. "Cara?" Ryan asked. "Why must all men fall for her?" She screeched. "Cora, what the hell?" Ryan replied. "Where are we?" He asked. "What is it about you?" Cora replied "Your human yet, there is something special about you, I can see it in your eyes." She replied. "You captured my sister's heart, you can love me too." She stated. "What?" "I am not interested in you and now I really understand why. "Ryan replied. She grabs hold of his hand and puts it on her chest. "My heart is also yours Ryan." She implied. Ryan pulls his hand back in repulse and disbelief. "Why can't you love me?" She yelled. "Your insane that's why." "You think that you can just force me or any man to love you?" Ryan replied. "You will never see her again, you are mine." She established. "My father will find us." Ryan replied. "Well if I can't have you, then neither can she." She considered. She then pulled a large dagger from her side pocket in her coat. "We could have been perfect together." She replied, as she raises her hands to stab him. "You kill me, Cara will never forgive you." Ryan replied. "She will move on, its what we do." She answered. "You're a cold bitch." Ryan said. "I am sorry, it had to end like this." She replied. As she goes to stab him the team kicked in the doors. Cora is with them as well. "You!" She yelled as she charged her knocking her to the ground and the dagger out of her hands. "Ryan are you ok?" Dylan asked. "Yeah I'm ok?" Ryan nodded as the team cuffed Cora. "It is not over." She said to Ryan. "Get her out of here!" Dylan commanded team takes her out, as Cara comes to Ryan. "You sure your ok?" she asked. "Yes, I'm just glad you're not a triplet. He joked. she kissed him. Now back in sickbay Paul checks his wound on his abdomen and is kind of thrown back. "Your wound is almost completely healed." He replied. "Does, that mean I can get out of this bed? Ryan asked. "If you have at least two more days of uninterrupted rest, then yes." Paul stated. Paul then goes to his office. Steven is by Ryan side. "Is he always like that?" Ryan asked. "Yes, I'm glad your ok." Steven replied. "So am I." Ryan added. Cara entered. "I'll let you two be alone." Steven said as he heads out, Cara sits beside him. "She is on her way to earth, it's over." Cora stated. "I was so scared, when I saw her with that dagger." Cara remembered. "How did I get so lucky?" she added. "Because, I am in love with you." Ryan acknowledged. She smiles as the kiss, she pulls back when vitals spike on equipment. "Wait should you be resting?" she asked. "So they keep telling me." Ryan replied. He leans in to kiss her and Paul comes out of office looks at them. Sternly. "I'll be back later." She replied as she gets up goes out. "I'll be here!" Ryan calls, meanwhile, at the prison on Earth. "Hey Guard!" Cora yells. "Shut up babor, no one wants to hear or see you, so just sit and rot." Guard replied. "I will get out of here." She stated as she looks around cell, she looks up to ceiling to notice a vent above her head. "That way." She replied as she jumps up to it and uses her hard head to break threw it, then she climbs into it and follows is till she comes across the docking bay. She then comes out behind some crates and sneaks aboard a ship. "Now he will be mine." She smiled. Now on the base the call comes in. "Sir, its earth there's been an escape." Jesse informed. "Who is it?" Biscus asked. Jesse checks report he cringes. "Cora Babor sir." He stated. "Where is Dylan?" Biscus demands. Meanwhile in Dylan's quarters he and Ryan, Steven and Cara are at the dinning room table eating dinner. "This is actually nice." Dylan admitted. "Yeah, who would've thought we'd all be eating together?" Steven replied. "Our father can be persuaded." Ryan disclosed. "Only by my sons." Dylan replied. Just then Jesse calls over com-link. "Sir sorry to interrupt but Biscus needs you in the control room." Jesse replied. "Excuse me, I will be back." Dylan heads out and down to control room. "What's going on?" Dylan asked. "Prison break, Cora Babor." Biscus says hesitantly. "Damm it, get out there and find her!" Dylan shouted. "Shoot to kill if need be." Dylan added. "We will find her." Charlie vows. "I will handle the search, you go enjoy your family." Biscus replied Dylan heads back to his quarters. "What was it?" Ryan asked. "Is it Grandfather?" Steven probed. Dylan looks to Cara. "She escaped didn't she?" Cara realized. "Yes an hour ago." Dylan confirmed. "Relax, the team will find her." Steven declares. "This is my fault, if I didn't love you." Cara blames. "No its not, everything will be fine." Ryan insists. "You can stay here on the base." Dylan replied. "You can stay with Amanda." Dylan added. Cara kisses Ryan good night. "I will see you in the morning." She replied then she goes out. "I am sorry son." Dylan replied. "So am I, why can't she let her sister be happy?" Ryan says frustrated. "You're a McKay, what can I say." Dylan says trying to lighten mood. Ryan smiled. "Thanks dad, for everything." Ryan replied. "Well she is not going to get you, I got your back." Steven insisted. Now as night falls on the planet, half of the team is still out searching for Cora as she managed to slip onto the base, threw the docking bay as Keyes is on guard duty. He catches her and aimed his weapon at her. "Hold it gorgeous." Keyes replied. "You got me." She stated. She looks him over. "You're new." She noticed. "Yes I am and you are going back to prison." He informed. "I haven't done anything." She paused "yet." She smiled. "Sure, just trying to break in so you can kidnap Ryan." Keyes replied. "I'm over him, I'm setting my sights higher." She is looking him over. "Seriously?" Keyes replied. "We will talk again soon." She hits a smoke device to cover her escape, now in the control room. "So what happened?" Biscus inquired. "Cora was trying to sneak in, I caught her she tried to flirt with me, and then she used a smoke bomb to escape." Keyes recapped. "What?" She just left?" Dylan asked in confusion. "Yes, I think she has changed her mind about Ryan." Amanda replied. "Well that's a good thing right?" Jon replied. "Well she has a new interested now." Amanda informed She looks to Keyes. "Whoa, Wait me?" Keyes replied. "Yes I read her thoughts, the things she was thinking about you would make you blush." Amanda stated. "Great, so I get my own psychotic stalker now?" Keyes asked. "Well you are an Aster." Shane replied. "I'm sure he can handle her." Jon stated. "I'll scan the area." Jesse said. "Keyes you are with me." Charlie ordered. "I am not afraid of Cora Babor." Keyes declared. "You should be, I am gonna use you as bait." Charlie added. "She is a girl, how scary can she be?" Keyes asked as he follows him. They then go to their quarters, which they share. Keyes goes into his bedroom and removes his gear and is just in his pants when he lies down on bed. Cora is there she managed to find his room with the help of the computer. "Well hello." She stated. Keyes opens his eyes and sits up. "Cora Babor?" He asked. "Don't call security just yet." She replied as she climbed into the bed. "Look, you and me are not happing." "You are a nut." Keyes replied. "We have a lot in common, we are both loners and abandoned. "She stated. "Yeah, I don't kill for fun." Keyes replied. "My brother will be in here any minute now." Keyes added. "Then I will comeback later." She pulls him in by back of his neck and steals a kiss and then she vanished with her device she retrieved. Charlie enters. "She's gone bro." Keyes replied. "What did she say?" Charlie asked. "She flirted, then kissed me." He replied. "Well next time, slap some cuffs on her while she is doing that." Charlie stated. Now the next day in the mess hall some of the team is at a table. "So wait, now she likes Keyes?" Cole asked. "Why not?" "He is strong and not bad to look at." Amanda replied. "Well then, why didn't she just hit on me?" Ralph insisted at the other table. "Please, we are trying to eat here." Cheryl replied. Over at another table; Dylan, Steven and Ryan sit. "So catch her yet?" Ryan asked. "No, but we will." Dylan assured. "I just feel bad for Keyes." Steven added. "Relax, Rick would kill her first." Dylan replied. Meanwhile in the rec room, Keyes is in their alone lifting weights when Charlie enters. "Hey, why didn't you wake me?" Charlie demands. "What, do I have to let you know when I pee too?" Keyes replied. "Hey this is not a joke." "Cora is dangerous, unstable, a psychopath." "Should I go on?" Charlie asked. "Are you always this uptight?" Keyes questioned. "When it is family, hell yes." Charlie replied. "Now lets get some breakfast." Charlie added. "Ok, mind if I shower first or do I need you to hold the soap?" Keyes said sarcastically. "Now you're showing your Aster." Charlie replied. Keyes put up weights and headed to locker room. Now later he is dressed with pants and t-shirt. When Cora appears. "Well, all wet and me wishing I was a towel." She replied. "Do you have a death wish?" Keyes asked. "Not at all, just trying to get your attention." She stated. "I don't think so." Keyes replied, "We could be magical." She implied. "Now I know why you kill men, they'd be bored otherwise you're not much for talking." Keyes said. "I only kill men I don't like." She replied. "I'd really rather, you not like me." Keyes asked. "I can wait." She stated. Charlie yelled for Keyes. "Big brother is watching you, we can talk later." She replied and then vanished. Keyes shakes his head in amazement and comes out. "What took so long?" Charlie asked, "Nothing lets eat." He replied they head to mess hall as they eat. "I'm thinking we should call Rick." Charlie stated. "Tell him about Cora." He added. "I thought you hated when he was overbearing?" Keyes replied. "Yeah, but he knows her better, how she thinks." "You need a rat to catch one so to speak." Charlie stated. "You do what you need to bro." Keyes replied. "You are not starting to like her, are you?" Charlie probed. "No, she is just all show, it's a cover a defense mechanism." "She is scared to be alone." Now that her sister has someone, I get it." Keyes identified.

"She has still killed hundreds of men in cold blood, don't forget that." Charlie answered. "Yeah, but so have a lot of people dad included." Keyes recapped. "Just please be careful." Charlie advised Jon comes to them. "Everything ok?" Jon asked. "Yeah, it will be once we get Cora locked up." Charlie replied. So I guess it would seem that all of us have bad girls after us, must be the Aster charm. Now we will meet a new addition to the family, Kyle McKay that would be Dylan's younger brother but we will also find another a young boy of thirteen, with some unbelievable power. It all began on Steven's sixteenth birthday; scene in the control room. "Octo has escaped." Biscus informed. "Then we'd better go find him.' Dylan replied. "I would like to help?" Kyle asked. "We can sure use the help." Biscus agreed. Meanwhile on the planet, Octo has managed to make his escape. He is hiding in an old abandoned office type building, on the outskirts of the city. Kyle is near by making his sweep of the area, when he noticed a shadow inside. He went in to investigate. He entered with gun in hand and goes step by step through the building. He did not notice Octo had seen him and snuck up behind him "You will do as a hostage." He replied. He knocked him unconscious. Amanda sensed his danger. "We need to move out." She replied. They do making their way to the building. "I am picking up three life readings in the building. Xavier replied. The team heads inside. "The alliance will find you." Kyle said as Octo has him on the ground. "Of course they will, I count on it but you will be dead." Octo proclaimed. Just then a young boy about thirteen comes out from hiding. He using powerful energy blast discharged from his hands and knocks Octo across the room and unconscious. "Who are you?" Kyle asked, as he got to his feet. "You saved my life." He added. "Nobody forget it." Kid replied. The team makes way to Kyle at that point. "You ok?" Dylan asked. The others see Octo on the ground in the distance. "Yes thanks to the kid." Kyle stated. "It was nothing." Kid replied. "What's your name kid?" Dylan asked. "Devon." He answered. "You look like, you could use a decent meal and clothes come with us." Dylan insisted. "I'm ok." Devon replied. "It's a free meal and not so sure it's decent." Ralph added. "Ok fine." Devon replied. Now back on the base in the mess hall. Devon is eating like there's no tomorrow as the team watches in astonishment, shock and amazement. "How long have you been in that building?" Dylan asked. "I scanned him." "He has not eaten any kind of decent meal in six days." Paul informed. "What, six days?" Kyle replied. "Amanda, what are you reading from him?" Jon asked. Amanda uses her powers to read his mind. "He is a good kid, lost his family a year ago." "There is something else, a connection to us." She stated. "Connection?" Jon asked. "Yes give me time, I'll figure it out." She replied. "Keep an eye on him." Dylan stated. "So this kid can eat huh?" Cole replied. "He must have no taste buds, if he's eating here." Ralph added. "He reminds me of someone." Shane probes. "Yeah I see it too." Charlie added. They watch Devon eating he has jet-black hair and sapphire blue eyes. Just then Moondeath appeared to them. "Hello boys." He replied. "What brings you to visit, not that were complaining."? Shane replied. "I am not really sure, I was drawn here." He answered. "I felt something." He added. "Like what?" Jon asked. He looks to Devon as he is eating. "Who is the boy?" Moondeath questioned. "His name is Devon." "We just found him, he saved Kyle's life." Shane recapped. "He reminds me of." He pauses. "What is it bad?" Charlie asked. "He has a familiar essence, how did he save Kyle?" Moondeath inquired. "He blasted Octo, with a type of energy that came from his hands." Charlie replied. "Could he be an Aster?" Shane asked. "Yes!" Amanda shouted. "That is it, he is your grandson." She replied. "Volrin's son I think." She added. "No way, he was lost in the zone." Shane replied. "Yes, but he was almost seventeen then." Jon stated. "We cannot tell him." Amanda replied. "We can't tell Volrin he is a nut." Charlie added. "I agree, but it is not our call." Jon reminded. "I think we should wait." "Volrin is still too unstable, he may try to convert him." Moondeath replied. "So, you want to lie to a kid?" Shane asked. "I'm sorry, but I know what lies can do first hand." "I had a breakdown remember?" Shane stated. "Your right, we must tell him." Jon replied. "Jon you should do it." Amanda insisted. "Why me?" Jon asked. "He knows you're the Valr Te Nesk, I think you can guide him." She replied. "He will trust you." She added. "Ok I will." Jon stated. They walk up to him at table. Devon stopped eating. "What, do I have to pay for it?" Devon asked. "No, you're our guest." Jon replied. "Your him right?" Devon asked as he stands up. "The Valr Te Nesk?" He added. "Yes I am." Jon replied. "So if you need to rest, you can use my spare bedroom." Jon offered. "I would be honored." Devon answered. He spends the night, now in the morning Devon is already up and going to leave when Jon comes out in his PJ's and robe. "Hey where are you going?" Jon asked. "I don't want to be a problem." Devon replied. "You are not, trust me." Jon stated. "Sit down, I'll explain." Jon replied. Devon goes to the couch and sits. "Look, you don't have to look out for me, were not family." Devon stated. Jon smiled. "Actually Devon, we are." Jon informed. "Look, you are here because you were meant to find us." "I've learned not to question the fates." Jon replied. "You are my cousin." He added. "No way." Devon replied in disbelief. "Yes your father is Volrin Aster." Jon added. "Hey I am not like him." Devon stated. "None of us are like our fathers." Jon replied. "I promise, you are safe here." Jon added. "I don't want to know him." Devon stated. "I understand." Jon answered. "Can I ask a question?" Devon said. "Of course." Jon responded. "Can you teach me?" Devon asked. "I'm not so great with control." He informed. "Of course I can." Jon prided as they smiled then Voltar appeared Devon is frightened. "Junior we need to speak." Voltar insisted. "Your Voltar Aster." Devon replied. "Can you excuse us for a moment, please." Jon asked. Devon gets up and goes out of Quarters. "What do you want?" Jon asked. "I was just checking on you." Voltar replied. "I am fine." Jon stated. "Well if your going to be so uptight about it, I will go." Voltar stated. He vanished Jon sighed as Devon came back in. "Did you tell him about me?" Devon asked. "No, like I said you are safe here." Jon replied. Just then Steven accompanied by Marie Jon's six-year-old cousin on his mother's side comes in. She has blonde hair and blue eyes. "Hey I'm Steven." He extends hand to Devon and Devon shakes it. "I'm Marie!" She shouted. "I guess, I'm your cousin Devon." Devon said. "Good, you can play dress up with me." She instructed as she grabbed his hand and pulls him. "Welcome to the family." Steven stated. "So, when can we work on my powers?" Devon asked. "We will start tomorrow, you have a dress up date today." Jon replied. "I won't be like him will I?" Devon worried. "Listen, our heart is what makes us who we are." "You showed that when you saved Kyle." Jon assured. "Volrin was good once, but the zone changed him." Jon replied at that moment Volrin appeared. Devon looks nervously. "Who is the kid?" Volrin probed. Moondeath also appeared "Volrin come with me." Moondeath insisted. "We need to talk." He added. "What do you want old man?" Volrin replied Moondeath grabs him by arm and they vanished. "Well let's go." Marie said as she pulls Devon out the door, meanwhile in the control room Dylan is in the office, when Ryan comes in. "Hey where is Cara?" Ryan asked. "She is with

Amanda shopping, I think." "I zoned out when they started talking clothes." Dylan stated. "I need to talk to you, its serious." Ryan replied. "Ok, should I sit?" Dylan worried. "I'm going to ask Cara, to marry me." Ryan stated. "I really want your blessing dad." He asked. "I know Cara has done things, but she has changed." Ryan added. "Yes I know, you bring that out in her." "Your good for her." Dylan replied. "Thanks dad." Ryan hugs him. "I have to go." He added and heads out Biscus walks in. "So what's going on?" He asked. "My son is getting married." "God I feel old." Dylan replied. "Well, you look it so it balances out." Biscus laughed. Now in the rec room, Devon is using his power to make the equipment rise off the floor and hover in the air. "Not bad kid." Jon replied. Then Devon lowers everything to the ground. "Do you think I should talk to him?" "Volrin I mean" Devon asked. "If you want to, just be careful." "You can control things when your not stressed, but we haven't battle tested you yet." Jon replied. "I'll go with you to see him, if you want?" Jon added just then Volrin appeared. "What is going on?" Volrin demanded. "I'm your son, Devon." He stated. "What?" Volrin replied confused. "Give him time to process this, Volrin." Jon insisted. "Fine, we will talk later." Volrin stated as he vanished. "That went not how I thought." Jon replied. "Should I be nervous?" Devon asked. Meanwhile back at the castle. "You have a son?" Rick replied in shock. "The galaxy may finally come to an end." He added. "Now is the time to crush the Alliance." Volrin commands. "Yes, family is everything." "Its time we took it back." Voltar agreed. Now back on the base in the rec room, Devon continues to learn control of his newly developing powers. "I hope there aren't anymore of you Asters, it's getting crowded on this base." Ralph jokes. "Hey we are all a family." Steven said. "I would like to go visit Moondeath, if it's ok?" Devon asked. "Of course." Jon replied. Now a little later, they come upon a small home in a village outside of the city. Devon knocks on the door to a small house it opens. "Hello?" Devon called out. "Come in Devon! "Moondeath exclaimed. Devon comes into the living room to see him seated on the couch. "Come sit with me." He replied. "Do you know, why I'm here?" Devon asked. "Yes, you want to know about him." Moondeath replied. "I think you can help him." Moondeath stated. "How?" Devon said. "You both need someone to care about you." He informed. Moondeath senses something. "You need to go before it's too late." Moondeath stated. "Why what's wrong?" Devon asked. Just then an explosion is heard outside and felt. Devon jumped to his feet. "What was that?" Devon shouted. "We'd better hurry." Moondeath replied. Meanwhile back at the base, Voltar and the others blast in the doors with their power. "What the hell are you doing."? Jon demanded as they met then at the doors. "It is time to end this junior." Voltar replied. "Where is my son?" Volrin demands. "Why are you doing this?" Jon asked. "Do you want him to hate you?" Jon added. Just then Moondeath and Devon appeared. "End this now, both of you!" Moondeath commands. "What are you doing?" Devon asked. "I'm sorry, I got caught up in the excitement of a son." Volrin confessed. Amanda rushes in. "Danny is dead!" She screamed. "You've killed yet another innocent." Moondeath replied. Devon begins to get angry his eyes glow a bright blue as he looses control of his powers "I should never trust you!" He yells "Devon No!" Jon shouted. "I hate you!" He cried as he used his power to blast Volrin out of base and at least 50 feet. "Devon!" Jon yells as he goes to him. Devon stops his eyes return to normal and he looks to Jon, and then looks around at everyone's fearful and stunned expressions. "I'm sorry." Devon replied. He then runs out of base into forest, Moondeath goes after him. Jon turned to Voltar. "Is that what you wanted?" "Are you satisfied now?" Jon asked. "Family is everything to me junior." Voltar stated. "No, controlling family is." "It is always gonna be about power for you." Jon replied. Rick comes over to Charlie and Keyes. "You need to go now." Charlie stated. "Yeah, before you loose what little respect and love we have for you." Keyes added. They go. Meanwhile Moondeath catches up to Devon sitting on a tree stump at the beginning of the forest. "Don't hate him." Moondeath asked. "He acts on impulse and idiocy, they both do." He added. "He killed Danny with that attack" Devon replied. "Yes, but I still believe there is good in him and you are the key all of you boys are." He stated. "You can save them." He added. Jon comes to them. "Hey you ok?" Jon asked. "How do you do it? "How do you still care about them?" Devon asked. "They are our family, no one is perfect but you only get one." Jon stated. "How many times have you forgiven him? Devon questioned. "More than he deserves." Jon replied. "Come on let's get back." Jon replied. Now as things began to settle at least for a little while, the team was planning a major bachelor party for Ryan before his big day. I on the other hand have the Overlord to deal with again. Scene it is night we go to Jon's bedroom as he sleeps she appeared to him, he sensed her and opens his eyes. "Go back to hell." Jon replied. "I can be who ever you desire Jon." She stated as she transforms into Jessica first, then Tracilla. "Which do you prefer?" She asked. "None of them, I want you to leave." Jon insisted. "It is fate, we will be together Jon." She replied. "You make me sick, I doubt that." Jon responded. "I will be yours as you, will be mine." She replied she then vanished Devon knocks and enters. "Hey, everything ok?" Devon asked. "The guys are gathering for the bachelor party planning in the rec room." Devon informed. Now all the guys are gathered in secret in the rec room. "Ok my boy needs a stripper." Ralph insisted. "Yeah and how do we get that past the girls?" Brent asked. "Hey, I'm the best man." Steven stated. "Yes he is so, what is your ideas bro?" Ryan asked. "Great cake and a piñata." Ralph replied. "I heard about this stripper named Skalia." He replied. The guys' mouths dropped to the floor in surprise and astonishment. "How do you know about her?" Marco asked. "Ah, again how do we get this passed the girls?" Brent replied. "They know I'm in charge of it." Steven smiles. "Why you little half Aster you." Ralph replied. As they continue talking Shane sees Jon by the window and heads over. "Hey you ok?" Shane asked. "What?" Jon replied. "You are a million miles away right now." Shane stated. "What is going on with you?" Shane asked. "Nothing, I'm fine." Jon insisted. "Sure you are." Shane says in disbelief. "Look, we have all fallen for the wrong girl, just saying." Shane replied. "Her and I can never be, not after all she's done." Jon responded, meanwhile at the castle. "I am going insane, I'm so bored." Rick stated. "Your also annoying." Volrin replied. "If I killed you, would anyone miss you?" Rick responded. "Quiet you two I am thinking." Voltar commanded. "What is it, something wrong?" Rick asked. "It's junior, I'll be back." As he vanished and reappeared to Jon's quarters, where he returned after the planning. Jon is about to go to bed. "Are you ok?" Voltar asked. "Father, what are you doing here? Jon demanded. "I am here as you're conscious, to remind you she is the Overlord pure evil, almost killed your father." Voltar replied. "I know all of that, thank you." Jon responded. "Then for the sake of your soul and my hairline forget her." Voltar pleaded. "Don't you think I'm trying? Jon replied. Just then Devon comes out of other bedroom. "Hey, am I interrupting?" Devon asked. "No not at all." "We have practice in the morning." Jon replied. "We are not done with this subject junior." Voltar stated then vanished. "He is interesting." Devon replied as he gets glass of water from frig in kitchen. "He is something." Jon stated they go to bed. Meanwhile Shane is in docking bay coming back from a shift when Voltar appeared. "Hello son how is your lady, Anilla right?" He asked. "She is fine, so what do you want?" Shane probed. "Just checking on your brother." He replied. "He is falling for her, isn't he?" Shane fears. "I'm afraid so, she is very tempting in her female form." Voltar remembers. "Ok, first off stop that." "I'm going to have strange dreams tonight, thanks." Shane replied. "You need to help him." Voltar instructs. "I'll do what I can, but you know us Asters were stubborn." Shane replied. So as my father and brother plotted to control my love life, I was spiraling out of control but that is the least of our worries there is a wedding happening let the fireworks commence. On the base in sickbay Anilla comes to Shane and hugs him tightly around his waist form behind. "I'm ok." He replied. She lets go. "You almost died I can't believe the Overlord of all people showed up to save you." She added. "Yeah she did, and I'm grateful even though I know she did it to score points with Jon." He added meanwhile outside sickbay. "So who is this Overlord?" Devon asked. "I'll tell you later." Jon replied. "So where are the love birds anyway?" Cole asked. Outside of the base we come upon Ryan and Cara sitting on a rock and kissing passionately. "So have you heard from Cora?" Ryan asked. "Or your mother?" He added. "No, it's fine your family is all I need." She replied. "Besides I have Cole." She added. "I heard about your mom, she seems interesting." Ryan smiled. "She is one of a kind trust me." She replied as they kiss. So next for us it should be a joyful celebration but it is about to go the way of the Asters. Which means disaster.

Chapter 12

WEDDING DAY

As we prepared for Ryan and Cora's wedding day others were working on ruining it. At a secret location on Mars Barbara Babor is with Cora Barbara is about 45 but, she is a hot mom. We hate to admit, with Blonde long straight hair and baby blue eyes. "So my daughter is getting married, and didn't invite me?" Barbara stated. "Who needs an invitation?" Cora replied. "We are family after all." She adds. "I think it's time I met my future son-in-law." Barbara said. Now later that day they land on Voltara in a small shuttle landing just outside the city they exit. "I will find him, he has never seen my face." Barbara recommended. "I will befriend him, and then stop this foolish union." She smiled. "I love how you manipulate mother." Cora replied. She goes toward city. Meanwhile Ryan and Steven are in the city when she sees them. "Well these McKay's get better looking every generation." Barbara replied. "Hey I'll be right back." Steven replied. He goes into a store; Ryan finds a bench near by and sits. Barbara comes over to him. "Mind if I sit here too?" She asked. "Of course you can." Ryan answered. As he moved down she sits. "So shopping alone?" She asked. "No, I'm with my brother." "He is getting my wedding gift so." Ryan replied. "Well aren't you lucky, to be young and in love." She replied. "Yes." Ryan stated. "I'm Ryan by the way." As he extended his hand she shakes it. "Barbara." She replied. "Nice to meet you." Ryan replied just then Steven comes out of store. "So lets go." He replied as he is holding a gift bag. Ryan stands and they go as Barbara goes as well and meets back up with Cora by shuttle. "He is sweet, I hate that." Barbara stated. "Still I can see why both of you fell for him." She added. "I think, it is also time to check on Cole." She replied. "He is disgustingly happy too," Cora informed. "Well not for long." Barbara replied. "We will change that, mother Babor is back." She added as she smiles. Meanwhile back on the base: Devon is practicing using his powers. He elevated Marie up and off the ground. "Spin me!" She yelled. "No spinning." Jon replied as Devon lowered her back down. "So, what or should I say who are you thinking about?" Devon asked. "Am I that obvious?" Jon asked. "Yeah, that overlord did a number on you." Devon stated. "Yes she did." Jon admitted. Meanwhile In the corridor Ryan comes up behind Cara and kissed her neck. "Hello beautiful." Her replied. "I recognize that touch." She responded. "You should, from now own I will be the only one doing that." Ryan replied with a smile as they kissed Ralph comes up. "Oh man, there goes my lunch." He said as Ryan and Cora laugh. Meanwhile at the mess hall Amanda and Cole are seated at a table when she gets the feeling of a presence. "Someone is here." Amanda replied. "Who is?" Cole asked. "A familiar person, someone close to you?" She replied. "We should check with Jesse, for any new escapes." Cole suggested. Now later that night, in Dylan's quarters where Ryan is staying in guest room alone until the wedding. Cora uses her teleport device to appear in his bedroom she stands for a moment to watch him sleep, when Barbara appeared. "Still lusting daughter?" She asked. "Trying to understand, how he could love her?" Cora replied as she gently touched his cheek. "You can ask him later." She informed as Cora takes his hand and all three vanish. Meanwhile in the control room Biscus is getting the reports on new escapees. "We know who escaped." Biscus stated. "Barbara and Cora Babor." He replied. "What!" Dylan exclaimed just then Steven rushes in. "Dad!" He shouted, "Ryan is gone." He added. "They took him." Dylan insisted. "Then we'd better find them." Cole replied. Meanwhile back at their secret location on Mars. Ryan is lying on a bed when he wakes up. "What the hell?" He replied as he sits up. "Hello Ryan." Barbara replies. "You're the woman form the bench." Ryan remembered as he tries to get up but one of his arms is chained to the bed rail. "Who are you?" Ryan demanded just then Cora comes in. "We are family, Ryan this is my mother." Cora informed. "I just had to meet the man, who could tear my girls apart." She replied. "My father and friends will kill you." Ryan stated. "So, how did you and Cara meet?" Barbara asked. "Go to hell." Ryan replied. "She is an fool, what is it about her?" Cora demands. "She is good." "Something you will never comprehend." Ryan stated. "You've got spirit boy" Barbara says impressed. Meanwhile back on the base, Cara is visibly upset and sitting in the briefing room. "This is my fault, I love him." Cora replied. "No its not." Amanda insisted. "I always wanted to be better, to be good." "When I met Ryan, I saw the potential for that life. "She added. "He will be fine." Amanda reassured. "He is a McKay." She added. 'I can't loose him." Cara replied. "You won't, that much I know." Amanda stated. Xavier comes in. "They found Cora, on Mars in a remote town." He said. Meanwhile back on Mars at secret location. "You won't get away with this" Ryan replied. "I always loved that positive McKay attitude." Barbara responded. "I just wanted to share in my daughter's happiness." She added innocently. "You and Cora only know chaos and malice. "You only came to ruin her happiness." Ryan stated. "Watch yourself boy." She replied. "Your no better than Voltar Aster." He added just then Voltar appeared. "Someone mention my name?" Voltar asked he sees Barbara. "So Barbara still alive I see." He replied. "This is not your concern, this is my family." She stated. "Actually it is, Steven is my grandson, this is his brother so I must assist." Voltar replied he then uses power to break the chain. "Consider this a wedding gift." Voltar stated. "Thanks." Ryan replied as the team busted in. "You bitch!" Dylan exclaimed as he goes after Cora and Barbara. Steven goes to Ryan. "Are you ok?" He asked. "Yeah thanks to him." Ryan replied as he gestured to Voltar. "Mother how could you?" Cole asked. "You will never understand, its Babor true nature." She answered. "Get her out of here!" Dylan shouted, and then Dylan looked to Voltar in surprise yet gratitude. "I guess I owe you one." Dylan replied. "No, just keep an eye on my family especially junior." Voltar stated then he vanished. "That guy never ceases to confuse me." Marco replied. Now back on the base as Ryan is brought into docking bay Cara is there and hugs him tight. "Your ok?" She asked. "I told you, your stuck with me." Ryan replied with a smile they kiss. Now its a few days later the wedding day and the base is all a buzz the guests are arriving including Dylan's admiral father the sparks will fly. Scene in Dylan's quarters Ryan is front of his mirror in bedroom in amazing suit trying to fix his tie as he struggles. "I hate this thing!" He exclaimed. Dylan then entered and helped to fix it. "Nervous are we?" Dylan asked. "So your ready?" He questioned. Ryan takes a deep breath. "Yes I am, I just hope I don't pass out." He added. Dylan lets out a laugh. "Thanks dad, for giving Cara a chance you will love her too." Ryan insisted. Steven enters all decked out in his suit. "So are we ready?" He asked. "Do I have to make a toast?" He added, "Yes its part of the best man duties." Ryan replied. Just then Paul walks in. "Excuse me Dylan, but your father has arrived." He said. "Oh no, why is he here?" Steven said. "He is not very nice." He added. "He is still your grandfather Steven." Dylan replied. "He probably won't approve of this wedding, it's probably why he is here." Dylan added. "He can leave then." Ryan stated. Just then his father entered, older gentlemen brown hair with grey mixed in and brown eyes. He is dressed in military uniform and stern look of disappointment on his face. "What the hell is going on here Dylan?" "You are letting this boy marry a babor of all woman?" He questioned. "Excuse me?" Ryan replied. "Father if you cannot be happy for him, you can leave." Dylan stated. "You have never listened to me." Father replied. "He is a boy." He added. "I am not a boy." Ryan fired back. "An undisciplined one at that." He stated. "That's it pops." Ryan replied as he goes toward him. "Stop!" Dylan yelled. "Not today, this is his day." Dylan stated. "Just go grandpa your ruining everything." Steven replied. "So I'm the bad guy?" Father asked. "I told you, my life and that of my sons is not yours to manipulate or control." Dylan stated. "If you want to stay you will be quiet." He added. Now it is time all are gathered in the mess hall, which has been converted to a church type set up. Ryan is at the archway with Dylan and Steven beside him all the team standing in front of their chairs standing; Cara walks in and down the aisle in a beautiful long flowing gown of glittery silver with Cole as her escort. Ryan watches her in sheer amazement. He smiles at her as she is standing beside him "You are so beautiful." He replied. She smiles back, now after the ceremony the party is on as they went to another hall for the reception. "Ok guys!" Steven shouted as they all settle down. "I'm the best man so I must make the toast." He replied. He raises his glass looks to Ryan and Cara. "You both had some troubled pasts, but you made it threw, now your lives together will be full of good things and last forever." Steven replied. All raise glasses and toast. "That was beautiful son." Dylan replied. "Alright ladies time to throw the bouquet!" Cara yells as all the girls gather in a group she throws it over her shoulder and Jenna catches it. They all scream in excitement. "Well looks like your next to be noosed man." Ralph replied. "I am not getting married." Charlie stated. "You think so?" Jenna said as she comes over. They all laugh, now time has passed my father continues to try and rule the galaxy while we, had new adventures and encountered new friends along the way as Keyes would meet and fall in love with Leeah but first things first, Charlie and Jenna are finally going to get married what will happen at these nuptials? The scene is set outside of the base it is beautifully decorated for an outdoor wedding flowers and chairs an amazing archway of Jenna's favorite flowers. The team is dressed in special military style dress suits. As the women are stunning in there dresses. "Whoa girl you look good." Ralph replied. "I know, put your tongue back in your mouth." Cheryl stated. Meanwhile in Jenna's quarters, as she is getting ready she has a gown of silk white with elegant beads lining its edges and a beautiful headpiece made of real diamonds with her dark blonde hair flowing behind it. "You look so beautiful." Lisette replied. "Thank you." Jenna smiled. "This is going to be the best wedding ever." Amanda replied meanwhile in Charlie's quarters he is pacing back and forth in a nervous panic. "Will you relax? Keyes insisted. "You are wearing a whole in the floor," Jon added. "I'm just so nervous." Charlie replied. "You will be fine." Shane replied. "Yeah your right." Charlie answered. Now it is time, as everyone is in positions Rick is standing, at the alter with Charlie and Keyes as Voltar, Volrin and Moondeath are in the crowd. "You are ready son so relax." Rick replied. "I know dad." Charlie answered. Now all the girls start walking down the aisle then Jenna comes out all are captivated, she comes to him as they take each other's hands. The priest begins the ceremony. "They have each written their own vows." He replied. "Jenna the first time we met there were defiantly sparks." He smiled, as did she and the crowd. "I knew you were the one, especially when you told me so." He added she lets out a giggle. "You keep my life exciting, you are my life." He continues. "I don't remember anything else before you and I cannot imagine anything else without you." "I cannot wait to see what lies ahead for us, I love you Jenna." He concluded. "Now Jenna." Priest replied. "When I first saw you, I could not believe how hot an alliance officer could be." She smiled as he did too. "I felt those sparks too, any man who was that brave and crazy to go up against me?" She continues. "I knew I would steal your heart, our adventures together have only just begun and I am ready, I love you Charlie

Aster." She ended. "With that said do you take this woman to be your lawfully wedded wife?" He asked. "I do." Charlie replied. "Do you take this man to be your lawfully wedded husband?" He asked. "I do." She replied. "Then by the powers vested in me by the Galactic Alliance, I pronounce you husband and wife, you may kiss your bride." He replied. They kiss as everyone cheered and yelled. "My man!" Ralph exclaimed. "Ok time to party!" He added. Now at the reception "I am so proud and happy for you son." Rick replied. "She is perfect for you." He added. "Not many woman can handle an Aster." He smiled. "Thanks dad." Charlie replied. Ryan and Cara come to them. "So that bouquet did this?" Ryan asked as he smiled, he and Charlie hugged. "Good to see you two." Jenna replied. "I will need some advice and marriage tips." Charlie replied as all laugh just then alarms go off. "What is going on?" Dylan asked Jesse over com-link. "Cora and Barbara Babor escaped sir." Jesse responded. "We need to find them now." Dylan insisted. Steven heads over to Ryan and Cara. "I'm guessing that alarm means an escape?" Ryan asked. "Yeah your mom and sister have escaped, we need to get everyone inside." Steven replied. All head inside, as team gets into battle gear and heads out to find them. Ryan is in Dylan in his Quarters, he watches out the window as fighters fly off in all directions. When Cora appears in front of the window. Ryan is startled. "Hello Ryan, I just had to see you one last time before I go you're still my weakness." She replied. "You need to be back in prison, where is your psychotic mother?" Ryan asked as he looked around. "She is looking for Cole." She replied. Meanwhile Cole is about to head out to look for them when, Barbara appeared in his living room. "Mother?" Cole replied. "We need to talk son." She asked. "I have to arrest you." Cole replied. She comes close touches his cheek. "I love you son." She replied then she disappeared. Meanwhile back in Dylan's quarters. "She was here?" Dylan stated. "Yes and crazy as ever." Ryan added. "We will find them." Steven insured. "Be careful." Ryan said to Steven as he heads out. "Don't worry, it helps she is nuts over you." Steven replied. "Where is Cara?" Dylan asked. "She is with Amanda." Ryan replied. "How are you holding up?" Dylan asked. "I'm ok dad." Ryan answered. "I'm sorry this ruined your return." Dylan stated. "I just can't believe she is still trying to come after me, I'm married." Ryan replied. Just then an explosion rocked the base it came from the south end. "Cara!" Ryan exclaimed as they rush out into corridor and toward it, dabree everywhere and smoke with smoldering flames they come upon Mary under some ruble. "Mary?" Dylan shouted as they lifted off console. "Where are Cara and Amanda? Ryan asked. "She was near me." Mary replied, Security comes and carry her to sickbay. Where is she?" Ryan worries, as he looks all around then he sees her under heavy Dabree. "Cara!" Ryan shouted as he rushes to her and digs her out Dylan helps "Cara?" He begs She is still and unresponsive. "Lets get her to sickbay." Dylan replied, Ryan lifts her and carries her to sickbay, now in sickbay. "Anyone else hurt?" Dylan questioned. "No she knew exactly where Cara was, she was trying to kill her." Amanda confirmed as Anilla is patching up her wounds. "Lets pray she didn't succeed." Dylan replied Paul and his assistant work feverishly on Cara as Ryan watches form a distance. "She has to be ok." Ryan insisted. "She is a fighter." Dylan stated Cole rushes in from docking bay. "How is she?" He asked. "We don't know yet." Ryan replied. "I can't believe Cora would do this." Cole replied. "She is obsessed with my brother." Steven replied. "She loves you Ryan, she will come back to you." Cole replied just then Paul comes out. "Paul?" Ryan asked. "She has internal bleeding and head trauma we have stabilized her for now." Paul replied. "Thank you." Ryan replied. "She is still critical." Paul reminds. "Can I see her?" Ryan asked. "Yes try talking to her." Paul replied. Ryan heads in he comes to her bedside and takes hold of her hand. "I'm here, you know I love to watch you sleep, but I'd rather you wake up so, I can see those beautiful blue eyes." Ryan replied. "Please be ok." Ryan begged, as he watches her noticing the monitors and her still body. Jon comes into sickbay. "How is she?" Jon asked. "Not good." Dylan replied Paul comes to Dylan. "We ran tests her body is healing but I suspect extensive brain trauma" Paul replied. "No." Dylan gasped, meanwhile as Ryan is with Cara. "Please wake up your scaring me, just squeeze my hand if you can hear me." Ryan begged eyes watered up. Dylan enters and comes beside him puts hand on his shoulder. "Something is wrong isn't it?" Ryan feared. "We have to keep faith son." Dylan insisted. "I'm trying to dad." Ryan replied as he lowered his head, meanwhile back in control room as Jesse is scanning Jon comes up to him. "Anything?" Jon asked. "No it's like they just vanished." Jesse replied. Cole turns to look at Amanda. "Are you getting anything?" Cole asked. "I'm not reading them they must be far." She replied. Now back in sickbay Paul comes to them. "I did an EEG."

Paul replied. "What is that?" Ryan asked. "To test for brain activity." Paul stated. "What did it show?" Dylan asked. "That there was none, I am so sorry Ryan." Paul replied. "I have to declare her brain dead." He added. Ryan's eyes are flooded with tears as he feels his body go numb then limp Dylan holds him close. "No" He denies as he shakes his head. Dylan hugs him tightly as he cries. "I am so sorry son." Dylan replied the team comes to sickbay. "Dad?" Steven said. "She is brain dead." Paul explained. "What?" Cole exclaimed, as he is in shock his eyes watering up Amanda hugs him. "Why did this happen?" Cole asked. "Cora only knows extreme emotions, love, hate jealousy. Amanda replied. Steven comes up to Ryan as he is sitting beside Cara now. "Ryan?" Steven said as he touched his shoulder. "She did not deserve to die this way." Ryan replied. "Not by her sister," "This is my fault." Ryan stated, just then Jesse called over com-link. "Sir we found them." He stated. "I'm on my way." Dylan replied. "Make her pay." Ryan replied. "I'll stay with him." Steven stated, as the team goes out. "She's at peace, she can't hurt her anymore." Ryan replied Meanwhile on Voltara itself in an abandoned village. "There it is!" Shane exclaimed. "Alright Babors come out its over!" Jon yells. Barbara then comes out with hands up. "Its just me." She stated. "Cora is gone." She added. "Where is she?" Jon demanded. "She knows her sister is gone, she has gone to mourn her." She replied. "Mourn her?" "She is the one who killed her." Shane responded. "Yes, but they were still sisters, twins they had a bond." She replied as the team takes her to prison. Dylan returned to sickbay. "Did you catch them?" Steven asked. "We found Barbara, Cora is still missing." Dylan replied. "She is still free?" Ryan asked. "We will find her." Dylan replied. "I need to lye down for awhile." Ryan stated with a look of exhaustion and overwhelming anguish. "Of course you do son." Dylan insisted as Ryan goes out. "I wish I could fix this." Steven replied. "All we can do is be here for him." Dylan stated. "I feel like I'm cursed like the others here." Ryan said out loud. As he sat down on the bed, he lies down and quickly falls asleep. Now back in the control room. Jesse is searching desperately for any trace of Cora. "Still nothing sir." Jesse said hesitantly. "Keep looking, she is coming here I know it." Dylan replied. Meanwhile Cora reappears to Dylan's quarters and into Ryan's bedroom she touched his hand and they vanished the alarms go off. "She was here." Jesse discovered. "Ryan." Dylan replied as they rush out of control room to his quarters. "Where is he Jesse?" Dylan demands. "I'm scanning sir." Jesse answered. "I lost his signal." He regrets. "Damm it!" Dylan exclaimed. "We need to find them." Dylan demanded. "Wait!" Jesse shouted. "I got his signal its on Earth." Jesse replied. "She is trying to throw us off." Marco said. "Lets go." Dylan asserted. Meanwhile on Earth Cora appears in an old abandoned home where she lies Ryan down on a bed. Ryan moves around then wakes up to see her. "You bitch!" Ryan exclaimed. "How could you murder your own sister?" He replied. "I needed to free you of her." She answered. "Your insane, you can't find a man of your own so you kill my wife, your sister for hers." Ryan stated. "You are pathetic." He added. Just then the team burst in. "No!" She yelled the team grabs her and cuff her. "Are you ok?" Dylan asked. "I'm ok." Ryan answered. Now back on the base Ryan is asleep Dylan checks on him and kissed his forehead, now the next day in the control room. "Hey where is Charlie, isn't he due back now?" Jon questioned. "He is out with Jenna having one last day of fun." Dylan replied. "Whoa Charlie and fun?" Jon asked. "Yes, he wanted to have fun he felt he was being to serious." Dylan added. "Ok then." Jon replied just the Keyes came in. "Hey where is Charlie?" Keyes asked. "He is out having fun." Jon replied. "My brother?" Keyes questioned. "Yes marriage agrees with him." Jon said, meanwhile Charlie and Jenna are on Earth at an amusement park on a roller coaster no less. Now we move ahead six months, as we find a less than enthusiastic Ryan and Steven in Dylan's quarters. "So are you going to go out?" Steven asked. "I know your trying to help but I am not ready." Ryan replied. "She wouldn't want you to be alone." Steven added. "I know, look you will be the first one I tell when I am ready ok?" Ryan promised. Now back in the control room. "Hey why didn't he take us to the park?" Ralph asked. "Hey I'm his brother." Keyes replied. "I just wish Ryan would go out." Dylan replied. "He will when he's ready, loosing someone especially your wife, it's gonna take time." Jon replied. "I just don't want him to give up." Dylan feared. "We won't let him." Jon replied just then alarms go off. "Sir an attack on Mars." Jesse informed. "We are on our way." Jon replied as team heads out Steven enters. "So how is he?" Dylan asked. "The same, I tried to get him to go out but." Steven replied. Meanwhile Ryan looked in the mirror and cleaned up, shaved and showered and then went out of the base and walked to the city. He saw a young couple on a bench kissing as he goes to turn to walk another way he bumped into a young woman beautiful with Raven hair and brown eyes. "I am so sorry.' Ryan replied, "Its ok nothing broken." She said. "It was my fault." Ryan added. "Its fine you looked distracted. She observed. "I'm Ryan." He extended hand she shakes it. "I'm Karin." She answered. "I should go." She added as she walks away as Ryan watched her Steven then comes up to him. "Here you are." Steven replied. "Who has got your attention?" Steven looks. "Just someone I bumped into." Ryan stated. "So did you get a name?" Steven inquired. "Karin." Ryan answered. "So go after her." Steven insisted. Meanwhile Karin entered a small secluded house, then went down in a secret elevator in the near by closet to reveal a secret compound, Barbara is seated at a computer console. "Well did you see him?" She asked, Karin then smiled as she removed a necklace from her neck and she was transformed back into Cora. "Of course and I can tell in his eyes he is ready to love again, this time it will be me." She replied. "Good, our plan is coming together perfectly." Barbara stated. "I should go find him so he doesn't loose interest. She puts the necklace back on and is Karin again. "I do love technology." She smiled she heads back up and out as Ryan is walking the streets looking for her. "Where did she go?" Ryan questioned as Karin comes toward him. "You again?" She replied. "I was hoping to find you." Ryan replied. "So, you were looking for me?" "Should I be worried?" She asked. "No, I'm sorry if I scared you." Ryan replied. "I think I can trust you." She smiled. "Are you thirsty?" "Maybe, we can go for a drink?" Ryan asked. "Alright why not." She answered as they go to a nearby tavern, meanwhile back in control room. Amanda gets a feeling something is not right. "Something is wrong." She replied. "What is it?" Cole asked. "Someone familiar." She answered. "I'll gather everyone. "Cole replied. Now all gather. "What is going on?" Dylan asked as she expressed a concern but could not pin point it. In the city Ryan and "Karin" were walking back to her place. "This is me." She replied. "Do you want to come in?" She asked. "I should go." Ryan replied she comes close leans in and kisses him he pulled back. "Whoa, this is all too fast." Ryan insisted. "We both lost someone we loved, why should we continue to suffer alone?" She asked. "There is something about you?" Ryan questioned. "I feel it too." She replied as they kissed again she opens the door and pulls him inside. "Are you sure?" Ryan asked. "Yes I am." She stated as she kissed him again leading him to the bedroom in back.

Meanwhile outside in the city the team is spread out trying to find him. "No sign of him yet." Cole said over com-link. "Cora is using this as a distraction to Barbara's bigger plan." Amanda warns Jesse picks up a signal. "Sir, someone is trying to enter north side." Jesse informed. Mark enters with Barbara Babor in custody. "What is going on?" Dylan demanded as Amanda realized what was going on by reading Barbara. "No, the girl Ryan met is Cora in disguise." She exclaimed. Meanwhile at the house as Ryan is lying in bed with "Karin" after sleeping with her. "Was that too fast? Ryan questioned. "I've waited long enough to get you into my bed." She replied she then smiles at Ryan as looks at her in confusion. "What?" Ryan said she then removed the necklace and changed back to Cora. "Cora?" Ryan replied in disbelief. "No." He added as he pulls away. "What were sisters, eventually we share everything." How could I have been so stupid?" Ryan questioned as he grabbed his clothes and gets dressed. "You're really going to just leave, after what we shared?" She asked. "I love you Ryan." She added. "You don't love me!" Ryan shouted. "You just wanted me because I loved Cara." He replied. "Admit it you felt something." She replied. "You know you did." She added. "You have no soul, you're just dark and callous." Ryan stated. "You can change me, like you did her." She replied. "You killed my wife, your sister I can never forgive you for that." Ryan answered. "I need to get out of here." Ryan stated as he headed out of room and to the door. He goes out and shuts it leans on it a moment and breathes. "I am so sorry Cara." He said then he goes. Now back on the base. "Where is he?" Dylan worries. "He is here." Amanda senses. "Something has happened." She replied. "Is he ok?" Dylan asked. "I'll go talk to him the rest of you, find her." He added as team headed out Ryan entered the control room with a look of disgust for himself and betrayal. "Dad I made the worst mistake of my life." Ryan replied. "What happened?" Dylan asked. "I met a woman Karin, or so I thought it was Cora in disguise dad." Ryan replied "I know, we caught Barbara just a few hours ago." Dylan informed. "No dad you don't understand. "He paused as he runs fingers threw his hair in frustration. "I felt something a connection to her, I slept with her dad before I knew it was Cora." He confessed Dylan is stunned. "I slept with Cora, the woman who killed my wife." Ryan sits in chair. "You didn't know it was her, how could you?" Dylan tried to reassure him. "I jumped into bed with the first woman I met dad." Ryan replied.

"Hey, no one here can judge especially me." Dylan answered. The others walk in Ryan rises and goes out of control room, Dylan goes to follow Jon stops him. "Let me talk to him?" Jon asked. Dylan nodded in agreement as Jon goes out after him to Dylan's quarters, he knocked and entered as Ryan sits devastated on the couch. "So everyone knows?" Ryan asked. "Look, I could write a book on sleeping with the wrong women." Jon replied. "Thanks." Ryan said. "I am just here to help." Jon added, meanwhile back at the control room. "She is in love with him." Amanda replied. "Great what about him?" Dylan asked. "He is confused, angry he needs time to sort it all out." She replied now back at Dylan's quarters Steven comes in. "Hey you ok?" He asked. "Not really no." Ryan replied. "I feel like it's my fault, I told you to go meet someone, to get out." Steven said. "I pushed you right into her bed." Steven added. "Hey, I make my own stupid mistakes ok." Ryan replied, meanwhile in the docking bay. "Its Ryan's choice he is an adult." Amanda replied. "Still, we are talking about Cora Babor here, she's insane." Ralph replied. "Hey, she is my sister." Cole said. "She also killed your other sister." Brent added. "I know, but deep down she regrets it." Cole replied. "Hey just look at my family, we never mean to hurt each other but we end up doing it." Keyes replied. "We need to just stay out of it." Amanda said just then Cora walked in. "Cora?" Jesse asked. "I'm here to turn myself in." She replied. Dylan comes in "You." Dylan replied. "She is turning herself in, sir." Jesse replied. "Then take her to a cell." Dylan commanded at that moment Ryan walked in. "Dad I." Ryan started to say then he stopped as he sees Cora being led away by security. "Why is she here?" Ryan questioned. "She surrendered." Dylan answered. "We should talk in private." Dylan said they go to Quarters. "I don't know why she did it." Dylan stated. "She just walked in?" Ryan asked. "Yes she did." Dylan answered. "I need to talk to her." Ryan replied. "No, I don't think that is a good idea." Dylan insisted. "I have to." Ryan replied. He goes out and heads to cell block Dylan follows him Amanda stops Dylan. "Let him do this." Amanda replied. "What is she up to?" Dylan demanded as Ryan enters cellblock and walks up to Cora in cell. Mark comes to him. "Ryan?" Mark asked. "Can I speak to her alone?" Ryan asked. "Are you sure?" Mark asked. "I'll be fine." Ryan said as Mark goes back to his post. "So you came to see me." Cora replied. "Why did you turn yourself in?' Ryan demanded. "It was the right thing to do." She replied. "It's time I tried it." She added. "Are you doing this for me?" Ryan asked. "Yes, I need to prove to you that, I love you." She stated meanwhile out in corridor. "You may not like what I tell you." Amanda replied. "Tell me anyway." Dylan said. "She loves him Dylan." She said As Dylan's face has a look of rejection and panic. "I'm sorry." She added. "Could it be a trick?" Dylan hoped. "No, she cannot hide her thoughts form me, she is not a telepath." Amanda answered. "Why did she fall for him?" Dylan asked. "He is an amazing, kind, good man." She said. "He gets that from his father." She added and smiled now back at the cell. "Why should I believe you?" Ryan asked. "You always lie." He added. "I know what I feel in my heart." She said. "I don't know what I feel right now." Ryan replied meanwhile in Jon's quarters "Ana?" He called out he sees a note on counter in kitchen. "Had to go into the city I'll be back soon love Ana." He read aloud Voltar then appeared. "Can we talk?" Voltar asked. "What is it now father?" Jon replied. "Can I not just check on my son?" He argued. "What are you up to?" Jon questioned, meanwhile at his castle "Alright when father returns we will discuss it." Rick insisted. "Where is our leader?" Volrin asked just then Voltar appeared. "I'm here." He stated. "Are we ready?" He asked. "The soldiers are, on your word father." Rick replied. "Then lets get back to business. Voltar demanded, meanwhile back on the base Jesse picks up multiple ships in the atmosphere. "Sir, I've got Voltarian cruisers traveling near multiple planets." He replied. "Where is Voltar's cruiser?' Dylan asked. "Its not among them sir?" Jesse said. "Their decoys have to be." Charlie insisted over com-link in his fighter with the others. "He is out here somewhere, we will find him as he signals Jon and Shane to follow him. "I should've known. Jon replied. "He keeps it interesting that's for sure." Shane added. "Lets find him fast." Charlie said well as my father attempted yet another take over of a newly found world Valtera, a world once thought a myth, it was hidden in a dimensional void until it was breeched by an explosion. It is where we discovered the existence of Derin my brother, whom we thought died as a small baby. We would also bring into the family Dylan's other brother Austin who unfortunately, caught the eye of a newly reborn Montra. That is not even the worst of it. We would loose a very brave yet vengeful girl named Rebecca who we tried to save. She went after a race of creatures she blamed for her parents death. We are still trying to protect Ryan from falling into Cora's deadly web, not to mention Barbara from trying to kidnap Cole. Now as months have gone by in control room. Dylan is at the main console watching the activity on the screen. Ryan entered. "Did you talk to the warden, about early release for Cora?" Ryan asked. "He said he would consider her good behavior." Dylan replied. "Thanks dad." Ryan said. "Are you going to see her?" Dylan asked. "Yes, but I'm going to take it slow." Ryan insisted. "I hope for your sake, she can change." Dylan replied meanwhile in sickbay as Paul is reviewing charts Anilla enters with a look of concern. "Paul I need you to run a blood test." She asked. "What's wrong?" He said as he looked up. "I think I may be pregnant." She smiled. Paul jumps to his feet in excitement. "Ok." He said. "I want to be sure before I tell Shane." She gleamed. "Of course." He said as he took a vile of her blood. "Don't say a word." She begged he agreed then she left as Paul is labeling vile Jenna also came in. "Paul I need a favor." She replied. "Are you ok?" He asked. "I think I'm pregnant." She exclaimed. Paul is in shock as his eyes widened with jaw dropped. "That's wonderful." He replied, "I need you to confirm, before I tell Charlie." She said. "Of course I'll draw some blood." He said now after he does. "I'll be back later and Paul don't tell anyone." She added then she goes out now a few moments late Leeah entered as Paul was putting up tubes. "Can I help you Leeah?" He asked. "I need to know if I'm pregnant." She replied Paul almost dropped his equipment in astonishment. "Are you ok?" She asked. "I'm fine, let's draw some blood." He said now after she asked him to keep it quiet. "Is there something in the water?" Paul wondered as he said that Steven came in. "Talking to yourself again Paul?" He joked. "I've just been busy this morning." Paul answered. "Is anyone sick?" Steven asked. "Not today I hope." Paul replied. "Ok, see you later." Steven goes he notices Paul smiling as he takes vials to the lab. "What is up?" Steven questioned, Meanwhile in the Rec Room. "Anyone seen my wife?" Charlie asked as Shane looks up from lifting weights. "No, but I'm looking for mine too." Shane replied then Keyes walked in. "Hey anyone seen Leeah?" He asked. "Is this too weird?" Charlie added. Meanwhile back at sickbay Paul has all three ladies together. "Jenna are you sick?" Anilla asked. "No are you ok?" Jenna responded. "What is going on?" Leeah said. Paul comes in with results "Well ladies, it would seem your all here for the same reason." Paul informed as they all look at each other in joy and surprise at that moment Steven was walking into the Rec Room, as the guys were still confused. "Have you seen our wives?" Charlie asked. "Yeah they are all in sickbay with Paul." He said the guys in a panic race out and to the sickbay. "I hope they are ok." Charlie replied. "Why are they all there?" Keyes questioned they all entered just in time to hear Paul say. "Congratulations, you are all pregnant." Paul said. The guys stand in shock and amazement. "A baby?" Charlie said and then fainted. Jenna rushed to him. "I'm going to need more beds." Paul replied with a laugh. "I'll get the smelling salts." He added. "I'm going to be a father?" Shane got woozy. Anilla sat him on bed. "Your ok." She said. "Whoa were gonna be parents?" Keyes replied. "I can't wait!" Steven shouted.

Chapter 13

SO MANY BABIES
SO LITTLE TIME

As our journey moves forward, we have faced many hardships. The lost of too many friends and loved ones, but we have kept our team, our family strong and united. This time is no different. Now we have babies coming, the future just might be what heals our entire family, or will it be a past love who will make my father see the light? Scene in the sickbay; Charlie starts to wake up on the floor of sickbay with Jenna kneeling over him. "Charlie are you alright?" She asked. "I am going to need a bigger sickbay." Paul replied. Now later all of the team gathered in the control room for the big news. "What's going on?" Jon asked. "I have no clue." Dylan answered. "We wanted all of you to be together for this." Charlie replied. "Is everyone ok?" Xavier asked? "Better than that, we are expecting a baby." Charlie informed, as he smiled. "That's great." Dylan said. "More than one." Shane replied. "Yes, we make three." Keyes added. Everyone is overjoyed and excited. "Well somebody needs to enforce the curfew around here." Ralph joked, as they all laugh. They each congratulated them. "How are we going to tell father? Jon asked. "Don't forget Rick, or should I say grandpa." Shane replied. "This calls for a celebration." Dylan insisted. Meanwhile at the castle as Voltar entered his throne room or A.K.A command center. "Junior just sent me a message, to come to the base." Voltar said. "I will stay and hold down the fort." Volrin volunteered. "Is everything ok?" Rick asked. "We will find out soon enough." Voltar replied. Now at the base in control room, Jesse sees on camera outside they have arrived. "Their here!" Jesse called. Jon goes out to docking bay doors and opens them. "What is it?" Voltar questioned. "Relax, it is good news." Jon insured. They go to briefing room. "Have a seat." Jon said. "Its something we need to sit for?" Rick questioned. "I would suggest you do." Jon replied. They sit in chairs by table when Charlie, Keyes and Shane enter the room. "Well, you are about to get an addition to the Aster clan." Charlie replied as they all smiled. "Son a baby?" Rick exclaimed. "Actually two." Keyes informed. Rick's eyes widened in stun and astonishment. "Both of you?" He asked. "This is good news." Voltar replied. "Glad you think so cause there are three." Shane replied. "You have been busy around here." Rick said. "This is a cause for celebration." Voltar chimed in. "No going overboard father." Jon insisted. "Me?" Votlar said innocently. "I know how you get." Jon stated. "A quiet family gathering, here with friends." Shane replied. "Fine, have it your way." Voltar said. Meanwhile back at the control room. "This is so exciting." Lisette said. "I've seen pregnant women, they are moody, hungry, and horny." Jesse informed as Lisette laughed. Now later that night in Shane's quarter he is in bed with Anilla. "So, I guess we will need a bigger place." Shane said, "We have plenty of time." Anilla said. "Its good to plan ahead." Shane replied as he touched her cheek. "You think your family can behave?" She asked "Of course...not." He said. Meanwhile over in Charlie's quarters, Jenna is staring at her stomach in the mirror in their bathroom. "I'm going to be huge." She dreaded. Charlie comes in and hugged her from behind. "Yes, but you will be cute." Charlie replied. "Will you still love me, when I am a whale?" She asked. He let a laugh. "Of course, I loved Moby Dick." He said as they both laughed. Meanwhile, over in Keyes bedroom. "Are you comfortable?" He asked as he fluffed up her pillows. "Will you relax, I'm the one who is suppose to be nervous." She stated. "Sorry do you need anything?" He asked. "No, just you here with me." She said she kissed him. Meanwhile Jon is training Devon, and Marie is watching also my daughter Vala, it is a long story a beautiful woman and a one-night stand. Now I have six-year-old daughter. "So, where do babies come form?" Marie asked "Mommy's tummy. Jon replied. "How did they get there?" Vala asked. "Careful on that one." Devon warned. "Lets finish training." Jon said. "Nice save." Devon replied. Meanwhile, at the docking bay Cora arrived.

"Sir, Cora Babor is here." Mark said over com-link. "Its alright, she has been released for good behavior." Dylan replied. "Inform my son." He added. "Yes sir." Mark responded. Now in the mess hall, Cora entered as Ryan was waiting there. "Hi." She said. "Hi, are you ok." Ryan asked. "Yes, I need to thank your father for speaking to the parole board." Cora replied. "I already did." Ryan stated. "So any plans." He asked. "I have a job lined up, not glamorous." "I'm working for an auto repair shop in town." "I was always good with my hands." She replied. "I hope you turn your life around." Ryan said. "I hope I still have a chance, with you?" She replied. Meanwhile back at Voltar's castle, he is sitting on throne reading baby name books. Rick is on the vidlink speaking to designers for clothes. "This is pathetic, we might as well retire." Volrin stated. "It looks like a baby store and not an evil lair." Volrin added. "Do be quiet Volrin." Voltar replied. "So what do you think of Voltran?" Voltar said. "Sounds good." Rick replied as he is looking at outfits. "I think the red robes say future ruler of the galaxy, yes?" Rick asked. "I will tend to business, as it appears you two have better things to do." Volrin bitched. Volrin stormed out. Now back on the base in the mess hall, Charlie, Keyes and Shane are carrying trays full of food. "You guys miss lunch?" Ralph asked. "No, this is for our wives." Charlie stated. "I have never seen her eat so much." Keyes confessed. "I'm afraid she will eat me, in my sleep." Charlie replied. "Guys, they are eating for two." Amanda reminds. "Two what, Qual beats?" Shane asked. "Only if your kids look like the Aster side." Ralph joked. Jon walks over to the table with Jenna, Anilla and Leeah. "How are our expected mother's doing?" He asked. "My back hurts." Jenna complained. "I feel bloated." Anilla gripes. "My feet are killing me." Leeah moaned. "Ok, I will just walk away now." Jon excuses himself as he goes. Now over at another table. "Poor guys." Cole said. "Yeah look at them, they look tired." Jesse added. "They have it easy." Lisette argued. "Yeah, women do all the work." Amanda stated. "Must be hard work, to complain and demand food all day." Ralph replied. "Shut up you fool, you try carrying a baby inside of you for nine months." Cheryl stated. "Hey, I saw a new vest out that can simulate carrying a baby for the dad." Steven informed. "Sounds like a good idea." Cheryl replied. "You guys think you can handle it?" Lisette asked. "Bring it on." Jesse stated. Now in the sickbay Jesse, Ralph and Cole turn around to reveal the Vest, it has a huge belly and breasts. "So how do you feel?" Lisette asked. "I am loving the breast part." Ralph stated as he touches them "Its fine." Jesse added. "So, we will just take them off now." Cole said. "Oh no, you guys get to wear them for a whole week." Amanda replied. "Say what?" Ralph replied. "A week?" Jesse asked. "We have patrols." Cole stated. "Don't worry, we spoke to Dylan he approved your time off." Amanda replied as Dylan entered. "Anything I can do to help." Dylan said. "We can handle this." Ralph confirmed. Now 2 days later in the Rec Room. "Ok, help me get it off." Ralph begged. "My back is killing me." Cole exclaimed. "This belly is pressing on my bladder." "I had to go to the bathroom six times, since breakfast." Jesse stated. "Hey, we cannot let them know we are hurting." Ralph replied. "I am hurting, last night I got in bed and almost couldn't get out." Cole said. "How do they stand it?" Jesse asked. "Come on we are men, we have been in gun fights." "We can do this." Ralph insisted, and then the girls come in. "So, how is it going boys?" Cheryl asked. Ralph smiles. "I feel good." He said. "We will see you later then." Lisette stated. "Are you ready to admit it?" Cheryl asked. "Never." Ralph said sternly. Now the next day, all three of them looking sleep deprived and in pain are on there knees begging. "Ok we admit it, you women are amazing." Ralph stated. "You deserve a metal." Jesse added. "Can we please, take them off now?" Cole pleads. "I think they suffered enough ladies." Cheryl said. "Yeah, you do look pathetic." Lisette added, meanwhile at the castle in the throne room. "So, is all right in the land of the goody goodies?" Volrin asked. "Go fall off the edge of the planet." Rick said. "We need to focus on evil, there are people out there ready to pounce." They could overthrow us." He added. "You are on the top of the list uncle." Rick replied. "Stop your bickering" Voltar commanded, meanwhile in the city at a run down apt building. Ryan comes up to a door and rings the doorbell. Cora opened it. "Hey you came, it's not great but it's livable." Cora replied as he comes in. "You forget, I lived on the streets." Ryan stated. "I can appreciate anything with four walls and a roof. He added he sits on couch in living room. "Dinner will be ready soon." She said. "So, how is everyone?" She asked as she checked oven in small kitchen "Well, its crazy hormonal town with all the babies coming." Ryan said. "Never a dull moment." She said "Its why I stayed, I love the vibe there." Ryan added. "That rush of adrenalin." He said. She comes with two beers and sits beside him on couch. She leaned in and kissed him as he kissed her back, Cora pulls back. "Are you sure?" She asked. "I'm a McKay, I'm never sure but I know what I want right now." He stated as he takes her head in his hands and goes in for a kiss. Meanwhile standing just outside of the building, a creature named Grelt with a large eye atop his head and sharp teeth that putrid out of the middle of his face, and a dark blue color all over his scaly body. "So, think you can take the straight path do you?" He said. "It will cost you my dear girl. He added as he slithered away, meanwhile at the castle. "I have a plan." Voltar replies. "Yes!" Volrin yelled in enthusiasm. "If, we choose yellow drapes that would be neutral and perfect." Voltar said. Volrin's mouth dropped in shock and disappointment, as he realizes his brother has grown soft over all the new babies to come. "Are you kidding me?" Volrin asked. "What?" "Perhaps we should go with green?" Voltar questioned. "Look at you, your support to be a cut throat ruler, yet your standing here planning a baby shower?" Volrin stated. "I once admired you." Volrin replied in shame. "Hey, we are always planning for this galaxy." Rick stated. "Yes, until you are derailed by pacifiers and pampers." Volrin replied. "Call me, when you're ready to kill something." He added as he walked out. "He is right, we need to gather plans for domination of this galaxy, if nothing else to secure the future clan." Voltar stated. "Tell Kravitz I expect weapons and creatures by the morning." Voltar commanded. Meanwhile back at Cora's apt, things have definitely gone to the next level. As we see Ryan lying in bed with Cora. "Are you having any regrets?" She asked. "No, I'm fine are you ok?" Ryan asked. "I am perfect." She replied as they kissed. "What if I screw up?" She said. "I'm here, to make sure you don't." Ryan replied with a smile then his com-link goes off by his clothes. "Sorry." Ryan said as he grabbed it and checked it. "Its fine, I have to be to work in a few hours." Cora stated as she got up and puts on robe Ryan gets dressed. "I will call you tonight." He promised, as they are now at doorway and he kisses her lips then he goes out. After a few moments Grelt comes to her door and knocks, Cora still in her robe opened door thinking it was Ryan. "Did you forget something?" She said then sees Grelt. "How did you get out of prison?" Grelt asked, Cora replies, "Good behavior." "What do you want Grelt?" she demanded. "So, interested in some action?" Grelt asks. "No, I'm legit now." She responded, "So, you go soft for an alliance officer?" He inquired. "I'm done with that life." She stated. "Perhaps you just need some inspiration." "I'll be in touch." He said as he slithers away leaving behind a trail of slime deposit, as she shuts the door. Now back on the base, in the Control Room, Ryan entered, Jesse turned to him, "Hey, where were you?" he asked. "I was with Cora." Ryan said. Dylan then comes out of his office; "Hey, I have an assignment for you." "Some illegal activity on Saturn." He said. "I'm on it." Ryan replied. He heads to the docking bay and then flies in a fighter to Saturn. He landed near the location and exited the fighter. "I'm going to check it out." He says over the com-link to Jesse. As he goes to the abandoned building, he hears a sudden noise and draws his weapon, "Galactic Alliance!" he yells. Grelt slithers out hands raised in the air, "Don't shoot!" he pleads. "Grelt?" Ryan said, as he recognized him. "When did you get out?" he asked. Grelt uses his magnetic ability to pull his weapon to him. "I have friends in low places." He stated, "Seems you have friends too." He adds. "Excuse me?" Ryan asked. "Always the gentlemen, even when you were on the streets." Grelt replied. "What's your game?" Ryan demanded. "Simple, You're in my way." "I need Cora's expertise, She's gone soft, then again you McKay's were always ladies' men." Grelt stated, "She won't help you." Ryan said. "I think she will, especially when I take her reason for not!" Grelt said. Ryan looks at him in confusion. "Dear naïve Ryan, I eliminate the distraction." He then pulls out his own weapon, aims it at him and says, "You, Nothing personal but she was mine first." "So, you can understand my problem." "You already cost me Cara, I can't lose my other twin." He stated. "You bastard!" Ryan exclaimed. "You, made her fall in love." He informed. "The heart is useless, in our line of work." He stated. "If you leave her, I won't kill you." Grelt offered. "Go to hell!" Ryan said sternly. "Been there and back boy." He boasts. "I can ruin so many lives, with your death." He implied. "Your father, Cora, and your friends!" "You would be so missed." He snickered. "My father will hunt you down!" He confirmed. "So would Cora." Ryan added. "Yes, That's why I won't kill you, but it will hurt a lot." He replied. "I miss the good old days, when you used to be one of us, a rebel." "Such a waste." He recalls. Then, he uses his long grotesque tongue to grab hold of him and slam him against the far wall, knocking him out. "I will get Cora." Then he goes. Meanwhile back at the control room, Dylan is at the main console, "Has Ryan checked in yet?" Dylan asked Jesse. "No, not since he landed sir." Jesse answered. Then Charlie enters, "Is there a problem?" he asked. "I don't know." Dylan responded. Just then a message appeared across the vid link. "Sir incoming!" Jess exclaimed then he puts it on the main screen; it is Grelt in all his hideous glory. "Greetings captain McKay!" "Grelt, how did you escape?" Dylan questioned. "All, will be explained, first a deal." Grelt said. "No deals you scum!" Dylan replied. "Oh, I beg to differ captain." As he moves to the side to reveal Ryan, tied to a pole while bloody and beaten. "Care to reconsider?" he stated. "Ryan. If you." Dylan threatens. Grelt interrupts, "Save it." "I don't want him, I want Cora." Grelt proposed. "It's your chance to be free of her." He added. "Tell her to work for me, and he lives." He concludes. Dylan responds, "You just signed your death warrant." "No I don't think so." He disclosed. "Mess with me, and you sign his." Grelt declares. He then cuts off communication. "Sir, I lost it." Jesse apologized. "Get me Cora." Dylan demands. "We'll get him back safe." Charlie assures. "I should've seen this, with Cora there's trouble." Dylan realized. He then notices Cole, "I'm sorry, I am just frustrated." Dylan replied. "I know, Cora will help she won't let anything happen to him." Cole replied. "None of us will." Cole adds. Now later Cora is in the Control Room, "I will do whatever you want." Cora swore. "I just want you to distract him, so we can find Ryan." Dylan stated. "I am sorry." Cora replied, "So am I." Dylan said, and then he walked away. Steven comes to Cora, "He'll be okay." He assured. Meanwhile back on Saturn, Ryan begins to come around. He opens his right eye, as his left is closed from swelling and has blood emanating from his nose, lip, and gash on his forehead. "So, you're awake?" Grelt said, "I'm just waiting, for your girlfriend to agree to your terms." He added with a sense of confidence. "You won't get away with it." Ryan mutters. Grelt hits him across the right cheek with closed fist, "shut up!" he shouted. "You got yourself into this mess." He recapped. "You should've just stayed away." He implied, as he punched him on the left side of the torso, "You're a McKay!" "Do you always have get the girl!" he barked. "You never will." He faintly replied. Grelt punches him in the face again. "Keep up that smart mouth, and I'll kill you for real!" he promised. Meanwhile in the Control Room, Dylan is with Cora and Jesse, "Send out the signal!" Dylan ordered. Jesse does as Grelt responds, "So, where is my favorite girl?" he asked. Cora moves forward, "I'm here, where is Ryan?" she asks. Grelt moves to reveal him tied up, "So, ready to meet?" he asked. "Where?" Cora replied as she held back her anger and fear. "Our old hangout, no alliance or he's dead!" he said as he cut off communication. "Let me handle it." Cora says, "Like hell I will!" Dylan shouts. "He's my son, I'm not gonna sit here!" Dylan demanded. "Let her go Dylan, we'll be back up!" Charlie replied. "He's right dad." Steven chimed in. "Fine, but if you get my son killed, back to prison." Dylan said firmly. "Okay let's move out!" Charlie ordered, "Steven, you stay with your dad." He added. "I will." Steven replied as the team goes. Little did we know Dylan was deciding Ryan's fate, just like my father attempted with me, to choose between Cora and him. Meanwhile on Saturn, "Cora, you go around back, we'll cover you." Charlie instructed. "Be careful." Charlie adds. Cora nods her head in agreement as she heads inside. Jesse tracks her on his handheld device, "I'll try to find Ryan!" Jesse says. "Good you and Ralph follow the signal, Xavier and I will go cover Cora." Charlie orders. "Cole and Amanda say out front." Charlie concludes, as Cora makes her way into the old bar. Grelt sits in chair at middle table, "This used to be a popular club for us." He reminisced. "Save your reminiscing, where is Ryan?" she demands. "Nearby, now to discuss our plans." He insisted. "You let Ryan go first, then we'll talk." Cora ordered. Meanwhile Jesse and Ralph got a lock on Ryan's com-link signal, which is imbedded, in all of their jackets. They arrive at an old house near by. "He's in here." Jesse said. "Figures, always the crappiest place you look." Ralph said. They draw weapons as they walk inside, to see run-down walls; cobwebs draped everywhere, old rundown furniture as they call out for Ryan. "Come on, I hate the smell of pee!" Ralph added. Jesse scanned, "This way!" he says, as they come up on a room that is empty. Only Ryan is there tied to a single pole in the center. As Jesse goes towards him, Ralph stopped him, "Hold on, it's too easy." Ralph grasped. "Got to be booby-trapped!" Ralph said. Jesse scans and picks up a device just beneath the floor, "You're right!" he said. "Hang on man!" Ralph said. Ryan opened his eyes, "Ralph?" he asked. "I'll disarm it!" Jesse says, as he uses his device to figure it out and he disarms the device. "Got it!" he said as Ralph goes to Ryan and unties him, "Well, you look horrible!" he says. "Where is Grelt?" Ryan asked as Ralph helps him out of the room. "Cora is taking care of him!" Ralph said. "We need to get to her!" Ryan insists barely able to stand on his own. "Charlie has her back, you are checking in to Hotel Sickbay, you know it well!" Ralph informed. "Yes, been there lousy food!"

Ryan said. "But Paul's face, is so cute!" Ralph added sarcastically as they get to the ship. Meanwhile at the bar, Jesse contacted Charlie to let him know that Ryan is safe. "Ryan is okay." Charlie said. "I will let everyone else know." Xavier replied. "Let's get Cora!" Charlie added. Meanwhile inside, "So are you in?" Grelt asked, as Charlie and Xavier enter. "Of course, not you second rate hood!" Cora says as she shoots him in the leg. Grelt says, "Then he dies!" he says pushing the detonation button, but nothing explodes. "No!!" he shouts. "You had backup!" he realized. "Unlike you, I have friends not toys to keep me company!" Cora replies. Charlie cuffs Grelt. "Time to go this time for good!" Charlie says. Now back on base in Sickbay, Paul is stitching the cut above Ryan's eye, as he is flinching. "Relax, I'm almost done." He said. Dylan and Steven enter, "He's okay." Paul confirms. "Thank god!" Dylan replied as Steven hugged him. "I'm fine, Is Cora okay?" Ryan asked, as Steven let go, "Yeah, Grelt is going away forever." Steven said. "Paul, Steven give us a moment please." Dylan asked. They both go out. "Don't say it." Ryan said. "Say what?" Dylan asked. "You've got that look, of father authority in your eyes." Ryan stated. "She is dangerous to you." Dylan insisted. "So, is everyone on this base!" Ryan reminded. "You are just using Cora, as a replacement for your dead wife!" Dylan exclaimed. "That's a low blow!" Ryan said coldly. "I won't stand here, and allow you to be a target for her old associates, and there will be others." Dylan stated. "My whole life has been risks dad, I'll be fine!" Ryan insists. "No you were lucky, luck runs out I know." Dylan replied. "She is not worth it son." Dylan said. "I won't give her up!" Ryan declared. Then Cora enters, they both look at her, "Ryan?" she said. "Make a choice son, I won't stand by and watch her get you killed!" Dylan said as he walked out. "What's going on?" Cora asked. She comes to his bedside. "I'll handle it." Ryan said as she hugs him. Meanwhile Dylan goes into the Control Room, into his office and slams the door. "Sounds like trouble." Lisette says. Steven goes into his office. "Dad are you okay?" he asked. "No, your brother insists on throwing his life away!" Dylan says. "He's not doing that dad, Cora makes him happy." Steven says. "They both need each other." Steven understands. "No. He doesn't need her." Dylan insists. Cole hears conversation and comes in, "My sister has changed Dylan, you of all people should understand, what its like to love the "wrong woman." Cole reminds. Then he walks out. "He's right dad, mom was no saint." Steven repeated. "I had to learn the hard way, that it doesn't work out." Dylan said. "It's his choice, not ours." Steven replied. Meanwhile in Sickbay, Cora and Ryan are kissing. "I was so scared." She said. "Me too." Ryan replied. "I'm sorry, my past is the problem." Cora added. "It's okay, it's over." As he caresses her cheek, "Until the next threat!" Cora admitted. "Hey, let's not think like that!" Ryan said. "We need to, your dad does." Cora replied. "I'll handle my dad." Ryan said. "You two just got your relationship on track, I don't want to ruin that." Cora replied. "I love my father, and I love you, he has to understand that." Ryan declared. Cole entered and said, "Hey are you okay?" "I will be." Ryan said as he noticed Cole is upset, "Did something happen?" Ryan asked. "Your dad is just angry" Cole replies." He is blaming Cora, for what happened." Cole explained. "I'm sorry, you're in the middle of it." Ryan said. "I'll be fine." Cole replied. "I don't want to destroy your family Ryan." Cora insists. "You won't, he'll come around once he's cooled off." Ryan assures. Just then two Galactic Alliance officers enter, "Cora Babor." One of them said, "Yes." She said. "I'm afraid you must come with us." He added. "What, no!" Ryan exclaimed. "Ryan don't." Cora said as they cuff her. "Where is my father?" Ryan demands. "His orders, your early release has been revoked I'm sorry." The officer said. "How can he do this?" Cole says. "I'm going to find out!" Ryan says as he tries to get up, but is too weak and sits down as the officers take Cora off the base. Paul comes out of his office, "Hey no moving, you need to heal!" Paul insisted. "No, I need to see my father now!" He tries to get up but falls out of bed and onto the floor. "Damn it!" He muttered. Paul helps him up onto bed, "I'll get him." Paul said. "No, I will." Cole said as he goes and heads into Control Room. Dylan is going over assignments. "Okay now today's mission...." He said. Cole storms in. "How could you!" Cole demands. "I'd expect that kind of act from Voltar Aster not you!" he said angrily. "What's going on?" Amanda asks. "Dad?" Steven questioned. "Your father revoked Cora's release." Cole informed. "They arrested her in front of me and Ryan in Sickbay!" he finished. "Dylan you didn't!" Charlie said. "I did, it was my word that released her, and so I can recant it." Dylan said. "Dad, how could you do that to him?" Steven questioned as he stormed out. Others followed. "Cole is right, that is something my father would pull not you!" Jon said. "I had to Jon, he is not safe with her." Dylan explained. "Even if he hates me he will be alive to do so." Dylan stated.

"This is not the way Dylan." Jon insisted. "It's the only way." Dylan says. Jon goes. Paul calls to Dylan on the com-link, "Ryan wants to see you now." Paul replied. Meanwhile in Sickbay, Steven enters. "Ryan, I am so sorry." He comes up and hugs him, "Are you okay?" he added. "I guess you heard." Ryan said as Steven let's go. "If I would have known…" Steven said. "Don't worry." Ryan ensures. Just then Dylan enters, Ryan gives him a cold stare. "I won't apologize for protecting you." Dylan explained. "Protecting me?" Ryan said in anger. "You sent the woman I love to prison!" he said in anger. "I had to, She brings danger every moment she's with you." Dylan explained. "How dare you?" Ryan replied. "You're judging her after your affair with Valtra Aster?" Ryan recapped. "I thought you, of all people would understand us!" Ryan said. "I do, that's why I sent her away." Dylan conveys." It always ends with one or both of you dead." Dylan said. "You have to release her." Ryan begs. "My decision is final." Dylan said as he goes to the doors. "I will never forgive you for this." Dramatic pause. "Ever!" he shouted as Dylan goes out. Ryan throws cup near by. "Damn it!" he said. Meanwhile back in Dylan's office, Steven is there waiting. Dylan enters. "Dad you have to let her go!" Steven insisted. "This is closed Steven." He said. "No!" he shouts, "You're going to make him leave again!" he continued. "If he does, at least he'll be safe." Dylan said. "Do you hear yourself?" Steven questions. "He loves her, you can't just stop that!" Steven exclaimed. "I've done the right thing." Dylan explains. "This is about you and mom isn't it?" Steven asked. "Stay out of it." Dylan insists. "No, I'm in it." Steven replied. "I won't let Ryan turn into you, a bitter man!" Steven shouted and he goes out. Meanwhile in the Rec Room, Amanda is with Cole. "I'm so sorry." She said putting her hand on his shoulder." "I still, can't believe he did it." Cole said. Charlie and Shane are also present, "None of us can." Charlie said. "He thinks he is doing the right thing." Shane said. Then Jon enters, "No he is not." Jon states. "He's doing what our father does, trying to control our fates." He adds. "He can not play god." Jon concludes. Meanwhile back in Sickbay, Ryan is again attempting to get out of bed, but he stops and lies back down in pain. Paul comes over, "You are asking for internal bleeding." He said. "I have to get out of here." Ryan says. "Not in your condition." Paul charges. "Now If I have to, I will sedate you!" Paul informed. "Fine." Ryan accepted. "Do you agree with my father?" Ryan asked. "No, I don't but I understand his motives." Paul said. "Then please explain them to me." Ryan replies. "He does not want you in danger." Paul said. "I'm not." Ryan insists. "Yes you are!" Paul said sternly as he looked away for a moment as Ryan noticed. "Why?" Ryan asked. "I can't discuss it." Paul says as he goes to leave, Ryan grabs his arm. "You're hiding something, I can see it." Ryan grasped. "There is more to this then just Cora." Ryan replied. "I've said enough." Paul said. "You haven't said anything." Ryan said, "Tell me." He stresses. "If I tell you, it will destroy everything your father and I tried to protect you from." Paul said. "Tell me Paul." Ryan demands, "This is about my life." He added. "I promised your mother as well." Paul said. "What does she have to do with this?" Ryan asked. "Alright fine." Paul closes the outer doors. "Your father only ever loved one woman." Paul replied. "She was his life, his everything." Paul said. "This is about Valtra, Steven's mother." Ryan complained. "I get it he loved her, he'll love her forever." Ryan moaned. . "She, is your mother too Ryan." Paul said. "What?" Ryan said as he tried to process it. "What are you saying about Paul?" Ryan asked. "It's the truth. Valtra is your mother." Paul stated. "No, I don't get it, Lorna was my mother, and she raised me." Ryan insisted. "She raised you, to keep the secret of your birth." Paul clarifies. "Valtra was afraid of Voltar finding out." He continues. "They were both too young then, don't you get it?" Paul replied. "You're the first born, of the first-born Aster." Paul adds. "That makes you, next in line to Voltar's throne." Paul explained. Ryan has a look of confusion as well as fear. "Where's my father?" Ryan demanded. "I'll get him." Paul goes to his office as Ryan is still stunned by the confession. Paul calls over com-link. "Dylan you need to get down here." Paul insisted. "What is it?" "Is Ryan alright?" Dylan asked. "The secret is out." Paul replied. As Dylan understands what he means, his eyes widened as he rushes to Sickbay in a panic. "Paul!" Dylan calls out as he comes to Ryan. "Is Valtra my mother?" Ryan asked. Dylan looks to Paul as he comes in, "Why did you tell him?" Dylan asked. "Talk to me dad." Ryan asserted. "Paul leave us." Ryan said. Paul goes out. "Answer the question." Ryan said. "We should talk, when you're better." Dylan said. "She is my mother." Ryan comprehended. Dylan sits beside him on bed. "How could you not tell me?" Ryan asked, "Why the secrets?" he added. "The time was different, your mother still served Voltar." He explains. "We were only sixteen, Paul was barely a medical student when he delivered you." Dylan recalls. "We had to hide you, if Voltar found out he would have killed me and taken you." Dylan explained. "Why not, tell me when I was older?" Ryan asked. "You were young and angry all the time, I was afraid you would join Voltar if you knew." Dylan said. "Did Valtra ever see me?" Ryan asked. "Of course, many times until she got sick." Dylan said as he takes Ryan's hand. "I couldn't tell anyone especially when you left." Dylan confessed. "Voltar would've hunted for you." Dylan said. "So you were protecting me?" Ryan said. "Cora is not a danger to me." Ryan said. "You are Voltar's first grandchild, I promised your mother I would keep you out of his world." Dylan said. "I want you to release Cora." Ryan demanded. "Ryan it's not that…" he says as Ryan cuts him off. "I'll go to Voltar then." "No, you are safe as long as he doesn't know who you are." Dylan pleads. "Steven is already in enough danger." Dylan says. Just then Steven enters. "What's going on?" Steven asked. "Go back to the Control Room." Dylan ordered. "He has a right to know." Ryan said. "Know what?" Steven asked. "Dad's been lying for years." Ryan explained. "Ryan, don't." Dylan said. "About what?" Steven says. "My mother." Ryan said. "What about her?" Steven asked. "Valtra is my mother." Ryan said. "What?" Steven is stunned, "Dad?" he asked. "Yes, it's true." Dylan confessed. "Why didn't you tell me, us?" Steven asked. "I was trying to protect you both." Dylan explained. "Voltar didn't know about Ryan, if I had my way he would not have known about you." Dylan said. "We had no authority over Voltara, we still don't." Dylan said. Steven sits on the other side of the bed. "This is, wow!" he said. "Tell me about it." Ryan replied. "No one else can know." Dylan insisted. "What about Jon and Charlie, The team their family?" Steven replied. "Voltar will find out, we can't risk it." Dylan said. "We may have to." Paul said.

Chapter 14

FIRST BORN

There are rules for many things, rules of engagement rules of love. For Asters, there are rules for firstborns no matter what. As my family has passed on rule from my great, great grandfather to his first born to his. Valtra is Voltar's first born; she would have inherited his empire. The rule of Voltara but she fell ill and died. With only one son too young to rule, at least until now as we discover she had another son. A young man strong willed and every bit an Aster as he is a human. Ryan is about to discover abilities he has not unlocked, power like his mother, but that will come later. First we must deal with my father, Scene back in sickbay. "What do you mean?" Dylan asked. "We will need to test him for Volvans, it is inherited, its what Valtra died from." Paul informed. "Only his scientists can test for it." Paul added. "I'm fine, I've never been sick." Ryan insisted. "It lies dormant for years." Paul explained. "We could say the test is for me?" Steven suggested. "Sorry son but Voltar had you tested as a baby." Dylan replied. "I think this is Ryan's decision." Paul said. "I don't want Voltar Aster in my life." Ryan stated. "I will make a deal, I'll release Cora just stay clear of Voltar, and he has ways of telling that you're related." Dylan replied. "What if, I show any signs of this Volvans later on?" Ryan asked. "I'll deal with it." Dylan insisted. "No, you've been dealing with my whole life." Ryan replies. "I will deal with it." Ryan informed. Meanwhile back in the control room Dylan comes up to Cole. "Cole I need to apologize." Dylan said. "Its ok, I get it." Cole replied as they shake hands. Cora comes back to sickbay after Dylan releases her. "Ryan!" She exclaimed as she hugs him then they kiss. "What happened?" She asked. "I have something to tell you." Ryan said. "This will change everything in our life." Ryan added. "Are you sick?" Cora fears. "No, at least not that I know of." Ryan assured. "I may have to be tested eventually." He added. "What is going on?" Cora asked. "My father lied about my mother." Ryan began. "Valtra Aster is my mother." He stated. "Valtra Aster?" Cora says in disbelief. "So the A as your middle initial, the one you didn't know what it was for is for Aster?" She replied. "Yes it is, my mother wanted me to know who I was eventually." Ryan said. "Voltar never needs to know about you." Cora insisted. "You sound like my dad." Ryan replied. "It would put you in too much danger, you have enough with me." She added as she touches his cheek. "If Voltar ever knew about you, he would take you from me from all of us." She informed. "I am nineteen, he can't do that." Ryan insisted. "I will need to be tested for Volvans at some point." Ryan said as he yawns form fatigue. "You, need to rest I will be back." She said as she kissed his lips and he lied back and fell asleep. He has a dream he is standing at a large crypt with title of Aster written across the top he sees where Valtra is buried along side countless others of the Aster clan. "I wish, I could have known you." Ryan said. "I guess I know, where I got that anger and rebellion streak from." He added just then Valtra's spirit appeared before him. "Hello my son." She replied. "How are you, even here?" He asked. "I am an Aster, even in death I can still watch over both my sons, as I always have in life." She replied. "You are so the image of your father." She added. "Do not blame him, I asked him to lie." She stated. "You, are a good strong man like your father, not to mention his way with the ladies." She smiled. "That what you loved about him?" Ryan asked. "When your father and I met, it was on the battlefield." "He was my prisoner but I could tell he was special, for a human." She said. "He broke through my cold heart, to fall in love with me and I with him." She added. "He and I did what we had to, to protect you." She stated as she touched his cheek. "I only wish, I could've seen you married." She sighed. "So do I." Ryan said. "I will always be with you." She added. "You did get one thing from me, my eyes good thing my father never looked too deeply into them, he would've figured it out." She replied. "I must go." She says as she vanished. "Good-bye mother." Ryan replied just then Voltar appeared to him, as Ryan was startled. "Why are you here McKay?" "Voltar demanded. Ryan's eyes full of fear and fright he begins to toss and turn in his sleep as Cora comes back in "Ryan?" She said. "Watch yourself boy." Voltar stated Cora shakes him and he jumps awake as he gasped for breath. "Are you ok?" She asked. "Yes, I'm fine." Ryan said as he calmed down. Meanwhile Dylan is in his quarters remembering when he and Valtra first met. They are sixteen and on Voltara after a great battle. She takes him to a secret chamber beneath the castle. "Why did you bring me here?" Dylan demanded. Valtra comes right up to him and steals a kiss. "You are tough for a human, you fought well." She said, "Untie my hands, I'll show you how well." Dylan stated. "I've decided to keep you." She said. "Keep me, I am not a pet." Dylan stated. "No, not as a pet." She replied. Now next scene they are sneaking away he is free of his cuffs and she leads him to secret chamber. ""Aren't you afraid, your father will find out about us?" Dylan asked. "I do not fear my father, I love who I want when I want." She stated as she pulls him in and they kiss. "So your saying you love me?" Dylan replied. "The great dark princess, in love with a human?" He smiled. "Shut up and kiss me." She demanded as he did. Now back to the present Dylan is in his office. "Voltar can never find out." Dylan says to himself. "Jesse get me Paul." Dylan ordered over the com-link. He calls Paul and he arrives at Dylan's office. "Yes sir?" Paul asked as Dylan rises and shuts the door. "Is there a way to test Ryan without Voltar knowing?" Dylan asked. "I may have a friend, I went to school with he works for Kravitz." Paul answered. Now later Paul goes into his lab grabs a vile of Ryan's blood, gets to the docking bay opens the doors heads out and makes contact via vidlink with his friend. "I need you to test some blood, for Volvans disease." Paul replied. "I will put a rush on it my friend." Man said. Meanwhile at Voltar's castle Voltar opens door to bedroom it is dusty and furniture is covered it was Valtra's bedroom he glances at old photos of her and her brothers and him. Rick then comes to the door. "Here you are, I've been looking for you father, why are you in here?" He asked. "I was drawn here I felt something." Voltar answered. "Ok, well Kravitz has caught one of his scientist performing an illegal test...for Volvans disease." He said. "What!" He shouted. Meanwhile in Kravitz lab as Kravitz's grabs the vile from the man. "What is this?' Kravitz demanded as he sees the name on it. "Ryan McKay?" He said. "Why would you test his?" Then he realizes. "No, it couldn't be." He questioned then he smiled "I knew that boy had a familiar fire about him." He stated just then Voltar bursts in. Kravitz puts vile in his lab coat pocket. Voltar goes to the man and grabs him up. "Explain yourself, before I snap your neck." Voltar commanded. "Whom are you working for?" He demanded man is scared and shaking can barely speak he drops him to the floor. "Kravitz!" He yells. "I will get to the bottom of this my lord." Kravitz assures. "Paul asked me to test the blood my lord." Man muttered. "Why would he need to?" Voltar asked. "My grandsons have all been tested." He added. "I will get to the bottom of this." Voltar stated as he leaves Kravitz pulls out the vile. "I guess I'd better run this, can't have anything wrong with our first born." He smiled. Meanwhile back at the base in sickbay. Ryan is healed up and sitting on side of the bed dressed he stands up. "Feeling better?" Dylan asked as he walks in. "Yes I am, Paul cleared me to get back to work." Ryan said. "You're sure your ok?" Dylan asked. "I'm fine, I did dream of her." Ryan added. "I talked to her spirit." He said. "She is always with you." Dylan stated. "I think she's been my lucky charm." Ryan replied. "I know she has." Dylan added just then Paul comes out of his office with a nervous frightened look on his face. "What is it?" Dylan asked. "My scientist friend, is dead." Paul answered. "What's going on dad?" Ryan asked. "Voltar will be headed here." Dylan realized. "For answers." He added. "Do you think he knows?" Paul asked. "Gather the team Paul." Dylan replied. Now in the control room all are present. "What's going on Dylan?" Jon asked as Ryan comes in and stands beside Dylan. "It's a long story, it started almost 20 years ago." "I told a lie, now its time to tell the truth." He continues, as everyone is intrigued yet confused. "Ryan is Valtra's and my son too." He stated all are completely stunned. "What?" Jon said. "Valtra and I were only sixteen at the time, its why we lied." Dylan explained. "That makes Ryan the first born." Charlie replied. "Does my father know?" Jon asked. "I'm not sure yet." Dylan answers just then alarms go off. "Ryan stay here." Dylan insisted. "I'm not afraid of him." Ryan stated. Dylan puts hand on Ryan's shoulder. "Just stay here, at least until we know what he does." Dylan pleads. "Fine." Ryan said as Dylan heads for docking bay. "Voltar is just outside." Jesse informed over com-link meanwhile as Ryan waits in Dylan's office Kravitz uses a teleportation device to appear to him. Ryan is startled. "So, I should've seen it." He said as he circles around him. "Your mother's eyes, that Aster fire behind them." He continued. "Who the hell are you?" Ryan asked. "I am Dr. lucandis Kravitz, I make it my life's work to study and know all things Aster." He informed. "I would love to have you on my table firstborn." He smiled. "Does Voltar know too?" Ryan asked. "Not yet, but he will see it too, your just too much like your mother, I can tell." He replied. "I cannot wait to see what you can do." He added. "What are you talking about?" Ryan questioned. "Your power will come soon enough, Ryan Aster McKay." He said then vanished as Ryan takes a deep breath, meanwhile outside the docking bay. "Where is he?" Dylan asked as he looks around just then Voltar appeared before him. "What are you up to McKay?" Voltar demanded. "None of your business." Dylan stated. "It is, when you use my scientist behind my back." Voltar replied. "Is Steven ok?" He asked. "He was already tested, all of them were." Voltar stated. "Just being cautious." Dylan replied. "You are hiding something McKay, I will find out." He informed meanwhile Ryan still in Dylan's office Cora entered. "Are you ok?" She asked. "Yes I'm fine, Voltar is here." "Its weird, I spent my life protecting Steven from him now, I will have to protect myself." Ryan said. "He doesn't know anything yet." Cora reminded him. "He has ways of finding out." Ryan said as he looks out the window. "I don't need this, someone else trying to control my life especially an Aster." Ryan stated. "I've watched Voltar in action, I was glad when I believed I was not one of them." He added as he takes Cora's hand. "He would probably try to kill you." Ryan feared. "He won't do anything to me, he's learned it never ends well when he interferes with his families happiness." She said. "He may even try to be my friend, I can't handle that." He replied as she hugs him a small drop of blood falls from his nose and onto the floor. "Lets not get ahead of ourselves yet." She said. "He maybe gone by now." She added. Meanwhile back at the docking bay after all have left except for Steven Voltar reappears. "Are you sure your ok?" Voltar asked. "I'm fine, grandfather really." Steven said. "Then why the test again?" He asked. "Are you having any nose bleeds, fatigue?" Voltar questioned. "I just felt a little sick, so dad got worried." Steven said. "Your father should know by now, I only want to keep you safe." Voltar explained. "You are all I have left of her." He added. "What were the results?" Steven asked. "I don't know, we didn't run them, no problem you can go with me now to my lab." Voltar insisted. "Ok, how about tomorrow?" Steven said. "Can't you use the blood we gave you?" Steven questioned. "Our blood is special it does not keep long outside of our bodies." He explained. "Good to know." Steven said. Meanwhile Dylan and Paul come back to docking bay. "Its ok really, I mean Steven is fine now, so you can go." Dylan stated. "Then I will go." Voltar says as he vanished then Paul and Dylan sighed with relief. "That was too close." Paul said. "I did get preliminary test sent to me, they were negative." He added. "We need to be sure Paul." Dylan stated. "I will go tell Ryan, see if he is ok." Steven says he goes to Dylan's office and enters to see Ryan sitting in chair holding a cloth soaked in blood to his nose. "Whoa, are you ok?" Steven panics. "Yeah, its just a nose bleed." Ryan said. Steven's eyes get wider in fear. "What is it?" Ryan asked. "We should go to sickbay." Steven said. "What is it Steven." Ryan insisted. "Nose bleeds are one of the symptoms." He replied reluctantly. "It could also be, the beating you got from Grelt right?" Steven added. "That's what it is." Cora insisted they take him to sickbay; Paul scans him with hand held device. "I think we need to finish the test." Paul replied. "Alright draw the blood and get it to him." Dylan concedes. "What do we do if it's positive?" Ryan asked. "Lets think negative ok?" Dylan said. "I'll do some other scans and x-rays, to make sure your healed up form your other injuries." Paul replied. Cora takes Ryan's hand and squeezes it, meanwhile back at the castle "McKay is hiding something, but how can Steven be sick?" "I had him tested." He contemplates. "I don't know father." Rick stated just then a currier from the base arrived with a package. "It's form McKay." Man replied, as Voltar takes it and opens to see a vile of blood. "That was fast?" Rick questioned. "Get this vile to Kravitz, I want it yesterday." He demanded. Rick takes vile personally to Kravitz as he is sitting at his desk looking at reports. "Hey father wants this yesterday." Rick ordered as he gives him vile. "Of course." Kravitz replied then Rick goes out Kravitz looks over vile. "Lets see what's going on inside that Aster/McKay interior shall we?" Kravitiz stated. Meanwhile back on the base in sickbay Jon enters. "I figured you would be here." Jon said. "I can't do this Jon, what if he is sick?" Dylan fears. "I will loose him like I did her." Dylan added. "Steven was ok, I just don't agree with the lies, I know my father it will be worse if he finds out like this." Jon stated. "He took it hard when Valtra died." Jon added. "I don't know if he could handle it, if Ryan has this disease too." Jon said. "I made a promise to your sister, to protect our son from your father and I will, I know about firstborns." Dylan stated. "He would not do anything to hurt him." Jon insisted. "He loves all his family." Jon added. "Yes and how does that end up?" Dylan reminded just then Voltar appeared before them in the sickbay with a look of anger and confusion. "I was going to be here for this." Voltar insisted as Ryan is sitting on a bed near by looking nervously at Voltar as he takes a deep breath. Voltar gives the envelope to Paul he opened it and reads it his face goes pale. "Its positive." He said as he lowers paper all are stunned and upset. "No." Dylan stated. "Oh my god." Cora gasped. "Alright McKay, start by telling me whose blood was in that vile cause it was not Steven." Voltar demanded. "A negative diagnosis does not change." He added. "I'm going to die." Ryan replies in a daze. Voltar realized what was going on. "No, you are not." Dylan insisted as he grabs Ryan's hand. "We will beat this." Dylan assured. "I will not loose you." Dylan added as he hugs him tight. "The blood was Ryan's." Voltar says. Jon pulls Voltar out into the corridor. "What is going on junior?" Voltar demanded. "How can he?" He added. "I think you know father." Jon stated. "He is Valtra's son." He admitted. "It explains why I saw him at Valtra's grave, why I felt something about him before." Voltar says angrily. "You need to calm down, Ryan does not need anger now, he will need your help." Jon stated. "My daughter lied to me, about her firstborn son." Voltar recognized. "I will kill McKay for this." He says. "You, will stay out here and cool down." Jon replied. "I cannot go threw that again, I will not." Voltar insists meanwhile back in sickbay. "How long to I have?" Ryan asked. "Its hard to know with this disease." Paul confessed. "A estimate?" Ryan said. "Could be years could be months." Paul admitted. "We will find a cure." Dylan stated. "Voltar hasn't." Ryan replied. Dylan takes Ryan's head in his hands as they both tear up. "I am not going to let you die." Dylan promised. "We need to be realistic dad, no one with this has survived." Ryan replied. "You will be the first." Steven stated as he wiped tears form his eyes. "I will get to work on a cure, I know Voltar will allow his scientist to help." Paul said. "You will be ok." Cora said as she kisses him. "I believe it when you say it." Ryan replied. Jon comes back in with Voltar. "My scientists are at your disposal." He stated as he looks to Ryan. "He is my daughter's son." He added. "Thank you." Ryan said. "I always take care of my blood." He replies, as he goes out. "That went, ok." Steven said. "Yes, for now." Jon reminded. Now back at the castle in the throne room. "Wait Ryan is Valtra's son?"

Rick says in shock. "Not another one." Volrin complained. "I had a feeling Valtra was hiding something form me." "I saw him at the crypt in a dream." Voltar said. "I should've seen it, we will find a cure." Voltar commanded. "We will father." Rick said. "I will not let my first grandson die." Voltar stated. "Neither will I my lord." Kravitz said as he comes in. "Tell me you have something." Voltar asked. "I believe so my lord, I will need to concur with their doctor." He added meanwhile back on the base in the mess hall Jenna is upset and eating. "I can't believe this poor Ryan." She replied. "I know." Charlie said. "Voltar will find a cure." Jenna insisted. "Of course he will." Anilla added as she is eating too, meanwhile in Ryan's room. Cora is sitting with him on the bed. "You need to rest, gather your strength." She insisted. "I know" Ryan says as he looks out the window. "I have to go, or I will be in trouble with my job." She apologizes and she kisses him. "Its ok, I'll be fine." Ryan said. "I will be back tonight." She promised as she goes. Voltar then appeared to him, as Ryan is surprised. "Don't you knock?" Ryan asked. "I'm sorry, I could sense you were alone." He replied. "So, do you just pop in when ever you want?" Ryan replied. "Yes, you will get use to it." Voltar says boldly. "So what do you want, take one last look at the corpse?" Ryan said. "What, no where do you get such twisted humor?" He thinks. "Never mind." He said. "Sorry, but I am not use to all this." Ryan said. "How are you feeling?" Voltar asked as he sits in chair next to him. "I'm tired." Ryan replied. "I know you saw Valtra's spirit." Voltar stated. "I should've realized it, when I saw you there." "I know my daughter, she only loved your father." Voltar stated. "You miss her don't you?" Ryan asked. "Of course, she was my daughter." He said. "How long did she live after she got sick?" Ryan asked. "Another year, she went down fighting." He replied. "Thanks, I needed to know that." Ryan said. "This is really weird, there was a time you would've killed me without a thought to get back at my dad." Ryan replied. "I would have regretted it." Voltar stated. "I can see her, in your eyes, you have the Aster fire." Voltar replied. "So, I can expect more of these visits?" Ryan asked. "Of course you are my blood." He replied as he rises up from chair. "I will let you rest." Voltar said. "So much like her." He added then he smiled and vanished. Dylan then entered. "Ryan?" Where is Cora?" Dylan asked. "She had to go to work." Ryan said. "Are you ok?" Dylan asked as he sits in chair beside him. "Yes, Voltar was here." Ryan stated. "What did he say?" Dylan questioned. "He just asked how I was." Ryan replied. "Do not trust him, no matter what." Dylan warned. "I'm not a kid dad, I've seen what he's done, and I'll be fine." He assured. "I love you son." Dylan said. "I love you too dad." Ryan responded. "You are too much like your mother and me." Dylan added, Meanwhile back at the castle in Kravitz's lab. Paul is also present looking over the data. "It's the answer, it has to be." Kravitz insisted. "Are you sure, it could be risky." Paul cautioned. "Not for the babies." Kravitz informed. "It's the best shot we have." Paul admitted now in the control room. "So what do we have?" Dylan asked. "It is possible we may have a cure, through one of the unborn babies placentas." Paul answered. "Is it dangerous?" Dylan asked. "No, we just need some of the fluid easily removed by a needle." Kravitz informed. "Its up to them, if they want to." Ryan insisted, as he looked extremely fatigued and pale. "I will do it." Anilla said. "Yes, so will I." Jenna stated. "Of course, you are family." Leeah agreed. "Thank you." Ryan replied. "We will begin immediately." Paul said as all the girls followed Paul to sickbay. "I need to call Cora." Ryan said as he heads out. "It has to work." Dylan said. "It will mom is looking out for him." Steven replied meanwhile Ryan arrived by shuttlecraft to Cora's apt. "Cora!" Ryan called out as he knocked on door. She opens it. "Good news." He said. "What?" She said excited. "They may have found a cure." Ryan said with a smile. She hugs him as they go inside, as she shut the door Grelt slithered up, he then kicked in the door. "Did anyone miss me?" He exclaimed, as Ryan and Cora are astonished. He then knocked Cora out with a stun from his weapon. "I hear a tale you're an Aster now?" He replied. Ryan's eyes widen in shock. "What?" Ryan said. "Word is out on you kid." He stated as he uses his tongue to grab his arm. "I think Voltar will pay big for you, first grandson." He added as he and Ryan vanish. Cora begins to come around. "Ryan!" She screamed. Now on the base Jesse gets the call from Cora. "Sir it's Cora." He said. "Cora what's going on?" He asked. "Grelt he escaped, he knows Ryan is an Aster he took him." She stated. "Damm it" Dylan exclaimed. "All officers full alert!" He commanded then he looks to Jesse and with regret and said. "Call Voltar he can help." Meanwhile at a secret location on Voltara itself Ryan wakes up after being knocked out by Grelt. "Where?" He asked as he focused his blurred vision he sees him. "Grelt how did you?" He asked. "I have friends my boy, so first grandson good thing I didn't blow you up huh?" He said. "You are worth more alive." He replied. "My father will kill you." Ryan stated. "Please, you are my ticket to fortune and power." He said. "You are just as crazy as you ever were." Ryan replied, meanwhile back on the base. Voltar is there he closes his eyes and concentrates to sense Ryan. He then opened his eyes. "I know where he is." Voltar informed. "He is good, you should market that Aster tracker." Ralph said. "I will bring him back." Voltar replied as he vanished. He reappeared to Grelt's lair. "Not so fast Voltar." Grelt cautioned as he pulled a detonator form his belt. "I am prepared, touch me I hit this button, he dies." Grelt informed. "What is your price?" Voltar asked. "All of Voltara." He boasted. Voltar lets out his sinister laugh. "You are very ambitious." Voltar stated then he swiftly grabbed him up with one hand and crushed the detonator with his, other which turned into a claw. "No deal." He said. The team then arrived as Voltar dropped him to the ground and the team cuffed and took him out. Dylan comes to Ryan and untied him. "Hey you ok?" Dylan asked. "Yeah, I'm ok." Ryan said now back in sickbay Paul and Kravitz are standing side by side as Paul has an injection. "Were going to inject this directly into your bloodstream." Paul explains. "In twenty four hours we will know if it's worked." He added. "Ok." Ryan said as he is lying on the bed. He takes Cora's hand as Paul injects him then after. "Now go to your room and rest, you also have a concussion." Paul informed. Cora walks him out and to his room. Now as Ryan slept Cora sat by his bedside she caresses his cheek. "You will be ok." She insisted. "You have to be." She added. Now in the morning Ryan in sitting on bed in sickbay as Paul is drawing his blood. "So now what?' Ryan asked. "We will test it for the disease try to relax." Paul said. "This will take a few hours." He adds. "I'll work on it." Ryan said just then Vala entered she comes to Ryan and takes his hand. "Are you ok?" Ryan asked. "Yes, I'm here for you." She said. "Thank you for that." Ryan smiled. "How about some lunch?" Ryan asked. "I can eat." She answered as the head out and to the mess hall. They get food sit at a table and then Dylan walked in with Jon. "There you are." Jon said. "Hi daddy, I was just keeping Ryan Company." She said. "That is very sweet of you." Jon replied. "So it went ok?" Dylan asked. "Yeah." Ryan said. "How long will the results take?" Jon asked. "Paul said a few hours so." Ryan replied just then the alarms go off. "Sounds like trouble." Dylan said. "Vala stay here with Ryan." Jon ordered as they head to the control room. "We have trouble on earth sir."

Jesse stated. "Alright sent the team to help." Dylan ordered. "I got this go be with Ryan." Jon insisted Dylan nodded and went back to sickbay. Now it's a few hours later and Paul has the result. "It worked, your blood tested negative for Volvans." He exclaimed as all sighed with relief. Cora hugged Ryan. "I knew you'd be ok." She said. "Thank you Paul." Dylan replied. "I'm just glad he is alright." Paul stated. "So, can I go back to work now?" Ryan asked. "Yes, you can go with Jesse to deliver some supplies to Jupiter." Dylan replied. "That was not what I meant dad." Ryan said. "Give me this ok?' Dylan asked. Now on Jupiter as Ryan and Jesse land a cargo shuttle they off load. "I can't believe he gave me this assignment." Ryan replied. "I get them everyday, it's nice to have company." Jesse said. "Yeah, but you are use to it." Ryan stated as they carry them to the drop off point. Jesse signs paperwork as Ryan waited. "Dylan is just trying to keep you safe." Jesse reminded. "He doesn't need to, I'm almost twenty." Ryan replied. "To our dad's we will always be kids." Jesse stated. "How about we grab some lunch?" Jesse said they head over to near by dinner type restaurant sit at a table and look over menu when the waitress comes over. She has blue skin blonde hair and brown eyes. "McKay?" She asked as Ryan realized who she was. "Carlee?" He replied. "It's been too long." She said. "It has, how are you?' Ryan asked. "I'm good, you your in the alliance now?" She asked. "Yes I am." Ryan stated. "So you followed the old man huh?" She smiled. "Yeah I guess so, this is Jesse." Ryan replied. "Hello." Jesse said. "Carlee and I grew up together." Ryan informed. "We were inseparable, so how is Steven?" She asked. "He's good." Ryan said. "It is so good to see you." She replied. "So what can I get for you?" She asked. "I will have a number two." Ryan said. "Still eating red meat huh?" She said. "I'll have a number six." Jesse said. "Coming up." She said as she smiled and went back to kitchen. "So, spill what's the story there?" Jesse asked. "What, we were friends." Ryan said. "She was not looking at you like a friend." Jesse stated. "She likes you," Jesse informed. "You're crazy, she was like a sister." Ryan replied. "I've seen that look before." Jesse insisted. "I'm with Cora." Ryan stated Carlee comes back with food. "Here you go gentlemen enjoy." She winked. "Anything else?" She asked with a smile. "No thanks." Ryan said she goes as Ryan starts to eat. "I am telling you, she has a major crush on you." Jesse stated. "Forget it and eat ok?" Ryan replied meanwhile back on Voltara at the castle in the throne room. "So he will be ok?" Rick asked. "Yes, he will be fine." Voltar stated. "Good, so can we get back to evil deeds now?" Volrin asked. "Yes of course." Voltar replied, just then he got a sense of danger. "What is it father?" Rick asked. "I felt a sense of danger." He replied. "Who?" Rick said. "I don't know." Voltar replied. "I should warn them." Voltar insisted now at the control room. Lisette is covering Jesse's station. "Sir, I have an incoming call from Rick Aster." She said. "On the vidlink." Dylan said she brings it up. "I have a warning of danger." Rick said. "Danger from what? To who?" Dylan questioned. "Father cannot be sure but something is going to happen soon." Rick replied. "Well, he must be off his game the team is back on the base." Dylan stated Steven entered. "Ahh dad Ryan and Jesse are still on Jupiter." Steven informed. "Lisette get them on the com-link." Dylan ordered she attempted to with no response. "No answer sir." She stated. "Alright Charlie and Shane get to Jupiter now." Dylan commanded meanwhile back on Jupiter as Jesse and Ryan headed back to shuttle. "You know I was right." Jesse insisted. "Just drop it ok." Ryan said as they rise up off the ground after a few seconds the engine shuts down and they hit the ground hard. "What the?" Ryan said as they are thrown form their seats. Jesse attempts to call on com-link but it's dead. "I think we've been sabotaged." Jesse stated. "Are you ok?' Ryan asked as they get to their feet. "Yeah I'm good." Jesse answered. "How bad is the damage?" Ryan asked. "It's fried, they knew what they were doing." Jesse admits. Ryan pulls out his weapon. "Then lets go back to that drop site." Ryan said as they pry open the doors. It is now night on the planet and very dark. "There won't be anyone there now." Jesse said just then a shadow comes toward them. "That's close enough." Ryan said as he pointed weapon. She removed her cloak. "Carlee?" Ryan said as he lowered weapon. "What are you doing out here?" He asked. "I'm going home, why are you still here?" She said. "Can we use your com-link?" Jesse asked. "Of course, follow me." She said as she goes to her apt. "It's in the living room." She replied. "Thanks, we appreciate this." Ryan said as Jesse goes to com-link it is not working. Jesse comes back to them. "Your com-link is dead." Jesse stated. "What?" Ryan replied. Then Carlee uses a mist that is emitted from her hands. It knocks them out. "I'll take care of you." She said meanwhile back on the base. "What did you find?" Dylan asked as he communicates over com-link. "I got the shuttlecraft, it looks like it's been sabotaged." Charlie said. "No one is here." He added. "I'm on my way."

Dylan said. "I'm going too." Steven said. "No, you stay put." Dylan insisted. "Can I go?" Cora asked. "Could I stop you?" Dylan stated meanwhile back at the apt Ryan starts to come around his hands are tied to the bedpost above him. "What the hell?" Ryan said as he tries to pull free. "Good your awake." Carlee said as she walked in she sits beside him on bed. "What is going on?" Ryan asked. Carlee leans in and kisses his lips. "I always knew you'd comeback to me." She said. "What?" Ryan said. "I've always loved you Ryan, since the day we met." She informed. "We were just friends that's all, I have a girlfriend." Ryan replied. "I can make you forget all about her." She said as she touches his cheek. "You need to let me and Jesse go before this gets worse." Ryan demanded. "You use to be such a rebel, taking risks joining the alliance has made you like your father." She stated. "Thanks for the compliment." Ryan said. "So, if this other girl was out of the picture you'd be free to love me?" She ponders as she gets up. "Carlee, what ever you are thinking please don't do it." Ryan pleaded. "You belong with me." She said then she goes out. "Carlee no!" He shouted, "Damm it." He said as he tries to pull loose of ropes. "Jesse!" He called out "I'm here, in the living room." He answered as he is tied to a chair. "Can you get free?" Ryan asked. "I'm trying." He said, meanwhile near by "I got something." Shane said as his scanner device goes off. "It's Jesse's tracker." He added they follow the signal to the apt they kick in the door. "Ryan? Jesse?" Dylan called out. "Dad?" Ryan yelled as they find them and untie them. "Who did this?" Dylan asked. "An old friend, so I thought." Ryan said. All gather outside apt. "Where is she?" Charlie asked. "She took off." Ryan said. "She?" Cora replied. "Yeah, a really nut, she was our waitress for lunch, she knew Ryan as a kid." Jesse explained. "Really?" Cora asked. "She was just a friend." Ryan reminded. "Yeah, she wanted to be more." Jesse said. "We will find her." Dylan replied now back on the base. "Any sign of this Carlee?" Dylan asked. "No sir, but we have her photo out there." Lisette added now in Ryan's quarters. "So, is she pretty?" Cora asked. "You have nothing to worry about, I love you." He stated as he kisses her lips. "I know." She smiled just then Voltar appeared they were startled. "Excuse me." Voltar said. "Did you want something?" Ryan asked. "A moment alone?" He asked. "Guess I should get use to this." Cora said. "Yes, you should." Voltar informed. "I will be outside." She said as she goes out. "What is it?" Ryan asked. "I heard about your problem, Carlee is it?"

Voltar replied. "She is not going to give up." Voltar added. "I'll deal with her." Ryan insisted. Voltar lets out a laugh. "No, I will." "Why does all of my blood think they can handle evil obsessed females, without me?" He questioned. "I will dispose of her quickly and discretely, don't worry." He added.

Chapter 15
OVERBEARING GRANDFATHER

Now that yet another Aster has been discovered, as usual my father tries to assert his control. Unfortunately, for him Ryan is too much like my sister, and even more like his father. He will not sit still for it, but that is not even the worst of it. My father had been busy or should I say Kravitz has, creating experimental creatures not to mention his obsession and disturbing curiosity for all things Aster. Will it put Ryan's life in danger?" Scene back in Ryan's bedroom, "I don't want her dead." Ryan insisted. Voltar touches Ryan's cheek. "You will learn my boy, that the only safe obsessed female, is a dead one." He stated. "That is not my way." Ryan informed. "I admire that humanity of yours, I hate it, but I do admire it." Voltar replied. "Don't hurt her, please." Ryan asked. "I will always keep my family safe." He stated then vanished as Cora comes back in. "What's going on?' Cora asked. "He is going to kill Carlee." Ryan said. "That sounds like a good solution." Cora replied. "No one deserves to die, for caring too much about someone." Ryan stated. "Yes, but she kidnapped you." She said. Ryan looks to Cora in disbelief. "Ok so did I, once but I've changed." Cora insisted. "She is my Friend." Ryan said. "She is also obsessed with you." She added. "Of course, cause one lunatic in love with me is enough?" He smiled. "Very funny." She replied. "I just, need to warn my dad what he is up to." Ryan stated as he heads out meanwhile on Jupiter Voltar finds where Carlee is hiding and kicks in the door. "Alright tramp, come out!" Voltar shouted. Carlee comes out of room to see him, as she is stunned and confused. "Voltar Aster?" She said. "What do you want?" She asked. "You to stay away from Ryan." He stated. "Who are you to make demands?" She said. "I guess you did not know, he is my grandson." He stated. "Now, you will go away or I will kill you." He added. "No, Ryan can't be one of you." She denies. "Trust me, he is." Voltar replied. "Now, do I have to kill you?" He asked. "It has been so long, since I've gotten my hands dirty." He stated. "We should not fight, Cora is the wrong one for him." She informed. "Yes I know, I will deal with her later, but I see you will be a problem." He stated as he grabbed her up by hey throat with one hand. "Nothing personal, really." Voltar said as he crushed her throat then dropped her and vanished. Now back on the base, months have passed and it is time for babies to be born. In sickbay "You are doing fine." Charlie says to Jenna, as she is on table, she then squeezes his hand really hard when a contraction hits. "Ok, you can let go anytime." He begged. Over at the other beds are Anilla and Leeah, also in labor with their husbands by their sides, meanwhile, outside in the control room. "So, who had all three on the same day?" Ralph asked. "I did actually." Jesse answered. "You guys bet on labor?" Lisette asked. "Hey, what else is going on right now?" Ralph replied. Just then, alarms go off the rest of the team heads out. "Does that include me too?" Ryan asked. "Yes." Dylan said reluctantly. Now as the team is battling some beasts that escaped from the zone on Mars. In the sickbay babies are coming. Paul delivers Jenna's baby first. "It's a girl!" He exclaimed as they both smiled. Then Paul rushes over to deliver Anilla's baby. "It's a boy!" He shouted. As she and Shane were excited. Then he comes to Leeah and delivers the baby. "It's a boy." He said, as everyone was so overjoyed, and cleaning off the babies and giving them to their mothers. On Mars there was major trouble, as Ryan is flying in his fighter trying to stop some of the creatures from attacking a village, another beast fires his long-range weapon at his ship taking it down to the ground. "Ryan!" Jon shouted, as Ryan is unconscious and bleeding form his head. Jon rushes to his fighter and uses his power to remove the cover. "Ryan can you hear me?" He asked as he checks his pulse, meanwhile back in the sickbay Voltar and Rick were also there even Moondeath came to see the babies. "It is the future." Voltar stated, just then Dylan calls into sickbay over com-link. "We have incoming wounded and casualties." He stated. "What?" Paul said as the medic teams and security roll in people on stretchers. Amanda is one of them also Marco and Ryan. Dylan rushes in. "Ryan?" He called as Paul is assessing them. "I need team two." Paul called as they enter and help care for the babies. Paul goes to Marco he scanned his still slightly burned body. "He is gone." Paul said as they covered him he then goes to Amanda who is conscious. "I'm ok, just a broken leg." She said as he scanned it. "Lets get her into the casting lab." He stated as staff members roll her away. Now he comes to Ryan, who is bruised and bloody. He scans him. "Ryan can you hear me?" Paul asked. Ryan lies still and unresponsive, with very shallow breathing. The med team begins to hook him up to IV's and attend his wounds. Paul comes to Dylan. "I will do all I can." Paul promised. As he goes back in and they pull curtain closed. "I should've sensed this." Voltar stated. "There was too much going on at once, father." Jon replied as Cora rushed in. "Is he ok?" She asked. "Paul is with him now." Jon replied. "This should not be happening, not when there are babies being born." Lisette said. "Ryan is strong, he'll be fine." Cole insisted just them Paul comes out from curtain all look to him with caution and fear. "I've stabilized him, but it is still critical." Paul informed. "The next twenty four hours will determine more." Paul added. "Determine what, if he survives?" Dylan asked. "Yes, I'm sorry." Paul answered, as he goes back behind the curtain. meanwhile back with the babies and parents. "Have we picked names?" Jon asked. "Yes, Alana." Jenna said. "That is beautiful." Jon said. "How is Ryan?" Charlie asked. "He is, holding his own." Jon replied, as he goes over to Anilla and Shane. "So, what is my little nephews name?" Jon asked. "Christopher Ryan." Shane said. "That's nice bro." Jon replied, and then he goes over to Keyes and Leeah. "What is his name?" Jon asked. "Richard Marco." Keyes said. "Sounds good and strong." Jon replied. Now back behind the curtain, you can see multiple tubes all over and blood all around. "Come on Ryan, you've got to live." Paul said just then Ryan opens his eyes and takes a deep breath. "Ryan!" Paul exclaimed, as he signals his med team to remove breathing tube. "Hey, welcome back." Paul said. "I feel like hell." Ryan whispered. "Yeah, you have looked better." Paul smiled. "Where is my dad?" He asked. "Outside, worrying as usual." Paul replied. Just then Shane comes over with baby in his arms. "Hey your awake, I thought you might like to meet Christopher Ryan." Shane replied. "Hey." Ryan smiled as he tries to take a deep breath. "You, need to not talk and rest." Paul stated, and then Dylan and Steven come in, as Shane goes back to Anilla. "He is awake." Paul said. "So far, he is ok." He added they both come to him. "So, I guess I'm on package duty forever?" Ryan said. "No, not forever, just till I'm dead." Dylan smiled as Steven hugged him. "You scared us." Steven said. "Me too." Ryan replied. "He needs to rest." Paul said as he comes back. They all go out, now later at night, as Ryan is sleeping and alone. Voltar appeared to his bedside. He looks at him for a moment to see the IV in his arm and the bandage above his right eye and oxygen tube in his nose. "I am so sorry." Voltar said as he touched Ryan's forehead. "I will protect you form now on." "I won't let you be hurt again." He vowed. Moondeath appears. "I know you will son." Moondeath replied. "I owe his mother this, for all the time I wasted keeping them apart." Voltar stated. "You should rest too son." Moondeath stated they go now next day Vala is sitting beside his bed in chair. Ryan slowly opens his eyes he sees her. "Hello Miss Vala." Ryan said she moves close to him. "Are you feeling better?" She asked. "I am now, thank you." He smiled. "Where, is your daddy?" He added. "He is still sleeping." She said just then Paul comes in. "Your father is looking for you Vala." Paul informed. "Got to go." She said, as she hops off chair and kissed Ryan's cheek, then goes out. Ryan smiled then he looked to Paul. "So what is the prognosis?" Ryan asked. "Your scans are clear, looks like your Aster genes are kicking in on the healing too." He added. "So, can I go back to work?" Ryan asked, as he attempts to get out of bed Dylan walks in. "Whoa, slow down you were in a major crash." Dylan reminded. "No work yet." He added. "I will go, check on the babies." Paul said as he goes out. "Speaking of babies, I'm not one." Ryan said, as he sits up and grabs his clothes lying on chair and gets dressed. "Did I say you were?" Dylan stated. "You had that look." Ryan said as he is dressed and stands up, he gets a rush come over him like he is being drained. "Whoa" He said as he sits back down on bed. "What is it, you ok?" Dylan asked. "Yeah, just dizzy for a second." Ryan replied. "Rest, that is an order as your captain." Dylan stated. "Fine." Ryan conceded, as he gets up and goes out slowly, and heads into corridor then he gets to quarters, to see Cora dressed in black. "Should you be up?" She said. "Marco's funeral." Ryan realized. "I'll change." He replied, as he goes into bedroom Cora follows him. "You should stay here." She insisted. "He was a friend, it will take me a minute." Ryan replied. Now at the funeral on Earth, behind the Alliance building the team is gathered in their dress uniforms, there is an urn on a table before them as Marco was cremated.

Dylan is at a podium. "What can I say about Marco Santana?" He began as we peer around to all the team, and the new moms holding their babies. Amanda with her cast and crutches. "He was a great pilot, he was an even better friend." "He was always ready to help, with no concern for his own safety." He continues. "He will be missed, by us all." Dylan stated. "It is always hard, to loose a team member, a friend, family." He added. "Even if not all of us, are family by blood, you are still our family." He acknowledged. "We must remember Marco, and carry him with us everyday." "To protect each other, as he did." He ended. Now after the funeral the team returned to the base. Ryan is sitting on couch in quarters Cora comes in. "Are you ok?" She asked. "Yes, I was just thinking." Ryan replied. "About me I hope." She said with a smile as they kiss, just then Voltar appears before them, they are surprised. "Don't you think he should rest?" Voltar stated. "What the hell?" Ryan said. "Do you mind?" Ryan added. "You could at least, let him heal before you." Voltar says, "Excuse me?" You're the one barging in, where you were not invited." Cora stated. "You will get use to it." Voltar informed. "Ok now, is not the time." Ryan insisted. "I could say the same to you." Voltar implied. "I am fine." Ryan stated. "You, were in a horrible nearly fatal crash, if you are not cleared for duty you are certainly not to…" Voltar said Ryan interrupted. "Ok, that is none of your business." Ryan stated. "Please just go." Ryan asked. "Fine, I am just trying to protect you." Voltar replied. "I know, and I appreciate it, but I am fine." Ryan insisted Voltar vanishes. "I can not believe him." Cora stated. "It's over, just forget it." Ryan said as he leans in toward her. "Now where were we?" He asked as he pulls her in closer they kiss. "Right here I think." Ryan said, as they kissed again and get up from the couch, and head into bedroom as he removes her shirt and she removes his. When Voltar appeared in front of them. "Again, I feel I really must protest." Voltar said. Ryan looks at him in anger and disbelief. "Will you go!" He exclaimed. "I am trying to help your recovery." He stated. "Don't you have, some evil you could be doing right now?" Ryan asked. "I have people for that." He informed. "This is insane." Cora stated as she grabs blouse and puts it on. "I, will be at my apt." She says as she goes out. "Cora wait!" Ryan yelled but she leaves Ryan looks back at Voltar. "Are you happy now?" Ryan asked. "You still have me." Voltar replied. Ryan is frustrated, meanwhile in Charlie's quarters in the baby's room he is staring down at her in her crib. "Hello my pretty girl, now you will go easy on your father right?" Charlie asked Jenna comes in. "Of course she will not, she is my daughter." She stated. "That is what I'm afraid of." Charlie replied. "Very funny." Jenna said as they both look down at her. "She has your green eyes." Jenna said. "Lucky for us, your looks." Charlie added, meanwhile over at Shane's quarters. He is sitting in rocking chair asleep holding the baby. Anilla walks in and touches his cheek he wakes up. "I'm up!" He exclaimed. "Shh." Anilla said. "I'll put him to bed." She added as she takes baby and puts him in the crib. She then turned to see Shane asleep again. She smiled. meanwhile over at Keyes's quarters he is attempting to change the baby's diaper when Leeah walks in. "So, how is it going?" She asked. "Great." Keyes said as he picks up baby and the diaper falls off. "Ok, maybe not." As he lays him back down. Leeah then changes him. "What would we do without you?" Keyes said now back at Steven's room Ryan knocks on his door. Steven opens it. "Hey, are you ok?" Steven asked. "No your..." he paused "I mean our, grandfather is driving me insane." Ryan admitted. "Of course he is." Steven said. "I need your help to distract him." Ryan begs. "I got it." Steven replied. Steven heads over to Ryan's room where Voltar is still there, As Ryan sneaks out of base to see Cora, where they continued uninterrupted where they left off, now after as Ryan is holding Cora in his arms. "I'm feeling much better." Ryan replied, "So am I." Cora smiled as she takes his hand. "No Voltar." She said. "Don't say his name, he might show up." Ryan warned. "I get the feeling, he hates me." Cora said. "Only because I love you." Ryan stated as he kissed her lips. "No, he doesn't think I'm good enough for you." She replied. "Hey, I have a checkered past too." Ryan replied. "I will handle the old man." Ryan assured, just then Voltar appeared. "Handle the old man?" Voltar stated. Ryan sits up as Cora covers up. "Unbelievable, don't you sleep?" Ryan asked. "It wastes time." Voltar said. "You, should get back to your room it's safer." He added as he looks around her apt. "You, need to leave." Cora demands. "Fine, you and I will talk later." Voltar informed then vanished. "I am so sorry." Ryan apologized. "It is not your fault." Cora stated as she kissed him. "Even for Voltar you apologize, that is why I fell for you, that compassion and fierce loyalty." She said now the next day Ryan is back out in the field he is just finishing his shift and headed into the docking bay when Voltar appears before him. "Am I interrupting?" Voltar asked. "No."

He replied as he is putting up gear. "What do you want?" Ryan said, he pulls out a photo album. "I thought, you might like to see your mother.' He stated as he gives it to him. "Thank you." Ryan said as he opened it. He sees a baby being held by a beautiful woman. "Was that her mother?" Ryan asked. "Yes, she was sweet actually liked me." He stated. "Must've not known you long." Ryan replied as he turns page. "Come to think of it she left me a few years later." Voltar remembered. "That would explain this." Ryan said as he sees photo of a six-year-old Valtra in full warrior gear. "I did not know about girls so, I raised her like her brother." He stated. "Wow, I thought I'd seen it all." Ryan said. "I'll go, keep the album it's yours." Voltar replied as he vanished. Now back at the castle Volrin is in the throne room as Voltar enters. "So is your plan working?" Volrin asked. "Of course it is, soon I'll get rid of that Babor slut, and then I will be choosing his bride." Voltar stated. Now the next day in sickbay Ryan is sitting on bed as Paul scans him. "I feel fine." Ryan insures. "Just a follow up." Paul said. "Alright, everything looks good." He said as he puts down scanner. "Good, can you tell my dad that?" Ryan said Dylan walks in. "Already heard." He replied. "So, can I come off light duty now?" Ryan asked. "Fine, next arrest is yours." Dylan replied meanwhile back at Voltar's castle in Kravitz lab he has Voltar and Volrin there. "So what is this plan?" Volrin asked. "We have an experiment, that Kravitz has been working on." Voltar stated. "Kravitz has been busy." Volrin said Kravitz then flips a switch to reveal a glass floor beneath their feet, under them they see a very beautiful young girl of nineteen, that is humanoid in appearance. "It's a girl?" "Surely Kravitz this, can not be your idea." Volrin replied. "It is not just a girl." Kravitz insisted as he hits a switch on the wall and a high pitch sound is omitted, which caused the girl to transform into a large beast with claw hands, a sharp tail and then it's eyes blasted from them a laser beam. "Whoa!" Volrin replied. "Cute, but deadly brother." Voltar stated. "You are a genius, as usual Kravitz." He added. "She will walk right up and into the alliance building, and destroy it from within." Voltar stated. "They will never see it coming." He added, as they all laugh. meanwhile back on the base Dylan is in his office when Biscus called over the vidlink. "So, I can count on you and the team attending." Biscus asked. "We have a choice?" Dylan questioned. "Of course not, be there at nine to help set up." Biscus instructed. "Why do we, have to go to these kiss ass functions?" Dylan asked. "You're the best team in the alliance." Biscus answered. "The delegates want to see, their favorite heroes." Biscus added. "So, see you soon." He said as he clicks off. Now Dylan has gathered the team in the briefing room. "Alright, it's time once again to attend the annual alliance gala." Dylan replied, as all of them moan and groan "Yeah, time to spread the love." Ralph stated. "So, your black ties gentlemen and dress your best ladies." Dylan stated. They all go out, Ryan comes up to Dylan. "So, another kiss ass function dad." Ryan asked. "You are my son." Dylan said, meanwhile at Cora's apt as Ryan heads to invite her to the gala, an old boyfriend is trying to stir up trouble, courtesy of my father of course, in an attempt to break them up. Ryan came to the door to see this guy kissing Cora passionately. "I'll just leave you two alone." Ryan stated as he walks away. "Ryan, no!" Cora cried. "Let him go." Derek said. Cora punched Derek in the face. "Don't you ever, touch me again." She stated as she goes after him, but he and the team have arrived on Earth for the gala. Biscus is there and comes up to them all dressed in their best. "Great you made it." Biscus said. "Yes, so how long is it?" Dylan asked. "Patience my friend." Biscus stated. Ryan is the last to walk in as the party is just beginning. He is clearly angry and upset; he didn't notice the young girl watching him, the same girl from Kravitz lab of horrors. He bumped into her. She has long raven hair and familiar blue eyes. "I'm sorry." Ryan said, as he went in, she just stared mesmerized for a moment, now inside. "Hey, where is Cora?" Steven asked. Ryan grabs champagne glass off the server's tray and drinks it down. "Kissing her new boyfriend." Ryan replied as he goes to a large table with more champagne. Biscus takes to the stage and steps up to the podium all applauded. Dylan looked to see Ryan drinking multiple glasses, as Steven rushed over. "Dad, something happened between Ryan and Cora, she was kissing a guy." Steven said. "What?" Dylan replied he goes over to Ryan. "Son, what happened?" He asked. "So, are you ready to say I told you so?" Ryan declared. "You did warn me about her." Ryan added as he sips from glass. "I should've listened to you." He said. "I'm sure it's not what you think son." Dylan replied. "I know she loves you." Dylan admitted. Ryan lets out a laugh. "That's a good one dad." Ryan responded. "Look, I know your upset but alcohol, is not the answer." Dylan said. Cora arrived in her gorgeous gown as they see her. "See, she is here to explain." Dylan said, as he took glass from him. She comes to them. "Ryan, it was not what you think." She said. "I'll leave you two alone." Dylan said, as he goes back to stage area. "He kissed me, to make you think there was something going on, but it's not." Cora insisted. "He is more your type right?" Ryan said as the alcohol kicks in. "Dark and brooding." He added, as the young girl comes closer to hear them. "It is Voltar." "He is trying to break us up, he sent him." Cora explained. "Don't let him win." She pleads. "So, you're going to use him as an excuse?" Ryan said. Cora shakes her head no with tears in her eyes. "What made me think, I could keep your heart?" Ryan asked. "You have my heart Ryan, I love you." She cried. "Why, should I believe you?" Ryan questioned. "You lied before." He added, just then the girl makes herself transform into her beast form, as the people scream and run for the exits. "Now that was not on the guest list." Ralph said. "Get the civilians to safety!" Dylan ordered, as the team works to clear them out. "What is that?" Biscus asked. "I'm guessing, a gift form Voltar." Dylan replied. She proceeded to trash the room and come up to Ryan and Cora. She knocked Cora across the room with her tail knocking her out. Then she grabbed Ryan in her clawed hands and crashes out through the concrete wall "Ryan!" Dylan yelled. "She won't hurt him." Amanda informed. "I know, Voltar must've sent it." Dylan said. "No, actually this was not his plan, she likes him." Amanda replied. "She is acting on her own." She added. "Great, can I just say, how glad I am not to be an Aster." Ralph stated. "Cause you people, attract the freaks." He added. "Lets go find them." Dylan said, as Cora comes to, Amanda helped her to her feet. "Are you alright?" Amanda asked. "Where is Ryan?" Cora replied. "That creature took him." Cole informed, as he comes over. "Come on." He added, meanwhile back at the castle as they saw this unfold. "Why is she not responding?" Voltar demanded. "I think she is rebelling." Rick replied. "Well, this went well." Volrin stated. "I will get her back under control, or kill her my lord." Kravitz swears. Meanwhile the creature lands far into the mountains, from where the alliance building is, and enters a cave near by. Where she lies Ryan down, as he was knocked out by the crash threw the wall. She touches his forehead, as Ryan starts to wake up she changes back to humanoid form. He sees her and jumps back. "Ahh!" He shouted. "You're the girl from the gala?" Ryan remembered. "Who are you?" He asked. "I was not given a name." She answered. "Let me guess, my Grandfather." Ryan replied. "Yes, he was my master." She said, just then Voltar appeared to them she changes back to beast form, and growled at Voltar and positioned herself in front of Ryan. "Now lets be easy girl." Voltar replied. . "Mine!" She stated. "You will not hurt him." She said. "No one will." She added, just then the team also shows up. "He is my son, just let him go." Dylan asked. "I will protect him." She insisted as she grabbed him up and flies over them, and out of the cave. "How do we stop her?" Dylan asked. "I will kill her." Voltar answered. "We need to find her first." Dylan said, meanwhile at another cave higher up. "You need to let me go." Ryan said. "They will kill you." Ryan stated. "I am going to keep you safe." She insists. "They are my family, my friends." Ryan explains. She changes back to humanoid. "Your heart is pure." She said, as she touches his chest. "This I know, do not trust Voltar he is always after power." She replied, just then the team makes way to them. She changes to beast and flies out without him. "You're ok?" Dylan asked. "Yes, I'm fine." Ryan said. "Good, lets go home then." Dylan stated, meanwhile back at the castle. "Every time we get the upper hand, you go soft." Volrin stated. "Even I, have loyalty to family." "Why do you think your still here?" He added. "We need to control this galaxy, before someone else does." Volrin replied. "We still own this galaxy." Voltar stated. Now the next day Dylan decided he and his sons needed some R&R. Scene in Dylan's quarters. "Sounds like a great idea." Steven said. "Yeah, I guess I'm in." Ryan replied. Now they go to their shuttle they climb in and strap in, when Ryan has his first vision of future events a power his mother possessed. He can see it as clear as day, the shuttle crashing to the planet and a shadow standing over him, then it ends as he clutched his forehead from the intense headache that followed. "Uh." He muttered. "Are you ok?" Steven asked. "I think I, just had a premonition." Ryan answered. "What?" Dylan said. "We were going down, we crashed." "It was like, I was there watching it." Ryan replied Dylan looks over the console, as they are flying toward Earth, suddenly the ship began to rattle, "So, I guess we know what your power is." Steven said. "I am not interested in one that shows me crashes." Ryan stated. "Relax, I've got control." Dylan assures, just then all the instruments go dark. "Damm it, brace for a hard landing." Dylan said. They crash out in the woods, the shuttle split into two parts, there are small flames still smoldering. All of them are unconscious. Dylan is the first to wake up. He looks over to see Steven and Ryan in the other half, still out cold. "Steven!" "Ryan!" He shouted. As they start to move. "I'm ok dad." Steven said as he sits up. Dylan comes to them. But the shuttle exploded behind Dylan, throwing him forward to the ground. Girl appeared and sees Ryan still out cold. She grabs him up and takes him away. As the team got the distress call and arrived moments later. "Dylan, are you ok?" Jon asked. "Yes, Ryan saw this before it happened." Dylan told. "He has Valtra's power of sight." Amanda replied. "Looks that way." Dylan said. "We need to find him." He added. "He is ok, that Girl Kravitz created pulled him to safety." Amanda confirmed. "Lets go get him." Dylan stated. Meanwhile as Ryan is still unconscious, she touches his forehead. "I will always take care of you." She says. Ryan has another vision, this time it's about Voltar. He sees him seated at his throne, when a powerful assassin enters and uses his power to blast him and kill him Ryan them jumps awake. "No!" Ryan shouted. "You're ok." She said. "I have to stop it." Ryan stated, as he tries to get up. "Stop what?" She asked. "Someone is going to kill him." Ryan replied. "I have to get back home." He stated. "I can see future events." Ryan explained. "I will help you." She says, as she transformed to creature and flies them up and away. She gets him back to Voltara and in front of the castle. "Thank you." Ryan said. "For you anything." She replied. Then she flies off, as Ryan goes inside and to the throne room. Voltar is seated exactly the way Ryan saw it in his vision. He sees the assassin in distance. Ryan rushes in. "Look out!" Ryan shouted, as the Assassin blast his power Voltar jumps out of the way, as the team also arrived. "You saved my life." Voltar replied, as the team grabbed the assassin and cuff him Dylan comes to Ryan as he rises, he also ducked from the blast. "Hey, are you ok?" Dylan said. "Yeah, is Voltar ok?" Ryan asked. "Yes." Dylan said. "I saw it happen dad." Ryan replied. "So, he has the gift." Rick replied. "Yes he does." Dylan said. Now back on the base in sickbay Paul checks Ryan who has a gash on his forehead. "Just a cut a couple of stiches, your good." Paul said. As we were recovering, Ryan was learning more about his gifts and the power that will come with them. He will learn he can control minds and have the power to control all things around him with his mind. Unfortunately, Ryan's vision could not always come in time to save a life. He lost Cora in an explosion, only to discover that Cara was alive. She is the girl that Kravitz created; He used her brain and brought her to back to life. That is not even the worst of it. There are others out there, beyond our galaxy. That has similar gifts as Ryan. One female in particular wants Ryan for herself. Her name is Dralla. Scene Ryan enters a cave on the outskirts of Voltara. He concentrates and can sense her. He goes into a cavern. Dralla comes up behind him. She is beautiful humanoid in appearance. She has blonde hair and blue eyes. "Well hello handsome." She replied. "I'm here to talk." Ryan said. "I'd like to listen." She stated. She leads him into her beautiful room filled with exotic furniture. "Nice place." Ryan replied. "Thank you, now what can I do for you?" She asked. "I understand that you, are one of the most powerful seers in this galaxy." Ryan said. "Yes I am." She stated. "I am too." Ryan replied. "Good for you." She said. "What is your name?' She asked. "Ryan." He said. "So, you learned how to lock your mind." She realizes as she tried to read him. "I've learned how to be cautious." Ryan stated. "How did they trap you?" He asked. She raised her hand to reveal a special steel bracelet. "This, it keeps abilities of any kind subdued." She said. "Try to control a few heads of the alliance and they leash you." She said. "Why not, use your powers for good?" Ryan asked she lets out a laugh. "Good?" "That is boring." She said. "I guess, I've wasted my time." Ryan replied, as he goes to leave. "You're a McKay, aren't you?" She read him. Ryan stopped. "And an Aster." She sensed. "I see it, Valtra was your mother." She stated. "I hope to see you again." She added. Ryan walked out. When he gets outside, Voltar was standing there. Ryan is surprised. "Are you insane?" Voltar asked. "No, she didn't hurt me." Ryan said. "Only because she can't, if she was free she'd kill you." Voltar added. "I can handle myself." Ryan stated. Now back on the base, Ryan is in his bedroom changing his shirt. Dylan entered. "Hey, are you ok?" Dylan asked. "Yes, I'm fine dad." Ryan answered. "She is evil son." Dylan stated. "I know." "She read my mind even with that bracelet." "She knows I'm a McKay and an Aster" Ryan said. "She had a thing for you, like mom didn't she?" Ryan realized. "She had a thing, for a lot of men." Dylan stated. Now later that night as Ryan sleeps he dreams. He is back in cavern only she has made it very romantic, with candles and comes out in a long sleek silk dress. "Care to join me?" She said, as Ryan is tossing and turning in his bed. "Come back to me Ryan. "She whispers, it echoes in his mind he wakes up "Whoa." Ryan replied as he caught his breath. Now in the morning, Jesse is at his console in the control room, when he gets the update on the com-link. "Sir, Dralla escaped." Jesse stated. "Find her." Dylan ordered. The team heads out. Meanwhile Ryan is out in the city, when Dralla walked right up to him. "So forgot me already?" She asked. "How did you escape?" Ryan replied. She holds up the broken open bracelet "I figured it out." She answered. Then she moves in closer and steals a kiss, as Ryan struggled to pull free. She managed to put another bracelet on his wrist. "I have what I want." She said. She grabs his hand and they vanish. Just as the team, gets to his location. "I lost them." Amanda replied. "I hope he can handle her." Ralph said. "He could, if she didn't bind his powers." Amanda realized. meanwhile, as Dralla appears on Saturn with Ryan In the center of a long abandon city. "Welcome to my old home." She said. "You realize, my father and my team will find us." Ryan replied. "You, are cute and arrogant, just like your father." She replied. "You should thank me, for keeping you safe from your grandfather." She said. "He is my family." "Why do I attract these women?" Ryan asked. meanwhile on an alliance cruiser. "Where are they?" Dylan demanded. "Amanda is trying to read him, but the bracelet blocks him." Cole said. "Where would she go?" Jon asked. "She, used to live in an old abandon city on Saturn." Jesse replied over the com-link. "Lets go." Dylan ordered. They arrive on Saturn Dralla sensed their landing. "Damm it." She exclaimed. They come toward them she pulls Ryan in and kisses him. It is powerful, and then she pulls back as his eyes glowed a deep green. She smiled and vanished as Ryan snapped out of it and took a breath. "Ryan, are you ok?" Jon asked. "Yeah, I'm ok." Ryan said. They open the Bracelet with a special key like device. Voltar comes up to him. "Don't worry, I will find her." Voltar vowed as he vanished. "That's our father, kill first then ask if it was ok." Shane replied. Now back on the base as Ryan is in his room. Voltar appears. "You are not really thinking about her right now?' Voltar asked. "Every time I let you boys handle them, you fall for them." Voltar stated. Just then Ryan has an intense vision. His eyes glow deep green and he clutches his head from the pain. He sees Cara walking in the city. Dralla comes up behind her and grabs her up by her throat then it ends. As he goes back to normal and breathes. "What did you see?" Voltar asked. Cara is in danger." Ryan replied. He rushes out. Voltar follows him. Dylan sees them in the corridor. What's going on?" As they rush right passed him. He follows them out of the base and into the city. They get to where he saw Cara walking. He sees Dralla coming at her. "Cara!" Ryan yelled. The power of his voice knocks

Dralla to the ground. Then the team cuffs her. "Are you ok?" Ryan asked. "I am now." She said as they hug. "You saw her coming after me." Cara said. "Yes, I would never let her hurt you." Ryan said as they hug. "Get her back to prison." Dylan ordered. Now things have gone back to a sort of normal, with a few bumps along the way, including evil creatures after our galaxy from another one, and many more Beautiful yet deadly females to deal with. Tracilla actually came back from the dead. Not the same as she was, in a good way. Now we will face even bigger challenges, the possible end of an era? Can it be, that my nephew Ryan is the key to making my father go legit? If he does, who will be waiting in the shadows to take his place? My nephew continues to hone his skills with the help of Moondeath. Vala has also proven very powerful and helped to save us from many of these new threats. Now comes the next journey, a journey to the underworld itself. It will prove a very traumatic experience for all of us. It is never a dull moment with my family. Lets hope we get threw this one alive.

Chapter 16
THE UNDERWORLD

The heart can easily be fooled; it is usually by someone we love. My father is a master at that. The heart can also be broken, by loss of love or a friend. I am afraid we will suffer many of these on our journey. Scene, on the base in the early morning hours, Ryan is still asleep in his bed. He has a vision. It starts out in Voltar's castle but then, hundreds of creatures rush into the long hallway led by one in a dark cloak. "Now it is mine." He claimed as he also laughs in triumph. Ryan wakes up, and jumps to his feet he gets dressed. As he is doing that, we go to a deep dark cavern on Voltara to see these very creatures. In a dark cloak, we see their leader. He is standing above them on the edge of a vast deeper cavern. These beasts have not been seen above ground, Hellish beings black as night and bruit in force. "Soon, we will control it all!" Leader exclaimed, as the beast howled and growled in support. "The boy is the key." He tells. "The key, to victory over the Asters." He explained. "His reign is over." He ends as the beast rejoice and cheered. Meanwhile back on the base in the docking bay, Ryan enters and grabs his gear and goes to head out when Dylan enters. "Ryan?" "Where are you going?" He asked. "There is trouble." He replied, as he climbed into one of the fighters. "You need to wait for some back up." Dylan insisted. "You are barely healed from your last go around." Dylan reminded. "There is no time." Ryan stated, as he then closes the hatch and the docking bay doors open he flies out. "We have trouble." Dylan called over the com-link. Now as Ryan lands his fighter near the castle, he then exits it and makes his way inside to the throne room. Down that same long hall, he saw in his vision. When suddenly, out of the shadows comes a figure toward him. He comes close enough to see, it is the leader in the cloak. Ryan is startled and quickly backs up. "I knew you would come." He said. "Who are you?" Ryan asked. "Where is Voltar?" Ryan demanded. "You are too late, Voltara is mine." He informed. "No, its not." Ryan said. Two creatures come out and grab Ryan by his arms. "You are the key." He said as Ryan tries to pull free of the creatures. "You won't win." Ryan replied. At that moment, he removed his cloak it is Volrin. Ryan's eyes widen in shock. "I already have kid." He said. "Are you insane?" Ryan replied. "Yes." Volrin admitted. "I am also going to be Voltara's next king." He added. "You see, when you are found dead, Voltar will be so distraught, so inconsolable." "I will just naturally assume power." He explains. "Well, with the help of these guys of course." "A king needs an army." He says. "He has protected, you and this is how you show your loyalty?" Ryan asked. "I will not be second!" He exclaimed. "Not anymore." Just then you can hear the engines of the teams fighters overhead. "Ahh the reinforcements." He replied with a smile. "Take care of them." He instructs the creatures. "Where is Voltar?" "Where is Rick?" Ryan questioned. "They are too busy, playing with the newborn brats." He answered. "So easily they are distracted now." "It's sad really." He added. "What about Devon, do you even care?" Ryan asked. "He will hate you." He added. "Of course he will, as I hate my father." "It's an Aster thing you realize." He replied. "You really don't care about anyone, but yourself." Ryan stated. "I am the only one who matters." He said. Meanwhile outside the castle walls the team is battling the creatures summoned by Volrin. "Who is in charge of this mess?" Ralph asked. "It's not Voltar, that's for sure." Cole replied. "Yeah, definitely not his style." Dylan stated. "That leaves Volrin." Amanda replied. "You mean that idiot is at it again?" Ralph replied. "When will he learn?" Xavier asked. "This time, he may have the upper hand." Amanda realized. "He has Ryan." She said. meanwhile back inside the castle. Volrin gets closer to Ryan. "Its time to die." He says. "How are you healing?" He asked as he punches him in the side. Ryan tries to hold back the pain, but you can see it on his face. "Your pathetic, comes from being half human." Volrin insulted. "You really need to learn, how to just not feel it." He added. "Like you?" Ryan said. "I use pain to my advantage, to gain control." Volrin replied. "Now, it's time to end you." Volrin stated as the creatures let him go. "You will die by my hands." He replied. "I want them all to remember, I killed you." He added as his hands glow and then a glow all over his body as he blasts it out threw his hands at Ryan knocking him to his knees. As outside Amanda can feel his pain. "He is killing him!" She screams, as the team finally blasts way into the castle. They come to him. "Meet your new ruler." He boasted and smiled a devilish grin. Then Voltar appeared before him. "Your last chance is gone brother." Voltar stated as he transformed into his Dregon and grabs Volrin up by his throat. The team helps Ryan. "Go ahead do it, coward." He stated. Voltar begins to tighten his claw and apply pressure, when Moondeath appeared. "He has had too many chances father." Voltar replied. "I know." Moondeath answered. Volrin is angered his eyes glow and blasted his power threw them at Moondeath. "Die old man!" He shouted, as Moondeath fell to the ground. "I will take you with me to hell." He indicated. He begins to generate so much heat and power, that Voltar had to drop him. "He's not going to stop!" Amanda yells. All run out of the castle just in time. He causes an explosion of power that takes out the whole castle, Volrin and Moondeath as well. "I can't believe he did that." Shane said. "I should've seen this." Ryan insisted. "No, this is not your fault." Voltar replied. "So, your castle is destroyed." "Where will you stay?" Jon asked. "I will stay with Ryan." "You did get new quarters all your own now." Voltar replied. "Just until my castle is rebuilt." Voltar promises. "You won't even know I'm there." He added. "I will be at my club." Rick stated. "I guess so, ok." Ryan said. Now later that night when, we all felt safe, at least we thought with Volrin dead. We will learn that even dead Asters, can still wreak havoc. At night as Ryan slept, with Voltar in the guest room. Ryan dreams he is back in the castle engulfed in flames. Moondeath and Volrin are standing their charred and burned reaching out to grab him. "You are coming with us." Volrin replied. Ryan jumps up in the bed and catches his breath. Voltar entered. "Are you alright?" He asked. "Yeah, just a nightmare." Ryan said. "Not about me I hope?" Voltar asked. "No, about me." Ryan confessed. now the next day in Dylan's office as he is sitting at his desk going over paperwork. Voltar walks in. "We need to pull our heads together, about Ryan." He stated. "What?" "Did something happen?" Dylan says frantically. "He had a nightmare last night." "He did not go into details, but he was in it." Voltar said. "You think he is in danger?"

Dylan asked. "I think so." Voltar answered. "I will talk to him." Dylan stated. "I don't think he will tell us." Voltar replied. "Who do you suggest?" Dylan asked. "Perhaps, your fellow psychic Amanda?" Voltar answered. They both go over to Amanda's quarters. "You know, I can't just probe his thoughts without his knowledge." Amanda stated. "Yes, but he has gotten really good at blocking his mind." "You're the only one who can get a glimpse." "He won't tell us." Dylan pleaded. "I don't want to have to order you, as your captain." Dylan replied. "He is my son, if he is endanger I need to know, please." He begged. Amanda sighs. "Ok, I will do it for you." She said. "Thank you." Dylan said. Now Amanda goes and sits on her couch. She closes her eyes and concentrates. She links her mind to Ryan's. She sees images of his nightmare, of Volrin and can feel intense fear and the death, she is so overwhelmed, and she must break the link. "Whoa." She said. "Are you ok?" Dylan asked. What did you see?" He demanded. "I saw fire, I saw death." "The ghosts of Volrin and Moondeath." She replied. "What does it mean?" Dylan asked. "He has so much guilt built up about their deaths, he is going to drive himself crazy." "It could even destroy his mind." She feared. "What can we do?" Dylan asked. "I think, I should talk to him." Amanda suggested. "Yes you should." Dylan agreed. Meanwhile in the Rec Room Ryan is lifting weights when Amanda enters. "So, did my dad or my grandfather send you?" Ryan asked as he put up weights. "Yes, we need to talk." She replied. "Do I have a choice?" Ryan asked as he grabs a towel and dries off. "I'm sorry I entered your mind." She said. "Its fine, I can hear everyone's thoughts in here so." Ryan replied. "You, need to stop blaming yourself." Amanda says. "Its easy to say." Ryan replied. "They don't blame you, no one does." She stated. "I can feel their sadness, they miss him." Ryan replied. "This, all happened because of who I am." "This is my fault, I am the first grandson." Ryan stated. "Just let me help you." Amanda asked. "Ok." Ryan accepted. Then she goes out; just then Volrin's charred remains are standing there before him. "You can't get rid of me." He laughs. "You are not really here." Ryan replied as he closed his eyes a moment, and then opened them and he is gone. Ryan breathes a sigh of relief as he goes to leave he hears. "See you in your dreams." Volrin voice echoed in his ears As Ryan's eyes widened in fear. Amanda in the corridor could feel Volrin's real presence. "No." She said she then rushes to Dylan's office. "I was wrong." She started. "Volrin is not a dream, his very soul is here form the underworld and it's after Ryan." She replied. Dylan's eyes widen in distress. Meanwhile back in Ryan's quarters Voltar is there. Volrin's spirit appears, but Voltar cannot see him. "He is mine, I'm going to take his soul to hell with me." He replied. "I will make him insane, like you did to me." He added. Then he vanished, now later that night as Ryan slept he began to toss and turn. Volrin appeared at the foot of his bed. "Time to. …Wake up! He exclaimed. Ryan jumped up in the bed. "It's time for the torcher to begin." He added. "You are not real"? Ryan insisted. "I am, in the underworld." "I can make my own rules" Volrin informed. "I will haunt you until I break you." He added. "You won't break me." Ryan stated. "Don't be so sure kid." He replied. "Get out of my head." Ryan shouted. Volrin vanished just then Voltar rushed in. "Are you alright?" Voltar asked. "No, I'm not." Ryan admitted. "Volrin was just here, at least his spirit was." Ryan explained. "He said, he is here to haunt me, until I break." He added. Now the next day the team is gathered in the in control room. "We need to figure out how to put Volrin back in the underworld, for good." Dylan said. "The only way I know is a Ervaltred." Jon stated. "It is what you humans would call, an exorcism." Jon explained. "What do we have to do?" Ryan asked. "I can find one of our Volcrats or a priest in your term." Jon answered as he headed out. "Yeah, we need to get rid of that jerk permanently." Ralph stated just then Volrin appeared but only Ryan can see him. "They can't get rid of me." "I'm not going anywhere, it's your fault I'm dead, so you're going to suffer." He replied as he laughed. Voltar noticed Ryan is agitated. "Ryan, is he here now?" Voltar asked. "Can you hear him?" he added. "Of course he can, how you ever got control of this galaxy is beyond me." Volrin said. "Yes he is." Ryan answered. "I will get rid of you for good." Voltar vowed. "Tell gramps, I'm not going anywhere." Volrin replied. "Yes you are." Ryan said. "Why don't you, have a look on this side?" Volrin suggested as he comes to Ryan and touches his forehead, giving him a blast of his negative energy causing him to see the underworld itself. To feel the pain and agony of the dead souls and see the horrors that exists there. It caused Ryan to pass out. "Ryan!" Dylan yelled as he kneels to him. "Volrin has linked his mind to his." Amanda sensed. "We have to do something." Steven said. "I don't know how we can?" Amanda admits. Meanwhile in the underworld itself Ryan is walking along its dark deep caverns. He can see fiery rivers on one side and the caverns are aligned with skeletal bones of the dead, as still zombie type creatures walk along passed him. He then saw Cora and Cara together. "No." Ryan denied as they saw him. "Join us my love." Cara replied as she reached for him with her decayed hand. Ryan shakes his head as if to try and wake up. "Stay with us." Cora added as she tried to grab him but he got away and down another cavern. As he entered it resembled his home as a kid on Earth, before he ran away. "What is this?" Ryan asked as he looks around he sees Montra the Moneconda there. "Stay with me!" She screeched as she grabbed hold of him. "I'm not dead!" He yells as he struggles to pull free. "No not yet." She replied at that moment back on the base, in sickbay he is hooked up to monitors as Paul is checking them. "How do we pull him out of this?" Dylan pleaded. "I don't know." Paul answered. "We will figure it out." "He is not taking him to hell." Voltar vowed. Meanwhile back in hell. "Please, help me to get out of here." Ryan begged. "Why would I do that?" She asked. "You know, I don't belong here, not yet." Ryan said. "No, you have much to do up there." She replied. "Please help me." He asked. "What do I get?" She said. "I have nothing to give you." Ryan replied. "I will settle for a kiss." She said. "What?" Ryan said as she pulled him in and kissed him. Volrin is in the distance. "Yes keep him distracted, so I can kill his body." Volrin said. "I feel weird." Ryan said, as he pulled free. "Its ok, it's just your body dying." She informed. "What!" Ryan exclaimed as back in the sickbay he codes. "Just let go Ryan." Montra insisted. "You can stay with me." She added. "No!" Ryan shouted with a powerful force, as concentrates and his eyes glow and he is transported back into his body by the sheer will and power of his mind. He then wakes up in sickbay as Paul is standing over him. "Thank god." Paul said. "I'm back?" Ryan asked, as Steven came up and hugged him. "Yes." He sighed relief. Jon is standing there with the Volcrats beside him. "We banished him." Jon said. "He won't be back." He added. Ryan takes a breath. "We should let you rest." Dylan said now the next day "So, you will be glad to know, I am going back to my castle it is finished." Voltar replied, "Ok sure, if you really want to." Ryan said with some disappointment. "Its best I think." "I've annoyed you and your new girlfriend Dralla long enough." He replied. "You haven't annoyed me." Ryan said. "I will trust me." Voltar admitted. meanwhile in the Rec Room Devon is with Jon. "Just tell me, I won't end up like him." Devon said. "You won't." Jon assured. "How can you be so sure?" Devon asked. "If I can fight the darkness within, so can you." Jon stated as he put his hand on Devon's shoulder. "We will protect you." Jon added. "I know, I just wish I could've changed him." "Like you guys did with Voltar." Devon said. "He has just gotten older, and we have been wearing on him." Jon smiled as Devon laughed. Now next day in the control room, in Dylan's office. "Hey dad." Ryan said as he entered. "Hey, it's quiet for once." He enjoyed. "Careful, we'd be out of a job." Ryan said. "That would not be a band thing." Dylan replied. "You sure, you don't want time off?" Dylan asked. "No, work is what I need." Ryan answered. "Oh by the way, my roommate is leaving." Ryan stated. "Halleluiah!" Dylan exclaimed. Ryan smiled and headed out. Now over at Jon's quarters, he is working on some notes when Voltar appeared. "Well junior, it's been a long reign." Voltar stated. "Are you ready to go legit?" Jon asked. "I think I did, awhile ago son." Voltar admitted. "Yeah, I think you did." Jon replied. "I guess, I'm just an old softy." He said. "No, you always had it in you to be good." "You were just too stubborn." Jon replied. "Yes, but so are you junior." Voltar stated. "I got that from you." Jon smiled. "Just don't let your guard down." "Volrin did get some creatures railed up for a take over." Jon warned. "Yes, but now that he is gone, they will fade back into the shadows." Voltar insisted. As he leaves, in a secret underground hideaway, Volrin's creatures are massing. "He is gone it's over." Beast replied "No, it's not his Grandson is still the key to the kingdom." Half human creature replied. "How do we get him?" Beast asked. "I know how, Volrin left me his secrets about that castle and the base." He explained. He pulls a map from his cloak. "All we have to do, is attack at night when they sleep." "We can walk right in and take him." He stated then laughed. Now back on the base in the Rec Room Ryan is lifting weights as Amanda enters. "Hey you ok?" She asked. "Yeah, I will be." Ryan answered. "Take your time, you went threw hell literally." She said. "I know, and I will thanks." Ryan said. Now later as all are sleeping a band of seven followers of Volrin sneak threw a drainage pipe and into the basement beneath the base. "Now we take over." Half human replies as suddenly the floor beneath Ryan's bed is blasted threw. He is thrown form the bed. "Uh." Ryan sighs dazed and dizzy. He looked up to see what happened. He is face to face with this creature his eyes widen in alarm and disbelief. "What are you?" Ryan asked. "The new order." He replied as he grabbed Ryan down threw the floor. Dralla entered as she heard the commotion. "Ryan!" She screamed. The team and Voltar come in. "He's been taken." Dralla said. Well it would appear that Volrin has managed to gather quiet a following you know what they say about a psychopath he leaves a following behind. Who will win this battle? Scene; back on the base in Ryan's quarters. "What happened?" Dylan demanded. "Some ugly creature blasted threw the floor and took him." She explained. "I should've taken the threat more seriously." Voltar admitted. "We will get him back, they have no real power they are just bruit force." Jon stated. "Yes, but Ryan is not immortal." "They can hurt or even kill him." Dylan reminded; meanwhile back at the creature's secret lair. Ryan is tied with rope to a single chair, in a dark barely lit room. The entire room filled with beast surrounding him. "Hard to believe, that you can control the future of a king." Half human said. "You've signed your death warrants." Ryan stated. "Perhaps, but you will die first." He replied. Ryan uses his power to enter one of the creature's minds and controls him he makes him lift up the half human one in the air. "Let him go." Creature replied. Just then one of the other creatures hit Ryan over the head and knocked him out releasing his hold on the other and creature puts him back down. "What happened?" Creature asked. "Keep him sedated." Half human instructed. "So he can not, do that again." He added. One of Karvitz former scientist comes in and sedated him with an injection. "Now, we call Voltar and the alliance and talk terms." He said. Meanwhile the team is out in their fighters searching for them. "Anything Amanda?" Dylan asked. "No, I can't read him." "I think he has been sedated." She fears. "We will find him." Jon insisted just then Voltar receives a message in his cruiser on his vidlink. "We have the boy Voltar." He states. "If, you surrender your power and planet he will live." He added. "When I find you, I will kill you." Voltar promises. Meanwhile in another room where they have Ryan sedated he begins to come around. "He is waking up." Creature replied. The scientist rushes over and injects him again. Amanda senses. "We must hurry." Amanda warned. "They will kill him with all of those drugs." She added. "How long do we have?" Dylan asked. "I'm not sure, few hours maybe." She answered. "They have turned one of my scientist." "He will die for that." Voltar said. "Lets just find Ryan." Jon replied. Meanwhile back in the secret hideaway our creatures are getting agitated. "Where is he?" Half human questioned. "If he does not contact me within the hour, the boy will die." He added. As everyone is scrambling to find Ryan, Vala is back on the base in Jon's quarters she is able to create a necklace of pure power that appears around Ryan's neck and it glows. "I'm coming." She said as she headed out into corridor and down passed the control room when Jesse saw her. "Vala?" He said. "Tell my dad to go to Mars." "I'll meet him there." She replied as she goes toward docking bay. "Whoa, wait Vala!" Jesse calls but she is gone. Jesse frantically calls Jon over com-link. "Ahh sir, Vala is headed to Mars." "She said to meet her there." Jesse informed. "What?" Jon exclaimed. "I think she knows where Ryan is." He added. "Get me her tracer location." Jon demanded as they head to Mars. Meanwhile Vala has landed on Mars right near the creatures' secret hideaway she exits craft and makes her way inside. She follows the light in the dark cavern to come upon Ryan, tied to chair unconscious. "Hang on." She said as she used her power to blast the scientist and knocks him out. The half human creature hears the noise. "What the?" He replied. He comes to where they are and Vala uses her power to blast him back. "Ryan, can you hear me?" Vala asked Ryan starts to move and wakes up opens his eyes. "Vala?" Ryan questioned. The team also makes way to them by tacking her. "Are you ok?' Dylan asks as he untied him. "Yeah, thanks to Vala," Ryan replied. Now back on the base in sickbay Ryan is sitting up on the edge of the bed as Paul checks him over with hand held scanner. "Your ok?" Dralla asked as she entered and hugs him. "Yeah, never a dull moment as an Aster." Ryan replied. "That is not even funny." She responded. "So, am I clear?" Ryan asked. "Yes, your fine." Paul stated. "Just take it easy for awhile." Paul added. "Hey, we should go to the beach." Steven suggested. Meanwhile outside the base under its surface, deep beneath it is the ocean floor is a beautiful hidden city. With it's glittering walls and caverns bright with colors. Fish and sea creatures never seen before, inside a particular structure are beautiful females, similar to mermaids but without the tails just webbed feet and gills along their necks. One on particular is about twenty years old, with beautiful lavender hair with speckles of silver throughout it and beautiful ocean blue eyes. "The time has come, our destiny awaits." She told. "What destiny is that my queen?" One of her warriors asked. "The one who brings us hope for the future, it is time to bring our king home." She informed. "He lives among the land dwellers?" Warrior asked. "He is more than just that, he is of two very different worlds." She replied. "It will not be easy, he will be protected by them." She stated. "He won't let you just take him my queen." Warrior warned. "Voltar's time is passed." "No one can stop what is meant to be." She said. "He will be mine, before it is too late." She vowed. "Too late?" Warrior asked. "Before he has a child with another." "He must have my child." "I was promised this long before, I was even born." She stated. "He made a vow to my mother, that the firstborn would be mine." She tells. "Now that he is revealed, it is time to take him." She replied. "We have waited long enough." She insisted. Meanwhile as the team takes some well-deserved R&R on the beaches of Voltar with its beautiful red seas the water is actually dark red. Vala comes over to Ryan. He sits on a blanket, while the other team members are in the water. "Aren't you getting in?" She asked in her adorable bathing suit. "Sorry Vala but, I have a thing about oceans." Ryan replied. "What thing?" She asked as Steven comes over. "He got pulled under by a rip current, almost drowned." Steven explained. "I swear, it felt like someone was pulling me down." Ryan remembers. "That sounds awful." Dralla said as she sat beside him. "Yeah, since then he never goes in the ocean." Steven said, "It's time to face your fears." Vala stated. "Dad says, it's the only way to conquer them." She added. "Yeah, besides it was years ago." Steven replied. "How about later?" "I've got a bad feeling." Ryan stated. "Ok later, but I'm holding you to it." She replied as she runs to the water. "She is right, you've got to get over it." Steven said. "I'll go in with you." Dralla replied. "You will?" he said as he leans in and they kiss. Meanwhile in the ocean off in the distance the Queen watches. "He is mine." She says angrily meanwhile back on the base Voltar enters control room and goes to Dylan in his office. "Where did everyone go?" Voltar asked. "To the ocean, for some relaxation." Dylan answered. "Why there?" Voltar asked in a nervous tone. "It was Vala's choice, believe me Ryan hates the ocean." He stated. "He does." Voltar inquired. "Yeah, when he was about twelve he nearly drowned." "So he stays on land." He explained. "Good." Voltar replied with a sigh of relief. "Why, what's this about?" Dylan asked. "Nothing." Voltar said meanwhile back outside at the ocean Ryan is laying on his towel in his shorts with his eyes closed relaxing. When he suddenly has a flash of the queen. "Ryan, come to me." "I'm waiting." She said. "Who are you?" he asked. "You don't remember?" She replied. He then has a flash of when he was a kid and being pulled underwater he was actually on Voltara in its very ocean and she was pulling him down. Ryan snaps out of it and sits up. "Are you ok?" Dralla asked. "Yeah, I'm fine." He replied as he glanced out at the ocean and looked around and catches a glimpse of her. "What the hell?" Ryan replied. She dives under the water. "I need to, go get something to eat." He said as he gets up and heads toward the base just then the queen appeared behind him in a beautiful dress of silver and pink. "Excuse me." She said. Ryan tuned to her "Have we met?" She asked. "I don't think so." Ryan replied. "So, are you enjoying the water?" She asked. "No, actually oceans and I have a bad history." He answered. "I'm just here with my family and team.' He added. "Such a shame, the water is cool and refreshing on a hot day as this." She replied. "Yeah, so is a shower and a lot safer." Ryan stated. "Don't be afraid Ryan, the ocean is your destiny." She said to him telepathically "Who are you?" Ryan said as he backed up. "I am yours." She added she then vanishes in a mist of ocean water that sprayed him lightly as Dralla comes to him. "Hey you ok?" She asked. "Yeah, I feel like heading home, if that's ok." Ryan replied. "Yes of course, are you sure your ok?" She asked. "I'm fine." Ryan said as Steven comes over. "Hey what's up?" Steven said. "We are gonna go back." Dralla said. "Ok sure, I'll see you later for dinner." Steven replied as they go meanwhile back in the ocean. "I must find a way, to lure him back to the water." She stated. "How, he fears the ocean." Warrior replied. "By making him love it again." She replied. "I will make him overcome his fears." She stated. Now later that night as Ryan slept. The queen entered his mind and manipulated his dreams. He is back at the ocean. "Come to the water, it is fine." She said. "I can't I don't swim." He replied. He is standing in swim shorts. "I will teach you, just trust me." She said. "I won't let anything happen to you." She promised. "Why should I believe you?" Ryan asked. "You belong with me, in the ocean Ryan." "We are pre destined." Ryan is tossing and turning on the bed getting agitated. "No." He said. Dralla wakes up and shakes him. "Ryan wake up." She said. Ryan wakes up. "What is happening to me?" Ryan asked. Dralla has a look of confusion on her face. Now next day in the control room, "I have no idea who she is." Ryan stated. "You saw her at the ocean yesterday?" Dylan asked. "Yes, she was telling me to remember." Ryan said. "What is that about?" Steven asked. "I know what is going on, and you need to stay as far from the water and her as possible." Voltar commanded. "What is it your not saying?" Jon demanded. "They are Vomarian warriors." Voltar explained. "What does this, have to do with me?" Ryan asked. "They think I owe them a king." He replied. "Why would they think that?" Steven asked. "I knew their queen long ago, that girl would be her daughter." "She desired an alliance between our clans." "I said no, she did not take rejection well, then again their warriors not too bright." Voltar replied. "So, why is she after me?' Ryan asked. "She must've known you were an Aster before I did." Voltar stated. "When I was twelve, I swear someone pulled me under." Ryan remembered. "So why now?" Dylan asked. "She is of age." "She figured this is the time to strike, but you are safe as long as you stay away from the ocean." Voltar guaranteed. "That is where her power is strongest." He insisted. "So, she wants a king?" Jon asked. "She is looking to solidify her future, since we are the power on land and they command the water." "She is looking to create a superior race." Dralla realized. "Ok, I still don't get why me?" Ryan asked. "You of age." "You're the first born of my firstborn." "You have no children yet." Voltar explained. "Wait, so she wants to have my child?" Ryan realized. "As long as you stay away from water, you'll be safe." Steven said. "Not a problem." Ryan replied. "Just be careful, they are very good at mind games and seduction." Voltar stated. "So, we got rid of one Psycho for another?" Dylan asked. "Sir, we have trouble by the city limits the dam has burst." Jesse stated. "She is trying to lure you." Voltar informed. "Then he will stay here." "The rest of you get out there and secure it." Dylan ordered. "Perhaps, I can handle the girl she is young and naive." Voltar suggested. "Yeah, just your type.' Dylan said meanwhile back in the ocean she noticed he did not come. "I must go to the base and continue to manipulate his dreams." "I will persuade him. She informed. "We should capture one if them, it will force him out." Warrior suggested. "You may be right, we will take one of them." She replied. "Alert my warriors." She stated. As she prepared to battle for Ryan, the youngest of our family went for a trip to the beach that we, didn't know about until it was too late for one of our team. Scene Devon and Marie and Vala are back at the beach alone. "Are you sure, we should be out here?" Marie asked. "Hey, I am thirteen and a very powerful Aster, I can protect us." Devon said. "Yeah right." Vala replied. "Look do you want to go swimming or what?" He asked. "I'm in!" Marie yells. "Yeah me too." Vala added. Meanwhile back in the base in the control room. "Ok, we need to find these warrior women." Dylan ordered. "Lets move out." Jon replied team heads out. Just then Ryan has a flash, he sees the kids at the beach and the warrior women rise out of the water and grab them. "No!" Ryan exclaimed. "Ryan what did you see?" Dralla asked, "The kids are in danger." Ryan replied as he rushes into the control room. "Dad, where are the kids?" Ryan asked. "With Lisette, she took them out." Dylan stated. "They are at the ocean?" Ryan said. "I'll call her." Jesse replied meanwhile at the beach Lisette catches up to them "Ok, just for a little while, don't go too far out." She said. "You are awesome." Devon replied as they run into the water and go about waist deep. When suddenly the warriors emerge form the water. Lisette sees them first, she rushes into water to protect them her gun drawn. "Get back to land!" She screams as she fired at them hitting one. Marie and Vala get back to the sand. "Devon, go!" She orders. "No, I can help." He insisted. He concentrates and uses his power to manipulate the water. He causes a huge wave to knock most of them back and further out to sea. Thinking they are safe they sigh relief until; the queen emerges in front of Lisette. "Lisette!" Devon yelled the queen then stabs Lisette in chest with her dagger and then she goes back under the water. "No!" Devon cried. He rushes to her and grabs her before she can go under. He pulls her back to shore and lies her down with tears in his eyes. "Lisette?" He cried. He can see the blood pouring from her side. "Tell Ryan to kill...she takes a breath "Kill that bitch." She closed her eyes and died. The team arrived Jesse sees her and rushes to her kneels down. "Lisette, no!" He says in denial "Wake up!" He yells as the team lower their heads in sadness. "I'm so sorry, I tried, I blasted them back but, the queen came out of no where." as Devon choked back tears. "It's ok." Jon assured him putting his hand on his shoulder. Ryan sees her too. "No." Ryan said. Jesse looks up to Ryan and a rush of anger takes over as he rises. "You." He stated. "Jesse take it easy." Jon said. "All of you Asters, we put our lives on the line!" He exclaimed. "Why is it you, never pay the price?" He demanded. "I am sorry Jesse." Ryan replied. "It doesn't bring her back." He said, "You live with that." He added. "I thought you, were different but you are just another Aster." Jesse stated "Jesse that's enough!" Dylan shouted. "Tell it to Lisette captain." Jesse replied as he walks off. "Ryan, he didn't mean it." "He is just upset." Jon insisted "No, he is right." "This is on me." Ryan replied. "I killed her." Ryan added. "We all suffered loss son." Dylan stated. "She wants revenge, we owe her that." Devon said. "Revenge is not the answer." Jon insisted. "No, I think it is." Ryan replied as he walked toward the water. "Ryan, no!" Dylan exclaimed. "Stop!" Steven yelled. "It's my fight." Ryan stated as he goes in waist deep. Jesse hears the commotion and turns back. "Ryan?" Jesse asked. "Here I am!" He yelled. "Its me you want!" "Come and get me!" He pleaded. Just then the queen, raises form the water. "Yes it is." She replied. "Leave them out of it." Ryan demanded. "Done." She answered as she grabs his hand and pulls him down into the water. "Ryan!" Dylan shouts. "We will get him back." Jon insisted. "I want to help I owe Lisette." Devon asked. "We need to get a team together, to go down there. "I got here as soon as I could." Voltar replied. "Not soon enough." Dylan informed. "Where is Ryan?" Voltar asked. Dylan pointed to the water. "No, we have to get him!" Voltar exclaimed. Meanwhile the queen and Ryan arrived to her underwater palace hidden inside of deep caverns. "Welcome, to your new home." She replied. Well now we must prepare for our battle on the queen's turf, but when we get rid of one psycho will we only gain another? Unfortunately, it is the aster curse. All of the male Asters in our clan for reasons we have yet to full comprehend have evil women that will lust after them. It goes back further than even us. So, as we get ready for this next challenge, it will only remind me of the role my family has played in this galaxy and the role we will play in its future survival.

Chapter 17

PSYCHOS PYSCHOS EVERYWHERE!

Well, if you haven't learned by now, Asters are cursed you will. We have issues when it comes to females. Yes, we can get it right sometimes and love a good girl, but it's that dark inner Aster that takes us to the Psychos. Now a woman scorned is bad, but a psycho scorned? To put in my father's terms "The only safe psycho female is a dead one." Scene back in the underwater palace where our queen has taken Ryan to be her king, "Who said, I was staying?" Ryan replied. "You are my destiny," "You're not leaving." She stated as her warriors surrounded him. "Now, lets get you some dry clothes." She said. One of her warriors brings clothes over. "Change, then we can talk further." She insisted. They put him in a room and close the door. They post a guard outside; meanwhile back on the surface by the water. "Ok, let's go." Voltar stated. Jesse comes back to them. "I'm going too." He said. "Jesse this is to…" Dylan begins. Jesse cut him off. "I'm going." Jesse informed. "Alright, we will need to split up." "We have no idea what it's like down there." They gear up Dylan, Jon, Steven, Devon, Jesse and Voltar go down into the water. Once they arrive at a cavern they can remove dive gear. The rest of the team works to distract the warriors from above. As they slip into the palace area. "Ok, stay sharp." Dylan instructed. They split up to take corridors in teams of two. Devon and Jesse are together. We follow them down a hall. They can see Ryan in a reflective window made of seawater and other sea elements. "Over here."

Devon said. Ryan looks up. He is dressed in a special pair of silk type pants and shirt he sees them. "Devon?" Ryan replied. They come to the door and Devon takes out the guard with his powers, and get inside. "Where are the others?" He asked. "On their way. Jesse paused. "Pal, I'm sorry I lost it on you." He added. "No, it was my fault." Ryan replied. "Ok, time to go." Devon said. They head to doorway, but the queen is there. She uses her power to throw Ryan and Devon back against a far wall. "Nice try." She stated. Jesse in anger charges for her "No!" Ryan yelled. The Queen uses her nails, which become claws to stab him in the chest. "Join your girlfriend." She replied. "Go to hell." Jesse said, as he takes a breath. Ryan rose from the floor and concentrates. He uses his power to enter her mind. He takes control of her and causes her to turn her claws on herself. She stabs into her chest. She yelled and falls to the ground. The rest of the team make way to them, as Ryan kneels to Jesse. "You are gonna be ok." Ryan said. "You never were a good liar." Jesse smiled. "You are gonna make it." Ryan insisted. Jesse coughed up blood. "Hey, I will be with Lisette." He replied. He then closed his eyes and passed. "Jesse?" Ryan said. He lowers his head. Jon comes to a confused and distraught Devon, puts his hand on his shoulder. "Why is this happening?" Devon asked. "I can't answer that one kid." Jon replied. Now next scene is the funeral. Two caskets side by side, all are in their black uniforms. All have tears rolling down their cheeks. Ryan flashes back to the time when, he and Jesse were at the restaurant just laughing. Everyone else remembers a time with Lisette and Jesse on the base. "We can take comfort, in the fact they died fighting." Biscus said. Now later back on Voltara Ryan is standing outside by the ocean. Dralla comes over to him. "Hey, it's getting late." She said. "I'll be there, in a little while." He replied. "You did what you could." She assured. "No, I let two innocent people die." "I have to live with that." Ryan stated. "They died fighting." She replied. "A battle, they never should've had to." Ryan stated. "I need to be alone please." Ryan asked. She nods in agreement and leaves, and then Voltar appeared. "It's never good to be alone." Voltar stated. "Didn't you hear me?" "I want to be alone?" Ryan insisted. "Of course, but you know I never listen to you kids." Voltar replied. "I killed them." Ryan said. "No, it's not your fault, if anything this is on me." Voltar stated. "My blood always suffers, for what I've done." He added. "They didn't deserve this." Ryan replied. "It's always the innocent who suffer."

Voltar said. "I won't let that happen again." Ryan vowed. Meanwhile back on the base in the Rec Room, Devon is practicing his telekinetic powers. He has the weights and chairs floating around him. Jon entered. "Hey are you ok?" Jon asked. Devon lowered the objects to the floor. "What good is having these powers, if people still die?" Devon asked. "I have watched many people I loved die." "I guess power or not we can't control our fate." Jon answered. "Yeah, but Asters don't die." Devon stated, "Even we will die." "We may live longer than our human friends, but we all do ascend." "Moondeath did." Jon replied. "I was right there next to her, I couldn't save her." Devon said. "I wish, I could tell you it won't happen again, but it will." Jon said. "Thanks, I need to get to bed." Devon replied. He heads out. Jon sits on bench when Voltar appeared. "It's been a rough day junior." Voltar stated. "Yes it has, how is Ryan?" Jon asked. "He, is blaming himself for everything." Voltar answered, "I know how that feels." Jon said. "What is done is done." "We can not live in the past." Voltar stated. Now the next day, Ryan is at the daycare on the base watching the babies in their playpens, just being babies. Paul comes over to him. "Yeah, they are cute huh?" Paul said. "Yes and innocent." "Don't know anything about death, still naïve." Ryan stated. "I wish I, could go back to those days." He added. "You can't go on blaming yourself for them." "We all will die only the fates know when." Paul replied. "I'll see you later." Ryan said. He goes. He sees Jon in the corridor. "Hey, how are you?" Jon asked. "I'm working on it." "How are Marie and Vala?" Ryan asked. "Playing dress up." "Vala is worried about you." Jon confessed. "Tell her, I'll be ok." Ryan stated meanwhile deep in the monster zone. Barbara Babor is standing with a tall lizard type beast. "We will escape tonight, then revenge is mine." She vowed. "I want all of them dead, except my son and Ryan McKay." She insisted. "Why let the McKay kid live?" He asked. "He is an Aster as well." She informed. "How is that?" He inquired. "Valtra is his mother." She stated. "Ah, she was the best warrior in this galaxy." He remembered. "Yes I know, all of you here admired her." She replied. "What about the other son?" He asked. "He has no powers to speak of, he is not important." She informed. "I see it all clearly now." He figured. "See what?" She asked. "You want his power." He implied. "Yes, he is powerful." "He can control minds." She replied. "So, is it personal too?" He asked. "What do you mean?" She asked. "You have a lust for him, I can tell. "Aren't you a bit old for him?" He replied. "You just do what I pay you for." She said. Just then over their heads a freighter from the alliance is flying it dropped off supplies "Ready?" She said. The creature nodded yes and grabs hold of her. He then used his tongue to stretch out and attach to the freighter, and it pulls them up. Meanwhile Ryan is in the docking bay checking his fighter, he gets a flash of people running and fires burning it is happening inside the base itself. He also saw the lizard beast then it stops. "Uh." Ryan sighed as he clutched his head. "No." Ryan adds. He then headed out into corridor, where he spotted Jon headed to the control room. "Jon!" He called. "What is it?" Jon asked. "There is trouble coming." "I saw a lizard beast." Ryan stated. "Let's go." Jon insisted. They go to control room, as they talk to Dylan at the command console. "It sounds like Drentarg, a lizard beast we put in the zone a long time ago." Dylan stated. "He wouldn't just leave on his own." Dylan reacted. "He is a mercenary for hire which means." Dylan thought. "Someone is controlling him." Jon answered. "Ok, but who?" Steven asked. Amanda is also present. She tries to concentrate on Drentrag and she also sees Barbara, seated with him in stolen freighter. "It's Barbara." She realized. "My mother?" Cole said. "Of course, she wants revenge." Dylan comprehended. "That is not all she is after." Amanda stated. "What did you sense?" Dylan asked. "Her plans are clear, kill all of us except Cole and Ryan." She answered. "Me?" Ryan asked in confusion. "She wants to control you, so she can use your power." She said. "Let's secure the base." Jon orders the team heads out. Amanda pulls Dylan to the side. "Dylan a moment." She asked. "What is it?" He said. "I'm afraid his power, is not all she wants." "She wants him." She revealed. "What!" Dylan exclaimed. "That is it, she is dead." Dylan vowed. Now later in the control room everyone is gathered for briefing. "Alright everyone weapon up." Dylan stated. "Ryan, you stay close to me." He insisted. "What?" "Why?" Ryan asked. "I'll explain, the rest of you go and be careful." He said as the team heads out. "Ok dad, what is going on?" Ryan demanded. Dylan goes into his office as Ryan followed. "You are staying here." He said. "Give me a reason." Ryan replied. "She is after you." Dylan said. "Yeah, she is after all of us, she is pissed." Ryan stated. "Yes but, she has developed a thing for you." Dylan replied. "That is crazy." Ryan disagreed. Dylan looks at him with sincerity. "You're serious." Ryan realized. "Amanda, sensed it from her." Dylan informed. "What makes you think,

I'm safer in here?" Ryan asked. At that instant the base is shaken and alarms go off. Then an explosion occurred near by. "Alright let's go." Dylan said as he draws his gun. "Stay behind me." Dylan ordered. Just then Drentrag entered the control room. He uses his tongue to grab the wall near them to collapse it on top of them, they are trapped underneath, and they struggle to get free. "We have trouble in the control room." Amanda sensed. "We've got to get back!" She shouted. The team heads back toward the control room, meanwhile in the control room. "Remember me McKay?" He shouted. "How could I forget that face?" Dylan answered. "I will enjoy killing you." Drentrag stated. He comes threw the damage up to them. Ryan concentrates and uses his power to control Drentrag. He makes him lift up the wall, so they can get free. Then Barbara comes up behind him, and hits him in the back of the head with the butt of her gun. "Hello captain." She said. Dylan turns to her. Drentrag is free of control and grabs Dylan with his tongue around his neck and begins to squeeze. "We need to go, their coming." She stated. Drentrag lets him go. He falls to his knees and coughs. Drentrag then picked up Ryan from the floor. "We will finish this McKay." He stated. They make their escape with one of Barbara's many gadgets she made, this one a portal leading back to her secret lair. The team then entered. "Dad!" Steven exclaimed as he kneeled to him. "Are you ok?" He added. "Yes, they took Ryan." Dylan acknowledged, as he rose to his feet. "Leave that bitch to me." Dralla said meanwhile, Barbara arrives at an abandon building on Mars. "In here." She ordered as Drentrag brings Ryan in. She then pulled out one of the power controlling Bracelets, which she herself found and put it on his wrist. "I knew stealing these would come in handy one day." She said. Ryan begins to wake up. "Well hello Ryan, we meet again." She replied. "Barbara." He said as saw bracelet on his wrist. "I stole it just for you." She replied. "This won't end well for you." Ryan stated. "I'll go keep watch." Drentrag said as he goes out. "So, lets talk about your power?" She said. "Go to hell." Ryan answered. "Such manners, I thought your father raised you better than that, or is that your mother's side." She replied. "I have manners, when there is a lady involved." Ryan clarified. "You are not one." Ryan said. meanwhile back at the base in a repaired control room. "Anything at all?" Dylan asked. "No, they must be too far." Amanda feared. Voltar is with them. "I will find him." Voltar replied as he Vanished, meanwhile back with Barbara.

"So, do you think because you are a McKay and an Aster, your better?" She asked. "No, but I'm not using people for their power or to profit." Ryan stated. "Of course not, you alliances think you're so superior." She said just then Voltar appeared. "Well, I guess I should've killed you a long time ago." Voltar said. "Voltar, I was only trying to defeat the alliance." She said as she rose up. "You, use to be in support of that." She added. "Yes I did once, but no one touches my blood." He replied. Drentrag attempted to sneak up on Voltar, Voltar reached behind him with his claw hand and blasted a hole right threw him, with his power as he falls dead. "It appears, you are working solo now." Voltar stated. He uses his power to remove the bracelet from Ryan's wrist, as you can hear the team flying overhead. "Fine you win." She said as she raised her hands up, the team comes in and take her away. "You ok?" Dylan asked. "I'm ok, thanks to him." Ryan said. "Thank you." Dylan said. "No need." He vanished now back on the base Dralla hugs Ryan. "You are ok?" Dralla asked. "Yes, I'm fine." Ryan answered as he sits on the couch. "What is it?" She asked as she sat beside him. "I'm not sure yet, just a feeling." Ryan said. "Did you have a vision?" She asked. "No, just a feeling." He replied. Now later that night he has a dream. He is back at the Aster family crypt when Valtra appeared. "Mother?" Ryan said. "You must be careful, don't go threw the wormhole." She warned. "What are you talking about?" Ryan asked. "It will lead to the past." She said. "What?" Ryan replied. "If you go into it, you will change our future." She feared. Voltar would know of you, when he was still evil." She explained. "I won't go then." Ryan stated. "You will be tempted." She said. "I will do as you ask." Ryan assured. "Be careful." She replied then Ryan wakes up. "Whoa." He said. Now in the morning he goes on his patrol at the edge of the galaxy with ralph in their fighters, after a few moments of looking around the wormhole appeared. "No way." Ryan said in disbelief. "What is that?" Ralph said. "It's a wormhole." Ryan replied. "Like a doorway, to another galaxy or dimension?" Ralph asked with enthusiasm. "No, it's the past." Ryan said. "Hell, let's check it out." Ralph said as he headed toward it. "Ralph no!" Ryan exclaimed but they were pulled into it. Meanwhile back on the base. "Dad, Ralph and Ryan's ships just vanished." Steven said as he checks the console. "What do you mean vanished?" Dylan demanded. "They are in the past." Amanda sensed. "What?" Dylan asked. "They went threw a wormhole, four years into the past." She said. "This could be dangerous, if he runs into Voltar when he was evil, he will change the future." She feared. Meanwhile back with Ralph and Ryan as the come out the other side of wormhole. "Damm it, looks the same." Ralph said in disappointment as he looked around. "Trust me it is not, it's the past." Ryan stated. "So, we will just go to earth and figure it out." Ralph said. "We need, to go back threw that wormhole." Ryan said just then Ralph saw a cruiser headed at them. "I think we go trouble." Ralph said as Ryan looked. "Those are Voltar's ships move!" Ryan exclaimed as they attempted to escape the ships opened fire. "Ralph!" Ryan yells, Ralph's ship is hit and going down on Voltara. Ryan also was hit and they hit hard on the planet. Ralph climbed out of his ship and over to Ryan's near by. He opened the hatch as Ryan was knocked out by the impact. "Ryan?" Ralph said. He then turned to see Voltar's army headed to them. "Oh crap." Ralph said, now next scene Ryan is lying on a bed with a towel across his forehead, as he comes to. "Ralph?" He said as he focused. "Dad?" He said as a figure came toward him. His vision is clear as he saw Valtra standing there. "Mother?" Ryan asked. "Hardly, I am Valtra." She said Ryan sits up. "You're alive." Ryan replied. "Of course I am, do I know you?" She asked. "You know of me." He answered. "I can feel something, a connection but you are older. "She touches his hand and can read him. She pulls her hand back. "Ryan, you should not be here." She replied. "I know, but how do we get out of here?" Ryan asked. "I will help you my son." She said as they heard troops coming. "No, it's father." She realized. "Do not let him touch you, or he will know who you are." She instructed. Voltar enters dressed in his robes with his guards. "Who are you?" He demanded. "I know you are with the alliance, but the other refused to talk." He added. "Ralph, no one just out flying around." Ryan said. "Yes, he is just a pilot father." Valtra insisted. "Leave us." He ordered Valtra she goes out hesitantly. "I will ask you one last time, who are you boy?" He demanded. "I'm just a pilot, out on my patrols." He answered. "You shot us down." He added. "You have, a familiar arrogance to you." "You remind me of someone." He thinks. "McKay." He said. Ryan's eyes widen in fear. "What is your relation to him?" He questioned. "Distant cousins, I don't even know him." Ryan insisted. "You are lying." He said. He grabs his hand. Ryan pulls free, but not before he sensed. "That is impossible, the rumor is true." He realized. "I don't know what you're talking about." Ryan said innocently. "You are my blood, my daughter's son." He replied. "Only you are older, where are you now?" He asked. "You can't, you'll destroy the future." Ryan insisted. "I will keep you here then" He stated. "You can't do that." Ryan said. "I am Voltar Aster, I can do anything." He replied as he grabs his arm. He can read some of his thoughts. "We are close in the future." He replied. "Yes, when you changed to our side." Ryan said. "Me do that?" Voltar laughed. "The future will change." He added. "You don't want to do this, read my memories see my future." Ryan replied as he used his power to show him. "My daughter is dead?" He replied. "I will change that, you can change that." He insisted. "What?" Ryan asked. "Your blood holds the cure." He stated. "I could save her?" Ryan realized. "Yes you can." Voltar replied. "No, I can't change the future." Ryan insisted. "You must, think of your family you could all be together." Voltar replied. "My mom and dad?" He said. "No, you hate my dad." Ryan stated. "I have to go." Ryan insisted as he heads for door. Voltar uses his power to stop him making him to pass out, as he catches him. "You are not going anywhere." He replied as his guards entered. "Put him in the other bedroom." He ordered as Valtra comes back. "Father no." She said. "He is your son, my blood the one you lied about." "Do you think I'm going to just, let him go?" "He belongs here." He commanded. "Father, don't do this." She begged. "He will be your cure." Voltar replied. "Do you not want to see them grow?" He added. "Yes, but not if you hurt Dylan." She replied. "You will understand." He said as he goes out and to the other bedroom to see Ryan still unconscious on bed. He gently touched his cheek and Ryan woke up. "Was this all a dream?" He asked. "No, you are home where you belong." Voltar replied as Ryan sits up. "What?" Ryan stated. "You will stay here with us." Voltar instructed. "You can't be serious?" Ryan said. "Yes I am." Voltar replied. "How do you plan on keeping me here?" Ryan asked as he tries to use his power but Voltar holds up his left hand to show him bracelet. "This prevents you form using your powers." He replied. "You are going to mess up the future." Ryan pleaded. "I will make it better." He replied. "Now that I found you, I'm not letting you go." Voltar said, "You are my blood." He added. "I love you grandfather, but not this version of you." "If you do this, I will not forgive you." Ryan vowed. "I can not let you hate me." He said as he undoes bracelet. Ryan is confused "You are free to go." He added. "What?" Ryan asked then Valtra walks in. "Go, while I have control of his mind." She said. "Wait, maybe he is right, I could still cure you." Ryan replied. "Please let me." Ryan begged. "I don't know, what kind of mother I will be?" She replied. "I know, you will be one who loves and protects us." Ryan said. "He doesn't need to know I did this." Ryan said she kisses his cheek. "You are your father's son." She replied. "I am yours too." He added he then followed her to the lab and gave her some of his blood; as Voltar was oblivious "Now, go quickly back home." She said as Ryan gets Ralph and she gives them a ship to escape in they go back threw the wormhole and are back in the future. "It's too quiet, are we dead?" Ralph asked just then over com-link. "Identify yourselves or we will fire. "Dad it's me." Ryan answered. "Thank god, where were you?" He asked. "Long story." He said. "Well your mother and Steven have been worried sick." Dylan replied. "Did you say mother?" Ryan asked. "Of course I did, not to mention Voltar too." He added as Ryan smiled now back on the base Ryan comes out of ship and Valtra is there he rushes to her and hugs her tight. "You act like you haven't seen me for ever." She said. "Just feels like it mom." Ryan said. "Alright, lets have dinner huh?" Dylan said. "Can I, get a minute with mom?" Ryan asked. "Sure." Dylan said as they go out. "Thanks for the save." He said. "You too." She answered as she kissed his cheek and they go to dinner. This is awesome my sister is back and they are a family again but did something change? Did my father go back to his evil ways? Scene it's late on the base Ryan is asleep with Dralla when Voltar appeared to them. He sits on his side of the bed in the chair. "Your future is with me." Voltar replied, then he touched his hand and they vanished. They reappear in the castle in his underground secret room. Ryan then wakes up on a smaller bed to see Voltar standing there he sits up looks around. "Grandfather?" "What going on?" He demanded. "The future has changed." Voltar answered. "What does that mean?" Ryan asked. "Just relax Ryan." Voltar replied. "Ryan goes to stand, when notices the bracelet from the past on his wrist. "What are you doing?" Ryan replied. "Something I should've done before, to protect the future." Voltar informed. "I don't understand?" Ryan questioned. "I will keep you safe." Voltar stated. "Why, do you think you need to do that?" Ryan asked. "I remember the past and the present." Voltar confesses. "I will change it all." "The old Voltar is back" He replied. "What?" "You can't do this." Ryan said. "I will not, let any of my blood be harmed again."

He vowed. "You will understand when you are older." He added. "No, I won't you need to let me go." Ryan demanded. "Just know, I love you and I'm doing this for you." Voltar stated as he goes out of room and locked the door. "Don't do this!" He shouted. Ryan tries to call to Valtra in her mind she wakes up in quarters with Dylan. "Ryan." She says as she sits up Dylan wakes up too. "What is it?" He asked. "My father, he took Ryan." She replied now next scene in control room with team gathered. "Apparently Voltar, has gone dark side again he took Ryan." Dylan said everyone is stunned and whisper. "Why now?" Steven asked. "Voltar remembers the past." "He knows what Ryan can do now." Valtra stated. "So my father has betrayed us yet again." Jon replied. "Then that means war." Dylan replied. "We need to find Ryan." Steven said meanwhile back at the castle in that room. Ryan keeps trying to get door open. Damm it! "Ryan yelled then Voltar comes in. "Relax, you can't escape Kravitz designed this room." He informed. "I thought you learned form your mistakes?" Ryan questioned. "I did, this time I will do it right." Voltar replied. "I won't help you to destroy the galaxy." Ryan stated. "You will understand why I've done this soon." Voltar insured. "Please, I know you're angry with them, but you have to let it go." Ryan pleaded. "You need to stay here, to be safe from my enemies." Voltar replied. "Do you know of someone?" Ryan probed. "When you came back from the past something else changed." Voltar revealed. "What?" Ryan demanded Voltar shows him what he saw. Monzee also escape after they went threw the wormhole. "Monzee form the past?" Ryan replied. "Yes, she is here now and alive." Voltar answered as Ryan's eyes widen in distress and anxieties, meanwhile back at the base Amanda has sensed Monzee's presence. "Monzee is alive." Amanda said. "What?" Jon responded. Just then she burst in threw the wall of the docking bay as alarms go off. "That is why father did it." Jon realized. "How can she be alive, she died." Dylan said. "She followed them back threw the wormhole." Valtra realized meanwhile as Monzee is battling the guards she grabbed one up. "Where is the first grandson of Voltar?" She demanded. "Shoot her!" Dylan ordered. They open fire on her and she flies off. "Get me Voltar now." Dylan commanded meanwhile back at the castle. "Why is she after me?" Ryan asked. "She knows who you are, she wants to claim you for herself." He answered. "You know, I'm really getting tired of these female creatures trying to claim me." Ryan responded. "Give me a chance to end her, then you can go home." Voltar vowed. "I can help, take off this." He raises wrist to show bracelet. "No, she will be able to track you, it protects you." Voltar explained. "Ok for now, but call mom and dad to let them know what's going on." Ryan insisted. "Alright." Voltar concedes as he called the base on his vidlink screen on the wall. "Ryan are you ok?" Dylan asked. "Yes, Voltar is insisting on keeping me here, until we can find Monzee." Ryan conveys. "I'll be back soon." Ryan said. "I have my people searching all her former hiding places, I will find her." Voltar stated meanwhile Monzee was close by and listening in on the message. "So, Voltar is trying to hid you from me." She replied she flies up and toward the castle lands near the drainage ditch and sneaks inside she battles the guards as Ryan can hear the chaos just outside the door. "What the?" He said as Monzee kicks in the door. "Hello firstborn." She replies as Ryan backs up "I have come from the past for you." She added as she backs him up against the wall and touches his cheek. "You don't want to do this." Ryan said. "Yes I do." She smiled she grabs his arm sees the bracelet. "He thought it could keep you safe from me, only thing he has done is made it easier for me to take you." She replied as she pulls him out of room and drags him back out the way she came and then flies off. "Monzee has Ryan." Valtra realized. "Let's move now!" He orders. "I'll bring him home." He says to Valtra. "I know." She replied meanwhile Monzee lands up in the mountains of Voltara and they go into a cave. "No one will find us here." She stated. "Look, you are going to end up dead for this." Ryan replied she comes in close and caresses his cheek "You are worth it." She replied. "Look just escape, go back threw the wormhole to your time." Ryan said. "Oh I will go home, and you're going with me." She stated. Ryan's eyes widen with horror she then pulls him in and kisses him. He struggles to get free she lets go as he catches his breath. "You will need your strength, for our wedding night." She replied as she pulls a quill form her back and sticks it into his neck causing him to pass out into her arms. "Now to go home." She said as she flies out of cave with him in her arms and to her vessel loads him up and they fly toward the wormhole as the team arrives. "We have to go in after her." Jon replied. "Ok, the rest stay and back us up." Dylan ordered as he, Jon, Shane, Amanda, Cole, and Voltar himself go in, meanwhile Monzee goes into the Monster Zone and to one of her caves lays Ryan on a long slab. Ryan begins to come out of it. "Welcome to my home." She stated as she transformed into her humanoid self she has blue skin long raven hair and hazel eyes. "What are you doing?" Ryan asked. "I am changing to please you." She answered. "I still know it's you." Ryan replied. "Yes you do but." She starts as she removes her clothing. "Whoa!" Ryan exclaimed as he turns away. She comes to him and touches his neck as she comes around to face him. "I will make you forget any other girl." She stated as she kisses him meanwhile outside in the Zone the team has landed. Voltar can sense Ryan's anxiety and stress he immediately appeared to them in the cave. "Get your filthy hands off my grandson." Voltar demanded as she lets him go "He is mine." she growls. Voltar blasts her with his power causing her to explode. "Lets get back." Voltar said. Now back threw the wormhole and back on the base Jon uses his power to collapse the wormhole and seal it for good. "Are you ok?" Valtra asked as she hugs him. "Yes I'm ok." Ryan replied. "I don't know, you did see Monzee naked." "You might be scared for life." Ralph stated. "Maybe if I, describe her to you it can lift some of the burden." Ryan suggested. "Oh hell no." Ralph rushes out as they all laugh. Now later Ryan is lying on his bed when he gets a flash of Barbara Babor escaping prison. He jumps to his feet and heads out his bedroom door to find Barbara standing in his living room. "Hello Ryan, I think we have unfinished business." She said. "How?" Ryan asked. "I have friends everywhere." She explained she pulls out the bracelet. "Remember this?" She asked as she used her stunner to knock him out and put it on his wrist they vanished. She gets to her escape shuttle that is piloted by Gunner Nelcon. "Hurry, before they realize he is gone." He said. Now at one of her undisclosed hideouts on Saturn. "You should go." She says to Gunner he goes, She turns back to Ryan as he is lying in a large bed. She uses a smelling salt under his nose to rouse him up. He wakes up he sits up to see her sitting beside him and the bracelet on his wrist. "You are insane." Ryan said. "Yes I know." as she moved in closer. "We could be good together." She suggested. "Not a chance in hell." Ryan stated. "I'm not that much older." She replied. "You fell for Dralla, she is older." She reminded. "What is so bad about me?" She asked. "I can be saved." She added. "Not interested." Ryan replied. "You will be." She said. Ryan looks at her in confusion. Dralla appears she proceeds to knock Barbara out with her mind power. "How did you find me?" Ryan asked as she goes to take off bracelet. "I heard her saying my name." She said as they kiss. "What about the bracelet?" Ryan said. "I kind of like you subdued." She smiled. "Your kidding right?" Ryan replied. She takes his hand and they vanish and reappear in the cave where they first met. "What are you doing?" He asked. "Having some fun." She replied as she pulls him over to her bed. "Is that allowed?" She asked. "Yes." He answered as they kiss. "I want you to move in permanently with me, but as my wife." Ryan replied. "Your wife?" She asked. "Yes, if you will marry me?" He asked. "Of course I will." She answered as they kiss, now later back on the base in control room. "You're getting married?" Dylan asked. "That is wonderful, I'm so happy." Valtra said as she hugs each of them. "That is cool, congratulations." Steven said. "Dad?" Ryan said. "Are you ok with this?" Ryan asked. "Yes I am." Dylan replied. "We have a wedding to plan!" Valtra exclaimed. Voltar appears. "So, I guess you heard?" Jon replied. "Yes I did but her?" Voltar questioned. "He loves her, you were in love too you know." Jon said. "Yes I was." Voltar replied. "Now behave yourself father." Jon stated as Ryan comes up to them. "Hey." Ryan said. "I'm happy for you." Jon says as he hugged him. "Thanks." Ryan replied. "I'll just be out there." Jon said as he goes. "So, you're going to marry her?" Voltar asked. "Yes I am, go ahead and say it." Ryan replied. "Say what?" Voltar answered. "You think it's a mistake." Ryan said. "Yes but, it is your choice so I will respect it." Voltar stated. "You will be there right?" Ryan asked. "Of course I will, I never got to see your first one." Voltar replied Ryan hugs him. "Thanks, I've got to get back or they will plan it without me." Ryan smiled. "Your mother loves a party." Voltar replied. Well what we thought would be an awesome union turned out to be a lie Dralla was still as dark and sinister as she ever was her goal was to have Ryan's baby the next heir to the Voltara throne, but my sister was not having that so she did what any good Dregon/Voltarian mother would do she snapped her neck. So now, we are all extra vigilant around the women who come into our lives and claim to love us just for us. Oh and Volrin did escape hell just for a little bit, but we took him down. So onto the next adventures to come, which will be a new girl actually, human is she the one to catch Ryan's heart and keep him away from the psychos? Or is Barbara still up to no good.

Chapter 18
TURNING POINT

Now that Ryan has learned about the dark side of our family and seen his mother, as a dregon. Will it spell trouble? Can Ryan deal with coming face to face with the Aster legacy? Who will pay the ultimate price? Now next day in the control room all are gathered. "We have a new member to our team." Dylan informed as she walked in "This is Lieutenant Alieah Mirah. "She will be our computer and communications specialist." He added. Ryan looks at her and is instantly mesmerized by her beauty. She has olive skin raven hair and hazel eyes. "Ok, all of you out on your patrols." Dylan ordered. Team heads out. "Ryan, wait one minute." Dylan said. "I'm sorry about being late." Ryan replied, "No this is not about that." "I need you to help our newest member." Dylan said. "Ok yeah sure." Ryan answered. "There is an s.o.s coming form an apt building on Mars." Dylan informed. "I got it." Ryan said as he headed to the docking bay. "Are you always late?" Alieah asked. "No, sorry I'm." He replied she cuts him off. "I know who you are, Lt McKay." "Can we go now?" She stated as she gets into a fighter. "Ouch." Ryan replied as he goes into his fighter. "Did, I do something wrong?" Ryan asked over com-link. "No, I'm just ready to get to work." She answered. "Ok then." Ryan said as they fly off and to Mars. Now at the building in question, they come to it Ryan draws his gun. "Stay behind me." Ryan ordered. "I know how to defend myself." She snapped. Ryan sighed as they enter building. They check around head, then upstairs to third floor. "Hello?" Ryan called out, as Alieah scanned with her gear. "Anything?" Ryan asked. "Yeah, ahead about ten feet." She said as they head toward it. Alieah sees a girl lying on floor. She kneels to her. "She's ok, just some scrapes and bruises." Alieah informed. Just then Ryan gets a flash and sees the roof falling down. "Look out!" He grabs hold of Alieah and the girl and pulls them out of the way with his telekinetic powers. Then roof falls taking him with it. Down to the main floor. Alieah helps the girl down to safety and rushes to Ryan. "McKay, can you hear me?" She yelled. No response as he in out cold and bloody and bruised. She calls over com-link. "I need help, officer down." She said. Now next scene is in sickbay. Paul comes out of exam room. "He has a clean break, it'll take four weeks to heal with him being only half Voltarian." Paul explained. "Thanks Paul." Dylan said. Valtra comes over to Alieah. She could tell she was shaken up. "He will be fine." She said. "I should get back to my station." Alieah replied. "Wait, I need to check you out lieutenant." Paul stated. "I'm fine doctor." She said. "It's procedure." He instructed she comes and sits on bed by Ryan's as Paul scans her. "Your clear." Paul replied. "Thank you." She said as Paul goes into his office. She rises and goes up to Ryan's bedside. Ryan wakes up. "Hey, is the girl ok?" Ryan asked. "Yes, she is fine." Alieah responded. "How did you know?" She asked. "I'm a seer, as my mom calls it." Ryan answered. "Thanks, for saving my life." She added. "Not a problem." Ryan smiled. Alieah heads out. "She is a lovely woman huh?" Paul said sarcastically. "Yeah." Ryan answered. "Uh no, I see that look." Paul cautions "She is a tough, by the book officer." "She is not your type." Paul insisted. "How would you know?" Ryan said. "She does not date pilots." Paul replied. "She just never met me." Ryan replied. "This is going to be trouble." Paul acknowledges. Now later in the day Ryan entered the Rec Room on crutches with his leg in a cast. He sees Alieah, working out. Ralph also there comes over to him. "Hey I heard you ok?" Ralph asked. "Yeah, I'm good." Ryan answered. He sits on bench watching Alieah lifting weights. "What are you up to?" Ralph asked. "Nothing." Ryan replied. "So, what do you know about her?" Ryan asked. "I would not waste my time." Ralph informed. "Why not?" Ryan said. "She does not date us man." Ralph stated. "So, let that one go." He added. "We'll see." Ryan replied. Now later on in control room as Alieah is at her console working. Ryan entered. "So busy?" Ryan asked. "Yes, I am actually." "Aren't you on sick leave." She replied. "Yes, so interested in dinner later?" Ryan said. "No thanks." She answered. "Why?" Ryan asked. "I don't date people I work with, especially pilots." "Now if you will excuse me." She said. She goes back to working. Ryan heads out and to his Quarters. He sits on couch when Voltar appeared. "She is a feisty one huh?" Voltar said. "Yeah, I guess." Ryan answered. "I wouldn't give up yet." Voltar replied. "She doesn't date pilots." Ryan said. "You, are an Aster and we are irresistible." Voltar stated. "Yeah ok." Ryan said then Voltar vanished. Meanwhile in Dylan's quarters, he is reviewing files on his hand held device. "Maybe I should check on him?" Valtra said. "He is a grown man Valtra." Dylan replied. "I am his mother." She said. "Don't overreact." Dylan pleaded. "I do not overreact." She stated. He looks up from device with a look of skepticism. "Ok I do." She admitted. "You are just a good mother." Dylan added. She sits beside him they kissed. Meanwhile Ryan is in bed asleep. Alieah is at her desk, remembering when they were in the building and he saved her. "Forget it Mirah, he is a pilot." She told herself. Then she thinks of scene in sickbay earlier. "He is also an Aster." She thought. "I need to get to work." She said. Now the next day Alieah entered the Rec Room to work out when she sees Ryan working with the lap pull down machine. He is shirtless and sweaty. "Are you sure, you should be doing that?" She said. Ryan lets go and grabs a towel of to the side and wipes some sweat from his chest. "Why are you concerned?" Ryan replied. "As, a fellow team member I was concerned, for your recovery." She answered. She heads over to lift weights on other end of the room. She watches as he continues his work out. Ralph noticed and comes over to Ryan. "Hey, you may just have a shot with her Romeo." Ralph said. "No, I'm not going to pursue her." Ryan stated. "What?" Why not?" Ralph exclaimed. "If she wants me, she knows where to find me." Ryan said as he smiled at ralph. "Oh, you are good." Ralph replied. Well our newest member of the team is beautiful, smart and tough. Can she resist the charms of Ryan however? Now after Ryan is done with his work out he grabbed his crutches and heads toward locker room. Alieah is staring hard. "What are you doing?" She said to herself. "He is nothing but trouble." She reminded, as she looked away. Now later in sickbay Alieah is passing by when she noticed Ryan is with Paul. "Ok, let's see how it's healed." Paul replied as Ryan sits on bed and puts up his leg she watched. Paul opened up the cast with his equipment. "Looks good, should be another week or two." Paul guaranteed. "Thanks." Ryan said as Paul used equipment to reseal cast. "You are a hero you know." Paul said. "Comes with the job." Ryan replied. "Just like your dad." Paul said.

"Look, do me a favor and don't tell my mom that I'm going to see my grandmother in prison." "She gets upset." Ryan asked. "Fine, just be careful, she is not trust worthy." Paul reminded. "I know I can handle it." Ryan stated as he gets up with crutches and heads out as Alieah hides. "What was that about?" Alieah spectacles. She followed him as he went to docking bay and took a shuttlecraft. She got in her fighter and followed as he went to the prison on Mars. She follows watched him enter. She also entered after him. Ryan goes to a cell where an older woman with gray in her raven hair and brown eyes is standing. "Hello Ryan." She said. Standing there with her restraint cuffs on. "What happened to you?" She asked. "I'm fine, look I came to see you because, I need to learn more about my powers." Ryan replied. "I will do what I can." She said. "It's just, now when I touch people I can see their futures, what they're thinking in that moment." Ryan continued. "You can control what you see." "You must learn to filter it." She stated. "To see what you need to." "I know how hard it is to see people's deaths." "I am sorry about your other grandmother." She replied. "Thanks, I should go, before they miss me." Ryan said. "I am glad, you still come to see me after the things I've done." She replied. "You are family no matter what." Ryan said he heads out. Alieah snuck back to the base as well. Now the next day in the docking bay as Ryan is checking his fighter. "Hey, have you been cleared yet?" Alieah asked. "I'm not good at sitting around." Ryan answered. "I see that, excuse me." She goes out as Ralph comes in. "It is working, what ever you are doing." "She is hot for you." Ralph said. "You think so?" Ryan asked. "Oh yeah, any girl who would follow a guy." Ralph began. Ryan interrupted. "Wait she did what?" Ryan questioned. "Where ever you took off to last night." Ralph said. "You didn't know?" Ralph realized. "No, excuse me." Ryan puts down gear and goes to control room and walked up to Alieah. "We need to talk." He insisted. "I'm busy." She said. "Yeah, spying on other people apparently." Ryan replied. Mary and Mark are looking up form their consoles. "Let's talk in private." Aleiah said. She gets up and they go across to the briefing room. "I wasn't spying on you." She said. "Ok, maybe I was, I was just curious." She added. "What I do, when I'm off is my business." Ryan stated. "I think its sweet, after all she did, to you and your family that you still go see her." Alieah replied. "Just stay the hell out of my business lieutenant Mirah." Ryan snapped, as he heads to the door. "Hey!" She shouted. He stopped and turned to her.

"I apologized, I don't know why I did it." "I don't usually do things like that." She added. "Good to know." Ryan said as he turned and walked out. She then slams her fist on table. "Way to go." She said. Now Ryan is at the mess hall, with Ralph sitting next to him. "So, you yelled at her?" Ralph asked. "Are you nuts!" Ralph shouted. "She is into you, you're pushing her away?" Ralph replied. "She followed me to the prison." "What if she told my mother?" Ryan worried. "You know how she gets." He added. Valtra enters and walked up behind him. "How do I get?" She asked. "I'm done." Ralph said as he grabbed food and rushed out. Valtra sits. "Nothing." Ryan said. "I know, you are hiding something from me." "I will find out what it is." She assured. "Ok fine, I went to see Alena." He paused. Valtra had a look of fury on her face. "See that, is how you get." Ryan replied. "You overreact." He added. "Of course I do, she is dangerous Ryan." "She will try to manipulate you." She warned. "She is not like that anymore." "I can feel it, she has changed." Ryan stated. "I wish I could believe that." She replied. "I have been going for awhile now." "I don't want you to worry ok?" Ryan said. "I am trying, but you don't make it easy." She replied. She kissed his forehead and gets up and goes out. Ryan sees Alieah enter. He gets up and goes over to her. "I was not ease dropping." She insisted. "I know, I'm here to apologize." Ryan replied. "I'm sorry I snapped at you." He added then goes out meanwhile at other table Ralph is sitting with Brent. "I give um two more days." Ralph said. "She is tough, I'll take that bet." Brent replied. They shake hands. Now later Ryan is in the rec Room doing lap pull downs when Alieah entered. "It's late isn't it?" She asked. "I'm fine thanks." He answered as he begins to breath harder. "Maybe, you should take a break." She suggested. "I know my limits." He said. He stopped then toweled off he stands to his feet. He then gets off balance from some fatigue and goes to fall. Alieah rushes to catch him as they fall down onto mat face to face. "See I'm fine." Ryan said as he still breathed a little heavy. "I can see that." She replied as she takes a breath she leaned in to kiss him, when he gets to his feet. "Good night Lieutenant." He said with a smile as he grabbed crutches and goes. She sits up and watched him in disbelief. "Uh." She sighed. Now the next day in the docking bay as Ryan puts up gear. Alieah entered in a fury and walked up to him and punched him in his arm. "What is it about you?" She yelled. "Oww, what the hell?" Ryan exclaimed. "What is your problem?" Ryan asked as he rubbed his arm. "You are McKay." She informed as Ralph, Shane and Brent look on. "You are so aggravating and reckless." She added. "So why are you talking to me?" Ryan asked. "Because, I think we should have dinner." She ordered. "My quarters, I'm cooking six thirty." She insisted then she walked out. Ralph looked to Brent and extended his hand. "I'll take my cash now please." Ralph said. "You always win." Brent said as he pulled out money from pocket and gives it to him. Shane walked over to Ryan "Are you ok?" Shane asked. "Yeah, I'm fine." He said with a grin. Now later at her quarters, Ryan arrived she opens doors she is dressed in a beautiful blue short dress her hair is done up. Ryan's eyes widen in amazement. "You said, something about dinner?" He asked nervously as he entered. "Have a seat, it's almost done." She said Ryan sits on couch. "Nice place." Ryan said. "Thanks." She replied as she comes form kitchen with two glasses of wine. She gives him one then sits beside him. "I'm sorry about hitting you earlier, I am just so new to all this." She confessed. "What is this?" Ryan questioned. "I know your not that dumb McKay." She said as she pulls him close by shirt and they kiss. "What took you so long lieutenant?" Ryan said with a smiled. "You are tough to resist for long." She answered. Just then dinner bell goes off they stop. "Dinner is ready." Ryan said. "Right." She replied as they get up and go to table. Now after dinner they are cuddled together on couch. "So, tell me about yourself?" Ryan asked. "I promise not to read your mind." He added. "Well, after the academy I was on the Jupiter base until I was assigned here." "I love classical music, my parents still live on Earth and you are just too cute." She said as she kissed his lips. "Ahh gentle, I am still healing." Ryan stated. "Not to mention funny." She said with a smile, now later as he goes to leave. "So next time dinner at my place?" Ryan said. "So you cook?" She asked. "No, not unless you want to end up in sickbay." He answered. "Ok until then" She said as they kissed. Now it's been two weeks and Ryan is in sickbay to remove the cast. "Ok, time to cut me loose Paul." Ryan said. Paul uses equipment to cut it open and remove it. "Ok you are back to 100%" He replied. "Yes, back to catching bad guys." Ryan replied. "Yeah." Leiah replied reluctantly. "What?" Ryan asked. "I suddenly remembered, why I don't date pilots." She said. "Relax, I'll be fine." Ryan replied as he hopped down off table and heads to docking bay. "Be careful!" She yelled. "I have a good reason to be." He answered now on their next mission he is flying on patrols with Ralph. "So, my man how is it going?" He asked. "Why is there a pool involved?" Ryan replied. "Now that hurts my feelings, I am just happy for you." Ralph said. "Yeah right." Ryan replied just them over the com-link. "We have trouble on Earth the Academy is under attack." Mark called. "We got it." Ryan responded as he and ralph headed to Earth where they see fires still smoldering and students cut and wounded as he and Ralph land and assist. "What the heck happened?" Ralph asked. "Some creatures attacked, I think Volrin Aster was among them." An injured student replied. "How did he escape?" Ryan said. "We better call for back up." Ralph replied they do and the team arrived. "I want him found!" Dylan demanded. Alieah pulls out mini computer "I can track him sir." She stated. "We had him implanted, with a chip all the prisoners are now." She added as she brings it up. "He is still here on Earth." She informed. "He is, inside the former white house sir." She added. "Let's move out!" He commanded. Now in the old white house almost completely destroyed by the battles fought with the aliens. The team busts in to the former oval office. "Welcome to my office, it needs a little work." Volrin replied as he sat in chair behind the desk. "Save it Volrin." "You're going back to prison." Dylan said. "I'm so scared captain, don't you see me shaking?" He says in jest. "It's over." Jon insisted. "Ahh yes, the noble Aster come to save the day." Volrin replied. "You are all so sickening really." Volrin added. "I need to introduce you to my friends." He said with a smile as a large group of alien criminals emerge from behind a door. "They hate you as much as I do." Volrin stated as a battle breaks out the team is fighting with them as Jon goes after Volrin. "I got Volrin." Jon replied as he uses his power to seal Volrin in a ring of energy. "How clever, you caught me or did you?" Volrin asked as he uses his power to break the seal. "You really need to try harder." Volrin replied. "How did you?" Voltar asked as he comes close to him and grabs him up by his neck. "I should've killed again." Voltar added. "Then do it brother." "I'll just make another deal with the overlord." Volrin said. "Yes, lets see if she will this time." Voltar answered as he uses his power to kill him body. Which sends Volrin's spirit back to the underworld. "That takes care of him." Voltar replied. "For now, until he finds a way to come back." Ryan stated. "Lets take the victory for today." Dylan said as they round up his followers. Now back on the base Ryan in his quarters when Voltar appeared to him. "So, when do I get to meet her?" Voltar asked. "What?" Ryan replied. "Your lady." Voltar said. "I don't think she is ready for you yet." Ryan answered.

"I don't bite unless asked." Voltar replied. "Sorry." Ryan said. "It's fine, I do tend to scare people." Voltar admitted. "Who you?" Ryan said with a smile. "Good night." Voltar replied as he vanished. Then Alieah comes to the door Ryan opens it. "Hey." He said. "So, everything ok?" She asked. "I'm fine, so about dinner pizza or Chinese?" He replied. "Doesn't matter." She answered. she sits on the couch as Ryan hits keypad in the kitchen, as Chinese food appeared they eat now after. "I was worried about you." Alieah confessed. "Yeah, my family can get rough." Ryan said. "Rough?" "They try to kill each other." She said. "Not all of them, look I know they can seem intimidating, but most of them are good now." Ryan explained. "You, are the one who helps to keep them that way." She stated. "They are lucky to have you." She added. "You can get lucky and have me too." Ryan replied as he smiled. "You are a piece of work McKay." She said. "Call me Ryan." He asked. "Ryan." She said as she leaned in and they kiss. Now the next day Ryan and Ralph are teamed up and on patrol. "Hey, we have trouble on Mars attempted robbery." Mary calls over the com-link. "We got it." Ralph answered as they arrive they see alliance cruisers battling with a large freighter. "You take the right, I got the left." Ryan stated as they move in a cannon is revealed out of the side of the freighter. "Scramble!" Ralph shouted but before Ryan could get clear he was hit by the blast. "Ryan!" Ralph yelled over com-link as his fighter crashes down on the planet. "Ryan, answer me!" Ralph replied frantically as he lands but no response. Next scene in sickbay Paul standing by a panel as he is reading the screen for his vitals. Ryan stands in front of him uniform is clean and he is fine. "Hey, am I clear to go?" Ryan asked. Paul does not respond. "Paul?" Ryan said as he waves his hand in front of him. Just then Moondeath appeared "He can't hear you or see you." He replied. "Why not?" Ryan asked. "Because your dead." Moondeath replied. "What?" Ryan exclaimed as Moondeath pointed to his body lying on the bed with tubes coming out of his mouth and side of chest with blood. Cuts, bruises and some burns he also sees Dylan, Valtra, and Steven standing there in tears. "No, I can't be dead." Ryan protested. "I'm sorry." Moondeath replied. "No, they need me." Ryan stated. "You, have done all you can." "They must find their own way." Moondeath said. "No I refuse to." Ryan stated. "Paul, will bring me back." Ryan said just then the computer goes crazy as they rush to him "What is happening." Ryan asked. "He is coding again move!" Paul demanded as they try twice to revive him. "Come on, stay with me." Paul said. "How do I get back?" Ryan stated. "It is not my decision." Moondeath explained. "No, I won't except it." Ryan replied as Paul gets a heartbeat. "See, I'm not dead." Ryan said. "You have to come with me." Moondeath said. "Who do I have to talk to, to get back?" Ryan demanded. "You need to talk to the one in charge." He answered. "Then lead the way." Ryan said meanwhile back in the sickbay as Dylan sits by Ryan's bedside "You need to get some rest." Paul insisted. "I'll rest when he wakes up." Dylan said. "We are doing all we can, his body has just taken too much." Paul admitted. "He is a fighter, he won't give up." Dylan replied. "Where is Valtra?" He asked. "I had to sedate her, she is resting now." Paul informed. "He can't die Paul, it would kill her." Dylan said just then Voltar appeared. "Any change?" He asked. "No but he is a fighter." Dylan stated. "Of course he is." Voltar agreed meanwhile Moondeath leads Ryan to the gates of the underworld then when he entered he was in a beautifully decorated room. "Ok, where's the one in charge?" Ryan asked just then the Overlord appeared in her beautiful female form. "Hello Ryan." She said. "I need to go back." Ryan replied. "You have done more than you needed to for them." She stated. "I refuse to go with you." Ryan said. "Why are you doing this?" Ryan asked as he looks at Moondeath. "This is not a punishment, this is your reward." He said. "I haven't done anything, I'm not done." Ryan insisted. "I will find my way back." Ryan added as he walked out of room. "He is one determined soul." She said. "Yes he is." Moondeath replied meanwhile back on the base. Vala enters the sickbay Dylan is asleep in the chair. "I will help you." Vala said as she comes to the other side of him she lays her hands on his head and concentrated as Ryan can sense her. "Vala?" Ryan said as Ryan is back in sickbay Jon entered. "There you are." Jon said. "I'm going to heal him." She replied. "I'm not sure you can." Jon said. "Don't give up Vala." Ryan said. "I can feel his spirit near." She stated. "She knows I'm here." Ryan realized. Just then Moondeath comes behind him. "Yes, you two have a bond." He added. "If you go back, your recovery will be long and painful." Moondeath informed. "I can handle it." Ryan replied. "Then you may go back." She said just then a glow of light then Ryan opens his eyes to see the sickbay and Dylan. "Dad?" Ryan said. Dylan wakes up. "Ryan!" Dylan exclaimed. "Paul!" He yelled as Paul comes over also Steven and Vala, Jon. "He's awake." Dylan said. Paul scans him. "I hope I didn't scare you?" Ryan replied. "I knew you'd be ok." Vala said with a smile. "Ok, lets let him rest." Paul stated others go out. "So how bad is it?" Ryan asked. "Lot of broken bones, but they will heal." Paul said. "You will be down for awhile, both your legs are broken." He added. "Ok I get it." Ryan said. Alieah entered. "Hey." Ryan said as he takes her hand. "I guess we will have to take it slow." Ryan replied. "You are something else." She said as she kissed him. "I have to get back to work." She said. "I'll be here." He replied she heads out then Voltar appeared. "Is it safe to come in." Voltar asked. "Yes." Ryan answered Voltar touches Ryan's forehead. "You had me nervous." Voltar said. "Yeah me too." Ryan replied. "If there is anything I can do?" Voltar asked. "No, I'm ok." Ryan stated. "How about a new line of work?" Voltar suggested. "Very funny." Ryan said. "I'm serious, I think this was a sign to change." Voltar said. "This, is what I do." "Who I am." Ryan replied. "There are other ways to help." Voltar replied. "I don't want to argue with you." Ryan said. "I'm sure your parents would agree." Voltar said. "You were lucky, very lucky you are an Aster but not invincible. "You almost died, more than once." Voltar reminded. "I know, but I will be back on this team." Ryan stated. "You are just too stubborn." Voltar argued. "Yes I am." Ryan said Valtra entered. "Hey no arguing." She said as she hugged Ryan. "I will be back later, to finish this discussion he vanished. "Was that what that was?" Ryan asked as he sees Valtra is upset with tears in her eyes. "Hey, I'm ok." Ryan replied. "Yes barely." She replied as she takes his hand. "You're not, gonna tell me what to do too are you?" Ryan asked. "You are my son, I almost lost you." "I don't want to go threw that again." She said. "I'm in as much danger, no matter what I do." Ryan claimed. "You have enemies from both sides." She added. "Please, don't go protective mode too." Ryan asked. "I'm your mother, that's my job." She replied as she kissed his forehead. "Fine, but when I'm back on my feet, I'm back to work." Ryan replied. "We can discuss this then." She said just then Marie, Vala, and Devon come in. "Hey, my favorite people." Ryan replied as they each hug him. "I'm glad your ok." Devon said. "So am I." Ryan replied. "Hey, where is dad and Steven?" Ryan asked. "Your father is trying to cool down, so he doesn't go ballistic on you." Valtra informed Steven enters. "Hey." Ryan said as Steven hugs him. "You scared me." Steven replied. "I'm not going anywhere, yet." Ryan stated. "I've got to get back so." Steven said as Dylan entered. "I will be back in a little bit." Valtra said. As all go out. "Go ahead and say it." Ryan replied. "No, I just want to sit here and watch you." Dylan said as he sits in chair and takes Ryan's hand. "I'm ok dad." Ryan assured. "I know you are." Dylan replied. "Paul says six months, I'll be back on my feet." Ryan stated. "You are a fighter like me." Dylan replied. "I'm sorry." Ryan added. "For what?" Dylan asked. "Giving you all your grey hair." Ryan smiled. "For scaring you." Ryan added. "You should be." Dylan said. "I know, you all wish I'd give this up but it is not me." Ryan stated. "I know you are my son." Dylan admitted. "I don't think Voltar gets that." Ryan said. "He does, he just doesn't like it." Dylan replied. They both let out a laugh Paul comes over. "Ok, let's get started on your rehab." Paul replied. "Good let's go." Ryan said. "Small steps kid, heat and ultrasound until your bones heal." Paul replied. "I'll be back." Dylan said as he goes now later. "So, where is the cute nurse?" Ryan asked. "You're looking at um." Paul said. Now it's late as Ryan sleeps Alieah entered Ryan wakes up. "Hey." Ryan said. "I know it's late but I couldn't sleep." She replied as she sat next to him. "It's ok." Ryan said. "This is why I hate falling for the pilots." She said. "What a coincidence, I hate falling." Ryan replied with a smile she laughed. "See I cheered you up." Ryan stated. "Yes you did." She admitted as she leaned in and they kiss. "I'm not going anywhere." Ryan replied. "I know, I'm just scared I don't want to loose you." She said. "You won't." Ryan stated. "I'm leaving, I decided to go back to Earth." She replied. "What?" Ryan asked as she stands up. "Alieah." He pleads. "I can't, watch you heal up and then get hurt again." "I'm leaving now, before I get too involved." She said. "No, we can." He started. "This, is hard enough It's better to do this now." She replied. "I can't handle this." She confessed. "I'm sorry she said as she goes out. "Aleiah!" Ryan yelled. "Damm it!" He shouted. Paul comes over from his office. "Are you ok?" Paul asked. "No, she's breaking up with me." Ryan said. "What, Why?" Paul said. "She's afraid to loose me." Ryan replied. "I have to stop her." Ryan sits up. "Get me a wheelchair." Ryan asked. "You are not ready to be moved, I just got you sewed up and stable you could bleed." Paul stated. "I can't let her leave." Ryan insisted. "Hey, if she loves you she will be back." Paul assured. "I guess she was right, painful long recovery." Ryan said. "Let's get to work then." Ryan added meanwhile at Voltar's castle he is blasting tables, chairs and walls with his power in anger and frustration. "Hey, you're going to destroy the place." Rick stated. Voltar stops. "I won't let him risk his life again." Voltar insisted. "You know, you can't stop him." Rick replied. "If I can get his parents on my side." Voltar considers. "Don't go starting trouble father." Rick replied. "That is my middle name." Voltar said as he goes out. "I thought it was Markavil?" Rick said meanwhile in docking bay Alieah is getting her bags loaded into a shuttle. "Hey, you're not really gonna go?" Paul asked. "I have to, I can't stand by and watch him get killed." She fears. "You are in love with him, he loves you." Paul replied. "I'm sorry." She said as she goes into shuttle. Well now comes the hard part getting my nephew back on his feet. But when he does will we let him fly again? Scene in sickbay Ryan lying in bed looking depressed and detached. "Hey, ready for your heating pad?" Paul asked. "Yeah I guess." Ryan said. "Hey positive thinking ok." Paul insisted. "Sure ok." Ralph enters. "Hey, where have you been?" Ryan asked. "I feel bad, I should've had your back." Ralph said. "It was not your fault." Ryan stated. "I know in my head, but I still feel guilty." Ralph said. "I'll be back out there in no time." Ryan replied. Valtra enters. "I've got to go." Ralph said as he goes out. "Hey." Valtra said. "Mom." Ryan replied as she kissed his cheek. "I'll let you talk." Paul goes into his office. "So, here to watch the slow yet exciting recovery process?" Ryan asked. "Of course." She answered. "I just wish you'd, consider something safer to return to." She added. "Mom, we talked about this." Ryan replied. "I want to keep you safe." She said. "Even when I'm here, I'm still in danger." He reminded. "At least we have time." She savored. "Time for what?" Ryan asked. "To get you, to see it my way." She answered. "That won't happen." Ryan insisted. Now later as Ryan is getting therapy Dylan entered looking upset. "What is it?" Ryan asked. "Volrin, he is back inside of a beast from the underworld." Dylan replied just then Ryan has a flash he sees the beast grab Devon in the city. "Volrin is going to take Devon." Ryan responded now in the control room. "I should've sent someone else." Jon stated. "Hey, you could not have seen this." Shane replied. "Devon can handle himself." Ralph said. Well now we have to deal with Uncle Volrin again, who has figured out how to jump into others bodies to escape his prison in the underworld, but we also have some other issues to deal with. Devon and our latest new threat a race of aliens called the Grelks. They will prove to be a formidable foe but not the only problem we will face.

Chapter 19

THE GRELKS

Let me tell you about our next threat the Grelks, creatures of enormous size and strength. They have the power to move in and out of space and time. We may not be able to defeat this threat. Volrin is also trying to sway Devon to doubt our intentions. Will he be taken in? Or will he find out a secret, so incredible it will spark his Aster rage to the surface. Scene: in the city as Devon is walking. Volrin in his creature body flies down to him as people see, and they run and scream in terror. He swoops in to grab Devon up in his claws, as he attempted to run. "Hello my son." He growled. Devon struggles to get free. "Let me go!" He shouted. "Not a chance, you're with me not them." Volrin insisted. "Like hell I am." Devon replied. He uses his power to electrify his body and shocks Volrin into releasing him. They both land in the forest. Volrin uses his power to change into humanoid form. "Nice blast son." Volrin complemented. "I knew you had that darkness in you, it increases your power." He added. "I am not like you, and I never will be." Devon replied. "Of course not." Volrin replied. He attempted to move closer to him "You are your own man, or do they still treat you as a child?" Volrin suspected. Devon considers his words. "I thought so." "They want to control you." Volrin resumes. "They are holding you back, from your true gifts." Volrin concluded. "Just shut-up, you're trying to twist things around." Devon said firmly. "I'm respected there." Devon insisted. "No, you are feared there." Volrin informed. "Your are feared, because you're my son." "They will never, fully trust you Devon." Volrin informed. "They do trust me." Devon assured. "They are watching you, waiting to see if it is in you." Volrin insisted. "They love and care about me." Devon said. "Then why are you, trying so hard to convince me?" Volrin asked. He then turns back to beast and flies off as the team arrived. "Devon, are you ok?" Jon asked. "Yeah I'm good." Devon stated. "How did he escape again?" Devon questioned. "He found a way to, jump into other bodies." Jon said. "He will be back." Devon stated. "Don't worry, we will catch him." Dylan answers. Now back on the base: Devon is passing by sickbay when Ryan saw him. "Hey Devon you ok?" Ryan asked as Devon comes in. "Yeah, I'm fine." Devon said. "I'm here if, you need to talk." Ryan insisted. "Thanks, how are you doing?" Devon asked. "Better, it's a slow process." "I just wish, I could get back out there to help find him." Ryan replied. "I wish they'd let me help, I'm a good pilot." Devon stated. "Don't be in a hurry to grow up, take a lesson from me." Ryan advised. "I'm almost fifteen now." Devon informed. "That was how old I was, when I was on the streets." Ryan replied. "I should let you rest." Devon said. He heads out into corridor, he is reminded of Volrin's words in the forest echoing in his head as Jon comes up to him. "Devon, are you alright?" Jon questioned. "I'm fine." Devon insisted. "Listen, don't let Volrin confuse you with his lies." Jon replied. "He can be very manipulative." Jon added. "I know, I'm not a stupid kid." Devon stated. "I never implied you were." Jon responded. "Where is that coming form?" Jon asked. "No where, forget it good-night." Devon said. He went down corridor to his room and shut the door. Volrin appeared in humanoid form. "So, was I right or what?" Volrin delighted. "Go away before I call security." Devon replied. "I am just trying to save you, from the foolish notion that you believe you belong here." Volrin stated. "I do belong here, and I'm not going to help you." Devon swore. "I would think long and hard about that son." Volrin stated. He vanished Devon turned to find Amanda standing in his doorway. "You don't really believe him, do you?" She asked. "No, I don't know some things he said." Devon answered. "We want you here Devon, we care about you." Amanda guaranteed. "But, do you trust me?" Devon asked. "Of course." Amanda answered. "Then, why am I not a pilot?" Devon inquiries. "Ryan is out of commission, I should be up there." Devon insisted. "We didn't let Steven fly, until he was sixteen." Amanda reminded him. "I feel like, I should be doing more than just back up." Devon replied. "You are needed here, to watch over Marie and Vala."

Amanda said. "So what, I'm a babysitter now great." Devon reacted. "Keep working hard, show them you are mature and ready, then they will let you fly." Amanda instructed. She goes, and then Moondeath spirit appears. "Hello Devon." He said. "I came to make sure, you do not go down the wrong path." He warned. "Don't let him trick you. "You know in your heart you are loved here." Moondeath stated. "I don't want them to fear, that I am my father's son." Devon responded. "They know you are not, trust them." Moondeath added then vanished. Now next day: Dylan comes up to Devon in control room. "Hey, I have a proposition for you." Dylan said. "Come in my office." He added. They go in Jon is there. "Sounds serious, am I in trouble?" Devon asked. "No, we just figured since we are a pilot down, you'd like to fill in?" Jon said with a smile. "Are you serious?" Devon said with excitement. "Ryan did recommend you to cover him, until he is healed." Dylan stated. "But, if you do good it could be a permanent spot." Jon added. "You won't regret this." Devon replied. "I know." Jon said. Meanwhile in sickbay: Ryan is on his feet holding onto the bars trying to walk slowly. "Uh." He grunts in intense pain. "Take it slow." Paul insisted. "I'm fine." Ryan assured then his leg starts to give way. "Damm it!" Ryan exclaimed. "I told you, to take it slow." Paul said as he helps him to steady back up. "I think you should quit for today." Paul suggested as Voltar appeared. "I agree with the good doctor." Voltar replied As Paul helps him back into bed. "I'm fine ok." Ryan said. "What is the rush?" Voltar asked. "I hate being cooped up." Ryan answered. "No one likes that, but if you want to recover fully." Voltar stated. "I know, so what did you want?" Ryan asked. "I was just checking on you, I talked with your mother recently." Voltar informed. "Why, are you two plotting something?" Ryan questioned. "Of course we are." Voltar admitted. "I should've known." Ryan replied. Voltar puts his hand on Ryan's shoulder. "We are only trying to keep you safe." Voltar said. "I hate when you try, to control my life." Ryan replied. "We know." Voltar said then Valtra enters. "I'll let you two talk." Voltar said as he vanished. "So here to use more guilt?" Ryan asked. "No, I'm here as your mother to check on you." She replied. "I'm sorry, I'm just frustrated." Ryan said. "I'm sorry for upsetting you." She replied. "You're my mother, it's your job." Ryan says with a smile. "I will, be back on my feet soon enough so, why rush it." Ryan stated Valtra hugged him. When Dylan entered. "Hey." He said "Dad, so how is my replacement doing?" Ryan asked. "Very good actually." Dylan admitted. "Have you heard from Alieah?" Ryan asked. "No son, I'm sorry." "All she did was send me her letter of transfer." Dylan replied. "She will be back, she loves you." Valtra informed. "I think, it's why she won't come back mom." Ryan admitted just then Jon rushed in. "We have trouble." Jon stated. Dylan steps outside with Jon. "What is it?" Dylan asked. "It's Barbara Babor, she escaped again." Jon answered. "What!" Dylan shouted. "Find her." He ordered. "I've got the team out looking." Jon informed. "I also, put extra guards on Cole and here at sickbay for Ryan." Jon replied. "He does not, need this not now." Dylan said in anger Valtra comes out. "What's going on?" "I could feel your anxiety." She said. "Barbara Babor has escaped." Dylan explained. "Who is she?" She asked "A sick twisted bitch, who has a lust for our son." Dylan answered. "I will kill her." Valtra stated. "If only it was that easy." "She is also highly intelligent, a genius at devices and gadgets to elude us." Dylan added just then alarms go off. "Stay with him." Dylan instructed. He and Jon headed to control room. Valtra comes back in. "What is it?" Ryan asked. "Your father will handle it." She replied. "Ok, who escaped?" Ryan demanded. "A Barbara Babor?" She said. "Great." Ryan replied. "Don't worry, I will protect you." She vowed. Meanwhile in control room: "Your sure it's her?" Cole asked. "Someone breeched our first gates." Dylan stated. "We will find her." Jon swore. "She is slippery, I know." Cole replied. "She won't get you." Amanda said. "My mother will never give up, until she dies." Cole replied. "I'm going to check Ryan's quarters." Dylan said as he heads out. "Come on, your staying with me." Amanda insisted. "Yeah ok." Cole agreed with a smile as they go out and down different corridor. Barbara appeared behind them knocking them both to the ground with a device she made. Amanda is knocked out but Cole is still conscious. "Hello my son." She said. "You are insane." Cole replied. "I'm still your mother." She stated. She uses device to knock him out, then signaled a huge fury beast to come in threw a side entrance she unlocked to grab Cole. She then uses her teleportation device to escape with them threw gateway. Jon comes around the corner to find Amanda. "Amanda!" Jon shouted as he helps her to her feet as she wakes up. "Barbara took him." She replied. "Then she will go after Ryan next." Jon said. Now in sickbay Dylan enters. "No sign of her yet." Dylan stated. Then the lights go out. Valtra can sense her. "She is here, she has help." Valtra informed.

"Where are the emergency lights?" Dylan demanded. Paul hits a switch and lights go on. "It's too quiet." Ryan said. Just then the big fury beast comes out of portal standing by Ryan's bed. "Whoa!" Ryan exclaimed Dylan draws weapon. "What the hell is that?" Dylan asked. Jon entered and blasted it with power form his hands as it vanished. "Looks like she, has made a friend." Jon said. "Ok, what does it get in return?" Dylan wonders. Just then Ryan gets a flash. He sees the beast with Voltar and it is blasting him. "It's after Voltar." Ryan disclosed. "I will warn him." Valtra said. "No, I will go." "You stay with Ryan." "They will still come after him." Jon said as he goes, meanwhile in another realm between space and time, a void of sorts. We see Barbara sitting next to Cole as he is lying on a bed. "Don't be angry." She begs. "I had to protect you from their plans." She explained. "They will be taking over the galaxy." She said. Now back in sickbay, as Amanda is getting a bandage on her forehead by Paul. "They are called Grelks." Amanda realized. "They came here to our galaxy once before, but thought it too weak." She continued. "Now something's changed." She finished. "Is they're a way to stop them?" Ryan asked. "No one has before, they have conquered other galaxies." She answers. "What I don't understand is, how'd Barbara met them?" Amanda questioned. "She is evil, they are using her." Valtra sensed. "Wait, you said they came to Barbara, she must've made a deal." "Maybe, that is how we can stop them." Ryan said. "Yes, your right." Amanda replied. "They can travel fast." Valtra sensed. Voltar then entered with Jon and Dylan. "I can keep Ryan safe." Voltar replied. "So, where are we going?" Ryan asked. "A void of my own creation, so let's go shall we?" Voltar said. "Ready when you are." Ryan replied they both vanish. "Are you sure they are safe." Dylan asked. "When he hid me there, you guys could not find me." Jon replied just then Creature appeared. "Look out!" Valtra yelled. Barbara also appears. "Where is Ryan?" She demanded. "If you do this, you will kill us all." Jon stated. "Not all just you." She replied. "Ryan and Cole will be safe." She added. "You are, a sick twisted bitch." Amanda said as she luges for her but Jon holds her back. "You will never see my son again." Barbara vowed. "Do you really think, they will honor that deal?" Jon stated. "We do honor our deals, Voltarian." Creature responded. "You will never find Ryan." Jon replied. "You are a powerful one." Creature replied. "Come find out." Jon answered as creature charged Jon. Jon transformed into his Dregon of pure blue light with wings "Get clear!" Amanda yelled. They rush out of sickbay as Jon blasts the creature, then it vanishes along with Barbara. "So, yours is blue." Paul understood. Jon changed back to his humanoid form. "We need to find Cole." Jon said. "I read Barbara in the chaos, they are near by." Amanda replied they go meanwhile in Voltar's void; it is royally decorated of course. "So how is therapy?" Voltar asked. "Ok, hard but I'm ok." Ryan stated. "I am sorry about Alieah." Voltar said. "I haven't given up yet." Ryan replied. "You and Jon have lost a lot too." Ryan asked. "It's the curse for our clan, to be alone." Voltar stated. "We all have paid a price, for being an Aster." Voltar admits. "Guess I will too." Ryan replied. "I hope not, maybe it can end with you." Voltar hoped. meanwhile back at their hiding place. "Where is he?" Barbara demanded. "He is out of our reach." Creature admitted. "You'll never complete your deal mother." Cole said. "So just let me go." Cole replied. "If she does not complete it, we will find another who will." Creature vowed. "You will be safe if I do." Barbara stated. "Ryan, will never be with you." Cole stated. "I will never forgive you, if you let them kill Amanda." Cole stated. "How can you be, so cruel to your mother?" She asked. "I wanted you to be my mother, but you can't let go of the evil, the power you hunger for." "I can't save you, so I'm giving up." Cole expressed. Meanwhile the team arrived on Pluto. "Anything?" Jon asked. "I can feel Cole's presence, we are close." Amanda said as they head toward it with Dylan, Ralph and Mary. They make way to a bright light a doorway of sorts, and go inside it. They find Cole chained to a wall by a shackle around his ankle. "Cole!" Amanda exclaimed as she rushed to him hugging him. They break chain. "Are you ok?" She asked. "Yes I'm ok." Cole replied. "I'm sorry, I know you wanted her to change." Amanda said. "Yes, but she won't, I have to except it." Cole replied. "Le's go." Jon advised. Just then creature appeared. "Now we have the bait." Creature replied as six other creatures appeared before them. "This was a trap." Dylan said. "Of course, now we have a powerful Voltarian resist, and we kill your friends." Creature promises as Voltar can sense what has happened. "Junior." He said. "What's going on?" Ryan asked. "It was a trap, they have him and the others." Voltar replied. "I have to help." Voltar stated as he vanished and reappeared to them "Father no." Jon said. "We need to be rid of these beasts, once and for all." Voltar stated as he and Jon concentrates and blasts their power at them. "This is only temporary!" Creature vowed as they exploded. Amanda puts cuffs on Barbara. "You took a big risk father." Jon said. "Of course I did, you're my son." Voltar replied. "I always protect, my most valued treasures." He added as he touches Jon's cheek. Now back on the base, just when we thought all was back to normal. We would discover an even more sinister plot underneath our very noses. "Daddy I'm sorry." Vala comes up and hugged him, as he entered quarters. "Sorry for what?" Jon says in confusion she lets go. "The lies." She answered as she transformed into Velana a beautiful humanoid woman that tried long ago to claim an Aster for a husband. "No, it can't be." Jon replied. She comes close with her light purple eyes and long blonde hair. "I am sorry son of Voltar but it was the only way to get close to all of you." She explained. "To gain your trust and learn your secrets." She explained. "What is it you want?" Jon asked. "The future." She says. "I thought that was you but I was wrong." She admitted. "Then who?" He paused and thought. "No." Jon realized. She blasts him knocking him out. "Now, I will claim my king." She replied as she vanished and reappeared in sickbay walks up to Ryan's bed as he sleeps. "I should've known." She replied as she caressed his cheek. "You are the true king." She said as Ryan wakes up. "Who are you?" Ryan asked. "I am your future queen." She answered. "Excuse me?" Ryan replied. "I have waited for you, when I found out your true lineage I knew you were the one." She stated. "When we met, I don't know you." Ryan contended. She then changed back to Vala. "No, this can't be your Vala?" Ryan asked. "You are the future ruler of us all." She replied. She changed back to Velana and touched his forehead her hand glows as she healed him. Ryan sits up then stands up. "How did you?" Ryan questioned. "This is insane." Ryan indicated. "We belong together Ryan." She insisted. Ryan grabs alarm on side of bed and pressed it. "You are crazy." Ryan said. Just then Voltar appeared. "Velana I should've known." Voltar said. "You are too late, our bond is set." Velana informed. "You know her?" Ryan asked. Jon and team enter. "It's over Velana." Jon said. "No it's just begun." She replied as she vanished. "Are you ok?" Valtra asked as she comes to Ryan. "Yeah, she healed me." Ryan replied. "Why didn't we sense her?" Jon asked. "She has powers of illusion, she fooled us." Amanda admitted. "We need to catch her." Dylan said. "I will." Voltar stated. "You need to be careful, she is a seductress." Jon reminded. "She seduced you, my grandfather and even Rick." Jon explained. "Am I, destined to rule the galaxy?" Ryan asked. "No one, in this family is destined to be with that witch." Valtra vowed. "We need to find her father?" Jon replied as he noticed he had vanished. "He went out looking for Velana." Valtra answered. "We can't let him go alone?" Jon replied. "Let him?" Dylan said. "Right, where would he go?" Jon thinks. "I'd start with Voltia her home turf." Amanda advised. "Help Valtra to protect Ryan." Jon asked. "Of course, you be careful." Dylan replied. "I've dealt with her before, and lived." Jon reminded him. "Yeah, but that was when she wanted you, now she doesn't big difference." He stated Jon vanished and reappeared on Voltia beside Voltar. "Any luck?" Jon asked. "Not yet, shouldn't you be guarding Ryan?" Voltar replied. "He is covered, I figured you could use back up." Jon stated. "I can handle her junior." Voltar insisted. "She is a real threat father." Jon replied. "I can't believe, how she fooled us." Voltar admitted. "She knew I wanted a child after Jessica and the baby died" Jon replied. "I am sorry son." Voltar said. "I know, but I am still young." "I mean if you can have kids and rick, Valtra." "I will too." Jon vowed. "She is close." Voltar senses. "Where?" Jon said as they look around and see a small hut type structure in the middle of the city. "Let's finish this." Voltar stated as they get to it and inside but it is empty. "She is quick, I will give her that." Voltar replied. "No, she is still here." Jon said as she appeared. "So ready to die?" Voltar asked. "How amusing you are Voltar, you always were." "I'm done playing games." She said. "You are not taking Ryan." Jon replied. "No, I'm not." She confessed. "This was all part of my plan." She admitted. Voltar and Jon are confused. "What twisted game are you playing witch?" Voltar asked. "You will find out boys." She said with a smile then vanished. "We need to regroup." Jon said. Now back on the base in control room. "What is she up to?" Jon questioned. "I don't get it, so she doesn't want me?" Ryan asked. "Why did she say she wanted him, then change her mind?" Voltar replied. "Who knows, who cares let's just kill her and be done with it." Rick stated. "I second that." Valtra replied. "First, we have to find her." Voltar said. "Maybe if we all concentrate, our power we can find her." Jon suggested. "Let's do that." Valtra agreed. As they all concentrate and they sense her. "So working together." She said she then sends an image into Ryan's mind of her true intensions. He sees Velana standing on a massive pile of dead bodies with a man in robes standing beside her. When man turns Ryan sees his face, it is Jon. "Whoa."

Ryan said as they all break link. "What did you see?" Valtra asked. "She sent me her vision, of the future she wants." Ryan replied. "What was it?" Voltar asked. "Jon, standing by her side." Ryan answered. "What?" Jon replied. "She is still after you." Voltar said. "I will kill her." Voltar vowed. "So, where is she?" Ryan asked. "She is close, I can feel that." Valtra confirmed. "We need to find her." Dylan said. "She will come here, we have someone she wants." Voltar stated. "Right." Jon replied. meanwhile Velana sneaks back on the base and into Jon's quarters where Tracilla is in bathroom coming out of the shower and puts on her robe. "Time to get rid of the competition." She said as she comes behind her and snapped her neck, sending her soul back to the underworld. Amanda can sense it. "No." Amanda said. "What is it?" Dylan asked. "She is here, she killed Tracilla." Amanda replied. "What?" Jon replied as he rushed out of control room to his quarters to find her in bathroom on the floor. "No." Jon cried as he kneeled to her. "I've been threw this too many times, but it never gets easier." Jon stated. "I am so sorry, we will kill her." Voltar promised just then alarms go off as they rise up. "She is here." Jon said. "I will take care of her." Voltar stated as he goes out ahead. "Father wait." Jon follows just then the lights go out. "Everyone stay put." Dylan ordered. "Mark where are the lights?" Dylan demands over the com-link. "Working on it captain." He answered. "Where is she?" Amanda said then the lights comeback on as they all get to the control room. "Alright, I need info where is everyone?" Dylan demanded as he goes to console checks all trackers. "Where is my father?" Jon asked. "He is not here." Dylan answered just then the large vidlink screen comes on its Velana. "Hello, not the Aster I want, but he will due for now." She said as she showed him chained against a wall in her lair. "Where do you want me to go?" Jon surrendered. "Jon no." Dylan ordered. "Meet me at your father's castle." She said then she cuts off transmission Jon goes to leave. "You are not going alone." Valtra instructed. "I have to, it's my battle." Jon stated. "Hey." Rick replied. "Stay here and protect them." Jon asked then he leaves. "We are not letting him go alone." Shane said. "No we're not." Valtra said as she and rick go after him meanwhile in lair. "I will kill you witch, you're not having my son." Voltar vowed. "I once respected your evil now, you're just pathetic." "You let your emotions rule you." She replied. "And you are not?" Voltar stated. "You act like you don't care, but you do." "He makes you fall in love with him, the way he treats people his heart." Voltar stated. "His power is why I want him." She stated. "Sure it is." Voltar replied just then Jon appeared. "Let him go." Jon demanded. "Your weakness is touching." She said. "I will never understand, after all he has done to you, why you still love him." She added. "He is my father, I will always love him." Jon answered. "How sweet, lets see how long it lasts after he is dead." She said as she pulls blade and puts it to his throat. "Why do you need to kill him?" "I'm here?" Jon replied. "I need to bring out the darkness inside of you." She explained. "I tried by killing your wife but." She said. "What?" Jon replied shocked. "Did you really think, I would let her have your child?" "She is not of royal Voltian blood." She replied. "You caused her crash?" Jon stated. "You have to be with me." She replied. "You are insane, if you think I would have a child with you." Jon responded. "You have no choice, if not me then no one." She vowed. Just then Valtra and Rick appeared and freed Voltar. "Take him, I have what I want." She said as she used her power to shake the castle walls then open a portal to her lair and grab Jon by arm and pull him in as they escape. "No!" Voltar shouts as it closed. "We must find them." Voltar commands. "He knows she killed his wife and child, she could unleash his darkness." Voltar replied meanwhile in her lair "So now what?" Jon said. "Nothing, I will leave you with your thoughts for a while." She replied. "To view your life." She added. "What does that mean?" Jon asked as she vanished he looks at the wall and it becomes a vidlink screen showing when he first met Carla and then her violent death, then showing when he met Jessica and then her death. "I am not my father." Jon replied then screen goes black Velana returns. "So was it worth it?" She asked. "To love and to lose them?" She replied. "I know what you are trying to do, my father tried it and it won't work." Jon stated. "I will destroy your life and those you care for, until all you have left is me." She vows as she vanished again and the screen comes on this time it shows the base where he sees Devon, Steven and Marie in the Rec Room. "No." Jon said, as Velana appears in front of them "Time to die kids." She stated. Devon steps in front of Steven and Marie "Stay behind me." Devon said as he raised his arms up and used his power to create a shield around them "Impressive kid." She replied as she blasted at it until Devon is weakened and falls back releasing the shield. "No!" Jon shouted as he transformed into his Dregon and escaped her lair. Then is on the base in the Rec room "Stop Velana."

He exclaimed. "So still good?" She asked. "Always." Jon answered. "Now get clear." He says to them. Steven and Marie go out. "I want to help." Devon insisted. "This is my fight Devon." Jon replied. Devon nods his head and goes. "You'll have to kill me." She stated. "I know." Jon said. "We could've ruled this galaxy." She replied. "What would be the fun in that?" Jon asked. "Such a waste." She replied. "I can say the same for you." Jon stated Velana let out a laugh. "You are your father's son." She said. "I will take that as a compliment." Jon replied as he uses his power and blasts her and she explodes shaking the base Devon comes back in. "Are you ok?" Devon asked. "Yes, thanks for the back up." He replied. "Anytime, so maybe your women streak will change for the good?" Devon asked. "I hope so." Jon replied as the rest of team enters. "Are you ok?" Steven asked. "Yeah I'm fine." Jon replied. "Is she gone?" Voltar asked. "Yes she is gone." Jon stated. "I'm sorry she put you threw all that." Valtra replied as she hugged him. "No, it's ok she tested my will, my very soul and I passed." Jon stated. "You passed, because your heart is true and pure." She insisted as they team heads back out of Rec Room. "If you need to talk." Voltar said. "I know." Jon replied Voltar vanished as Devon stayed behind. "How do you do it?" Devon questioned. "Do what?" Jon asked. "Keep from being like him." Devon answered. "I believe my mother was the key." Jon replied. "I wish I knew, who mine was." Devon said. "You have us, we will help you." Jon promised. "I hope so." Devon replied. "I see it in you, you are not your father." Jon insisted. "I'm afraid, when I get angry that, I will become him." Devon worried. "Just because we get angry, does not mean we will be evil." Jon reminded. "I'm glad I have you." Devon stated. "I'm glad too." Jon said with a smile as Devon smiled too now later that night as Devon slept he dreamed, he sees himself as a baby he can see walls of gold and white a beautiful palace. He sees the outline of a female then wakes up. "Mom?" Devon said. Now in the morning Devon is up and headed into the control room he comes to Amanda. "I need your help." Devon said. "What is it? "Is Volrin back?" She feared. "No, this is not about him." "Its about my mother." Devon replied. "Your mother?" She asked. "I'm dreaming about her, I feel like I need to find her." Devon insisted. "I will do what I can, take my hand." She said when he gives it to her she gets a flash of his dream she can see the palace of gold and white and sees her face then she lets go. "What did you see?" Devon asked. "I saw her." Amanda replied. "Do you know who she is?" Devon begged. "All I know is that you can not try to find her, or you will be in danger." She revealed. "I need to know who I am." Devon stated. "I don't know if you should." She feared. meanwhile Ryan arrived to the Earth base and sees Alieah headed into it. "Alieah!" He shouted as she turned to see him. "Ryan?" She said as he comes over. "You're walking?" She replied. "Yes, I am." "We need to talk." He said. "Ryan I can't do this." She replied "Tell me you don't feel anything for me, and I will walk away and never look back." Ryan stated. "You know I do, but I'm afraid." She answered. "You don't have to be, I decided to not be the first line." Ryan replied. "What?" She said. "Let's just say, you are not the only one who's afraid of dying." Ryan admitted as she kissed him then hugged him in overwhelming joy. Meanwhile back on the base Devon comes to Jon in Dylan's office alone. "Can we talk?" Devon asked. "Of course, what is it?" Jon replied. "I had a dream, about my mother I think it was a memory," "I asked Amanda to help, and when she read my mind she freaked out." Devon explained. "She freaked out?" Jon replied. "If she feels that strongly, maybe you should drop it." Jon suggested. "I need to know who she was Jon." Devon stated. "Let me talk to Amanda." Jon replied. "Thank you." Devon said then Devon left. Now Jon heads to Amanda's quarters she opens door. "Jon, what brings you here?" She asked. "Devon actually, what did you see?" Jon asked. "I saw, someone who is very admit about him not being revealed." "I could tell in her eyes she was afraid Jon." Amanda revealed. "I will talk to him." Jon replied as he heads out to his quarters Voltar is there. "Hello father, what brings you here?" Jon asked. "I'm here about Devon, you need to stop him from searching for his mother." Voltar demanded. "Why would you care, who his mother is?" Jon asked. "I am concerned, for his well being is all." "He is family." Voltar replied. "I will handle it." Jon assured. "Let me do it." Voltar insisted then he vanished Jon goes to control room and into Dylan's office. "There is something my father is hiding, it's about Devon's mother." Jon replied. "That man has too many secrets." Dylan stated Amanda comes to the doorway. "Including Devon." She revealed. "What is it?" Jon asked. "Devon is not your cousin, he is your brother." She realized. "What?" Jon replied just then Devon was by the door and heard her. "What?" Devon asked in disbelief. "Does my father know this?" Jon asked. "Yes he does." Amanda admitted. "Why didn't he say anything?" Devon demanded, "He is trying to protect you, form something greater than just our galaxy." Amanda confessed. "What does that mean?" Dylan asked. "I get it, he doesn't want me." "I'm use to that." Devon replied as he walked out. "Devon!" Jon called as he goes after him. "Wait, I know my father can be confusing, but we need to talk to him." Jon replied. "What kind of father doesn't acknowledge his own son?" Devon questioned Voltar appeared before them. "One, who is still trying to keep him safe." Voltar answered. Well my father has some major explaining to do but that is only half the story. We still need to find out who that woman in Devon's dream really is and why we need to keep it secret. This is about to get really intense and take us back to a time when they're where three major beings in our universe the gods, the titans and the ancients.

Chapter 20

THE ANCIENTS

The universe began with three types of beings; the Gods who created the creatures and worlds we have come to know, and yet to discover. The Titans fierce warriors, that protected the gods and other creatures in the universe, until they were banished for their betrayal. Then there are the allusive Ancients, they exist among the stars and rarely take humanoid form. They do so If, there is a threat to the balance of good and evil. They are the mediators, who have no high opinion of dark or light. They are supposed to stay neutral. Only once did they interfere, when a Goddess dared to love a Titan and spawned a dark abomination upon the universe, which happened to be our Patriarch. Scene we go back fifteen years to Voltara where a younger Voltar has a darkness in his eyes and recruited a scientist with intentions of his own. Scene in the castle we come to a throne room, where Voltar stands with a young Valtra and Rick, also an older man, "You will have your lab below Kravitz." Voltar informed. "Yes my lord, I am eager to serve the Aster royal family." He replied as he goes out of hall. "Can we trust him father?" Valtra questioned in her black battle armor. "He is loyal to Aster blood, that is all I require." Voltar stated meanwhile above the very planet high in the stars. We come close to one of them. We find large golden doors which lead to a palace, which when we enter it is pure gold and white, as a young beautiful female looks out of a clear crystal wall is watching them. She has raven hair and beautiful sapphire eyes. "I must stop this." She replied. She then goes into a room where a single throne sat and upon it sits an older man, with white hair that has streaks of raven color and sapphire eyes. "Father, I believe it has begun again." She stated. "What do you mean?" He demanded. "I saw the clan known as Aster, they have dark plans for this universe." She admitted. "I should not have let them live." He replied. "We will gather the army, and wipe them from this universe." He exclaimed as he raised form his throne. "No!" She shouted. "I have also, seen goodness in many of their hearts." "We can not destroy all of them." "I've seen there potential, for greatness." She informed. "What do you suggest then?" He replied. "I will go to them, speak on your behalf." She answered. "I will allow it, but if they can not be reasoned with." "They will be destroyed." He vowed. "Yes, father." She replied as she departed and made her journey in a great ball of light, crashing to the surface of Voltara as she emerged from the blast wearing a dress of gold and flecks of white through out. Meanwhile inside the castle, a young boy of seven comes out of his room running and bumps into Voltar. "Junior, what are you doing?" He commanded. "Sorry father, I was headed out to play." He answered. "Then go to it." He said with a smile and a wink. "Yes sir." He rushed by and out the castle doors. He played in the near by forest, where he came upon Mordra. "Well, hello young one are you all alone?" She asked. "Yes, I'm just playing." "I live there." Jon replied as he pointed to the castle. "What is your name young one?" She asked as she kneeled to him. "I am Voltar Aster Jr." He identified. "Ahh I see." She replied. She touched his hand and saw his fate. "You will do great things." She informed. "You are pretty." Jon said. "Thank you." She said as he rushed off toward the city. Mordra continued on to the castle. She walked inside as the doors were opened. She could here yelling in the distance, as she came upon the throne room. "You will do as I say!" Voltar shouted. "Yes father." Valtra replied as she left. "You were too soft on her." Rick insisted. "If I had taken prisoners from the alliance, you would have me whipped." Rick reminded. "She knows now, so she will kill all next time." Voltar replied. Rick goes out as Mordra entered. "Who are you?" Voltar demanded. "I am Mordra, I am here to stop what you are planning for this galaxy." She stated. "You?" "I mere woman." Voltar replied. "I am an Ancient." She announced as her eyes glow blue. "So I see, forgive me I've never seen one so beautiful." He replied. "I have seen from the stars, what darkness you have conspired here." She informed. "You will end it." She ordered. "Of course, you should stay for dinner." Voltar suggested. "I really must return." She declined. "I do not bite." Voltar promised, just then Jon entered. "Hey, you are the lady from the forest." Jon replied. "This is one of my sons." Voltar replied. "Junior, go get cleaned up for dinner." He said. "Yes father, are you staying?" He asked. "I believe I will." She answered with a smile as he went out meanwhile back at the palace. "My king she has not returned." Marcel replied. "What is taking her so long?" Zavaris questioned. "Should I go after her?" Marcel asked. "No she is capable." Zavaris replied. Now back at the castle, at a large dinner table Jon is eating. "Slow down junior, chew your food." Voltar replied. "So is he your oldest?" She asked. "No, I have three older." "They serve in my army, which is why we are alone for dinner." Voltar replied. "What of your plans?" She demanded. "I will not destroy the galaxy." He insisted. "I hope I can believe you." She said. "It is late, I should return." She said. "You can wait till morning, I have many guest rooms." He suggested. "I really should not." She replied. "Stay, it's been too long since there was a lady as pretty as you here." Jon begged. "Well since you asked." She replied. "It is settled then." Voltar stated meanwhile back at the Ancients palace. "She is staying the night?" Marcel asked. "Yes she is, I see no harm in it." Zavaris replied. "It is unwise, to spent too much time among them my king." Marcel warned. "I trust my daughter." He stated, now later as Voltar has tucked Jon into bed. "You like her father, don't you?" Jon asked. "I like many woman." Voltar answered. "She is different, I can tell." Jon said. "I think so too." Voltar replied. He goes out and down the hall, he heads to where Mordra is staying. "I hope it is to your liking?" Voltar asked. "It is beautiful," she said as she looked at the artwork on the walls. "So are you." He replied. "Why Voltar Aster, are you flirting with me?" She asked. "I had hoped we were past that." Voltar answered as he comes closer. "There is something about you." She replied. "I sense it too." He said. She touches his cheek. She can read his thoughts, some dark yet not all. "So my dear, what did you see in me?" Voltar asked. "I saw a man divided." She replied. "I hope also something more." He stated as he kissed her and the kiss was powerful. "We should stop." She said as she pulled away. "If that is what you want." Voltar replied as he walked toward the door. "No, it is not." She admitted as he came back and they kissed. Now the next morning, they were lying together in the bed when she woke first. "What have I done?" She said as she looked to a sleeping Voltar. "I am sorry, but I must go." She whispered in his ear as she kissed his cheek and vanished. A few moments later Voltar awoke, he turned to see she was gone. "Mordra?" He said as he gets up. He puts on his robe and heads out into hall looks all around. "Where did she go?" He said. Where did who go father?" Rick asked as he headed to breakfast. "She is gone?" Voltar questioned meanwhile back at the palace. "So now you are back." Zavaris replied as she entered the doors. "Yes father, I took care of the balance." She replied. "I had no doubts." He said as he kissed her cheek. "Now, back to watching the other galaxies I think." Zavaris replied. "Of course father." She said as she walked off. "Are you sure she is alright?" Marcel asked. "Yes she is fine." Zavaris replied. Now months have gone by, and Mordra has begun to show. She has been avoiding her father and confided in one other Ancient she could trust. "So are you sure this was wise?" Gallya asked. "I saw light in him, I think our child will help to keep him there." Mordra replied. "This child, is going to have great power when he is older." "Are you sure he can handle it?" Gallya replied. "I have already seen his fate and that of his brothers and sister." "He will be loved and protected." She assured. "I hope love has not blinded you." She said. Now back to Voltara and the present day. "So, what are you protecting me form exactly?" Devon asked. "I promised Mordra when she told me of you, that no one would know what you were." Voltar replied. "What am I...dad? Devon demanded. "You are our son, half god, half ancient." He confessed. "If others knew this, they would come after you." Voltar stated. "He is a target, just for being an aster." Jon replied. "I want to meet her." Devon asked. "Did you hear nothing I said?" Voltar replied. "Yes I did, but I want to meet her." Devon maintained. "I don't even know, how to go about that." Voltar admitted. "I think I can help." Amanda said as she entered. "I think Devon, you can find your way to their palace." She added. "Tell me how." Devon said. "First, you need to practice." "It is going to take all your power to get there." She advised. "I'm ready to do it." Devon said. "Please, be careful son." Voltar replied. "You don't get to call me that." Devon stated, as he walked out with Amanda. "Let him do this father." Jon replied. "He doesn't realize, how many enemies I have, that we both have." Voltar warned. He is nothing that this galaxy has seen before junior." He added. "When he is older he will command the gods, as well as the Ancients." Voltar informed. "Then he will need us, to have his back." Jon said.

Meanwhile in the palace, "My king, I have discovered a force in this galaxy." Marcel replied. "What kind of force?" Zavaris demanded. "It can not be." Marcel alleged. "What is it?" Zavaris insisted. "I am getting, the power of a god and of us together." Marcel replied. "That is not possible." Zavaris dismissed. "I swear to you my king." Marcel said. "I must see this." Zavaris insisted as he vanished meanwhile on the base in Amanda's quarters she is helping him to concentrate. "Just, let the power flow threw you." She instructed as Devon concentrated he began to glow all over his body. He opened his eyes and they glowed a brilliant blue as the base itself shook, Then Devon blasted out the walls all around him. "Devon, you must stop now." Mordra appeared and said. Devon stops. "You're her aren't you?" Devon asked. "I am your mother, but if you don't stop using your power this way, he will know." She pleaded. "Who will know?" Devon replied just then Zavaris appeared a towering man of six foot seven. "Whoa." Devon said. "What is going on here?" Zavaris demanded. "Please father, let me explain." She replied. "Wait father?" Devon said confused. Zavaris comes up to Devon looks into his eyes and touched his forehead. He could read everything, then he let go. "Father?" Mordra said. "You lied to me?" He replied as Jon and Voltar and others rush over. "Whoa, dude did you blow out the walls?" "Cause that is, wow." Ralph asked. "Who is that?" Jon asked. "This is my father, Zavaris king of the Ancients." Mordra replied Zavaris looks into the crowd to see Voltar. "You!" He shouted as he comes after him. "Father no!" She pleaded as Zavaris lifts him up. "You seduced my daughter, you Aster." He replied. "Whoa, I was not alone in that." Voltar stated. "Father, you are not helping your case." Jon replied. "Stop!" Devon yelled as the ground itself shook beneath them. "Look, I am just as pissed at him as you are, but I don't want him dead." Devon reacted. Zavaris looks to Voltar and dropped him down hard. "Why did you not tell me?" Zavaris demanded of Mordra. "I was, afraid of your retaliation on them." She answered. "We should let them talk." Jon suggested. "No way, this is getting good." Ralph said. "Move it." Dylan ordered the team goes inside the base. "I'm sorry about your apartment." Devon apologized. "It's ok, we'll fix it later." Amanda said so it is now just Mordra, Devon, and Voltar. "So, I sent you to fix a dark creature, and you slept with him?" Zavaris replied. "I did not go there with that intention father." She insisted. "Then please, explain this to me?" Zavaris asked. "I looked into his heart, his soul." "He is not all darkness." She said. "Thank you my love." Voltar replied. "You be quiet." Zavaris demanded. "Can I ask a question?" Devon replied. "Of course my son." Mordra said. "What happens to me?" "I mean, am I going to turn dark, or follow you up there?" Devon said. "I don't know how to answer that, this has never happened." Zavaris said. "We are observers, we keep the balance." "We never get involved in your affairs." He explained. "Well that has changed." Voltar stated. "Please, stop talking." Devon asked. "I need time to process this." Zavaris replied. "I understand, an outcast again." Devon stated. "No never." Mordra replied. "Lets face it, I'm a once in a lifetime mistake." "What is my destiny really?" Devon questioned. "That we will figure out together." Mordra insisted. "I will return." Zavaris vanished in a brilliant blast of light. "Oh please, he is just showing off now." Voltar replied. "What ever you need to ask you may." She said. "How did I end up abandoned?" Devon said. "That was not my plan." She assured. "I came back to Voltara to bring you to your father, but he was darker then." "I knew it was not safe, so I found loving parents, who could not have a child." "They raised you, I did not know what happened after." "I was sent to watch another galaxy." She explained. "Ok, so what happens now?" Devon asked. "You are an Aster, first and foremost." Voltar stated. "I really, want you to go away right now." Devon said as his eyes glowed blue. "Let us talk Devon alone, Voltar please." She asked. "Fine, I will be at my castle but, we will talk later Devon." He informed. "I wouldn't hold your breath." Devon responded. Voltar vanished. "Do not be angry with him, I am as much to blame." Mordra replied. "I just want to know, who I am what I am." Devon replied. "You are the best of both of us." She answered, meanwhile inside the castle. "So, yet another son you lied about father?" Rick asked. "I had no choice, it was to protect him." Voltar insisted. "Ok, so do we need to worry about these Ancients?" Rick replied. "I can handle them." Voltar argued. "I need to figure out how to gain my son's trust." Voltar stated. "It took you years with the others, so I'd say a decade?" Rick said in jest. "Not amusing at all son." Voltar replied Meanwhile under there feet in Kravitz's lab. "So, yet another son for him." He said. "I must study this boy, learn what makes him tick." He smiled meanwhile back at the base Devon used his power to rebuild the walls in Amanda's room. "All done." Devon replied. "Hey, can you fix my place too?" Ralph asked. "Yeah, no." Devon answered. "So, how'd your talk go with your mother?" She asked. "Ok I guess, I just don't get what she saw in him. Devon questions. "I mean she must've had to look, really deep into him to find goodness." Devon stated. "Hey Voltar is arrogant, annoying, and overbearing but, he loves all of you that much I can see." She said. "I should get back to work." Devon replied. "You can't avoid him for ever." She said. "It's a big galaxy, of course I can." Devon said as he heads out to his quarters to change. When he walked in Kravitz was there. "What are you doing in my room?" Devon said as his hands glowed. "Wait, I come in peace." He replied. "You work for him, what did he send you to talk for him?" Devon asked as he stopped glowing. "No, he doesn't even know I am here." He answered. "I just had to see, the half god half Ancient for myself." He said. "Why do you care?" Devon asked. "My boy, do you not realize how powerful you will be?" Kravitz tells. "Why you, will command the respect of beings higher than any of us." Kravitz explained. "You can do all the things of Gods and Of the Ancients." He added. "Do you not see the potential?" He asked. "I'm not interested in power or what ever else you're thinking." Devon said. "I should've known, when I saw your eyes." Kravitz added. "My eyes, what are you talking about?" Devon asked. "No Aster has blue eyes, in fact the only blue eyes on your Aster side would be your great, great grandmother, the goddess Relana. He answered. "You, are the only one of any of these beings with the potential to rule a universe, if you wanted?" Kravitz specified. "You need to go, I am not interested." Devon stated as he made the ground beneath Kravitz shake. "As you command my lord." He replied and vanished just then Zavaris appeared to him. "What do you want?" Devon asked. "I would like to talk, if that is alright?" He asked. "I guess so." Devon said as Zavaris sits on couch. "What do you want to know?" Devon replied. "I can feel the power, growing inside you it concerns me." He stated. "What, you think I will go dark?" Devon asked. "No I know you will not, but I can feel others gathering, they will come from other galaxies to claim you and your blood." Zavaris revealed. "Tell me what to do?" Devon asked. "I can not interfere my boy, I am an Ancient." He explained. "Yeah, I forgot you sit back and watch." Devon replied. "We can not risk a shift in the balance of the universe." He explained. "Well, I guess I'm more Aster than Ancient." "I don't stand by, and let people get hurt." Devon replied. "I'm sorry, I wish I could help." Zavaris said. "Yeah me to." Devon said as he goes out. "That boy is defiant and noble." Marcel replied as he appeared to Zavrais. "Yes he is, which is exactly what we will need for our future." Zavaris replied. Now in the Rec Room Jon is there working with weights. When Devon comes in. "Hey, how did it go with your other family?" Jon asked. "They are something else." Devon answered. "What are you going to do about our father?" Jon questioned. "I haven't decided on him yet, I still have anger there." Devon admitted. "Trust me, I can understand." Jon replied meanwhile at the castle Voltar entered Kravitz's lab. "Where were you earlier?" Voltar demanded. "I apologize my lord, but I had to collect specimens for my research." He answered. "Of course, well I will be going out for awhile." Voltar informed. "I understand my lord." Kravitz replied as Voltar goes; now later that night as the team slept a shadow comes up standing over Devon as he slept. He wakes up to see Voltar standing there. "What the?" He said as he turned on his light. "I'm sorry, I just wanted to watch you." Voltar replied. "Watch me?" Devon replied. Devon rises. "Look, I know you are angry believe me." "I can feel it even now, but I am your father and I love you." Voltar stated. "You think, that I will forgive you just like that?" Devon asked, "You let me believe, that Volrin was my father, lied about my mother." Devon continued. "Now I'm supposed to just, let it go and be an Aster?" Devon replied. "I am not fooled by you, I will never trust you." Devon stated. "I am sorry you feel this way, but I will not give up on us." Voltar said then he vanished Devon sighed as Mordra appeared. "Great, both of you in one night." Devon observes. "This is more than I've seen either of you in my whole life." Devon replied. "This bitterness will only make you more angry." Mordra observes. "You must let it go." Mordra insisted. "I can't help it, maybe it's the Aster in me?" Devon said. Mordra touched his forehead and showed him a glimpse of his destiny. "That is the man you will be, remember that." She said. "Whoa." Devon sat on his bed. "I will have a family?" Devon said. "You will be a large part of the fate of this galaxy Devon, but you must remove all doubt, all fear and anger from your path." She advised. "He is trying, why can't you?" She asked. "Ok, I get it I will try." Devon compromises. "I'm sorry." Devon replied Mordra kissed his forehead. "Get some sleep my son." She said as he lied back and she vanished as Devon slept the Ancients were watching as well. "So, when will you tell him?" Marcel asked. "There is time, he is not ready." Zavaris replied. "He will face many battles and temptresses, don't you think he should know why?" Marcel asked. "He must become the man, that we know he will be." Zavaris affirmed. "He must go this path on his own." Zavaris said. "When he needs us, he will come." Zavaris replied, now next day in the control room. "So, how are you doing?" Amanda asked. "I'm ok." Devon said, "I need to go out for awhile." Devon told Dylan. "Ok, where are you going?" Dylan asked. "I need to, talk to my father." Devon answered as he headed out and to the castle. He comes to throne room to find Rick. "So, hello little brother." Rick replied. "Yeah I guess so." Devon responded. "Our father is not here." Rick informed. "Where did he go?" Devon asked. "He'll be back later, you're welcome to hang around explore, if you want." Rick welcomes. "I have to get back to my club." Rick says with a smile and vanished. Devon goes out of throne room and walked down the long hall. He saw many rooms. He looked in a few, then came upon a locked door at the end of the hall he used power omitted from his hand to break it open. He went inside it was an elevator, which lowered down as he stepped into it and stopped after several levels and doors opened to a dark damp laboratory. He walked down hall to see, cages with all types of awful experimental creatures. "What is this?" Devon said as Kravitz came up behind him. "Welcome to my lab Devon." He said as Devon was startled. "I am honored by your visit." He added. "What are you doing for my father exactly?" Devon asked. "What ever he requires." Kravitz answered. "I can give you a proper tour." He smiled. "No thanks." Devon said as Kravitz reached up to brush his cheek and touched his hair." What are you doing?" Devon demanded as Kravitz has stolen a lock of his hair. "I thought, I saw one of my experiments." Kravitz replied. "I would love to study your DNA." He added. "I should go." Devon said as he headed back to elevator. "Come back anytime!" He shouted as Devon got in elevator and doors closed. "Now let us see what makes you tick my handsome Aster." He replied now back on the base alarms go off "What do we have?" Dylan said. "We have creatures attacking the city of Voltia." Mary replied. "Alright get over there people." Dylan ordered as Brent, Devon, Steven and Shane land on Voltia. "Alright, lets break up this mess." Shane ordered. Brent comes up form the north side and Devon comes form the south as Steven took the west they came upon a group of Garlocks. "Whoa, how did they escape the zone?" Shane replied. "I have no idea." Brent said. "We'd better round them up."

Steven said. "I got this." Devon replied as his eyes glow and the ground beneath the Garlocks feet shook and they fell. "Ok then." Shane said as they cuffed them and loaded them in the shuttle. "Nice work bro." Shane replied. "Yeah that was kick butt." Brent added. Just then a type of Moneconda but younger emerged from the shadows. "You will not stop me!" Mona exclaimed as he jumped out and at them. "What the hell is that?" Shane replied. "I think she is a Moneconda like Monzee." Steven said. "No way, how many of these things are in there?" Brent said. "I have no idea, but I got this." Devon said as his eyes glowed. Mona saw him. "Who are you?" She asked. "Time to go back to the zone." Devon said as he blasted her back against a building with his power and knocked her out. "Ok, let's get her loaded up." Shane said now back on the base in the control room. "So, I heard you took down a few Garlocks." Jon asked. "Yeah, no big deal." Devon said. "He also, took out a Moneconda." Brent added. "How did one of those get out?" Dylan asked. "We need to get her back in now." Amanda replied. "Why, what is it?" Jon said. "I think, she's decided on her first Aster crush." She added as she looked at Devon. "What me?" Devon replied. "Great, welcome to the club brother." Shane replied. "I don't get it." Devon said. "She is a female, that can shape shift." Amanda explained. "Yeah, too bad she's ugly in her true from." Ralph stated. "Your kidding right?" Devon asked. "Sorry, I wish we were." Jon answered. Meanwhile on the shuttle with the prisoners headed back to the Zone "We must escape." Mona replied as she changed into a young pretty girl of fifteen with blonde hair and green eyes. "I have found the one." She said. She then got free of her cuffs and tackled the pilot forcing him to crash near the base in the forest. She made her escape with her Garlocks meanwhile: back on the base in the mess hall. "Yeah be careful moneconda are very affectionate" Shane informed. "Come on man, I am trying to eat here." Ralph said. "Just be glad, she is back in the zone." Charlie replied. "So they like Asters?" Devon asked. "They seem to gravitate more toward them yes." Jon answered. Now later that night as Devon slept in his bed. Mona sniffed out which room was his and came up to his bedroom window. As she watched him sleep she used her power to make the window vanish. She then, still in her humanoid form sat beside him on the bed. She touched his cheek gently. Devon woke up saw her and jumped up so fast, that he fell over and out of the bed on the other side. "Are you ok?"

She said as Devon got to his feet. "Who are you?" Devon asked. "I am Mona and you are?" She asked. "I'm Devon, how did you get in here? He looks around noticed window was gone. "Whoa." He replied as he turned back toward her and she was right in his face. "You have beautiful eyes." She said. "Thanks." Devon responded. "Are you married?" She asked as she moved closer Devon moved away and fell back onto bed then sat up. "No, I'm fifteen." Devon stated." "Who are you?" Devon demanded. "I am your destiny." She answered. "Ok, look I am tired so, how about you go back to your home, I will go back to bed." He replied as she kneeled down to his level and pulled him to her and kissed him. "Whoa!" Devon yelled, as he pulled free. "Why did you do that?" Devon asked. "So, you will not be claimed by any other." She stated. "What?" Devon said in confusion. "You are mine Devon, as I am yours." She explained. "Ok first off, my parents won't let me even date." Devon said. "There will be no need for a courtship." She replied. "We will marry once we arrive in the zone." She said. "Wait, what?" Devon said as she pulled him up to his feet. "Where do you think you're taking me?" Devon said. "To our new home." She smiled as she pulled a quill from her hair and stuck it into his neck. "Why did you?" Devon feels affects of quill's sleep potion and passes out and into her arms. "Now to return home." She said as she transformed back into her beast form and vanished. Now in the morning Jon comes to Devon's bedroom. "Hey you're gonna be late!" Jon said as he opened the door to see the window is gone. "Oh my god." Jon replied now in the control room. "She just took him?" Dylan said. "She is a moneconda, she has powers." Amanda reminded. "We have to get him back, he's a kid he can't marry that." Shane stated. "Yeah, can you imagine the kids?" Ralph replied. "Hey he is not marrying her, we will find him." Jon said just then Voltar appeared. "Junior, what is going on?" Voltar asked. "Oh nothing dad, just a young moneconda that fell in love with Devon." Shane answered. "What!" Voltar exclaimed. "We will find him." Jon assured. "How did you let it happen in the first place?" Voltar demanded. "We didn't know, until we captured her Garlocks." Shane explained. "That is it, when this is over he is living with me." Voltar commanded. "Good luck with that father." Jon replied. "Now lets go." He added meanwhile in a cavern in the monster zone Mona has Devon lying in a bed as she touches his forehead. She looks humanoid again. Devon begins to come around. "What a dream I had."

Devon said as he looked up and saw her. "Whoa!" He yelled as he jumped up and out of the bed. "This was real?" Devon said. "Of course, you are with me now." She smiled. "Sorry but, I am not ready to settle down." Devon insisted. "I am an Aster you realize." Devon replied as he goes to use his power but can't. "What's going on?" Devon said. "It's the bracelet," she pointed out. Devon looks down at his wrist. "Well get it off." As he tries to remove it but can't. "Sorry but, I can't let you escape, or have your family find us." She explained. "What is wrong with the women in this galaxy?" Devon replied. "I will love you until I die Devon." She vowed. "I am not in love with you ok, I haven't even started shaving yet." Devon replied. She comes up to him and pinned him against the wall and kisses him it is very powerful. "Wow, you really need to stop doing that." Devon replied trying to gather his composure. "Why did you not enjoy it?" She asked. "Yes, I mean no." Devon responded. "I can be yours forever." She stated. "Forever is a really long time, I mean I need to weigh my options." Devon replied. "I'm sure my father has my wife all picked out." Devon suggested. "I will kill any other rival." She vowed. "Ok, what is with the dark streak? Devon probed. "We don't need to kill everyone ok." Devon said. "I will not give you up." She swore. "I am really not, worth dying for." Devon said as she caressed his cheek. "You are to me." She said as she kissed him again. This time he kissed her as he was swept up in the emotions then pulled back. "Ok whoa, lets slow down here, I need to think." Devon said as she tried to kiss him again. "Seriously, stop doing that I can't focus." Devon said just then Voltar and Jon And Shane appeared. "Thank god." Devon replied as he took a deep breath. "Alright beast, let my son go." Voltar ordered. "No he is mine." She stated. "I guess we will have to do this the hard way." Voltar draws his power to his hands. "Wait!" Devon shouted as he stepped in front of her. "You can't just kill her." Devon said. "Yes I can, son she is a moneconda, they do not stop until they are dead." Voltar explained. "I get it, but can't we just lock her up?" Devon requested. "She is still a kid." Devon reminded. "He has a point dad." Shane agreed. "Have you two, forgotten what they have done?" Voltar asked. "No, but all she has done is fall in love father." Jon stated. Voltar lowers his hands. "Fine, lock her away." Voltar conceded as Jon put a bracelet on Mona and Shane removed Devon's bracelet. "I will find you again." She promised as Shane took her to a shuttle near by. "I will kill you then!" Voltar vowed.

"Thank you, for not killing her." Devon replied. "I have gone soft for you boys." Voltar stated as he vanished. "So, are you really ok?" Jon asked. "Yeah, I saw what she looks like in beast for, I am not letting her be my first ok." Devon replied. "Ok then lets get back. As we got threw our first of many battles with the Moneconda females, we must now focus our attentions to what lay ahead for us. We will have to deal with Betrayal, Jealousy and many, many more females that are after the Aster bloodline. We must also deal with the discovery of new galaxies outside of ours, where we will find even more hideous and bizarre beings that either want us dead or for their own gain. So though we have just begun, as a family of Asters trying to change our dark past to a brighter future we can only hope the generations to come will learn form the mistakes we make along the way. Until we meet again for our next journey my human friends.